# THE STONE OF EXISTENCE

## FRAGMENTS OF IMAGINATION BOOK ONE

*To Judy*

*Jolene Reed*

### WRITTEN BY JOLENE REED

*Fragments of Imagination*

*The Stone of Existence*

*By Jolene Reed*

*Dedicated to R.S.R. for giving me the idea of this entire universe.*

*Other novels by Jolene Reed:*

*Crazy*

## Im·ag·ine
/iˈmajən/
*Verb*
Form a mental image or concept of.

## Cre·ate
/krēˈāt/
*Verb*
To bring (something) into existence.

## In·no·vate
/ˈinəˌvāt/
*Verb*
Make changes in something established, especially by introducing new methods, ideas, or products.

# Prologue

The terminals hummed all around him, their multi-colored lights blinking every few seconds with no pattern or unison, making small pools of light for a split second every time one of them lit up. The room was dark, the lights on the terminals the only source of illumination in the entire space. There were no lights in the room because there was simply no point in putting them there. After all, nobody was supposed to be inside anyway.

He moved soundlessly through the room, ducking around terminals in order to not be spotted by the cameras on the walls. His eyes darted around the room, scanning for threats, but more importantly, the thing he was looking for. His feet slid over the black tiles, making no noise. He had trained himself to move and step a certain way over the past few years that way he wouldn't be heard when he carried out his grand plan. Silence was key. The terminals were arranged to make a sort of maze, that way if anybody ever did try to find the treasure inside it, they would get lost and be doomed to wander around the vast room forever, always looking for a way out, but never finding one.

But this one was different. He was smart. He had a purpose, a plan greater than him. He knew he would find it. He had a feeling he would. And whenever he had a gut feeling about something, he was almost always right. He turned right, the tugging sensation getting stronger. He came to a fork in the maze. He stopped, his brow creasing slightly as he looked between each path. He knew that one wrong turn could make him doomed to roam this place forever. So, messing up was not something he wanted to do.

After a moment, he decided to take the left side. He prayed that he had chosen the right path. He glided through the maze, his eyes gazing around him until- there! There it was! The treasure! Well, it wasn't exactly a treasure, more of a life source for all of Imagine. But that made it special, and it was a treasure because it was special. It was the first step in his plan. He stopped, frozen in place. There were books describing the Stone of Existence, but there weren't any pictures. It was something of a fairy tale in Imagine, something that everyone knew and heard about, but also something that nobody had seen in a very long time. The oldest imaginary friends had seen it, but they had locked it away, hoping that it would never see the light of day again. Sure, it was a wonderful thing, allowing the existence of Imagine, Create, and Innovate. But it was also a dangerous thing, holding powers that no imaginary friend should ever possess. Nobody knew for sure what powers it held, except for the oldest imaginary friends, but they never spoke about what powers it held, saying that they'd rather forget what they saw all those years ago. But he had heard stories. Old stories passed down through generations. He had listened to every single one ever since he was discarded all those years ago. Before he was discarded, he thought they were rubbish and paid no attention to them, like most other imaginary friends. But after being discarded, he became desperate, listening to almost anything in hopes of finding something. He had to be careful who he asked, because most imaginary friends would get suspicious of him and report him to the Imaginists. Because *most* imaginary friends were fine with their lives, their lot in this world. But he wasn't. He had heard enough stories to know that it would be perfect for his plan.

He stared at it. It was everything he had ever imagined it to be, and more. It was on a stand in the middle of the space between two terminals. There wasn't a light shining down on it, because it didn't need it. It didn't give off light, per se, it just seemed to… glow. It was blood-red, glinting in the soft lights of the terminals. It was small, about the size of his palm, and shaped like a pendant. Because it *was* a pendant, really. It hung from a simple silver chain, part of it rusted from all the years of no use. There were three symbols carved into it, one for Imagine, one for Create, and one for Innovate. Most people thought it was because it represented all three of the lands. But he knew the real thing it stood for. It meant, '*I have the power to bring all three of these lands down to their knees.*' Now, that wasn't what he meant to use it for. He had nothing against Imagine, Create, and Innovate. Well, besides the fact that he was growing tired of Imagine. No, he was going to use it to bring something else to its knees. *Someone* else. He took one step towards it, then another, growing more confident of no traps with each step he took.

Some of the stories said that there were protective spells around the Stone of Existence. He hoped they were false, though he knew they probably weren't. He walked right up to it and looked down at it. The urge to snatch it up was so strong it almost took over him, but he resisted it. It seemed to snag him on an invisible hook and pull him towards it, make him want to put it around his neck. He closed his eyes, feeling for a spell. He had been trained by a few imaginary friends to detect spells, something only very old and powerful imaginary friends could even cast. He felt a trace, as if a spell was there once before, but it no longer existed. He opened his eyes and they flew to the Stone, resting hungrily on it. He slowly raised his arm and touched the Stone. He felt a shock of power surge through him, knocking him off his feet just as an alarm began to wail. He laid on the floor in shock. All of that power, all of that feeling, it was amazing. It was overwhelming, but he was sure he'd get used to it. He was shaking, but he got to his feet and grabbed the chain, knowing that touching the chain was probably less of a shock than touching the actual Stone. Sure enough, he felt a wave of power when he touched it, but it was far less than when he had touched the Stone itself. Taking a deep breath, he slipped it over his head, feeling the Stone thump against his chest a second later. A bloodcurdling scream was ripped out of him as power ran through him, making him squeeze his eyes shut in pain. This was what it felt like to have power. This was what it felt like to be alive. This is what it felt like to be real. Then, a second later, he heard the footsteps of I.P.O.'s running through the maze.

Breathing hard, he placed one hand on the Stone of Existence and opened his eyes. They were closer now. He could feel them. An evil grin spread across his face as he looked up. Some of the stories at least were true. To feel imaginary friend-presence was a major advantage that he would need in his plan. They rounded the corner a second later, firing nets that would have restrained him if he hadn't been wearing the Stone of Existence. If he hadn't been *real*. The nets passed right through him, not affecting him at all. He laughed, but there was no mirth in it. It sounded evil and dangerous; the laugh of a man who was about to do something terrible. One of them saw the Stone. He swore.

"He has the Stone of Existence! Take cover!" he yelled. Some ducked out of the way, but most didn't hear the I.P.O. The man extended his hand and a beam of bright red energy shot out of his palm, tendrils of red energy dancing down his arm as his eyes glowed red. It speared through three I.P.O.s at once. They fell to the cold tile floor, their forms fading within a few seconds to nothing. A few of the I.P.O.s froze as they watched their comrades fade in shock. The man took the opportunity to blast them with energy beams, their net guns clattering to the floor as they collapsed. There had been about twenty, but within ten seconds, every one of them was dead except for one that had run, fumbling with his walkie-talkie as he tried not to trip on the smooth floor. The man was smiling maniacally now as he looked around at the empty floor that had held bodies moments before. Then he rolled his eyes and sighed as he remembered one running. He took a deep breath and set off after him, the Stone of Existence giving him extra speed and sharpening his senses. He could hear the lone I.P.O., running through the maze towards the exit. But with the speed from the Stone of Existence, the I.P.O. didn't stand a chance. The man found him within a minute, the I.P.O. sprinting towards the door as he yelled into his radio.

"It's too late! He's gotten the Stone of Existence! Shut down all exits! I repeat, shut down a-" he yelled, but the man shot out a wave of invisible force that knocked the man off his feet. The walkie-talkie flew out of the I.P.O.'s grip, sliding across the floor, but the light was still glowing indicating the button was still engaged as though it was stuck or something.

*It's still on. Good. I want them to hear everything,* the man thought as he stopped walking. He stood over the I.P.O. on the floor, who was looking up at him with terror. The man with the stone looked to be around twenty, but with imaginary friends, you never knew how old they actually were. They were as old as their Creator imagined them, so an imaginary friend could look ten and really be fifty.

"W-who are you?" the I.P.O. asked, his voice wavering with fear. The man didn't answer, letting the silence make the I.P.O.'s nervousness shoot-up a few levels. The I.P.O. licked his dry lips and spoke again.

"Why? Why did you take it and what do you want to do with it?" he asked, his breathing fast.

"That's for me to know and for all of Imagine to find out," the man said, then shot the I.P.O. with a smaller beam of energy, keeping it going and watching him writhe in pain. The I.P.O. screamed as the white-hot beam ate away at him, making him fade slowly from where the beam hit his chest. The I.P.O. howled in pain, tears running down his face. The man looked down at him and laughed at the I.P.O.'s suffering.

When the I.P.O. was almost completely faded, the man locked eyes with him and spoke in a soft, dangerous tone with a slight German accent.

"I am the end of the world. I am the end of Imagine. I am Kile."

The I.P.O.'s eyes widened, and then he faded into nothingness. Kile looked up and left the maze, entering the vault that had kept the door to the maze hidden. He extended his hands towards the wall and beams of energy shot out of his hands, tearing into the wall and making a huge, gaping hole that overlooked a street. Clicks and shouts suddenly could be heard from the vault door. Kile, figuring he was out of time, drew up the hood on his cloak, and knowing that the Stone of

Existence would save him, he ran across the room and jumped out of the hole, disappearing into the night.

# Chapter One

*I'm going to go blind if she doesn't turn on the lights,* Joanne thought. The glow of lamps and the promethean boards around the room provided just enough light to draw by in the corner where Joanne sat but not enough to draw comfortably. The room smelled of tap water and paint, and also a hint of cinnamon from the air freshener that the art teacher, Ms. Loke tried to use to make the room smell better; though most of the time it didn't work very well. High school art class wasn't exactly easy, but to Joanne it wasn't very hard either. Ms. Loke usually gave them a prompt at the start of class each Monday, and she let them draw whatever came to mind for about twenty minutes. The prompt for today was simply "Paper", which was a bit odd, considering the fact that they were drawing on paper. Joanne had chewed on the tip of her pencil for a few seconds, an old habit of hers, as she tried to think of an idea. Something came to her soon enough. She started drawing a City made entirely of paper, the people and animals origami looking in the drawing. There was no point in adding color to this drawing because the City was made of simple computer paper. Joanne's pencil flew over the page, sketching it out first, then darkening the lines and adding more details.

She finished drawing the last origami bird just as Ms. Loke announced, "Time is up! Please turn your papers into the red basket and go back to your seats!" The students got up and turned in their papers. Joanne, looking at the other students' papers, knew that hers was one of the best. She had been told she was very creative and imaginative, sometimes too much for her own good. She was also a better artist than most of the kids in her class. There were a few that were better than her, but she was one of the best. She went back to her seat after dropping her paper in the basket and looked at Ms. Loke, ready for instructions. After everyone was seated, she clapped her hands together.

"Okay, as you all know, I am assigning you a project today. For this week, you will be designing and making a pillow. Now, I know you all did something like this in middle school, but this time, you have to hand stitch the design, and I must approve it first, because it must be creative, and it must look good. We are going to give these to teachers for Christmas, so I don't want any half-done, sloppy pillows. I am going to assign you each a teacher, and you're going to make a pillow that you think they'd like. Don't worry, I'm not going to give you a teacher you didn't have. I'll give you a teacher you've had before. Okay, here's the list of what teachers each of you have, and the supplies are on the back counters. This is due on Friday. I expect the best. Now get to work, because you really don't have time to goof around," she said, waving a paper, then setting it down on a small table. Then she walked to her desk, her blond hair bouncing as she walked. She sat down and pushed her red glasses up her nose, then started working on a painting. The students got up and surged towards the list.

"Hey! No shoving! One at a time, people!" Ms. Loke called from her desk. The students grumbled and made a sort of line. Joanne was near the back of it, since she had been farthest away from the front of the room. When she got to the list, she scanned for her name. *Joanne Raider... Mrs. Hallamon.* A smile spread across her face. Mrs. Hallamon was her science teacher, and everyone loved her. An idea began to form in her head of what she could do, but she moved out of the way and went back to her seat so the students behind her could see the list.

"Aw, Joanne got Mrs. Hallamon! Lucky!" one student muttered. Joanne tried not to act too happy about it, because she knew that some kids were unlucky and got somebody like Mr. McKolfer for their pillows. She sat down, already picking up her pencil and starting to sketch out a pillow design.

Ms. Loke started walking around the room, looking at student's papers and pointing out things they could do to improve their design as she passed by them. Joanne started sketching out a science-type look, then decided that Mrs. Hallamon would probably like something more of a mix of science and her love for kids. She started to erase her design, but she got interrupted by the bell. *Crap! I'm going to be late to Mrs. Gran's again!* Joanne thought as she swept her things into her backpack and threw it on her back. She joined the wave of students in the hallway that went all directions at once. You were supposed to stay to the right side of the hallway, but most kids ignored that rule, shoving and elbowing their way through the crowd. Joanne winced as one kid elbowed her in the ribs to get past her. She huffed and glared at them as they disappeared into the crowd. She knew they all had places to get to, but he didn't *have* to *shove* his way through everyone!

"Rude," Joanne muttered as she turned down into another hallway. She made it into Mrs. Gran's class just as the tardy bell rang. She sunk into her seat, slinging her backpack over her chair. Her seat was at the back of the room with her best friend, Lola. Even though there were four seats at their table, they were the only two occupants.

"Tsk, tsk. Almost late again. You should be ashamed," Lola said, shaking her head.

"Really? Says the person who's late basically every day?!" Joanne teased.

"Well, how am I supposed to make it on time? The strings classroom is all the way on the other side of the school!" Lola protested.

"That's no excuse, young lady! Just be glad you aren't in athletics when that bell rings! Then it'd be twice as hard for you to make it to your history class on time!" Joanne exclaimed, gesturing to the sweaty athletics boys in the room. Thankfully, Mrs. Gran had an air freshener that smelled like apple pie that actually worked for a little while before it left behind a terrible after smell, so at the moment, the apple pie smell drowned out the sweaty teenage boy smell. The room had round tables, each one with four chairs, and history decorations on the walls. There was also a promethean board, a white board, and a teacher's desk.

Mrs. Gran closed the door and said, "Everyone, take out your history journals. Today we will be discussing the Civil War. Take good notes because there might be a pop quiz over them tomorrow!" Mrs. Gran said, then turned on the promethean board and started the slide show on the Civil War as she begun to talk about it. Joanne was usually very focused in class, but she found her attention wandering and had to silently remind herself that she was in history now, and she should focus on history and take notes, or the quiz tomorrow would not turn out very good for her. She kept thinking about designs for her pillow, which was not something that would help her in history the next day. Thankfully, Joanne usually paid attention in history, so when Mrs. Gran suddenly sprang a question on her, she was able to answer it.

"Joanne! You look like you're not with us today! Tell me, what day did the Battle of Gettysburg end?" Mrs. Gran asked, smiling at Joanne, though the smile said that she knew Joanne hadn't been paying attention. Joanne blinked.

"Oh! Um- July 3rd, 1863," Joanne stuttered.

"Yes, that is correct. You all might want to write that down," Mrs. Gran said, giving Joanne a true smile and a thumbs up when everyone looked down at their journals to write down the date. Joanne smiled back before writing down the date herself.

"You are such a nerd," Lola muttered, shaking her head and smiling.

"I am not!" Joanne whispered.

"Then tell me how you knew that off the top of your head when you weren't paying attention!" Lola said.

"I... I read," Joanne said.

"Really? I didn't notice," Lola said sarcastically as her eyes came to rest on the eight-hundred-page book Joanne was currently reading, her bookmark sticking out of it at around page two-hundred.

"Oh, shut up!" Joanne said, lightly hitting Lola's shoulder before returning her attention to the promethean board. She tried to pay attention and had more success than the day before, but not much. When the bus bell rang, she didn't even notice. Lola shook her shoulder.

"Joanne! Joanne! Earth to Joanne!" Lola exclaimed.

Joanne looked up, blinking.

"Pardon? My apologies, did you say something?" she said, looking at Lola. Lola sighed at her choice of words.

"I swear, sometimes you sound like you're eighty, not sixteen. But anyways, *what* are you thinking about? You've been off in your own world for most of class!" Lola said, her eyebrows raised as she waited for an answer.

"Oh! Ms. Loke gave us an assignment in art, and I was just trying to think of ideas for it," Joanne replied.

"Okay. How big of a project is this if it was taking your attention away that much?" Lola asked, looking at Joanne expectantly.

"It's actually not that big of a project," Joanne said, shrugging.

"Then why are you- you know what, never mind. Put your journal up before the car bell rings," Lola said, zipping up her seafoam green backpack.

"Okay," Joanne said, putting her stuff in her backpack and slinging it over her shoulder. A few seconds later, the bell rang, and the few car students left all stood up and rushed out of the room as if they couldn't stand to be inside of class one second later.

"See you tomorrow!" Lola called over her shoulder as she walked to her mother's classroom.

"Ta-ta!" Joanne said as she went in the direction of the doors leading to the parking lot. She walked out of the doors with the tide of kids who were car riders or had cars they were going to drive home. There were at least two hundred heads around her, some of them she recognized while others she didn't know at all. She spotted the blond-dyed-brown head of her friend Penny, but she was too far ahead to catch up with her.

A few heads away from Penny, she spotted someone shorter than most other kids in the crowd. Her gaze slid over him at first, then her eyes shot back to him as she recognized his messy brown hair. She felt her blood run cold and she paled, but just like that, he was gone. Joanne shook her head and rubbed her eyes. *I must have imagined it. It couldn't have been him… he's gone, he's not here, he never was here. It must have just been some short freshman or something.* She thought, her steps now shaky. But then again, what kind of freshman was as short as a sixth grader? Joanne shook her head again, clearing her thoughts as she walked to her car. Thank goodness, Joanne had been able to drive for a few months now. She preferred to drive herself around than have her parents drive her. She felt safer with herself in control over the vehicle. She had a small silver car that she had saved for, for a few years. She walked over to it, took out her keys, and got in after she unlocked it. She started the engine and pulled out of the parking lot, starting the seven-mile drive to her house. She turned on the pop radio, but quickly turned it off when she discovered it was just "Girls Like You", again. Her phone buzzed. She glanced over at it. Some unknown number of 266-462-4463 had texted her. She looked back at the road, deciding to ignore it, but curiosity had rooted in her mind and wouldn't let her forget about it. *It's probably just some person who has the wrong number. Or a salesperson.* She thought, but when she got to a red light, she picked up her phone and read the text.

Her screen said, *Meet me at Schlotzsky's.* She stared down at it. Who would be telling her to meet her at Schlotzsky's?

*Um… who is this?* Joanne texted back… the light still red.

*Just trust me and meet me there.* They texted a few seconds later. *This doesn't seem like a salesperson… who the heck is this?* Joanne wondered. She was seriously considering this. She had always been told she was too curious, but she couldn't help it. Who was texting her and why did they want to meet at Schlotzsky's?

*I'm not meeting you unless you tell me who you are!* Joanne declared.

*I'm an old friend of yours, Joanne. Please, just meet me at Schlotzsky's. It's urgent.* They texted just as the light turned green. Joanne pressed down on the gas as she drove towards her house. *I am not meeting this stranger at Schlotzsky's. They could be a kidnapper or rapist or- wait. How did they know my name? Dear God, I can't take this.* Joanne thought as she pulled over into a parking lot. She picked up her phone.

*How do you know my name?* She asked.

*I told you, I'm an old friend of yours.* They replied.

*Really? Prove it. If you get this right, I'll meet with you. What is my favorite movie?* Joanne said, then thought smugly, *there's no way this creep is going to know this.* About thirty seconds later, they replied.

*Let me think…Courageous.* They texted. Joanne's phone slid out of her grip and landed in her lap in surprise. *How did they possibly know that? I don't think any of my close friends could get that one right!* She thought as she picked up her phone.

*How did you know that?* She demanded.

*No more questions until you show up at Schlotzsky's.* They texted.

After a moment's hesitation, she asked, '*When do you want to meet?'*

They replied, *Nine-Thirty. Be there or no more questions of yours will be answered.*

Joanne stared down at the phone. *I know I probably shouldn't go… but who is it? I won't know unless I go.* Joanne thought, still staring at the texts. She shook her head and muttered, "I should just drive home. I'll go home, and I might go meet them… I shouldn't, but I'm intrigued now…" She pulled out of the parking spot and drove the rest of the way home. She parked in the garage and went inside. Her dad wasn't home yet. *He's probably picking up Jasmine.* She thought as she walked to her room, ignoring her dogs yipping at her from their cage. She threw her backpack down on her bed and took out her phone again. *I might need somebody's opinion on this.* She thought, taking a screenshot of the texts. She scrolled through her contacts, wondering who she should send it to. *Probably Mom and Dad. Well, no. They wouldn't let me go. I'll just put it in the group chat or something.* Joanne thought as she clicked on the group chat with six of her close friends. There was Lola, Penny, Alexa, Adele, Asha, and Karrie.

She sent out the picture of the texts and said, '*Idk who this person is. Should I go meet them?*' It was only a few moments before some of her friends answered.

*Sounds like some weirdo pervert. I wouldn't, if I were you.* Karrie said.

*Woah. I don't think you should. What if it's a stalker or something?* Penny said.

*Hmm. It could be a scam.* Alexa said.

*It's so weird that they know that about you. How do they know that?* Lola asked.

*I have no idea.* Joanne replied.

*They know your name... that's really weird. I wouldn't show up if I were you,* Asha said.

*Yeah, I probably won't show up.* Joanne said.

*Yeah, don't.* Karrie said. Then Lola started talking about her latest celebrity crush, so Joanne turned her phone off and started trying to work on her project. She kept trying to design the pillow, but her mind kept wandering to the stranger that texted her. What was their deal? Who were they? The time seemed to stretch on. She'd glance at her watch, thinking that ten minutes had passed, but all that had passed was two minutes. She fell back on her bed and closed her eyes.

A few seconds later, she heard her dad call, "Joanne! Jasmine! Time for dinner!" Joanne laid there for a few more seconds, then opened her eyes and got up, walking to the dining room. There was a plate of beans and chicken at her spot at the dining table. She sat down, noticing her mother's empty seat.

"When will Mom be home?" Joanne asked her dad as she picked up her fork.

"In about ten minutes. So, how was school?" he said.

"Oh! Umm… it was fine. I got a project to make a pillow for art, but nothing else out of the ordinary," Joanne said, trying to push her thoughts of the texts away.

"That's nice," he said, then started talking with Jasmine about some big project going on at her school. Jasmine was in seventh grade now, and Joanne was in tenth. She finished her meal quickly and went back to her room, deciding to do some of her English homework. She finished after about an hour, sighing as she checked her watch. It read 8:49.

*Less than an hour until I leave if I'm going to meet them,* Joanne thought, swallowing. She put her homework back in her bag and decided to just sit down and read. It was growing dark now, the sun almost completely gone over the horizon, making the sky a dark blue and making the lamps around her neighborhood turn on, their yellowish light providing some illumination in the darkness. She shut the blinds and sat down on her bed with her book. She opened it up and started reading, trying to lose herself in the world her book provided her with. She tried to concentrate on the events but found that she couldn't. Frustrated, she slammed her book shut and looked at her watch again. Now it read 9:14. *I can get there in ten minutes. Screw it, I'm going and I'm leaving now,* Joanne thought, grabbing her phone and rolling off her bed. She opened the door to the garage but was stopped by her dad's voice.

"What are you doing, Joanne?" her dad asked. Joanne froze, slowly turning to see her dad standing in the hallway with his eyebrows raised.

"Oh. Um, I was just going to Schlotzsky's," Joanne said. She didn't mind lying about most things, but she didn't like lying about where she was going. Well, she wasn't lying. More of a half-truth.

"Why? It's nine at night, Joanne," her dad said, staring at her with a look that would get most people to spill their guts. *Crap. I'm going to have to lie to get myself out of this one,* she thought.

"Oh, I was just going to see some of my friends," she lied, praying she looked and sounded casual. Hopefully her theatre class experience was making her a better liar, otherwise she'd surely get in trouble for this one.

He stared at her for a moment before he said, "I hope you're not lying to me, Joanne. I told you not to betray my trust when you got your car and your phone. I pray you aren't doing so now." then he turned on his heel and left. Joanne stared after him, not believing that she had just gotten away with that. But after a moment's hesitation, she went into the garage and got in her car, starting it up and pulling out of the garage.

When she was about to turn out of the driveway, her phone rang. She glanced down at the screen. It was Lola. Joanne sighed and picked it up.

"Hello?" she said.

"Joanne! You better not be going to Schlotzsky's!" Lola's voice yelled through the speaker.

"Now why would you think that?" Joanne asked, feeling uneasy.

"Because! I know you and I don't want you doing something stupid! It's a trap, I'm sure of it! Don't! Go!" Lola replied.

"Don't worry, I'm not going," Joanne said as she turned out onto the street.

"Are you lying to me?" Lola asked with a tone that could cut metal.

"No!" Joanne lied, sick guilt settling into her stomach. She really didn't like lying to her friends, but sometimes it was necessary in order to keep their feelings from getting hurt or to keep them from worrying.

"Are you sure?" Lola asked.

"Yes, Lola. I'm sure," Joanne said.

"Okay. I believe you. I have to go now, so I'll see you later," Lola said after a moment of silence. Joanne slumped with relief.

"Alright. Bye," she said.

"Bye," Lola said, then hung up. Joanne put the phone down, feeling sick about lying to her friends. *She said she believed me. Well, I guess that's her mistake. She should be able to believe me. God, I disgust myself. Whatever this person has to say better be good.* She thought as she turned out of her neighborhood and out onto the streets. The streets were quiet, almost no other cars driving on them at this hour. Her headlights were two spots of light in the darkness, lighting her path. She knew how to get to Schlotzsky's by heart, since her dad loved it there so much that they went often. She parked in the Schlotzsky's parking lot and took a deep breath. *This is it. My last chance to just go back home and forget about this whole thing.* She thought, blowing out her cheeks. But she found herself getting out of the car anyways. It was a bit chilly, the wind blowing her chin-length platinum blond hair around her face like a halo of some sort. She drew her army-green denim jacket closer to her and regretted not wearing something warmer than leggings. She pushed open the doors and a wave of heat washed over her. *Thank god it's warm in here.* She thought. When she walked in, the manager of the store said,

"Joanne! How are you doing honey?" The manager was a middle-aged man with a kind face and an even kinder personality named Cab. It was short for something, but Joanne had never asked what it was short for. Since Joanne and her family went there so much, she knew Cab well.

"Um, I'm doing good. How about you?" she asked, her eyes darting around the room for the person that had wanted to meet with her.

"I'm good. I'm always good. It always brightens my day to see you or your family. Speaking of your family, where are they?" he said, his brow furrowing slightly as he peered around her in search of her family.

"Oh, they're not here. I came here to meet an old friend," Joanne said.

"Ah, okay. Do you want anything, or did you already eat?" he asked.

"Uh, I'll have a cookie," Joanne said, glancing towards the display case with brownies, drinks, and cookies.

"Sugar?" he asked as he went around the counter.

"Yup," she confirmed. He handed it to her, and she handed him a dollar.

"Thanks," she said.

"Sure thing, sweet pea," he said, then went back behind the counter. Joanne gave him a smile before walking around the booths in search of the person that might have wanted to meet with her. But there was nobody there except for an elderly couple.

*Well, there's still two minutes until 9:30...* Joanne thought as she shrugged and sat down at one of the booths. She looked around, waiting. Two minutes passed. Then five. Then ten. *Where the crap are they?* Joanne wondered. Finally, she gave up and stood up. She started walking out when she saw a person that hadn't been there when she walked in. She froze. They were alone in a booth, wearing jeans and a hoodie with the hood pulled up. *But how? I was watching the door, I would have seen or heard them come in.* Joanne thought as cold dread began to trickle into her stomach. The person looked up but she couldn't see their face since it was covered in so much shadow. They gestured for her to sit across from them in the booth. Joanne obeyed, despite her brain screaming at her to run because this couldn't be real, it shouldn't be real, it couldn't be happening, and it shouldn't be happening. She stared at them and they stared at her. Then they spoke.

"If I pull down my hood, you have to promise not to scream," they said. Joanne knew the voice more than she knew her own. She paled and felt like a bucket of ice water had been dumped on her head. She just nodded, not feeling like she could talk. They reached up and she saw the familiar Batman logo on the hoodie, making her breath catch. They dropped the hood and her mouth dropped open. She balled her hands into fists and shoved them in her mouth to keep herself from screaming. Across from her sat her old imaginary friend. He grinned his crooked grin at her, his blue green eyes flashing. He was just the way she remembered him. Brown messy hair, blue green eyes, pale skin, a few freckles, and a crooked grin. Then he spoke.

"Hey, big sis. Did you miss me?"

# Chapter Two

She just stared at him in shock and horror before shooting out of her chair.

"No! No! You're not real! You never were real! You can't be here! You aren't here! I'm imagining things! Yes, I must be imagining things. Go away! One, two, three, four. One, two, three, four. One, two, th-" she started saying desperately.

"Really? Trying to use the counselor's counting to get me to go away again? Sorry sis, but I'm here on my own time this time. Counting won't make me go away anymore," he said, sighing. She stopped counting, her breathing fast.

"But-but *how*? This *can't* be happening! I watched you go! I said goodbye three years ago! You *can't* be back!" Joanne ranted. He held up a hand as if to shut her up.

"Calm. Down. It is happening, honey, and if you'll just let me explain and quit freaking out, then all of this will make sense," he said, using a tone one would use around a scared wild animal.

"Nope, nope, nope! I got rid of you, you're not here, goodbye!" Joanne said, then ran out of the restaurant despite Cab's concerned calls behind her, the cool night air making her hair fly behind her. She sprinted to her car and got inside, slamming the door behind her, her breaths fast and quick. *This can't be real. He's gone. He's dead. I watched him die! He can't come back! This can't b-* Joanne started thinking desperately but stopped with a scream when she saw him sitting in her front seat.

She screamed again and climbed out of the car, slamming the door behind her as he sighed and said, "Wait! Joanne! Oh, god. This could be harder than I thought." She ran down the sidewalk, trying to get away from him. She wasn't paying much attention to the fact that she was running on a slick sidewalk, and next thing she knew, the ground was gone from underneath her feet and she hit the pavement with a sickening *thud*! She laid on the ground, breathing hard, as a wave of pain went through her.

"Ouch, my elbow," she muttered, looking at her elbow where her jacket had torn and seeing a huge bloody spot where her skin had gotten scraped off. Suddenly she saw him standing over her, panting and clutching his side.

"Come on, really? You know I hate running, Joanne. Why'd you have to do that?" He said between breaths.

She was about to scream again when he said, "Please don't scream! Good lord! Somebody's gonna call the frickin' police if you don't *shut up*! Because believe me, *nobody* but *you* can see or hear me, so you look *literally insane* right now!" Joanne shut her mouth as her breathing slowed back to a normal pace.

"But… I watched you die. How are you back?" she asked, her brow furrowed in confusion as she stared up at him in a mixture of awe and horror.

"Just… let me explain. I'll tell you everything, but first we have to get you off the side of the road," he said, extending a hand to her. She nodded and tried to take his hand, but her hand grasped empty air. He took his hand back, looking embarrassed.

"Right, I can't touch you. Sorry, I forgot. You're gonna have to get back up yourself," he said. She nodded, feeling like she was in a daze. Slowly, she got up and stood beside him. *This can't be real, s*he thought.

"Okay, now let's go to your car so we can talk privately," he said, then turned on his heel and walked across the road to get to the parking lot. With no other good options, Joanne followed him, making sure no cars were coming before she crossed the road. She got in her car and found that he was already inside. She remembered his name, but she didn't want to say it. She couldn't bring herself to. After knowing him for eight years, she knew his name and his voice as well as she knew her own, if not better. She shut the car door and turned to look at him.

"Okay. I'm going to listen to you, but I also want to know why you're here. Because you shouldn't be here at all. I watched you die. You should be gone forever," Joanne said, trying to sound calm, though she was sure that she didn't look it.

"I know I should be gone forever. But one thing you should know about imaginary friends is that we're never *really* gone. So, I'm just going to start from the beginning. Don't freak out and no questions until the end, okay?" he said. Joanne nodded. He took a deep breath, then began.

"This is complicated, so get ready. Okay, so… basically, there are … um, ***realms***. Three of them, actually. There's Imagine, Create, and Innovate. Imagine is kind of like a little retirement home for imaginary friends. When we're discarded, which is… when we aren't used anymore, we just go to Imagine for the rest of forever and we're considered 'discarded.' We also go there when we aren't being imagined or as we call it, 'in play.' So, it's like a hang-out until we retire.

When we're discarded, it's permanent and we can't go back to the normal world anymore. We might be able to see or feel or Creator's emotions sometimes, but that's about as far as it goes. But while we're still in play, we can go there whenever our Creator uses us. Our Creator is the person that imagined us. So, you are my Creator, as weird and messed-up as that sounds.

Let me think... ahh, yes, another realm is called Create. This is the place for the oblivious people who know nothing and are so absorbed in their own little world that it's not even funny. Every character from every single book, every single movie, all of those people go to Create. Like, even the unfinished ones that random people make. And Create is kind of divided into millions and millions of sections, their size depending on how complex the world is. Like Star Wars, that one is a huge section, while some little short story would be very small in comparison. Of course, they don't know about each other. They think their world is the only world and they have no idea that somebody created them. They also have no idea about Innovate or Imagine. Innovate is where all of the inventions and designs for stuff go. Building design? Innovate. Fashion design? Innovate. Design for a robot? Innovate. So, nobody really lives there except for some robots that have been invented. They don't know about Imagine or Create. They just kind of exist in their little realm. There are borders between the three, so we don't collide. If we collided... it would be bad. Like, really bad. There'd suddenly be robots in Harry Potter and talking rabbits in the Walking Dead. It would be bad. Not to mention confusing.

So yes, you *did* discard me three years ago. So, technically, I'm discarded. And technically, I'm really not supposed to be here. I shouldn't be able to get here. But because of... certain events, I *can* be here. I came here to ask you for help, Joanne. There's a Stone that is called the Stone of Existence. It lets Imagine, Create, and Innovate live together in harmony and keeps them from spilling out into the normal world. Us imaginary friends keep it because we know what it is, so we can keep it safe. We kept it on a stand in the middle of a maze in the middle of the vault. It has been safe for hundreds of years, since when Imagine was created. But somehow, somebody stole it. The first imaginary friends anchored the three realms' power to the table, so if it was removed from the table, then all three of the realms start to slowly die. Like, crumble away until they're gone. That means everything in it dies, too. And you're probably thinking, 'Oh, that's not a big deal.' Believe me, honey, it is. If Innovate dies, that means no more designs, no more inventions, none of that jazz. So, mankind will basically be stuck where it is if Innovate dies. Like, forever. If Create dies, then all characters, all movies, all games and video games, all of that is gone. Imagine opening a book only to find all of the pages blank. Or trying to play a movie and all you see is a blank screen. So, all entertainment… or most entertainment would just disappear. You don't want that, do you? Don't answer that, by the way. If Imagine dies, then all imaginary friends go away. I know it doesn't seem like a big deal, but without imaginary friends, nobody would be there to keep Create and Innovate in check. And a bunch of little kids would be alone. Just think of those sad, lonely, little kids. So, if all three died, most of the new generations would be lonely and depressed and have no social skills whatsoever, there would be no entertainment … which could lead to people trying dangerous things for entertainment, and mankind would be stuck where they are forever. So, we're in kind of a bad situation. I mean, you know Gods and stuff way back in the day before Jesus? And then all of those weird phenomenal occurrences? That was Create's characters getting out of hand because Imagine wasn't a thing yet.

You know what, I'm better give you a quick history lesson. First there was Innovate, when the first person tried to make something. Then a little bit down the road when they started telling stories, Create was born. But with no imaginary friends yet, they had nobody to keep them under control. So, dragons and gods and all of that crap ran around for a little bit. Then, a little later, the first imaginary friends were made. They got in there, they found the Stone of Existence, and they got a hold of it. Because if a character from Create or an imaginary friend from Imagine or even a robot from Innovate is touching the Stone of Existence, they become real. That's why it was so chaotic back in the day. The Stone of Existence was getting tossed from character to character with nobody to stop them from wreaking havoc if they got their hands on it. But yeah, imaginary friends got it and they used its power to bind Innovate, Create, and Imagine together that way the characters would stop causing trouble. Then they anchored it to the table and prayed that nobody would ever find it. Well, like I told you earlier, somebody took it, and now all three realms are dying. So, I came to ask you for help in finding it. We have about three weeks until all three realms are completely gone. So, will you come to me with Imagine to help us find it?" he said, then looked at her hopefully when he was finished. Joanne was quiet for a second, letting his words sink in.

"Why me? Why not somebody else? Why can't you guys do it yourselves?" she asked quietly.

"Well, there's a bit of an issue. Remember how I told you that if a character, imaginary friend, or some random robot held it they'd become real? Well, now that imaginary friend is real and they're going around killing imaginary friends and we can't do anything about it," he said seriously.

"Why not? Can't you …*kill him*?" Joanne asked, her eyebrows raised.

"Well… it's not that easy. Imaginary friends are all imaginary, so we can't kill each other. We can catch rogue imaginary friends who've lost it and lock them up forever, but we can't kill other imaginary friends. But since this imaginary friend has the Stone of Existence and they're real, they can hurt and kill us. So, we're kind of helpless and have no chance," he said sheepishly.

"You've got to be kidding me! Who even *made up that system*? That means if *anybody* got a hold of it, you guys have *no* hope!" Joanne said indecorously, throwing her hands up in the air. He cringed away from her.

"Yeah, I know, I know, it wasn't very smart, but nobody thought that anybody would ever get a hold of it, so they didn't consider this situation!" he said, leaning away from her due to her outburst. Joanne sighed and slumped down in her seat.

"Great. That's just great. So, you need somebody real to defeat them or something?" she said tiredly.

"Yeah, basically," he said.

"But, why me? Why not some other person?" Joanne asked.

"Well… technically you're not supposed to go or know about Imagine. The Imaginists, which are like the leaders of Imagine, don't know I'm here, and they definitely don't know that I'm trying to get you to come with me. They're trying to find ways to capture him, but all they're doing is getting imaginary friends faded, which is basically imaginary friends dying. Heck, me and some of my buddies have tried suggesting bringing a real person in to help, but they think it's a terrible idea," he replied.

"Why?" Joanne asked.

"Because, no real people are supposed to know about us. If one knows, then they could mention it to another, and before you know it, everyone knows about the three realms and they're trying to get there. It would be a disaster. Like, even worse than when *Darth Vader* discovered the rebel base on *Hoth*," he answered. Joanne decided to ignore the *Star Wars* metaphor.

"So how did you even get here if you can't go back here after you get discarded?" Joanne asked.

"The Stone of Existence was stolen, so the three realms have started dying. That means there are cracks we can slip through now to get back to this world. So, I got here that way and I can take you there that way," he explained.

"Oh. So, you're telling me you want me to come and be some sort of superhero to all of you imaginary friends and everything else?" she asked.

"Basically," he said, shrugging.

"I won't do it," Joanne said.

His eyebrows shot up in surprise.

"What?" he asked, shock on his face.

"You heard me. I won't do it," she said.

"Wha- why?" he asked.

"Because. I got rid of you three years ago so people wouldn't think I was crazy. I'm not about to get sucked into some big mess just so you can come back and haunt me again because you can't just stay dead!" she exclaimed, her tone firm.

"That's not why I'm here-"

"Yes, it is! I'm sorry, but I think my mind is just playing tricks on me right now. I'm tired, I've had a long day, and I really can't do this right now, and I need to just go home and sleep," Joanne said sharply, cutting him off.

"It's not your head, Joan-"

"Yes, it is! Go! Get out of my car!" she said shrilly. He looked at her, hurt on his face.

"But Joanne-"

"LEAVE!" she screamed. He looked at her, opened his mouth like he was going to say something, then sighed.

"I remember when you said that we'd be together forever. I remember when you said that we'd do everything together. I remember when you said I was your favorite person in the whole world," he said, his voice raw with something like sadness and pain put together.

"I was in first grade, Rumple! Nobody knows what they're talking about in first grade!" Joanne said, then inhaled sharply. She had said his name, something she hadn't wanted to say. Something she hadn't said in three years.

"But you… you said you were sure of it. And that's not all I remember. I remember going to school and talking to you in the hallways. I remember you dragging me out of bed on Christmas morning before anybody else was awake. I remember you crying into my shoulder when you were alone during the summertime. I remember going on rides with you at amusement parks and whenever you got scared, I'd count to three with you over and over again, telling you to pretend we were just waltzing until you weren't scared anymore. I remember watching you learning to swim, and how you begged me to get in the water with you. I remember waltzing with you in the church restroom to keep you from getting lonely and bored. I remember how you used to draw me all the time. I remember how you'd laugh when I got icing all over my mouth from a cupcake. I remember-" Rumple started saying, his voice softer and gentler now.

"Stop! I can't take it anymore! I can't deal with *you* anymore! Please, just go!" Joanne said, feeling tears well up in her eyes. He stared at her with a sadness so strong it made her want to reach over and hug him.

"Fine. I will. Because I love you, and I want you to be happy. Don't think I forgot when you told me you loved me, because I've never forgotten, and I never will," Rumple said, his voice cracking. And then suddenly he wasn't there, as if somebody had wiped away fog from a window and saw that what they thought was a person was really nothing. Joanne stared at where he had been sitting, her breaths quick and fast. His words echoed through her head. *Don't think I forgot when you told me you loved me, because I've never forgotten, and I never will.*

She felt her eyes water. She wiped at them furiously. *How can he still upset me after three years? Why does he still matter to me?* Joanne wondered. She sat there for a few more minutes, then drove home. She went to her bedroom, closing the door behind her, and went into her closet, ignoring her dad calling out after her, asking her what had happened. She reached down and picked up an old, beaten-up cardboard box. She looked down at it and realized her hands were shaking. *Stop that!* She thought, and her hands stopped shaking. She opened the box and took out the pictures inside. Her parents didn't know that once every year on his birthday, she took it out and cried. Even though he was imaginary, even though he wasn't real, she had still cared for Rumple. He had been her imaginary adopted brother that she had for eight years. How could she not care about him? How could she not keep a box with every single drawing of him she ever did, everything she found that she knew he would've liked? She stared at them for a second before she gently set them back down and shut the box. She heard somebody knock on the door.

"Joanne? Are you okay?" her mother asked.

"What? Oh, yeah, I'm fine. I'm just going to bed," Joanne replied, hoping she didn't sound like she had been crying or screaming.

"Um, okay. See you tomorrow. Good night," her mother said.

"Night," Joanne said back. Joanne heard her mother walk away. Joanne took off her combat boots and laid down on her bed. She closed her eyes and tried to push away her memories of the past hour. Soon enough, she fell asleep. She dreamed of a world where everything was gray and dead, and all of her family and friends were dead. She collapsed to the ground, crying, and suddenly she saw Rumple standing over her.

"You could have stopped this," he said.

Joanne woke up with a start, her breathing hard and her clothes drenched with sweat. She looked around wildly, then realized she was just in her room.

"Oh, my God. Oh, my God. What *was* that? Is that really going to happen? Surely it can't… but what if it does happen? What if I really could have stopped all of that? Will it even happen? Oh, Lord, I don't know what to do!" she muttered, running her hands through her short hair. Her elbow throbbed slowly. She looked at it and saw her jacket stained with dried blood and that the wound had started to scab over.

She got up from her bed and picked up her phone. She clicked on the number 266-462-4463 and stared at their texts. *How is this possibly him texting me? He can't… or he shouldn't be able to because he's not real, he's imaginary. Right?* Joanne thought in confusion. She looked at them for a little bit longer before she turned her phone off. *Nope. I don't want anything to do with him anymore. I'm just going to go back to sleep and forget any of this ever happened,* she thought, then went back to sleep.

She woke up to her alarm blaring in her ears. She slowly opened her eyes and then got up. She got dressed and ate breakfast, then drove to school, pushing thoughts of Rumple and what he had said last night far from her mind. She parked and got out, slinging her backpack over her shoulder. She walked into the school and headed to the gym; the place students were supposed to go if they showed up before the first period bell rang. The gym was huge, with shiny wood floors, blue bleachers, and a few big windows to let in sunlight. She looked up and saw her friends Penny and Alexa sitting in their normal spot in the bleachers. She climbed up the bleachers and sat down beside them. Alexa had shoulder length dark brown hair, chocolate-brown eyes, and pale skin. She was kind of a music nerd and was a loud person, and she was always ready to argue if she didn't agree with you on something. But even though it might not seem like it at first, she was a good person. Penny had chin length blond hair that had been dyed brown and wore glasses. She seemed a little quiet until you got to know her. She was very talented at drawing but had a bit of a temper at times. She was kind otherwise.

"Well, you look disturbed," Alexa said after a moment. Joanne blinked in surprise at how quickly they had been able to tell something was off.

"Really? I'm fine," Joanne said, a little too casually to be believable. Penny and Alexa exchanged a look.

"Please tell me you didn't go and meet that weirdo that was texting you yesterday," Penny said.

"Don't worry, I didn't," Joanne lied, feeling sick as she felt another lie land on her conscious.

"Are you sure about that?" Alexa asked, squinting at her. Squinting at people was something Alexa did because she couldn't raise her eyebrows. So, if she was squinting at you, she was really just trying to raise her eyebrows at you. Most people didn't know that, so then they'd ask her why she was squinting at them.

"Yes," Joanne said, swallowing.

"Come on, Joanne. You're a terrible liar and we all know it. Who was it that you met last night?" Alexa said. Joanne sighed, knowing she couldn't escape their questions now. She opened her mouth to make up some story when the bell rang. She stood up, relief on her face.

"Don't think you're going to get away. You are going to spill some tea and tell me who it was that you met …during math class!" Alexa said, pointing a finger at her and also standing up.

"Aw, dang. I wanted to ask her more questions," Penny said with mock disappointment.

"Don't worry. I'll get it out of her, and I'll tell you what creeper she met," Alexa assured Penny as they walked down the bleachers.

"I didn't meet a creeper!" Joanne said, rolling her eyes.

"Then who did you meet?" Alexa asked, squinting at her again.

"I don't want to tell you!" Joanne said. They branched off into the hallway. They said goodbye to Penny as she went to her history class.

"Why not? Oh, wait. I know! Let me guess, you've finally given into your teenage hormones and you're dating your crush!" Alexa said, fake realization on her face.

"Dear Lord. No, Alexa, that isn't it either," Joanne said, sighing.

Alexa smirked at her.

"Well, I had to try," she said as they walked into math. Their math class was decorated with cheerful signs on the walls, offering inspiring quotes to discouraged students. There were about seven tables, all of them round except for the rectangular one in the middle of the classroom. Karrie and Lola were already sitting at their table. Lola looked at Joanne with a look that a father would give his daughter if she got home late.

"Joanne! You went and met that pervert last night, didn't you?" she asked, her tone firm.

"Um…" Joanne said, looking away from Lola in an attempt to not meet her gaze that currently had fire in it.

"You did, didn't you?" Lola asked, her tone a deadly calm.

"She did," Alexa said simply. Lola shot up out of her seat.

"Joanne Raider, I am going to literally kill you since they didn't!" she exclaimed.

"Calm down! They didn't kill me, and it wasn't a pervert!" Joanne said, trying desperately to get Lola to calm down, who could get very fired up sometimes. Once Lola got going, there was no getting her back until she was completely done ranting to you about how angry she was.

"Then who was it? We told you not to go and you did it anyways!" Lola exclaimed. Karrie was looking back and forth between Lola and Joanne with a surprised look on her face while Alexa had just taken out her book and was reading it, completely ignoring the conversation at hand.

"Yeah, I know, I know. I probably shouldn't have done it," Joanne said apologetically, trying to make up a believable story about who she saw there while she talked.

"Yeah, you shouldn't have! I mean, five people telling you that you shouldn't go just wasn't enough for you, was it?" Lola asked, her eyebrows raised and her tone sarcastic. Alexa looked up from her book.

"Come on, Lola. Go easy on her. You know she's pretty headstrong, and no matter what we told her, she probably would have gone anyways," she said, shrugging.

*Thank you,* Joanne mouthed to Alexa.

"Yeah... well, yeah, but what if it had been a creep? She could have gotten hurt!" Lola said, struggling to find the right words.

"But she didn't. And please stop. I'm trying to draw and you're starting to sound like my mom," Karrie said politely. Joanne looked over at Karrie, and sure enough, she had taken out some paper and a pencil and had started drawing an animal. Karrie was always drawing animals, never objects or people. According to her, that's why she wasn't in art. Because she said she'd have to draw things she didn't want to draw. She was currently working on an animal that was a mix of an owl, a fox, a whale, and a lion.

"Sorry, I'm just trying to keep Joanne from doing something stupid that gets her killed!" Lola said.

"Just calm down. Mrs. Cook is going to tell you to be quiet if you don't shut up," Karrie said, jerking her head in the direction of their math teacher, Mrs. Cook. Lola opened her mouth like she was about to say something, then sat down and closed her mouth. Thankfully, Mrs. Cook was teaching them something new that day, so there wasn't any time for Joanne's friends to ask her any more questions, because she still didn't have a story that they would think was real.

*Even if I told them the truth, they wouldn't believe me. They'd think that I finally lost it, or I was lying to them. Because really, what kind of story where your past imaginary adopted brother comes and asks you to help save three magical realms is believable? It's not. I'm going to have to lie to them either way,* Joanne thought glumly.

When class ended, Lola said, "I will figure this out in theatre! Mark my words, Joanne, I will figure out who you met last night!" Then Lola, Joanne, and Karrie walked to theatre. Alexa had to go to her band class, since she didn't have theatre with Lola, Karrie, and Joanne. Penny was also in theatre, and she was waiting for Joanne when Joanne arrived.

"Okay, spill the tea on who the heck you met last night," Penny said.

"I already told you three that I don't want to tell you!" Joanne exclaimed, throwing her backpack down onto the stage.

"Guys, maybe we should just leave her alone. She doesn't seem like she wants to talk about it," Karrie said, looking around at her friends nervously as if she expected somebody to start throwing punches at any second.

"Thank you, Karrie," Joanne said gratefully.

"Well, I want to know!" Lola said.

"Maybe it's none of our business! Maybe it's personal!" Karrie said, her voice rising.

"Is it personal, Joanne?" Lola asked, whirling around to face her.

"Yes, actually!" Joanne said. Then she saw out of the corner of her eye, a head of brown hair. Joanne froze. Then very slowly, she turned and saw him putting his backpack down with everyone else's. He looked up and she met his gaze.

"What are you looking at? You look like you just saw a ghost," Penny said, turning and trying to see what Joanne was looking at.

"Um… nothing. I'm going to go to the bathroom. I'll return in a moment," Joanne said hurriedly, then started walking towards the bathroom. She jerked her head in the direction of the bathroom, hoping that Rumple would get the message. She walked into the bathroom and saw him hesitate, then follow. The bathroom was small and dimly lit, the light blue stalls covered with papers that had inspiring quotes on them. She went in a stall, letting him in with her, and turned on him, furious.

"Dang, it's been a while since I've been in a girl's bathroom," Rumple said, looking around. Joanne just stared at him indecorously, her mouth open.

"What the *heck*?" she said angrily.

"Oh, I was just saying that it's been a while since you brought me into a bathroom to talk to me," Rumple said casually.

"What? No! I meant, what the heck are you doing here?" Joanne asked, annoyed.

"Oh! Right! Well, I thought about what you said last night, and I decided that I should try again," Rumple said, not meeting her eyes.

"Rumple! The answer is still no! I'm not going to do it!" Joanne exclaimed, crossing her arms and turning to leave.

"Please! It's getting worse every day. Old imaginary friends are starting to fade because of how weak they're getting. There are holes in Imagine where there didn't used to be! We need your help!" he pleaded. She turned to him and saw genuine fear in his blue green eyes. The fear made her stop dead in her tracks.

"Please. Please help us," he said quietly. She looked at him, shaking her head with sad eyes.

"I'm sorry, but… I can't," she said, then rushed out of the stall and out of the bathroom. Rumple just watched her leave, sadness and disappointment on his face.

"Then we are all doomed," he muttered sadly, then disappeared.

# Chapter Three

"Woah, are you okay?" Karrie asked her as she walked back to the stage.

"What? I'm fine," Joanne said, trying to smooth out her features.

"Um, no you're not. I can see it in your eyes. What exactly is going on, Joanne?" Karrie asked, peering at her with concern. Joanne opened her mouth, then shut it.

"Come on, you know you can tell us anything," Penny said gently.

"Well... I can't tell you this," Joanne said, her voice cracking as Rumple's pleas echoed through her head.

"Why not?" Penny, Lola, and Karrie asked in unison.

"It's... crazy. You wouldn't believe me," Joanne said in dismay, shaking her head. Her friends exchanged a look.

"Um... did the person you met last night do something to you?" Lola asked.

"Wh- no! No!" Joanne said, surprised that they had thought that.

"Did they tell you something?" Penny asked.

"*I don't want to tell you*!" Joanne shouted. Her friends flinched, surprised by her outburst. Joanne was surprised, too. But she couldn't get Rumple's words out of her head, and her friends questioning her about it was making her feel quite ruffled. Before she knew what she was doing, she turned and ran away from the stage, snatching her bag and running towards the double doors. She shoved them open and sprinted out of them and into the parking lot, the sun shining in her eyes as she climbed into her car. She sighed with relief at the quiet in her car. She was finally away from their prodding. *I need to go somewhere to calm down. How about the library? Yes, I'll go there,* she thought. She started up her engine and began to drive away. She saw in her rearview mirror her friends standing by the doors, watching her leave. She inhaled shakily and turned down onto the road that would take her to the library. There weren't many people out, since it was a Tuesday and most people were at work or at school.

The reality of skipping school and driving off hit her. *Oh god, what did I just do? I'm so dead. I'm going to get in* so *much trouble,* she thought in despair, regret lacing through her. She parked at the library and went inside. It was a building that was a little smaller than her school, with windows and bricks, the paint off-white and the trim dark green. The familiar smell of cleaning products and books washed over her. She inhaled deeply. The library had an adult section, a kid section, and an intermediate section. Its floors were carpeted and a light gray color. The walls were an off-white, and the shelves were shades of grays and light purples. There was a big window by the adult section that took up the entire wall. There were a few windows with blinds that let light filter into the kid's section over by where there were some toy animals. There were computers in the adult section, waiting to be used. The intermediate section had some booths from a restaurant, a few soft chairs, and a checkerboard table with rickety seats. The intermediate rarely had visitors, while the adult and kids' section usually had somebody browsing through the books. She walked over to the intermediate section, her eyes running over the spines of the books. She had read a lot of them, but not all of them. She selected one off the shelf and sat down in one of the soft chairs in the corner. She took a deep breath and started reading, losing herself in the book and forgetting everything that was going on.

She had been reading for a good hour before her stomach growled. She tried to ignore it, but she got hungrier by the second until she couldn't shut it out anymore. She stood up, putting the book back in its place. She walked out and got into her car, ignoring the stare she got from an elderly man walking his dog. She drove over to Subway and went inside. There was one other person inside, eating a sandwich in the corner. Joanne sat down and ordered a sandwich, paying for it with some of her cash, then got some sweet tea and sat down. She chewed her sandwich in silence. Suddenly her phone buzzed. She picked it up. Lola was calling her. It was lunch time at school, and students were allowed to take out their phones during lunch. So, it appeared that Lola was taking this time to call Joanne. Joanne's finger hovered over the hang up button before she sighed. *She'll just get worried if I don't pick up. Frick,* Joanne thought as she pressed the pick-up button.

"Hel-"

"JOANNE RAIDER!" Lola's voice shouted through the phone. Joanne winced and held the phone away from her ear in order to not damage her hearing.

"Uh… yes?" Joanne said sheepishly, trying not to provoke Lola to scream at her more.

"WHAT THE HECK DO YOU THINK YOU'RE DOING WALKING OUT OF SCHOOL LIKE THAT?" she screeched. The other person in the corner looked up from their sandwich and stared at Joanne.

"Well, I didn't exactly walk out-" Joanne began, but Lola cut her off.

"YES, YOU DID!"

"Um… technically I ran out," Joanne said, then realized a second later she shouldn't have said that.

"OH MY GOD! *JOANNE*! I- I can't even deal with you right now. Penny, *you* talk to her," Lola said, sounding tired and annoyed at Joanne. Joanne heard noises and suddenly Penny's voice was on the phone, her tone firm.

"Okay, Joanne. Lola's *really* mad at you and we're all wondering where the heck you are or why you ran. So, could you please tell us *where you are and why you ran out of school during school hours*?"

"Um, I'm currently at Subway and I ran away because you guys wouldn't leave me alone," Joanne said.

"Really? That's why you ran away? You could have just told us that you didn't want to talk about it!" Penny exclaimed.

"I did!" Joanne said.

"Oh, yeah…" Penny said in realization. Joanne resisted the urge to roll her eyes.

"But won't you come back to school?" Penny asked.

"I'm already out. I'm not going back today," Joanne said dryly.

"You need to come back! People keep asking where you are and eventually *somebody's* going to find out that you're skipping, and you are going to get in *serious trouble*!" Penny hissed.

"I know, I know, but I can't go back now," Joanne said, running a hand through her hair. Penny sighed.

"Joanne. Please don't lie. Did something upset you last night? You don't have to get into details, but did this person tell you something you didn't want to hear?" she asked slowly. Joanne's breath caught in her throat as Rumple's words rang through her head for what felt like the hundredth time that day.

"Yeah. Yeah, they did," Joanne said after a moment, her voice just above a whisper. There was silence for a second.

"What did they say to you?" Penny asked.

"I... well. Basically, they told me that there's this little m-" Joanne started saying, but suddenly, her phone clicked, as if they had hung up. Joanne took the phone away from her ear and saw that she had hung up.

*What the heck?* Joanne wondered. She was about to press the call button when she saw a hand on hers. But she couldn't feel the weight or warmth of the hand, she could only see it. She looked up. Rumple was standing there, looking pissed.

"Don't you ever tell *anyone* about what I told you! Anyone! *This* is why the Imaginists didn't want to bring real people into it! Because *this* would happen!" he shouted. Joanne stared at him in shock, her mouth open. Then she came to her senses and anger flared up inside her.

"I'm sorry, but you come and tell me that the fate of the world rests on my shoulders and I'm supposed to not tell anyone and do nothing?" Joanne asked angrily. The person in the corner was now definitely staring at Joanne, though she didn't care.

"You can do something if you would just help! You have to realize that if you don't help us, then all is lost for my world and yours!" Rumple said, anger flashing in his eyes.

"But why me? I don't want to get involved in this! I don't want to get involved with you again! When I said goodbye that night, I meant it!" she growled. He looked as if he had been slapped. The person in the corner grabbed their things and left hurriedly.

"Did you? I know that *every year* on my birthday and the day I died you take out a box of some pictures of me and *cry*! I know for *days* after my death you cried whenever you were alone! About *me*! You wished for me to come back! You talked to the stars *every night*, telling me how your day was, and how much you missed me and wanted me to come back for *weeks*! So, *don't* tell me that you want nothing to do with me, because I *know* you do!" Rumple shouted, his voice cracking and his breathing fast and hard. Joanne stared at him in shock.

"I know that I'm asking a lot. And you're confused and you're hurt. But believe me when I say that I need you. Every imaginary friend needs you. Every person in this world needs you. And I know that's a lot to take on, but I just want you to know that if you change your mind, I'm here," he said, his tone becoming gentler. Joanne looked at him with an unreadable expression.

"How much longer do you think the three realms have?" she asked.

"About three weeks," Rumple said, his tone serious and his expression somber.

*Three weeks,* Joanne thought.

"Do you know where the Stone is?" Joanne asked.

"Well, we know it's with the person who stole it," Rumple said sheepishly.

"Who stole it?" Joanne asked.

"Um… somebody heard something about some imaginary friend named Kile. We don't know anything else about who he is. Or where he might be. We just know that he took it for some reason. We don't know why or what he's going to use it for, but we're pretty sure that it's not good," he replied, his brow furrowed slightly as he remembered as many details as he could. Joanne nodded and was quiet.

"Rumple, I'm really sorry, but I shouldn't get involved in this. I should live a normal life, without worrying about that… and without you," she said, biting her lip. Rumple sighed a sad sigh.

"Okay. I had to try one more time. So… goodbye, I guess. Goodbye f-" he started saying but broke off into a fit of wild coughs. He clutched at his stomach as if it was the source of his coughs. His face contorted in pain as cough after cough racked his body. Joanne's eyes widened in concern and surprise.

"Rumple, are yo-" she started saying, but stopped when he started flickering rapidly, like a TV with bad reception, only this was her imaginary brother, not just a show on some channel that she could care less about. He collapsed to the floor as he flickered, his eyes wide with fear. She fell down on her knees to the floor beside him.

"Rumple! Oh, my God, Rumple! Can you hear me? Are you okay? Rumple!" She said, her voice frantic. She reached out to touch his shoulder, only for her hand to pass right through him. She jerked her hand back in shock, her mouth wide open. Suddenly he stopped flickering. He gasped as if he had just been underwater and looked up at Joanne, his breathing quick and shallow.

His breathing slowed as he looked at her, the fear starting to leave his eyes.

"Are you-" Joanne started, but he sat up and held up a hand.

"I'm fine now. But that. That is what is happening to imaginary friends everywhere right now. We're flickering, and some don't reappear when they stop flickering, and they just disappear forever. They fade. And that is going to happen to every book character, every design, and every imaginary friend unless the Stone is found. Unless it's put back on the stand. That is why I'm asking for your help, Joanne, because you're the only one that can stop this. Please. Be a hero and save us all," Rumple said, his voice rising with emotion. Then he looked at her, hope in his eyes.

Joanne shut her eyes. Then she said so softly even she could barely hear her own words, "I'll do it."

Rumple blinked at her; his eyebrows raised in surprise.

"What?" he asked, as if he didn't believe what she just said. Joanne wasn't sure she believed herself either. She opened her eyes and looked at him, her gaze filled with determination.

"I said I'll do it," she said, louder than before. Suddenly he reached over and hugged her like he used to hug her before. Before he had to leave. Before they said goodbye. Of course, she couldn't feel him. She was real and he was imaginary, so all she felt was air. But she tried to hug him back anyway, even though her arms went through his back a little bit. She closed her eyes for a second before he let go of her.

She couldn't tell he had let go until he stood up.

"You don't have to hold your arms up anymore. Come on, let's go," he said. She opened her eyes and saw that there was nothing in front of her anymore. Rumple was standing in front of her, trying not to smile.

"Oh, shut up. You know I can't feel you, so I have no idea when you let go," Joanne said grumpily as she dropped her arms and stood up, but her eyes looked happy, giving away her true emotions. She tried to punch his arm, but her hand just passed right through him.

"Ha! Benefits of being imaginary!" he said, a smirk on his face.

"Just be quiet!" she said as he started to walk outside. Of course, he just passed through the door like it wasn't there, while Joanne had to push it open. He also just sat down in the front seat, completely ignoring the door. Joanne climbed into the car, closing her door behind her.

"Okay, what now? I agreed to help you. Do you pick me up in a tornado and take me there? Does some weirdo imaginary friend team come and throw me in a sack and then bring me there? Wait, I know! You tell me to drive off a bridge to get there?!" she said sarcastically.

"Okay, there's no need to be sarcastic. You drive somewhere, for the record," he said wryly.

"And where is that?" Joanne asked.

"The old mall on the side of the interstate," Rumple answered. Joanne started.

"The old mall on the side of the interstate is the way to get to Imagine?" she asked, disbelief coloring her voice.

"Um, yeah," Rumple said, looking at her strangely, as if he thought she was weird for thinking something was weird.

"You're serious?" Joanne asked, her eyebrows raised.

"Yes!" he insisted.

"The one that's shut down?" she asked.

"It's the only frickin' mall in this whole town! Yes, that one!" Rumple exclaimed.

"Um, okay then. So, I just drive there?" Joanne asked.

"Oh, my lord. Yes. Haven't you driven before?" Rumple said dryly, looking slightly annoyed.

"*No, I haven't driven before!*" she said sarcastically. "Sorry, I just haven't driven to a closed mall to go to some magical land before," she continued.

"Okay, you can take the sarcasm down a notch now. Let's just go," he said, reaching over to buckle himself up before realizing that he couldn't touch anything without passing through it. He just sighed and slumped back in the seat.

"You're not going to buckle up?" Joanne asked.

"Um, boy! Does it *look* like I can buckle up?" he asked, trying to grab the seatbelt for show as his hand went right through it. *I forgot he still acts like he's twelve. I guess he'll always be twelve, because that's how old he was when he died...* Joanne thought.

"Oh. Sorry," Joanne muttered. He sighed again, louder this time.

"It's fine. Let's just move out," he said.

*I forgot he used to say, 'Let's move out.' I've forgotten a lot about him...* Joanne thought. She started the car and began the drive to the shutdown mall. They drove in silence before Rumple reached over and turned on an 80's pop radio. Joanne turned her head and looked at him strangely.

"What?" he asked as a Michael Jackson song started playing. Joanne shook her head and sighed, looking back at the road.

"Nothing," she muttered. Rumple smirked beside her as he started to sing along with the song. Thankfully, they arrived at the mall shortly afterwards, so she didn't have to listen to Rumple sing anymore. She switched off the radio as the mall became visible. Rumple pouted at the sudden cut-off of the music but didn't say anything.

"Park behind it so nobody sees you," Rumple suggested as she pulled into the parking lot.

"Oh, that would be smart," Joanne muttered.

"Honey, I know I'm smart," Rumple said, a smug expression on his face.

"That is *not* what I said," Joanne protested.

"Well, it was implied," he said, shrugging.

"Where was that implied?" Joanne asked, staring at him weird as she parked in a spot on the other side of the mall.

"Well, usually only smart people say smart things," he replied, shrugging. She just nodded.

"Right," she muttered. She got out of the car while Rumple just stepped through the door.

"Okay, lead the way, genius," Joanne said, gesturing towards the mall as she grabbed her backpack and slung it over her shoulder, shutting the car door behind her.

"Gladly," Rumple said, then set off towards the mall.

*How is this the way imaginary friends get to Imagine?* Joanne wondered.

"So, do all imaginary friends come through here to get to Imagine?" she asked as they walked towards the locked double doors.

"Well, there are old buildings all around the world that imaginary friends go through. So, no, not all of them go in this way. But most in this area do. I went this way every time you weren't imagining me," he explained, talking about it like it was the most normal thing in the world. Joanne guessed that for him it was the most normal thing. He had gone this way for eight years. How could it not be normal for him?

"So, do they walk or drive here? That sounds like it would take a while," Joanne said.

"No, imaginary friends can teleport in this world. These are just like gateways that we can teleport right to. Then we just step through and bam! We're in Imagine," he said.

"You can teleport?" Joanne asked, her eyebrows raised.

"Um, honey, do you think these babies could walk all over this earth every time you went on vacation? No, we can teleport, because we're cooler than real people like that," he said, smirking and gesturing to his feet. Joanne rolled her eyes, her eyebrows dropping back down. Joanne stopped at the double doors, but Rumple just walked right through them. Joanne stared at the space where he had just been.

"Wait! Rumple! I can't walk through the door!" Joanne called out, banging her fists on the double doors. His head popped out, the rest of him inside. It was a strange sight, one that made Joanne start even though she knew Rumple just passed through things as if they weren't even there.

"Oh, right. Sorry. Are the doors locked?" he said sheepishly. Joanne tried pulling on the handle, then pushing it. The door remained firmly in place.

"Do you really think they'd just leave a mall unlocked?" Joanne asked, crossing her arms as she stared at the door.

"Hmm… I don't know. Sometimes real people are really stupid," Rumple said with fake thoughtfulness. She gave him a look.

"Really? Okay, is there a way to unlock the doors?" Joanne asked.

"If you had a key, then yes, there would be a way to unlock the doors," Rumple said with a voice somebody would use when talking to a dog or a small kid.

"O- Rumple! Seriously, quit with the snarky comments!" Joanne said, annoyed.

"Fine. I surrender," he said, sounding very bored.

"So, I guess there's no way to get in the mall without breaking a window or something," Joanne sighed as she said.

"I never said that," Rumple said.

"But you told me that I need a k-"

"Yes, you *would* need a key to get through the doors. Lucky for you, I know another way. Follow me, dear sister," Rumple said, cutting her off. He walked back out into the parking lot and began strolling along the side of the mall. Joanne let out a huff and gritted her teeth. Then, with no better options, she followed him. He peered at the side of the building as he walked, as if he was looking for something. He suddenly stopped and muttered,

"A-ha!" Then he stepped back and gestured theatrically to the side of the mall.

"I present to you a way to get in. You may all applaud now," he said. Joanne just glanced at him before looking at the wall. It looked completely normal to her.

"I don't see anything," Joanne said flatly.

Rumple scowled at her. "Your imagination has seriously gone downhill the past three years. Look. Like, don't just glance at it like you're better than it. Actually *look*," Rumple said. Joanne squinted at the wall. Suddenly, she could see it. It was a section of wall that was painted a slightly different shade than the rest of the mall, and it was about five feet tall and three feet wide. You wouldn't notice it unless someone pointed it out to you.

"Oh. I see it now," Joanne said.

Rumple rolled his eyes.

"I was hoping you did, otherwise we'd be standing here for a *very* long time as I tried to explain to you the difference between colors. Now come on, the clock is ticking," he said, clapping his hands and passing through the wall. Joanne took a step towards the section of wall and put her hand against it. It *felt* like the rest of the wall did. She pushed against it, and it swung open like a door. Joanne's eyes widened in surprise. She walked through it into the mall as it closed behind her, ducking down a little bit to fit inside. It was dark inside, the air dusty and smelling of decay. She could barely see anything except for silhouettes of counters and furniture. She looked around, but she didn't see Rumple anywhere.

"Rumple? Rumple, where are you?" Joanne asked, her voice echoing back to her in the empty mall. She felt her heartbeat quicken as she whirled around, scanning the dark room for him.

"Um, right here," Rumple's voice said from behind her. Joanne, not expecting his voice to come from behind her, jumped, then whirled around and punched him, a pure reaction from the self-defense class she took in middle school. Her fist moved right through his stomach. He looked down, looking slightly surprised.

"Umm, okay then. I mean, your aim was great. Totally would have made me double over if I was actually here. But then there's the fact that I'm your brother and I'm imaginary, so…" he said, his voice trailing off. Joanne slumped with relief, dropping her fist so it was no longer through Rumple.

"Don't do that again!" she said, straightening up and giving him a glare.

"Give you tips? Okay, I won't," he said, shrugging.

"No! I meant don't sneak up on me again!" Joanne hissed.

"Wow, I snuck up on you? I wasn't even trying. I'm impressed with myself," Rumple said, smiling and nodding proudly.

"N- where were you anyway?" Joanne demanded.

"Oh, I was just teleporting around and seeing if that homeless guy still lived here. He was on the sexual offender list, so I was just making sure the area was safe before you went any farther in here," he said casually, as if that was something most people did every day. Joanne opened her mouth, then shut it, deciding that she wasn't in the mood to say something sharp back.

"Let's just go," Joanne said, sighing.

"Okay. Ladies first," Rumple said.

"Um, no. *You* know the way. *You* are leading the way, not me," Joanne said, raising her eyebrows and gesturing towards the darkness. Rumple sighed.

"Fine. Follow me, then," he said, then suddenly pulled a flashlight out of thin air. He flicked it on, but nothing happened. "Right. These don't work unless I'm in Imagine. Well, maybe just watch where you're stepping and follow my silhouette," he said, dropping the flashlight. It disappeared before it hit the ground.

"How...?"

"I can pull my things from Imagine whenever I wish. Some of them don't work when I'm here though, because I'm imaginary and so is it, so if it was to perform something that would affect others, like a flashlight, then it doesn't work," Rumple explained, sounding like he was reading from a textbook and also sounding bored.

"Oh. That kind of makes sense," Joanne said after letting the words sink in.

"It does if you were listening. Now, follow my little silhouette," he said, then set off into the inky blackness of the mall. Joanne swallowed, and trying to ignore her fear of the dark, followed him. She stepped over pieces of broken furniture and old mannequins, shards of glass and small dead animals that had gotten lost in the mall and never found their way back out. Joanne tried not to shiver. Finally, she saw a light up ahead.

"We're getting close. Come on," Rumple said.

"To what?" Joanne asked.

"The gates," he said. Joanne's brow creased as she tried to remember gates in the mall when it was still open, but she came up empty handed.

"Since when are there gates in this mall?" Joanne asked.

"They're not legitimate gates, stupid. It's something on the floor in the middle of the mall," he replied. Joanne narrowed her eyes at him to keep herself from calling him something worse than 'stupid'.

"Well, where are we in the mall right now?" Joanne asked.

"The old Ivan Smith Furniture Store," Rumple replied without any hesitation.

"Oh," was all Joanne said. They continued trekking through what was left of the Ivan Smith Furniture Store until they reached the place that was supposed to have bars that would've come down when the mall closed to protect the store from the rest of the mall. Some of the bars were still there, but most of them had broken away and rusted. Rumple carefully stepped over the bars and turned to face her.

"Alright, move it. We're almost there," he said. Joanne leaped over the last of the bars and squinted in the light. They were in the main part of the mall now. There were benches where people had once sat, a play area where children had once played, fountains, trees that were once alive, and skylights above to let in natural light. Looking up, Joanne saw that some of the skylights were broken, but most were still intact. Now that Joanne could see, she saw how much of a mess the mall was. It had been about six or seven years since the mall closed, simply because it wasn't getting enough business anymore. There were rumors of a new mall, but nothing had ever happened. The walls were cracked, plants slowly taking over them. There was also some mildew here and there. The tiles on the floor were cracked, dirt scattered on top of them from small animals running through the mall. The fountains were off and had dirty, stinky water in them now, nothing like the clear, clean water from Joanne's memories.

"Wow," Joanne breathed.

"Yup. It's pretty impressive," Rumple said, looking around.

"So, did imaginary friends use this place even when it was open?" Joanne asked.

"Yes, they did. Nobody could see us, so it's not like we were disturbing anything," he replied, shrugging. Joanne gazed around the old mall for a few more moments before looking back at Rumple.

"Should we go now?" she asked.

"Yeah. Come on," he said, then started walking to the center of the mall. After one last look at the sight around her, Joanne followed him. He stopped when they were in the very middle of the mall. There was a huge, dome-like skylight over the middle of the mall, letting the most light hit the design on the floor in the center of the light. It was a compass, only, instead of an N, an E, a S, and a W, there was an Im, an In, a No, and a Cr. Joanne stared at it.

"That's weird. I never noticed that it didn't have the right letters," she said, cocking her head to the side like a dog.

"Yeah, most people don't. Those who do assume it's pointing to something else. Which, it technically is. Imagine, Innovate, Normal, and Create," he said. There were ropes around the compass design, meant only for people to look at and not step on. Rumple ducked under the ropes even though he didn't need to.

"Come here. The rope won't kill you if you duck under it," Rumple said to Joanne. She ducked under the rope and stood on the compass beside Rumple. She felt a strange sensation around her legs that felt like she was standing in a river, but instead of water, it was energy.

"What the?" she muttered.

"All people that have had imaginary friends feel it if they stand on the compass. The more developed their imaginary friend was, the more they feel it. That's why it's roped off. It'd raise too many questions," Rumple explained.

"Oh," Joanne said.

"Okay. Repeat after me," Rumple said.

"Um, okay," Joanne said, unsure of what she was going to be repeating. Rumple cleared his throat, shutting his eyes briefly before opening them, and started singing:

> *"Take me to the place where I can Create*
>
> *Take me to the place where I can Imagine*
>
> *Take me to the place where I can Innovate*
>
> *Take me to the place where I don't have to be normal*
>
> *Where I can just be free*
>
> *Imagine, you call to me*
>
> *I am answering your plea*
>
> *So, come on and take me to the place I long to be*
>
> *Imagine is the only place for me."*

Joanne echoed the lyrics to the song as he sang them.

Then he finished and she finished and they looked at each other. Rumple's crooked smile spread across his face.

"Hang on," he said.

"To wha--?"

A sudden beam of white-hot light shot up from the compass, swallowing up Joanne and Rumple. Joanne gasped, not expecting it as she reflexively shut her eyes. The light didn't feel warm or cold. It felt like nothing, just like Rumple did. Then, just as suddenly as it started, it stopped.

"Umm. You can open your eyes now," Rumple said.

Joanne slowly opened her eyes and gasped at the scenery around her.

"Welcome to Imagine," he said, gesturing around them, a lively glint in his eye.

Chapter Four

Their surroundings stunned Joanne, since they didn't really make any sense. She and Rumple both stood on the compass, but it seemed to be in the center of... everything. The world around her seemed to be divided into five sections. There was a Tundra, a Beach that led to an ocean, a Forest, a Desert, and a City. Joanne's mouth hung open as she looked at it all.

"But how..." she wondered aloud as she stared at the drastic climate changes around her.

"Well, we are currently in the very center of Imagine. Think of it as a pie with five slices. They start here, and then they slowly branch out in a pie shape. So even though you can see the other sections of Imagine now, once you pass into one, you can't really see the others any more. And if you accidently pass into another section, then just step right back into yours," Rumple said, looking at the sight around them fondly.

"But why are there different sections?" Joanne asked, her brow creasing.

"Because. Not all imaginary friends are people. There are sea creature imaginary friends for some kids that live by the beach. There are Desert creature imaginary friends for kids that live in the desert and have never seen anything else. Forest creatures for kids who live in the woods or near the woods. And the City is where almost all human or almost-human imaginary friends live," he answered, pointing to each section as he talked about it.

"Wait, are there things here that aren't real?" Joanne asked.

"Um, this is children's imagination we're talking about. So, of course. Mermaids? We got it. Fairies or giants? That too. Random blobs? Weird, but yes. Elves or vampires? Sure thing. Though, the vampires are usually very grumpy and there aren't too many of them," Rumple said casually, smiling as he talked, as if talking about where he lived brought him joy. A smile slowly spread across Joanne's face.

"This is... amazing," she said, looking around.

Her phone suddenly rang. She sighed and pulled it out of her pocket. It was her dad calling her.

"Should I pick it up?" Joanne asked.

"Um. I never had parents. Well, I did, but I never knew them. So, I don't know what to do in this situation," Rumple said sheepishly.

Joanne sighed at his unhelpfulness and answered it.

"Where are you?" her dad's voice asked sharply.

"Umm, where do you think I am?" Joanne asked, dodging the question.

"I know you're not at school. I'm tracking your location and it says you're at the old mall. Why are you there? How did you even get in there?" her dad demanded.

"I… I can't tell you," Joanne said, closing her eyes.

"What do you mean, *you can't tell me*? What's going on, Joanne?" he asked, confusion in his voice.

"I can't-" Joanne started saying, but Rumple yanked the phone out of her grip and hung up. The phone rang again, showing her dad's name again, and before she could do anything, Rumple pressed the pick-up button and held it in front of his face, letting Joanne's father see Rumple for about two seconds before Rumple hung up and blocked her father's number.

"Rumple! My dad is going to be *freaking out* now!" Joanne said.

"Now why would he do that?" Rumple asked.

"Umm. You just hung up on him and blocked his number and *showed him your face,* when I should be at school! *Why do you think*?" Joanne demanded.

"Oh, right. Sorry. But we really can't have you contacting your parents. It'll throw this whole thing into danger," he said, grimacing.

"You don't say! I'm never going to be able to go back home now!" Joanne wailed.

"Why would you want to go back there?" Rumple asked.

"Because, it's my home! It's where my family is-"

"Well, I'm right here. *I'm* your family. And don't say it doesn't count just because I'm not real. Besides, after this is all sorted out, you'll get to go back to them and we'll craft some master story that doesn't involve any of this or something like you doing drugs," he said, cutting her off.

"But… I'm so screwed. My dad's going to think I'm *on something* now, and when he can't find me at the mall, he's going to report me missing… oh, Lord, *what* have I gotten myself into? I should have never come! *Why* did I think I could be a hero and save everyone? I've read too many books. I let myself get sucked up into a fantasy world and now here I am, with somebody that's not even real and… wait. How did you take my phone from me?" Joanne rambled, then looked at Rumple with curiosity.

"Oh. It's simple. We're in Imagine. This is my world. I can touch things, including you," he replied, reaching out and tapping Joanne on the shoulder. Joanne flinched at his touch, feeling freaked out by how he felt. She *felt* him. His finger felt *warm*. It felt *real*. Rumple pulled his hand back, something like hurt flashing across his face, but he quickly covered it up.

"Oh," Joanne said.

"Oh, indeed. Now come on. Let me take you to where I live. Then we'll start trying to figure out a plan on finding this Kile guy," Rumple said, gesturing for her to follow before he set off into the City part of Imagine. After one last look around her, she stepped into the City after him. She could sense the difference as soon as she crossed into the City. The air was cool, around eighty degrees. She could suddenly hear sounds in the City. Sounds of vehicles, people, and everyday life swirled around her. The sun was getting low in the sky, about an hour from beginning to set, caressing everything below with its warm glow. And the City itself was another thing entirely. It seemed to be a blend of every culture and every era. Some of the streets were dirt roads, some were railroad tracks, some were cobblestone, and some were pavement. A few buildings were wooden or small huts from about two hundred years ago, but most were more modern. Houses, skyscrapers, stores, temples, churches, treehouses, you name it. It was all there. The people were from everywhere, too. There were English, American, Jamaican, Egyptian, Chinese, Russian, and Canadian people, and so many more different ethnicities and races. Joanne could hear accents of people on the wind. There were trees and plants of all different kinds by the sidewalk, shading the imaginary friends walking on the sidewalks from the sun. Some imaginary friends were obviously normal people, while others looked a bit off.

There was one person that looked unusually pale and was wearing all black. The person glared at Joanne when they saw her staring at them before taking a swig from a bottle they had with them that was filled with a dark red liquid. Joanne shuddered and tried not to imagine what was in the bottle. Some of the imaginary friends had strangely colored eyes, skin tones, or hair. Rumple and Joanne even passed by two girls that had just come out of a shop that had pastel colored hair that were wearing clothes that looked like they were made of petals.

"Fairies. Don't stare at them. They'll start trying to sell you plants that make you pass out for two hours if they see you looking at them. Trust me when I say you *don't* want that," Rumple muttered, eyeing the fairies warily.

"You sound like you've done that before," Joanne muttered back, smirking. He lightly hit her arm.

"Shut up. I was seven and I didn't know any better," he mumbled, his face flushing with embarrassment. Joanne just laughed.

"This place is… extraordinary," she said. Rumple nodded.

"Yeah, it is," he said. Joanne looked at the imaginary friends. Most of them looked carefree and smiling, as if they didn't have a care in the world.

"They all look so happy," Joanne said in wonder.

"Yeah. That's because most of them don't know about the Stone of Existence going missing. Most people don't know was has happened," he whispered so only Joanne could hear.

"Wait, seriously? How do *you* know about it then?" she asked as they walked along the sidewalk to wherever Rumple was taking them to.

"Well… I'm in a type of group that knows stuff," he said carefully, as if he was trying to tell her something but not tell her too much.

"Wait! Are you one of those *Imaginists* things?" Joanne asked. Rumple stared at her for a second before he busted out laughing. Joanne jumped at his outburst.

"What's so funny?" Joanne asked, her brow furrowing. He doubled over and slapped his knee.

"It's just… *me*!? An *Imaginist*!? It's just *so* stupid!" he said between laughs.

"Why is it stupid?" Joanne asked, feeling ridiculous even though she didn't know what was so funny.

"Because the Imaginists are *idiots*!" he said loudly. Some imaginary friends looked shocked at him saying such a thing and glared at him as they passed by. Rumple's laughter died down, a look of embarrassment reaching his face.

"I probably shouldn't have said that so loudly. But, anyways, come on," he said sheepishly.

"Why shouldn't you have said that?" Joanne asked.

"Okay, let me tell you how things work here so you won't be confused and so you won't have some angry imaginary friends on your tail. Number one, nobody likes to joke about being discarded. It does happen to everyone eventually, but it isn't something to joke about," he said.

"Why not?" Joanne asked.

"Because being discarded is... not embarrassing, but it usually hurts the imaginary friend's feelings. Being discarded is basically your Creator saying that you're just not good enough for them anymore. It *does* hurt an imaginary friend's feelings, and they're usually down for a little while. Kind of like a temporary depression. It happens to all imaginary friends, whether they existed for one day or ten years. So, it's not something you should joke about, whether you're talking about yourself or the other imaginary friend you're with," Rumple explained, his eyes looking sad for a second.

A question tugged at Joanne's mind. *Did you miss me that much? Did you miss me like I missed you, or was it worse?* She wondered, but kept her mouth shut.

"Second thing. The Imaginists are the closest thing to celebrities here. They lead us, or try to. They make decisions for the good of Imagine, so everyone adores them and knows them. Of course, not everybody loves them, but the majority of Imagine does, so it's not wise to voice if you don't like the Imaginists. It's kind of like politics in the normal world, but it's more evenly divided there. It'd be like if you have a room of fifty people, maybe only two or three people don't care for the Imaginists. So, the majority of imaginary friends like the Imaginists. So, if you want to stay out of trouble, *don't* say that you don't like them," he said.

"So, you don't like them?" Joanne whispered.

"Why are you whispering?" Rumple asked, not answering her question and looking at her strangely.

"Because I thought you said it was frowned upon," Joanne replied.

"Oh. I mean, you don't need to *whisper*. But no, I don't care for them too much," he said casually. Then he began talking again.

"Third thing. Don't discriminate against imaginary friends just because they might not be human. Most imaginary friends are human, but some aren't. So, if you discriminate against them or say they're weird, it is considered *extremely* rude. Because they can't help it. Their Creator just had a *very* vivid imagination. Fourth thing. *Don't* start fights with imaginary friends because you can't get hurt by them, because you can hurt and kill them. It's not smart. So, *do not* get into fights, because you *will* hurt that imaginary friend and they won't hurt you and *everyone* will know that you're real," he said as he turned down a cobblestone road.

"Wait, they're not supposed to know that I'm…"

"Real? Yeah, that's the fourth thing. Remember how earlier I told you they didn't want to bring real people into this? So, don't tell people you're real or suggest you're real or do anything that would make it obvious that you're real," he said, answering her unfinished question.

"What would I do that would make it obvious that I was real?" Joanne asked.

"Um… get into a fight. Or get shot with the Stone of Existence and nothing happen. Those are the only ways I'm thinking of right now. So, stay away from those two things and you should be good to go," he replied, sounding confident in his answer. They turned down another street, this one pavement.

"Anything else I should know?" Joanne asked.

"Umm. *Don't* mention the Stone of Existence being missing. And also, make up a story," Rumple said.

"What do you mean?" she asked.

"Like, we have to pretend that you're not real. We have to say you're imaginary. So, let's pretend you're some brand-new imaginary friend fresh off the street that some lonely little seven-year-old imagined," Rumple said.

"Oh. Okay," Joanne said. He turned down another road.

"Hey, Rumple, why is the sun setting here?" Joanne asked.

"Oh. It's just a different time zone kind of thing. We're three hours ahead of you guys. So, it's like… four here," Rumple answered, taking out his phone and glancing at the time his phone screen showed. Joanne nodded as they turned down yet another road, this one still pavement, but more worn down, falling away at places. The buildings were smaller and more run-down than they had been earlier.

There were almost no imaginary friends walking around here, and those that did looked shady and dangerous to Joanne.

"Rumple, where are we going?" Joanne asked as she started to feel uneasy.

"Where I live. Come on," he said, not slowing and not looking back at her. She jogged to catch up with him, her footsteps the only sound in this part of the City. She passed by something that looked suspiciously like blood splattered on the pavement and she quickly looked away. Rumple led her deeper and deeper into the dart part of the City until most of the buildings were crumbled, and almost all were graffitied with art. It would have been pretty if some of the art hadn't been so sinister. Scenes of blood, skulls, and death were what most of the art consisted of. It almost seemed like the poor part of the City.

"Rumple, is there poverty here?" Joanne asked as they passed by a man slumped against a wall, who Joanne hoped was asleep. He looked at her with sad eyes. "Joanne, there's poverty everywhere," he said. He suddenly veered to the left. Joanne almost tripped as she tried to follow him. He walked into the grass, most of which was dead and yellow. It scratched and crunched against her boots, the only noise besides the wind. Rumple kept walking, the ground beneath them sloping downwards. Then Joanne saw it. It was a huge building, an old hotel by the looks of it in the middle of the valley. Some of the windows were broken, the sign that once hung on the hotel now lying on the ground. The parking lot was filled with vehicles that looked old and broken, all shapes and sizes. Joanne couldn't tell if the lights were on inside, since the sun wasn't down yet. The walls were also spray-painted and had some splatters of what looked like blood. There seemed to be an arena behind it, and a stable of some sort beside it.

"You *live* here?" Joanne asked, her eyebrows raising in surprise.

"Uh, yeah," Rumple said, giving her a weird look.

"It's just... so big," she said, looking at it in wonder.

"Oh. I'm not the only one that lives here," he said, smiling.

"You aren't?" she asked.

"Nope, there's a lot more people that live here. Did you really think that I lived in that hotel all by myself?" he said, chuckling.

"Well, I wasn't sure what to think!" Joanne said, huffing.

"You're hilarious. Anyways, come on. And just a warning, some people may look mean, but they won't hurt you. Unless you hurt them first," he said, smirking when he saw Joanne's eyes widen. They approached the hotel doors and Rumple stopped when he was in front of them.

He put his hand on the door and muttered, "Hail, King Kafa."

The doors swung open.

"Who's King Kafa?" asked Joanne.

"I'll tell you later," Rumple muttered as he walked through the doors. Joanne's eyes widened when she saw inside of the hotel. They were standing in the lobby, but it had clearly been decorated. The walls had been painted with multiple designs, some of them dark like the ones on the buildings Joanne had seen earlier, but most were simple designs. There were chandeliers with strips of cloth hanging from them, casting multicolored light to the ground. There were some rugs on the floor that were colored with stains of all different colors. There was a table and a leather couch on one side of it, two leather loveseats on the other. The reception desk had multiple computers on it now, each one with headphones for gaming or something like gaming. There was a snack machine, but it was busted open, the snacks that were once there long gone. There was a drink machine, though, with water, tea, and some sodas inside. There were also tapestries nailed to the wall, each one gray and black with gold lettering that spelled out something in a language Joanne couldn't understand. *Χαίρε βασιλιά Kafa*, it read. And in the center of the lobby was a throne. Like, a golden throne with a red carpet leading up to it. A man was sitting on it, talking with other imaginary friends. He laughed at something one of them said. His laugh reminded Joanne of how Hyenas sounded. He had wild, long brown hair that stuck out in every direction that reminded Joanne of a lion's mane that had one streak of gold through it. His eyes were a mischievous green. Not the same green as Rumple's, but close enough that anyone could see the similarities. He was wearing a heavy cape that was gold on the inside with leopard fur lining, along with a black sleeveless shirt, gray pants, and shiny black boots. He also had some armor on, including wrist gauntlets, so he looked like something from ancient times. He looked to be in his late twenties, or very early thirties. He looked up and saw Rumple. A smile lit his face that looked like one of a fox when it was about to spring upon a rabbit. Everything about this guy seemed, almost... *evil*... to Joanne.

"Ah, Rumple! Back at last. Tell me, where have you been?" he said. Rumple froze and turned to face the man.

"Oh! King Kafa! I've been showing this new imaginary friend around the City the entire day," he said, giving a bow that looked way too theatrical to be believable to Joanne. Kafa's eyes slid over to Joanne where they widened a fraction. His gaze was hungry and evil looking, full of sick thoughts. Joanne swallowed and bowed the way Rumple had earlier. He laughed again, the sound of it reverberating through the room.

"Oh, there's no need for that. Come closer, I want to see you better," he said, chuckling, though it sounded dark. Joanne was sure she paled, but she rose and glanced at Rumple, who nodded, though she couldn't help but see the worry in his gaze. She approached Kafa and the throne, stopping a few feet in front of him. His eyes ran up and down her, the smile on his face never faltering, only widening even more. But something did flash in his eyes, though it was only there for a second, so Joanne figured it was just her imagination. Joanne resisted the urge to slap him, since she figured doing so would not be good for her. She suddenly wished that she had worn a baggy T-shirt and had her jacket zipped up. His eyes finally rested back on her face. Now that she was closer, she could see him better. He was wearing eyeliner and black eyeshadow and he had stubble on his face. Why he was wearing eyeliner, Joanne didn't know, and she figured she didn't want to know. He was a lean and had some muscles on his arms, but he didn't look like he would be able to win a fight against some of the people in the room.

"Well, aren't you a pretty little thing? What's your name, dear?" he asked. Joanne felt her face flush at the term "pretty little thing" and it wasn't from flattery, though she was sure Kafa thought so. She felt a bit humiliated, standing in front of everyone like that with him looking at her that way.

"Joanne," she replied shortly.

"Joanne. That's a beautiful name. Is this your first time in Imagine, Joanne?" he said, beaming at her.

"Yes, it is," Joanne said curtly.

"And how do you like it so far? Being imaginary and all?" he asked, grinning like a schoolboy as he leaned forward a little to hear her reply.

"It's been pretty great. I mean, Imagine is beautiful and I never got lost with Rumple showing me around. I think I might like being imaginary," she said after pretending to give it some thought. He laughed a short laugh without mirth.

"I think we all loved being imaginary once. So, tell me, how did you stumble upon the Unavenged?" he said, earning a few chuckles around the room.

"Rumple brought me here," she said, glancing back at him. Rumple looked so small, like a sheep in a pack of wolves, due to the fact that everyone else in the room looked older than twelve.

"Oh, yes. Rumple is one of my best men. *Very* clever. Were you looking to join the Unavenged?" Kafa said.

"Well, I don't really know what the Unavenged is," Joanne said, looking at Rumple and flashing him a *help me* look. Kafa looked back at Rumple, his eyebrows raised.

"Aw, you didn't even bother to tell her what we do? Come on, Rumple. You just dragged the poor girl here without even telling her what all of this is about? You know what, I'll tell her. Come a little closer, darling, I hate having to lean forward so much," Kafa said, beckoning for Joanne to come even closer. Joanne took a few steps forward so now she was only about a foot away from the throne. *If he calls me darling one more time...* Joanne thought, trying not to spit on his smiling face.

"That's good. So, this is the Unavenged, a group I started around twenty years ago. We're a group of imaginary friends that disagrees with the ways of the Imaginists. We rule over the dark part of the City, but trust me when I tell you it's very safe here. We occasionally do some things around the City just to remind everyone that we exist and we are not to be ignored. Most of us are discarded, though it's fine if you're not. If you join, you'll be given a home, food, and a family. So, what do you say Joanne?" he explained.

"Do I have to *do* something to join?" Joanne asked. Kafa laughed like it was the funniest joke he ever heard, and most of the Unavenged in the room also laughed.

"Of course, you do! We can't let just anybody into the Unavenged, can we? To get into the Unavenged, you must win a fight against one of my people," he said, his eyes sparking dangerously. Joanne felt herself pale a little. She gulped and looked back at Rumple, who looked like he was trying to keep calm, but it wasn't working. She felt a hand on her face that turned her face back to face forwards. It was Kafa's hand. He had long, thin pianist hands, though she doubted he actually played the piano. She clenched her hands in fists to keep herself from slapping his hand away.

"What are you looking at, Joanne? *Do you* want to join the Unavenged?" Kafa asked. The room fell silent as everyone waited with breaths held for her answer.

*Well, I'm sure that if I said no, I would look weak, and I don't think I want to look that way around these people. So, I don't guess I have a choice,* Joanne thought. She was pretty sure Rumple was shaking his head behind her, but she didn't pay him any notice.

"Yes. I'll do it," she said more bravely than she felt. Kafa smiled, though it looked malicious, and everyone in the room began cheering.

"Very good. Come! Unavenged! Assemble to the arena!" he said, letting go of her face and standing up. Joanne tried not to look surprised. He was only about five foot, while Joanne was five three. The Unavenged surged towards the exit, including Rumple.

"Come, Joanne, I'll lead you to the competitor's arena entrance," Kafa said, gesturing for her to follow him as he went out a different exit. Joanne followed him.

"What will the fight be like?" Joanne asked.

"What? Oh, you'll each have a sword you can use, and you duel until one person is on the ground with a sword pointed at their throat," he said cheerfully, as if the thought was pleasant. He led her down into a type of underground tunnel place that Joanne would easily get lost in without Kafa.

"Oh," Joanne said, trying not to sound nervous. He seemed to sense her nervousness.

"Don't be nervous. We have healers. And besides. I feel like you'll win," he said casually.

"And why is that?" Joanne asked. His eyes darted to her elbow for a second.

"Oh, no reason. You just seem like you have something special in store for the fight," Kafa said, then opened a wooden door and led her inside. It was a room with armor and swords, the floor dirt and the walls made of wood. It was dimly lit with some lanterns on some ledges.

"This is the place where you choose a sword and put on some armor. I don't suggest too much armor, or else you won't be able to move around much. Here's an earpiece to put in. Now, I must get to the king's box. I'll be watching. Good luck," he said, giving her a pat on the shoulder and an attempt at a reassuring smile before he turned on his heel and walked away, the sounds of his boots muffled by the dirt floor. Joanne watched him leave, glad that his perverted gazes left with him, but also confused on why she needed an earpiece. She put it on anyway. She looked around and chose a chest plate. She put it on, praying her years of theatre taught her how to put it on the right way. Then she grabbed a sword that had a blade as long as her arm.

*I could hurt this person. I have to go easy on them. Not too much. I still have to win this thing, just I can't necessarily hurt them too much without revealing that I'm real. This is going to be very difficult,* Joanne thought.

Suddenly she heard a loud, booming voice.

"Ladies and gentlemen of the Unavenged! Today we have a fight for a place in the Unavenged! Today we have Joanne and Barthemius! Let the fighting commence!" Kafa announced, and then a door that Joanne hadn't noticed creaked open.

*I guess I go,* Joanne thought. She walked out of it and was greeted by blinding stadium lights and the roar of the crowd. It looked like an old football field, the Unavenged sitting in the bleachers. There looked to be about three hundred of them, if not more. Across the field, she could see a man who was extremely buff with muscles. He was easily twice Joanne's size, and he looked like he could probably smash her between two of his fingers if he wanted to. Joanne swallowed, feeling the sword in her hand. She had taken tennis for one year in middle school, so she prayed that sword fighting was similar to tennis, otherwise she was screwed. The cheers got louder as he began walking towards her. Joanne took a deep breath and started walking towards him, wishing that she had something on other than boots. They reached the middle and they stopped when they were about six yards apart.

"Good luck, little girl," Barthemius said, his smile smug, as if he was sure he was going to win. Then in one swift movement, he lunged at her, sword out. Joanne dropped and rolled, springing back to her feet a few feet away, her feet sliding a little in the dirt. He whirled around and looked surprised to see Joanne standing there. Sure, she was covered in dirt now, but she was still in one piece. He lunged again, this time coming in from the side. Joanne couldn't move fast enough to duck, so she brought her sword up, blocking it. But he was stronger than her, and his force on the blade pushed her backwards, her boots sliding in the dirt.

*Maybe I should take a different approach,* Joanne thought, and she kicked as hard as she could. Barthemius, not expecting it, howled in pain and fell to the ground. His eyes looked surprised and... scared. Of Joanne. Joanne moved to point her sword at his throat, but he was too fast, springing up and tackling her to the ground. Her sword flew out of her grip, skidding away from her.

"You can imagine, Joanne. Use it," Kafa's voice whispered in her ear from her earpiece.

*I can imagine. What does that mean? Wait,* Joanne wondered, then realized what Kafa had meant. *Nothing too unbelievable. Just something to let me win this,* Joanne thought. She imagined pushing Barthemius off her, and suddenly she did, her arms full of strength she didn't know she had. Barthemius flew off her, his eyes big with shock. She imagined she was fast, and she sprinted to her sword, kicking up dirt behind her. She wrapped her hand around the hilt and ran back to him, imagining she could leap far. She pushed off the ground when she was about twenty feet away from him, and she leaped through the air, her feet landing on his chest just as he started to get up. His head slammed against the ground, hard enough to knock him unconscious. He went limp and suddenly loud cheers rose up and the crowd began chanting her name. They all looked surprised. So was Joanne.

*What the heck did I just do?* she wondered.

"Well done, Joanne," Kafa said approvingly in her ear. She held up her sword, beaming. She saw Rumple in the crowd, his mouth hanging open in shock. The sight made her laugh.

"Joanne has defeated Barthemius! Welcome to the Unavenged, Joanne!" Kafa announced. Joanne looked up at the king's box and saw him nodding and smiling, but unlike everyone else, he didn't look surprised at all, as if he had been expecting Joanne to beat Barthemius.

*How did he know to tell me to Imagine?* Joanne wondered as the cheers rose up, stronger. The sun was beginning to go down, tinging the sky with pink.

"Alright! Everyone to the dining hall! It's time to eat and celebrate our new member!" Kafa announced, then disappeared from the king's box.

Joanne heard Kafa whisper in her ear to go back to the place where she found her armor and sword. Joanne turned and walked back to the room, the door shutting behind her. Joanne tried not to jump. Kafa was already there, a smirk on his face as he clapped.

"Very good job out there, Joanne. I told you that you had nothing to worry about. I was right, wasn't I?" Kafa said.

"Yeah, you were. How did you…" she said, thinking about how he had told her to imagine, and suddenly everything she imagined had happened.

"Joanne, you have to realize that I am not king for no reason. I know things that most others don't. I, for example, am the only one that knows your little secret. Well, I guess your brother knows, but nobody else does. It gives me leverage against you. In case you were to ever do something that displeases me, I would simply report you to the Imaginists. I may not like them, but they know what they're doing. Sometimes. Sometimes it's not strength that makes power, but knowledge," Kafa said, then turned to walk away, but Joanne stopped him, leaping to land in front of him, her super-leaping still working.

"Wait! How did you know?" Joanne asked, her face a mask of shock. Kafa laughed.

"Simple. First off, when I felt your face, you felt different. Imaginary friends feel warm, but you felt cold due to the wind outside. Imaginary friends don't get cold. Well, I guess vampires feel cold, but I could tell you weren't a vampire. Second off, Rumple was looking at you as if he had known you for years, not just a few days. I remember when he was discarded, he came to the Unavenged and I remember him mentioning how he was a girl's imaginary friend. And third, you didn't get hurt by Barthemius at all. You should have a bruise or a scratch, but no, nothing hurt you. So, I just connected the dots. Now, take your armor off and get ready for dinner," he said, then stepped around her and disappeared in the tunnels, leaving Joanne alone in the empty arena.

# Chapter Five

He felt it deep in his bones. A stir. Something different, something… off. Something was most definitely wrong. Kile's eyes snapped open, surveying the room around him as his eyes adjusted to the dimness. It looked the same, but he could feel in the pendant he wore around his neck that it didn't feel right. He got up from his bed and wiped his runny nose as he went to his window, his footsteps silent on the carpet floor. He threw open the curtains, the light of the sunset spilling into the room as he looked down at the City below. He felt it again. Somebody was channeling Imagine's power, somebody else that wasn't him.

*Impossible! No imaginary friend can channel Imagine's power unless they have the Stone! I have it, so that's not possible. Unless… hmm. Most curious. I will have to find this person. Why they're here, I don't know, but I will soon find out. And I will end them before they have the chance to end me.*

# Chapter Six

*What the heck was that? How did she even do that? How did she know to do that?*
Rumple wondered as the throng of people carried him to the dining hall. *She
shouldn't have been able to defeat Barthemius. But she did. She's not athletic at
all, so that doesn't even make sense. She was doing something; I just don't know
what...* Rumple was jostled out of his thoughts when the Unavenged entered the
dining hall and saw Kafa sitting at the head of the long table. Rumple shoved his
way through the crowd, apologizing whenever somebody complained or told him
to watch it until he reached Kafa.

"What did you think you were doing?" he said angrily. "Pairing her up against
Barthemius like that? *Nobody* can beat Barthemius! You knew she probably
wouldn't win! Wh-"

"I knew she would win, Rumple. Calm down. Now go take a seat," Kafa said,
cutting him off as he examined his sharp fingernails; sounding very bored. Rumple
sputtered, not suspecting that answer.

"B-but how? How did you know she could do that? I didn't know she could d-" he
stuttered, but was cut off by Kafa yet again.

"I am king, I don't tell my secrets. Now, if you know what's good for you, go sit
down and do stop acting like you're twelve," Kafa interrupted, his tone one that
nobody smart would question. Rumple flinched when he said twelve and almost
said that he was fifteen, thank you very much, but swallowed and went to his seat
at the table.

The dining hall had a gigantic chandelier, far larger than the small ones in the
hallway. Expensive oil paintings adorned the walls, some depicting death while
most showed portraits of famous imaginary friends, including Kafa. The floors
were a polished dark wood, so dark that if blood were to be spilled on it, nobody
would be able to tell it was blood unless one stuck their finger in it or smelled it.
There were two windows, though heavy velvet curtains always blocked their view
from sight. The faded wallpaper was a light red with a pattern on it. The table itself
was terribly long, long enough to seat around three hundred people. There were a
few chairs that were empty for new recruits and some were empty because the
owner had left the Unavenged. The seat to the left of Kafa was always empty for a

new Unavenged member, while the seat to the right was for the strongest warrior. Barthemius had sat in that seat, but due to his defeat from Joanne, it was now empty, ready for her to sit. Rumple was close to Kafa, one of his most trusted Unavenged. He was about eight chairs away from Kafa's left side, showing his status in the Unavenged. Though Rumple had only been in the Unavenged for three years, Kafa had taken a particular liking to him and he had risen through the ranks of the Unavenged quickly.

Rumple sat down, the sound of his chair scraping against the floor joining the noise of many other chairs doing the same. The food was already laid out on the table, as it always was, in order to not displease Kafa. Kafa may have been a bit short and thin, but he really wasn't somebody you wanted to displease, agitate, or have as an enemy. He was lethal, cruel, and cunning. Those three qualities in one person made him very dangerous indeed, which was why Kafa had been able to keep his position as leader in the first few years of the Unavenged when some imaginary friends had been stupid enough to try and challenge him for the position.

The food was Roman that day, as it always was whenever a new imaginary friend joined the Unavenged. Apparently Kafa had been Roman, so whenever a new imaginary friend was victorious, he always liked to serve food that was served to victors where he and his Creator were from.

Most imaginary friends were talking to one another, excitedly chattering about Joanne defeating Barthemius. Nobody ate yet. It was custom for Kafa to eat first, and then everyone else was allowed to eat. There were jugs of posca and wine, and plates of breads, meats, vegetables, fruits, and fish. There were even small saucers of olive oil, though most imaginary friends didn't use it on their food. Kafa was a very old imaginary friend, one of the first to exist from around 120 AD. He had seen a lot, adapted a lot, but he always kept his love for the food of the country he had been created in.

Imaginary friends began using spoons and other utensils to pile food onto their plates. Rumple poured himself some posca since he wasn't twenty-one yet, though most imaginary friends in the Unavenged didn't care if you were underage. Technically posca was watered down wine, but there was no other drink available, so Rumple had it anyways. He put some trout on his plate along with some asparagus and a slice of bread, then leaned back in his chair and waited. He looked around, but Joanne still wasn't back from the prepping room of the arena. Rumple remembered his fight to get into the Unavenged. He had only won because of his speed and his small size, but he had won all the same, and Kafa had later praised him for using his size to his advantage, since Kafa wasn't much taller than Rumple.

Suddenly the doors swung open and Joanne peered in as if making sure it was the right room. Kafa noticed her first.

"Behold our new champion, Joanne! Joanne, welcome to the Unavenged! Please, come and join me!" he announced, the chattering dying down at the sound of Kafa's voice and applause rising as he said Joanne's name. Joanne stumbled back a little, not expecting the applause.

*Good job, Joanne. Smooth as always,* Rumple thought fondly as he began to clap. She looked surprised and a little embarrassed, but she blushed a little anyways and smiled a little as she walked over to Kafa. He patted the seat to his right and she sat down in it, her platinum blond hair shining in the light from the chandelier.

"That is the seat for our champion! I am proud to tell you that you now have the right to sit in that seat, Joanne! This feast is to honor you! Enjoy yourself! You may all eat now!" he said, and chatter burst out around the table as people began to eat their food. Joanne looked a little uneasy as she sat next to Kafa, but he said something to her that made her laugh and most of it went away, though some of it still remained in her eyes.

*None of this was what I planned. I was supposed to get Joanne in here, make a plan, and then we'd carry it out and hopefully save all of Imagine. But frickin' Kafa had to notice her and now this is going to be a lot harder than I thought. Crap, Kafa. Crap!* Rumple thought as he watched the two of them eat and talk. Rumple began to eat his food, keeping an eye on Joanne as he did so, hoping that if she noticed him, she would feel better.

"Are you alright? You look a bit ill," Kafa said when Joanne sat down, earning a halfhearted laugh from her.

"I'm fine, thank you," she said, feeling a little bit less uncomfortable.

"Oh, alright. I know this might all seem new and strange to you, but you'll get the hang of how things are done here soon enough," Kafa said reassuringly, putting a hand on her shoulder that Joanne wanted to shrug off. She couldn't help but feel exposed and uneasy ever since Kafa told her he knew her secret.

*What if he does report me to the Imaginists? What will they do? What will happen to me?* Joanne wondered nervously. Her thoughts were interrupted by Kafa.

"So, Joanne, tell me about yourself. Where are you from? How old are you? That sort of thing," he said, his eyes sparking with genuine interest. Joanne began to put some food on her plate as she talked.

"Um. I'm sixteen. I'm from South Carolina. There's not that much to tell. I'm pretty normal, honestly," she said. Kafa's brow furrowed in slight confusion as he drank from his glass.

"Hm. Where is this... South Carolina? Is it over in the new world? Or rather, the United States of America?" he asked. Joanne blinked in surprise when he called it the new world. *How old is this guy?* Joanne wondered.

"Oh. Yeah, it's over in America. Where are you from?" she said.

"I'm from Rome back around 120 AD. I may not talk or dress like it, but believe me, I'm quite old. I've simply lost the accent over the years. So many more imaginary friends spoke English that I just learned the language and stopped speaking Greek. Do tell me, what year is it now?" he replied, a small smile on his face as if he were remembering something.

"2017," Joanne replied. Kafa whistled.

"I am getting old. Shoot, I'm still just as athletic as I was back in the day, though; so, I suppose I'm fine. But anyways, tell me about your town, your family, your hobbies. Surely, you're not that dull if you had an imaginary friend." he said, shrugging.

"Uh, I live in a town of about twenty thousand people. I like drawing and reading an- is this wine?" Joanne said as she took a sip of her drink.

"*That* is posca," Kafa said, pointing to her cup.

"What's that?" Joanne asked.

"Watered down wine with some spices," he said as he drank some wine.

"Don't you guys have water?" Joanne asked, setting the posca back down.

"But of course. Do you not like wine?" Kafa said as he set his own glass down.

"Well, I'm underage..." Joanne said, trailing off, but he just looked at her blankly.

"For what?" he asked, looking confused.

"For what age you can drink alcohol!" Joanne exclaimed. Kafa frowned. "When did that come into play?" he asked.

"I don't know! Point is, I'm too young to drink this, so may I please have some water?" she asked.

"You may," he said, then clapped his hands. Suddenly an elf girl was standing behind him with a pitcher of water as if she had appeared out of thin air. He took the pitcher from her hands, thanking her, and poured Joanne some water, then handed it back to the elf girl, who disappeared.

"Thank you," Joanne said, sipping some water.

"You're welcome. Please continue about your life, because I do find it quite interesting," Kafa said, leaning forward a little. Joanne put some food on her plate and then began to talk.

"Well, I like drawing, reading, and writing. I'm in tenth grade. I work at Subway in the summer. I have a sister and three dogs. I- woah, are you okay?" Joanne said as she ate, stopping when Kafa began coughing.

"I'm- I'm-" he tried to say between coughs, though he wasn't getting hardly anywhere in Joanne's opinion. She did something she'd seen other people do and started whacking his back.

"I'm- n-not choking!" he coughed. He took his hand away from his mouth to get a napkin, which to Joanne's horror, was covered in blood. She gasped and was about to call for a nurse or something when he held up a hand, as if he had sensed her train of thought.

"D-don't. One se-second," he said, still coughing as he pressed the napkin to his mouth. After a few moments, the coughing ceased and he set the napkin down, folding it over to hide the red stain on it. He wiped his hand on his napkin and then wiped it across his mouth, setting it back down. He looked over at Joanne, and there was something she couldn't read in his eyes.

"Please don't tell anyone about that," he said, leaning forwards so only she could hear him.

"Why not? What was that?" Joanne asked. He waved his hand as if there was a fly in the air.

"We shall discuss it later. For now, just forget about it and enjoy your food. Now, excuse me while I go… clean up," he said, giving her a smile and looking at her with a strange look in his eyes before getting up and leaving the room. Joanne could have sworn that there was worry and fear in his eyes, but she wasn't sure. She looked around, now surrounded by people she didn't know, and quickly finished her food, the feeling of unease growing in her stomach. Not only was she in some land for magical imaginary friends with a crazy imaginary friend running around, a super-powerful imaginary friend knew that she was real and could tell anyone, and it looked like he was dying. Just like Rumple. Which was why they had to catch the crazy imaginary friend. Because Joanne now saw that if they didn't, then everything would surely die. Rumple had told her that, but her brain hadn't fully believed him until that moment. She paled and was glad she was sitting down, or else she was sure she would have collapsed.

*This entire place is a world. A world with thousands of inhabitants. They all have thoughts, feelings, lives… and if I don't hurry, they will all die. Everyone in this room will be dead,* Joanne thought darkly, running a hand through her hair. She suddenly felt sick. She got up, trying not to run, knowing that imaginary friends were staring at her but not caring. As soon as the dining hall doors closed behind her, she ran through the hotel until she was outside, the cool night air hitting her face. It was around seven now, and the sun was almost completely gone, the last rays of light touching the land. She looked around and decided she needed to take a walk. She set off down the sidewalk, drawing her jacket closer to her and forgetting about the shady figures she had seen earlier, her mind occupied on the thought of Imagine dying. So, she didn't notice when two figures fell into step behind her, their pace matching hers so she wouldn't hear their footsteps. The moon began to rise, or rather, the two moons.

*I guess Imagine has two moons… weird,* Joanne thought, pausing to stare at them. Her followers, not expecting her to stop, stopped a second too late. Joanne, hearing them behind her, whirled around, but she was too late. Her legs were knocked out from underneath her and something dark and scratchy came over her head. She tried to scream, but something was pressed against her mouth and the wind was knocked out of her as she hit the ground. Darkness enveloped her, almost like a wanted peace from her scattered thoughts earlier as she felt herself being lifted up, up, up…

Kafa splashed cold water on his face for the fifth time, trying to get the sick feeling to go away. He felt hot all over, and there was an annoying burning sensation in his throat where his blood had come up. He wiped his face with his hand towel and looked up in the mirror. Some of his eyeliner had smeared.

*Ahh, delightful,* he thought sourly, reaching over to his makeup on the counter to grab his eyeliner. He took the cap off and reapplied it, then with one last look at himself, he walked into his room. It had a thirty-six-inch TV, a wooden desk, a queen-sized bed, a mini fridge, a mirror, a nightstand with a lamp, paintings on the walls, expensive rugs, and a balcony that overlooked the dark part of the City. His territory. His domain. He sat down on his bed, the sheets still a mess from last night. *I hate nightmares,* he thought as he remembered his dream. He picked up his cell phone from the nightstand and stared at it before setting it back down, deciding that him coughing up blood wasn't worth calling someone up. It's not like he was dying. But then again, Kafa supposed things had been changing since the Stone of Existence went missing. Imaginary friends had been fading, mainly old ones, some young, and Kafa knew that he was very old, and if the Stone wasn't returned soon, he would fade soon, something he had thought would never happen to him.

Kafa stood up, going to the balcony in hopes of the cool air helping cool him off. He sat down on the chair on the balcony and began thinking about Joanne. He had known she was different the moment she had walked in the Unavenged base. She had a spark in her eyes that he had never seen in an imaginary friend before, something he had only seen in his Creator centuries ago. Just the thought of his Creator made him smile. The thought of his laugh, his smile, made Kafa happy. He had felt it when his Creator had died, just a few years after he had been discarded. His Creator had been too young when he passed. But Joanne... she was the first real person he had seen since his Creator. In a way, she was like his Creator. A fighting spark in her eyes, the color of her eyes, the way she talked and handled situations... it was all so familiar to him. But she was too young for him. He had been hoping that she was a little bit older, but sixteen was simply too young. Besides, he didn't really feel like settling down and committing to anybody at the moment anyways. He didn't want to report Joanne to the Imaginists, but it was good for her to be scared of what he could do. Then she wouldn't do anything against him, and he wouldn't have to worry about her ever challenging him. Because deep down, he knew that because she was real, she could beat him. But she didn't know that. It would be even easier, this being the second time that he had started coughing up blood. He was getting weaker by the day, and nobody knew.

*Oh, Joanne. What will I do with y..?* he was thinking.

"Joanne?" Kafa muttered, squinting in the darkness. About half a mile away, he could see someone with platinum blond hair walking with two people following. He swore softly and stood up, jogging to the phone on his desk. He scrolled through his contacts until he found the right person. He pressed call and they picked up after a ring.

"Hello?"

"Rumple! Where's your sister?" Kafa demanded.

"My what?" Rumple asked, his already high-pitched voice jumping an octave. Kafa rolled his eyes.

*Dear Jupiter, how could I not know?* Kafa wondered.

"Your sister, Joanne! Is she with you?" Kafa asked, his tone sharp.

"Um… no. Why?" Rumple replied, a note of fear creeping into his voice. Kafa swore again.

"Meet me in the lobby. Get there as fast as you can!" Kafa said.

"Wait, how did y-" Rumple started asking, but Kafa hung up, cutting him off. He put his cell phone in his pocket and walked to his door, grabbing his cloak on the way out and then leaving the room and locking the door behind him. He walked down the hallway at a fast pace, shrugging on his robe as he walked. He slid down the banister on the staircase and into the lobby. Rumple was already there, looking confused and scared. Kafa walked right past him, shoving the doors open.

"Wait! W-"

"Come on!" Kafa said, interrupting Rumple again. He could hear Rumple jogging to catch up with him. Rumple jogged until he was beside Kafa, who was still just fast-walking.

"What's happening? Did something happen to Joanne?" Rumple asked worriedly as he tried not to trip over the worn, uneven sidewalk.

"Well… I think she might be in trouble. I saw two strange figures following her," Kafa said. Rumple tripped and Kafa's hand shot out to steady him.

"WHAT?" Rumple exclaimed.

"Silence! Whoever is following her might hear us!" Kafa hissed as he led them to his horse. Kafa preferred horses over cars. He swung himself onto his jet-black horse and helped Rumple up.

"Why do they want Joanne?" Rumple asked quietly.

"You told her about the missing Stone of Existence, correct?" Kafa asked.

"How did you know?" Rumple asked. Kafa sighed.

"Do all of you think I'm *that* oblivious? I mean, really, I haven't stayed king without being a bit observant, and I'm smarter than you might think. I was able to connect the dots on why you brought her here. Little do you know, that puts her in danger," Kafa said, kicking the horse in the side, making it rear up and then take off in the direction Joanne was seen.

"How does it put her in danger? And how did you even know she was real? Like, *legit*, I thought we had her story *down*!" Rumple exclaimed. Kafa sighed again.

"First, her skin felt cool when I touched her face. Second, you too seemed far too close to have met each other earlier that day. Third, she didn't get hurt at all when she was in that arena. She should have at least gotten some scratches," Kafa said quickly, as if he didn't want to waste breath explaining the clues again.

"Wait, when did you touch her face?" Rumple asked. Kafa looked at him indecorously.

"That's what you have to say? Seriously?" he said.

"Well, she's my sister, and I know you get around with the ladies sometimes, so I was just making sure-"

"Please. As if I would ever do that with your sister. I touched her face before she fought in the arena, remember?" Kafa said dismissively.

"Oh, yeah… I remember now. But back to this whole shebang. What do you mean, she's in danger?" Rumple asked, concern and fear creeping into his voice.

"Well, she is real. Therefore, she is the only one who has even a slight chance in defeating the thief and getting the Stone of Existence back. When she imagines things, the Stone can feel it. So, whoever has the Stone will be able to feel that she imagined something and they'll know that somebody real is in Imagine. Then they'll want to track her down before she has any idea that she's in trouble, and probably kill her so she can't kill them," Kafa explained.

"Just like now. She doesn't know she's in trouble," Rumple said, suddenly sounding very distant.

"Yes. That's why I arranged the fight so quickly. I wanted her to get accepted into the Unavenged so she could stay with us and be safe in the hotel. But, well… then I had to excuse myself and she wandered off for some reason," Kafa said, looking away from Rumple as he remembered coughing blood onto a napkin.

"How did you know … where did you see someone following her, though?" Rumple asked.

"I was on my balcony and I saw two people following her as she walked down a sidewalk, but I don't know if it could be the same person who took the Stone. It could just be a simple mugger, as you know this isn't the safest part of Imagine. People walking alone get mugged all the time, so we drive or ride. You didn't tell Joanne about that, did you?" Kafa said, the wind whipping at his face, making his long, wild hair fly into Rumple's face. Rumple sputtered, trying to hold onto the back of Kafa's shirt while also trying to swat his hair away.

"Well, no. I didn't think she'd go outside by herself," Rumple said.

"Shouldn't you be keeping an eye on your own sister?" Kafa asked, shooting Rumple a look over his shoulder.

"Well, I had to pee. So, I left. I came back, and she was gone," Rumple explained.

"Perfect. Rumple had to take a potty break and our only chance of saving this place suddenly disappears. You may not have known that, but that's another reason the Imaginists didn't want to bring a real person into this. They'd be a danger, and in the end, it'd just be a big mess. So, good job, Rumple," Kafa said dryly.

"Well, I didn't know! And you have to realize, we are all *dying*! I know you're dying more than most because you're older than most! *Don't* think I didn't see you cough blood into a napkin! I brought her because I'm trying to stop this before you and others die! *She* is our *only* hope! We all know that if a real person does not intervene, we will all surely fade away as if *we never existed*!" Rumple exclaimed. Kafa paled and was quiet for a moment.

"Yes, I know. Believe me, I know. I don't wish to die. I've done too many things to go to heaven, so I'll surely burn in hell. I want to stop this as much as you do, but I'm not sure if it'll be enough. Because you have to realize, we still don't know where this thief is …or what he plans to do. I mean, if he's real, he could destroy all three realms in an instant. Why he would do that, I don't know. But I'm sure there's a motive. There's always one. But I just have no idea what that might be," he said softly. Kafa almost never spoke softly. Always sharp, always firm. If he was speaking softly, then he was trying to get you to listen.

"Yeah. I'm sure he has some master plan, but who knows what it is," Rumple said. Kafa nodded, then swore.

"Wha-aahhhh!" Rumple yelled as Kafa kicked the horse and it took off. Rumple clutched to Kafa's shirt, trying desperately to not fall off the horse as it tore through the street. Rumple peered over Kafa's shoulder and saw in the light of the two moons, two figures loading a limp body into a van. Rumple swore, too. The figures climbed into the van and it took off like a bullet from a gun. Kafa kicked the horse, making it go even faster as they chased after the van.

"Can you ride a horse?" Kafa yelled over the howl of the wind as he steered the horse sharply to the right as the van turned right.

"Umm, I'm riding one right now, dude," Rumple said.

"No! I meant, can you drive a horse?" he asked, agitation creeping into his voice.

"Oh! I don't know, I've never tried before," Rumple said.

"Well, you're about to have to try," Kafa said.

"Wait, what?" Rumple exclaimed as Kafa suddenly stood up, balancing on the saddle with the skill of someone who had done it for years. Rumple stared up at him open-mouthed.

"Now grab the reins and steer if they steer!" Kafa instructed as the horse drew steadily closer to the van until they were about three feet apart.

"Okay, I'm going to jump! Then you jump after me!" Kafa shouted over the noise of the wind and the van's engine.

"Are you crazy? We'll die!" Rumple exclaimed. Kafa just looked at him like he was an idiot. Then Rumple realized what he meant.

"Just steer! Okay, I'm jumping… now!" Kafa said, then launched himself off the horse just as the van turned left. Kafa flew over the edge and scrambled for a hold on the roof as he slid over its smooth surface. Rumple's stomach contracted in fear as he watched Kafa. Kafa finally managed to get a grip on the side of the van, so he was now dangling over the road on the side of a van going around fifty miles an hour that was slowly increasing speed.

"Kafa!" Rumple exclaimed as he steered the horse to follow the van again.

"What?" Kafa asked, looking as if it was quite an effort to hold on.

"Are you okay?" Rumple asked.

"DO I LOOK OKAY RIGHT NOW?!" Kafa yelled.

"Um… I mean, you're doing pretty good so far. Just hang in there, buddy! I'll be there in a second," Rumple said.

"I don't really have much of a choice!" Kafa exclaimed.

"Oh, yeah. Okay, here goes," Rumple said, muttering the last part to himself as he slowly and shakily stood up. His arms pinwheeled through the air as he tried to keep his balance.

*Jupiter help us all; he's trying to stand on the horse,* Kafa thought as he strained to hold onto the side of the van. If he had been any taller, his feet would have been dragging along the road. For once, he was glad for his size. Rumple took a deep breath as he balanced precariously on the saddle. Then he jumped, rolling onto the roof of the van. He clung to it, afraid to move as he thought that it was a miracle that he had made it.

"Rumple! Could you lend a hand?" Kafa asked.

"Um… oh, yeah. One second," Rumple said, steeling himself. The horse was now far behind the van, turning to go back to the hotel. Rumple wished *he* was in the hotel. Gathering his courage, he inched his way across the roof until he was peeking over the side Kafa was clinging to with one hand.

"Alright, I'm going to give you my hand. You take it and I'll try to pull you up!" Rumple said, extending one of his hands to Kafa. Kafa took his other hand and put it in Rumple's. Rumple swore.

"You're heavy!" he said.

"No, you're just an unathletic twelve-year-old and I'm a full-grown man!" Kafa exclaimed.

"Tell yourself what you need to," Rumple muttered as he tried to pull Kafa up. Kafa did most of the getting up, sort of using Rumple as a ladder to get back up. After a few agonizing seconds, Kafa was on the roof with Rumple. They were both panting, Rumple more than Kafa. Kafa looked over at Rumple.

"I think you might want to work-out sometime," he said.

"Hey!" Rumple exclaimed.

"It's true," Kafa said, shrugging.

"Well... doesn't mean you have to acknowledge it," Rumple muttered. Kafa snickered before his face grew serious again.

"Alright, lay on your stomach and spread out like this," Kafa said, doing so. Rumple followed his instructions.

"Why?" he asked.

"It'll be easier not to be seen this way," Kafa replied.

"Oh, okay. Where do you think they're taking us?" Rumple asked.

"I don't know," Kafa said, his voice uneasy as they watched their surroundings race past them.

"This is bad," Rumple said. Kafa looked at him as if he was an idiot again, but said nothing. The van turned again and then began to slow. Kafa and Rumple looked at each other, anticipation on their faces. The van pulled into a clearing that had a single tree, the tree and all the grass dead and dry. The two figures got out of the car and went around to the back, taking the body out. The person had a sack over their head, but it was clearly Joanne. Kafa felt Rumple stiffen beside him. He put a hand on Rumple's shoulder to steady him. The two figures carried Joanne out to the tree, where there was another figure waiting in the shadow of the tree. Kafa slid down the side of the van, beckoning for Rumple to follow him. Rumple did the same, landing on his face instead of on his feet like Kafa did.

"Ow," he muttered before springing to his feet. Kafa took his sword out of its sheath and began to creep towards the figures. Rumple followed, trying to be just as silent as Kafa was being. The figures took the sack off Joanne's head. Kafa and Rumple stopped when they were on the other side of the tree. The figures dropped their hoods.

*Ugh. Vampires. How disgusting,* he thought. They lowered Joanne and then crouched down to feed on her blood. Rumple made a retching sound beside him. Kafa elbowed Rumple, but it was too late.

# Chapter Seven

The vampires' heads snapped in Kafa and Rumple's direction. Rumple swore softly as Kafa leaped into action. Kafa swiped at them with his sword, making them jump back. The third vampire's eyes widened.

"King Kafa! To what do we owe the pleasure?" he asked, giving a stiff bow and looking nervous.

"The pleasure is nobody's! What is the law about feeding?" Kafa demanded, holding the sword point to the vampire's throat. The vampire looked at the sword uneasily.

"Um… jump, boys!" the vampire ordered, and suddenly Kafa heard Rumple yell as two vampires leaped on his back, knocking Kafa to the ground. Kafa swore and Rumple started trying to kick the vampires.

*Jupiter, help that boy,* Kafa thought dryly as he tried to get out from underneath the vampires. He tried to swing at them with his sword, but the third vampire put his foot down over it, making it impossible for him to move it.

"Go ahead and feed, boys. The girl and the runt are mine," he said.

"Hey! Who are you calling runt?" Rumple exclaimed. Kafa resisted the urge to roll his eyes.

"Be still and it'll be over soon," the third vampire said, whipping out a dagger. Rumple paled considerably.

"Rumple! Move it!" Kafa called as one of the vampires moved down to his neck. Kafa tried not to recoil in disgust. *I have one shot. Hopefully this works. Dear Jupiter, let this work,* Kafa thought as the second vampire positioned their mouth over his neck. As he moved down to feed, Kafa moved his head and slammed it against the vampire's. The second vampire rolled off him in surprise, clutching his head. The one vampire left on him was not enough. Kafa rolled over pinning him underneath him before he sprung up and kicked them in the nose, making black vampire blood spray everywhere. The vampire cried out and Kafa stepped on his face, the crunch of bone under the heel of his boot silencing them for the time being. The third vampire whirled on him, forgetting that Kafa's sword was under his shoe as he moved towards Kafa. Rumple, not knowing what else to do, leaped onto the vampire's back, wrapping his arms around the vampire's neck in an attempt to choke him.

"Vampires don't need to breathe, you idiot!" Kafa called over his shoulder as he grabbed his sword off the ground.

"They don't?" Rumple shrieked as the vampire tried to throw him off it's back.

"No!" Kafa exclaimed as he began fighting the second vampire.

"Oh! Maybe I should take a different approach…" Rumple shouted, trailing off before he started trying to elbow the vampire's face. The vampire, looking just as confused as Kafa, simply grabbed Rumple's elbow and threw him to the ground. Then the vampire descended on him. Kafa swore yet again.

"No! Rumple! Don't get his blood in your mouth!" Kafa said as he cut the fast-moving vampire across the chest, making him crumple to the ground. He rushed over the vampire that was on Rumple and make a slash across his back. The vampire howled and leaped, trying to tackle Kafa, but Kafa shoved his sword through the vampire's middle, making him join the other two vampires on the ground. Kafa and Rumple looked at them, breathing hard, then looked at each other. Kafa wiped his black blood slicked blade on the grass and shoved it back in its sheath.

"You. We need to train you in combat sometime. Now come on, help me get your sister into the van," Kafa said, jerking a thumb towards Joanne.

"Okay. You know what, I never thought I'd piggy-back ride a vampire. Now that I have, I wish that I didn't," Rumple said as he lifted Joanne's arms and Kafa lifted her feet.

"What?" Kafa sighed.

"Sometimes I forget you're stuck at twelve, and then I am *brutally* reminded," Kafa said, shaking his head as they carried her to the van.

"Technically, I'm fifteen," Rumple said.

"But you're still stuck at twelve," Kafa reminded him. Rumple muttered something under his breath that Kafa couldn't make out, but he then decided he didn't care to ask what he said. They put her in the backseat and buckled her up, then went around to the front. Kafa got into the driver's seat and started the engine. Thankfully, the keys were still in the ignition. Kafa drove them out of the clearing and back to the road. He drove in silence, he and Rumple not saying a word, until suddenly he felt someone's hands around his throat. He gagged, yanking the steering wheel to the left in an attempt to throw them off. It worked. They let go of his neck, tumbling to the other side of the van. Kafa's head whipped to the backseat in search of who had just tried to strangle him as he was driving. Joanne laid on the ground, having unbuckled. She was breathing hard and her eyes looked unfocused. Rumple looked behind him.

"Joanne! You're awake!" he said happily, as if he didn't notice that she had just tried to choke Kafa. Kafa gave him a look. Her eyes focused on Rumple, then Kafa.

"Oh! Oh my god, I'm so sorry! I thought that you were one of those guys! I was just walking and- wait, how did I get in a van with you two? Joanne said apologetically before she seemed to realize where she was. Kafa and Rumple looked at each other.

"Well, long story short, you went outside for some reason, Kafa saw you, you got kidnapped, we got on a horse and started chasing a van with it, Kafa lost his mind and told me that we had to jump off the horse and onto the van, and when he tried he failed miserably, and then he used me as a human ladder to get back up, then the van stopped and we saw some vampires had kidnapped you so then we beat the crap out of them and then you tried to choke Kafa on the way back to the hotel, and yeah, here we are," Rumple said in one breath.

Joanne stared at him.

"What?" she asked. Rumple gave her an exasperated look.

"Dude, if you think I'm going to say all of that aga-" Rumple started, but Kafa talked over him.

"Basically, you got kidnapped by some vampires and we saved you. You're welcome," Kafa said.

"Oh. Umm, ...thank you. I wouldn't want to be food for vampires," Joanne said.

"Sure thing. But back to the whole being-outside-without-somebody-else talk. *Why* were you out there alone?" Rumple asked.

"Oh. I just... needed some air, so I took a walk," Joanne explained.

Kafa blinked at her.

"You needn't go outside again," he said.

"Why?" she asked.

"In case you've forgotten, I rule over the dark part of the City. There are dangers everywhere, especially at night. If you want to go outside, somebody needs to go with you," Kafa said.

"Oh. Yeah, I probably won't be doing that again," she said.

"Good. And please, no more trying to choke me," Kafa said as he drove back onto the road.

"Yeah, I won't be doing that again either," Joanne muttered. They drove back to the hotel and when they parked, Joanne asked,

"Didn't you just steal this van?"

"Yes, I suppose I did. They tried to steal you first, so it's their fault they lost their van," Kafa said, shrugging as he got out.

"Hmm. Okay, then," Joanne said as she got out.

"Now, we were originally going to have a Run tonight, but after all that, I don't think I'll have the energy to pull it off. But I do wish to speak with the two of you privately. Please, follow me," Kafa said, turning and walking into the hotel. Some Unavenged members were in the lobby throwing paper planes at each other, which Kafa ignored completely. He led them through the lobby, through a hallway, and then up a staircase. They arrived at a door and he unlocked it, holding it open for them to go inside. Joanne guessed that this was his room, from the looks of it. There was a huge TV, paintings, a queen-sized bed, a balcony, a bathroom, a nightstand, a mini fridge, and a desk. Kafa pointed to two chairs by the desk.

"Sit," he commanded. Rumple and Joanne sat in the chairs and looked at him. Joanne noticed that he looked very tired. He had shadows under his eyes, his cape was splattered with black blood, his hair was even more of a mess than it had been earlier, and his eyes looked exhausted. He didn't show it, though, when he spoke.

"Okay. I'm just going to tell the two of you now that I know your little secret and your little plan. I know Joanne's real, and I know that Rumple brought Joanne here in an attempt to try and defeat the person that stole the Stone of Existence. Here is the flaw in your plan. I believe that I know the imaginary friend that took the Stone of Existence, and you're going to need a lot more than just Joanne to defeat him.

Joanne is one person. He is too, but he is a very clever and intelligent imaginary friend. He will find a way to either stay in the shadows and carry out his plan, or he will carry out his plan by force. The first way would make it extremely hard to find him, and unless Joanne gets any training, she won't be able to defeat him, whether we find him and the Stone or not. The second way, you won't be able to get to him. I know him well enough. He's the type of person who plans the dirty work and lets others carry it out for him. So, he'll be hiding behind something, puppeteering the entire thing.

Another flaw: Joanne can imagine things, and since this is Imagine, they will actually happen. The Stone will allow him to feel that she's imagining things. He'll know that there is a real person in Imagine, and he will want to exterminate her before she has a chance to defeat him. So, he will track her down and kill her before we even have a chance to find him. By bringing Joanne here, she is in terrible danger. But now that she's here, it won't be easy to get her back out if that's what we wish to do. He'll be guarding the exits to the normal world, making sure that she can't leave.

So, at this point, we have to make a plan. A real plan, one that has a chance of winning against this imaginary friend. I'm telling you that you will need me and the Unavenged to assist you. So, I offer you our help in finding and defeating this imaginary friend. Do you accept?" Kafa said, pacing in front of them, his boots echoing on the wood floors.

"Umm, why would we say no?" Rumple asked.

"Hmm, I don't know. Perhaps you're headstrong and think that you can tackle Kile on your own. But let me tell you now, alone, you will not win," he said after a moment's consideration.

Rumple looked at Joanne.

"Do we want to do this?" he asked.

"It's probably our only chance if we want to defeat this guy. Yes, we accept," Joanne said.

"Excellent! Excellent! We shall start training the two of you tomorrow. For now, it would be best for us all to get some rest," he said, a smile lighting his face.

"Yeah, probably. See you tomorrow?" Rumple said.

Kafa laughed a short laugh.

"You forget that I am your king. Of course, you'll see me tomorrow!" Kafa said.

"Right! See you then!" Rumple said, getting up. Joanne did the same.

"And Joanne! Do remember *not* to go around without somebody else!" Kafa said, smiling as they walked out of the door.

"Umm- alright!" she said, giving him the first genuine smile that she had given him since she met him.

"Bye, now!" Kafa said.

"Bye!" Joanne said as the door shut behind her.

The smile stayed on Kafa's face after they left. He shook his head, smiling to himself now.

"Trying to choke me when I had just rescued her... she is truly an interesting figure," he muttered to himself. Suddenly his phone rang. He took it out of his pocket and looked down at the screen. *Unknown number* it said. Kafa pressed the answer button and held it to his ear.

"Hello?" he said.

"This is Kafa, correct?" a male voice with a slight German accent asked.

*He sounds awfully familiar...* Kafa thought.

"Why yes. Who is this?" Kafa asked, his brow furrowing.

"An old friend. But that doesn't matter. I have a deal for you, Kafa," the man said.

"I'm listening," Kafa said.

"Give me the Joanne Raider," the man said.

"That's not a deal!" Kafa scoffed.

"I'm not finished. Give us Joanne Raider. *Or* I will shoot you with this little rock here," the man said, the voice no longer coming from the phone but behind Kafa. Kafa whirled around and almost dropped the phone in surprise, his eyes wide before they narrowed to slits. A man stood behind him; the balcony door wide open. His pitch-black hair flew in the gust of wind from outside, his gray eyes unreadable. He looked to be in his late twenties. He was wearing all black, looking like a shadow come to life. Kafa had seen a few of those back when children's imagination wasn't as imaginative as it is these days. The man removed the cell phone from his ear, pressing the hang up button. Kafa heard a click in his ear, and a voice said, "Call ended."

The man was wearing a long-sleeved black shirt, black pants, black boots, and a red stone glinted on a necklace around his neck. Kafa paled when his eyes slid over the rock.

"Hello, Kafa. Did you miss me?" the man asked, his teeth pearly white when he smiled. Kafa lowered the phone.

*Of course, I did,* Kafa thought, but he didn't say it aloud.

"I can't say I did. Rumor is you're running around with the Stone of Existence," Kafa said, feeling as if all the air had been sucked from his lungs. The man gestured to the necklace he wore.

"Ah, you've lost your observant nature over the years. But the rumors *are* true," the man said, smirking as he touched the Stone.

"I see that. I'm not stupid," Kafa said dryly.

"Oh, of course you're not, Kafa. I wouldn't have given you the pleasure of my company if you were," the man said smoothly.

"You gave me your company because we were friends, not because you thought I wasn't stupid," Kafa growled.

"Yes, I suppose we were friends. For a while. Then I saw the light and realized how ridiculous I was being," the man said.

"You saw the light? You didn't see any light, you changed for the worse! There was never a moment when you improved!" Kafa exclaimed.

"Maybe. But you went downhill, too. Really. What kind of King are you? Ruling over only half of the City and then rampaging the other half! Come on, Kafa, I thought you were better than that," the man said with mock disappointment.

"You knew those were my plans! It wasn't something I planned after you changed! I've always been that way. Ambitious. But look at me, I have *power*. I *rule* over the dark part of Imagine. I don't think you can say that," Kafa said, his hands curling into fists.

"You're right, I can't. Soon I will rule over all of Imagine and more," the man said, an evil smile splitting his face.

"What do you mean?" Kafa asked, trying not to let fear creep into his voice.

"I am far younger than you, Kafa. You are growing old. I have plans that I will carry out. Plans that you could never dream of. Now, give me Joanne- *or* I shoot you with this," the man said.

"Kile, I thought you were better than this," Kafa said, hurt creeping into his voice as memories of the old Kile raced through his head. The one that had a heart. The one that would have never hurt anything. His best friend.

"I was. I am no longer," Kile said flatly, as if the emotions had been sucked right out of him.

"Could you really kill me? After *everything* we've been through, after *everything* we did... I thought you felt the same way about me I felt about you, Kile. I thought you *cared*," Kafa said, looking heartbroken.

"I did once. But I don't anymore," Kile said.

"What did she say to you? You never told me; you didn't want to be around me. What happened that night?" Kafa asked.

"*Do not* talk about her!" Kile exclaimed, his eyes flashing with rage.

"What did she say that made you break the way you did?" Kafa asked, concern in his voice as he took a step towards Kile.

"SHUT UP!" Kile shouted, his breaths fast and his eyes wild and angry. Then he took a deep breath, seeming to regain control of himself.

"Now. Joanne or your death. You choose, Kafa," Kile said coldly. Kafa was silent for a moment, then sighed as he realized that he didn't have much of a choice.

"Fine. I will give you Joanne on one condition. Leave the Unavenged alone when you carry out your plan," Kafa said slowly.

Kile laughed.

"Oh, Kafa. You are in no position to bargain with me. But very well, I accept. Now, bring her to me," he said.

"I can't give her to you now. I just dismissed her. Give me a week and I will have her delivered to you," Kafa said.

Kile sighed.

"Fine. I will be watching you to make sure you don't pull any tricks. Step out of line, and this whole hotel burns with you in it," Kile said, then just as quickly as he came, left through the balcony.

Kafa collapsed onto his bed after Kile left, running a hand through his long hair. *Dear Jupiter, what have I done?* he wondered hopelessly as the blankness of Kile's voice echoed through his head. *I was. I am no longer.* Kafa closed his eyes. *What did she say to you to change you the way it did? What did she do?*

~~~

"And here it is," Rumple said proudly as he opened the door to his room. Joanne looked around, pretending to be amazed.

"Wow. It's beautiful, Rumple," she said sarcastically. It was basically Kafa's room, but without the mini fridge, the balcony, or the large TV. Just a small TV instead. And it was a mess.

"I know, right? I chill here when I'm not needed," Rumple said as he plopped down onto the queen-sized bed. There was a gigantic Batman poster over the bed.

*Of course. What else could I expect from him?* Joanne thought, a smile tugging at the corner of her mouth. She remembered how he used to sleep in a Batman sleeping bag on her floor and she felt a pang as she remembered imagining it after he left and it being empty.

"Okay, so I was thinking that you sleep on the ground, because I'm not giving up my bed. Or since you're my sister, you could share the bed with me as long as you stay on the other side of the bed and don't touch me," Rumple said as he took off his shoes, tossing them to the ground.

"I think I'll take the floor," Joanne said.

"Good. I wasn't going to let you sleep with me anyways. It'd be too weird," Rumple said happily. Joanne rolled her eyes. Typical Rumple. She took off her shoes and laid down on the ground, closing her eyes.

"Are you really just going to sleep on the floor?" Rumple asked. She opened her eyes.

"That was the choice, so yeah," she said.

"I was gonna get you a sleeping bag or something…" Rumple said, trailing off.

"That would be much better," Joanne said, getting up.

"One second, let me find it," he said, opening the drawers of his desk. A second later, he took out a bundle and rolled it out on the ground. The familiar gray fabric with the Batman logo on it made Joanne gasp.

"Oh, my gosh! This was your sleeping bag!" she exclaimed.

"Yeah, I know. I only used it for like, eight years," he said, smiling.

"I- I remember watching you as you slept. I remember kicking it out of the way when I wanted to sit down and looking at it after you left…" Joanne said, trailing off. Rumple put a hand on her shoulder.

"Hey, it's okay. I didn't actually die. Besides, I'm here now, so it's okay," he said softly. Joanne nodded and smiled at him.

"Yeah, I know," she said, then yawned.

Rumple's eyebrows raised an inch.

"You good?" he asked.

"Yes, I'm just tired," Joanne said.

"Me, too. I'm going to hit the sack. See you in the morning," Rumple said, dropping his hand and climbing into bed. Joanne climbed into the sleeping bag, smelling Rumple on it. She had always imagined he smelled faintly of B.O., but mainly like old comics. He smelled exactly like that. She closed her eyes as Rumple flicked off the lights and tried to fall asleep.

"Good night," she said.

"Night, dude. Don't say anything else, because I will kill you. The Rumple needs his beauty sleep," he said.

Joanne smiled, even though she knew he couldn't see it in the darkness. *I forgot how much I missed you,* she thought as she drifted off to sleep.

# Chapter Eight

"Rise and shine! Come on! We've got to go! Unavenged breakfast is only served until eight! If you don't hurry, you won't get breakfast!" Rumple exclaimed, jolting Joanne awake. She cracked her eyes open to see Rumple standing over her. Her eyes flew open and she jumped.

"I know, my face is scary. Come on, hurry up," Rumple said, then walked away.

"What about new clothes?" Joanne asked as she got up.

He looked at her and gestured to what he was wearing.

"You do realize that most imaginary friends don't change outfits. We wear whatever our people imagine us wearing. So. It would look weird if you changed clothing," Rumple said.

"Oh. Okay, that's… different," Joanne said.

"Yeah, I know it's weird for you. Now come on, we have got to go," Rumple said, opening the door and walking out of it. Joanne shoved her shoes on and hurried after him to the dining hall. Most of the imaginary friends had already eaten, leaving only a few that were there when Rumple and Joanne arrived.

"Do I sit in the seat I sat at yesterday?" Joanne asked.

"It's only custom if Kafa's here. He is not, so you can sit by me, since that person isn't here either," Rumple said as he sat down in his seat. Joanne sat down beside Rumple and began putting things on her plate. She put two fluffy chocolate chip pancakes and poured herself a glass of apple juice, the liquid sparkling in the light from the chandelier.

She drank it, and then Rumple started talking about the day.

"Okay, Kafa is going to personally train the two of us today. That may not seem like a big deal to you because he saved you yesterday, but trust me, it is still a big deal. So, treat him with respect and don't be dumb. Okay?"

"Got it," Joanne said, then drank some of her apple juice.

"He'll probably train us in hand-to-hand combat and also some weaponry. He does not go easy on people though, so just because he's training you doesn't mean he'll let you win deals and stuff," Rumple said.

"How good of a fighter is he?" Joanne asked.

"Um, pretty frickin' good, or else he wouldn't still have the position of King," Rumple said.

"Oh, yeah… this could end badly for me," Joanne said. Rumple shrugged.

"It very well could," he said casually.

"Thanks for the confidence," Joanne muttered.

"I didn't mean it that way. I just meant that he's strong enough that even with two of us attacking him, we might not win," Rumple stated.

"How is he *that* strong? He's *shorter than me*, for crying out loud!" Joanne exclaimed.

"Well, some of it comes from the fact that he is extremely cunning and has a bunch of strategies that he's learned over the past one-thousand-and-nine-hundred-years." Rumple said.

"That makes sense," Joanne said.

"Yeah. Don't challenge him ever, okay? You *will* lose, and you *will* be kicked out of the Unavenged. Got it?" Rumple said.

"Got it," Joanne said, then finished her food. Rumple finished shortly afterwards.

"Okay, let's go to the lobby. He's probably lounging on his throne," Rumple said as they left the dining hall.

"Does he do that a lot?" Joanne asked.

"Honey, he's king. He's not gonna let anybody forget that for one second," Rumple said with a short laugh. They walked into the lobby to find a bunch of imaginary friends hanging out on the couch but no Kafa.

"That's weird. He's usually here…" Rumple said, trailing off.

"Could you call him?" Joanne asked.

"Oh, yeah. Stupid me," Rumple muttered, taking out his phone and calling Kafa. He picked up after the first ring.

"Hello?" Kafa asked. He sounded weary and tired, something Kafa almost never sounded.

"Hey, Kafa, it's Rumple. Me and Joanne were wondering when we're gonna train with you," Rumple said.

"Oh. Right. Are you two in the lobby?" Kafa asked.

"Yup," Rumple replied.

"Umm, okay. Stay there, I'll be there soon," Kafa said, then hung up.

"We are supposed to stay here because apparently he'll be here soon," Rumple said to Joanne.

"Alright. Do we just sit somewhere?" Joanne asked.

"Umm, I guess," Rumple said, then walked over to one of the loveseats and sat down in it. Joanne sat down in the other one, and then they waited. About two minutes later, Kafa walked in the lobby in all of his glory, his cape grazing the floor as he walked.

Two imaginary friends on the couch stood up and bowed.

"Hail, King Kafa," they said in unison. Rumple stood up and did it, too, so Joanne did it as well so she wouldn't look weird. He nodded at the other imaginary friends in thanks, a smile on his face. Then he turned to Joanne and Rumple.

"Okay, you two, let's go to the arena," he said, then turned on his heel for the tunnels. Joanne remembered how yesterday she had to follow Kafa's footprints in order to get back to the Unavenged and not get lost in the winding tunnels.

"I will train you two in hand-to-hand combat and weaponry. I will also teach you some methods in escaping some situations," Kafa said as they walked.

"Like what?" Rumple asked.

"Oh, the usual. Kidnapping. Being held at gunpoint. Being blackmailed. That kind of thing. I'm sure you're familiar with at least one of them," Kafa said casually, as if he was talking about ways to make friends.

"Oh. Whoopee," Rumple said with false enthusiasm. Suddenly Kafa stopped and kicked at the ground. A hatch that had been completely covered in dirt was revealed.

"Wh-" Rumple started saying, but Kafa slapped a hand over his mouth. Joanne would have laughed if she hadn't been so confused.

"In here," he hissed, opening the hatch and looking around, as if making sure they weren't being followed. Rumple and Joanne went down into the darkness. Kafa shut it behind them and flicked on a light.

"So, this is where they keep the wine," Rumple observed. They were obviously in a wine cellar. A tiny wine cellar, so they were all crammed against each other.

"Okay, I'm going to tell you this now because I'm not going to betray you two. And I hate being blackmailed. You are our only hope, and I'm not about to throw that away. Last night Kile paid me a visit. He held me at Stonepoint and told me to give him Joanne or else he would shoot me with the Stone of Existence. I had no choice but to agree. He said he would be watching me, but I don't think he'd be watching me here. So, in one week, I'm supposed to hand you over to him. But I don't intend for that to ever happen. I have a plan. You stay with the Unavenged, act completely normal for around five days. I contact the Imaginists to help you get out of here. A day before I'm supposed to hand you over, we get you out of Imagine and back to the normal world, where you'll be safe. What do you say?" Kafa explained, looking pained when he said he agreed to Kile's deal.

"But you need me to defeat Kile," Joanne said.

"We do. Believe me, we do. But your safety is worth more than our own," Kafa said.

"But if I leave, you'll all die. I don't want that to happen any more than you do," Joanne said.

"Yes, I know. But I don't want you to die if we could get you to safety," Kafa said, looking at her like he was remembering something from a long time ago.

"I deny your offer," Joanne said. Kafa and Rumple's eyebrows raised.

"What?" Rumple asked.

"Why?" Kafa asked, taken aback by her response.

"I'm already here. Yes, I am in danger, and I know that. But how about a different plan: I suggest we do some of the things in Kafa's plan, but we make some adjustments. We will keep me for the next five days, and you will train me as much as you can. We will also meet up with the Imaginists and we will tell them our plan. With the combined forces of the Unavenged and the Imaginists, we can surely make a trap for Kile. When you hand me over to him, we will ambush him and capture him, taking the Stone away from him. We return the Stone to the stand, and then I can go back home," Joanne said. Rumple and Kafa looked at each other, thinking.

"It's not bad, I'll give you that. But how do you expect us to defeat Kile? Even with the Unavenged and the Imaginists, it won't be an easy task," Kafa said.

"Sheer force. If there's enough of us, he won't be able to kill all of us. I slip into the crowd disguised as another imaginary friend, and I catch him off guard. I take the Stone, and I kill him with it. The end," Joanne said.

Kafa nodded slowly.

"One question. How do we meet with the Imaginists? Like, they hate us and we hate them. How would they agree to meet? And when would we meet?" Rumple asked.

"Well, there's a ball coming up. If they don't agree to meet with us, we sneak into the ball and meet up with them there instead," Kafa said.

"So, we're meeting up with them either way?" Joanne asked, laughing.

"Pretty much. This is something they don't have much of a choice on. They'll just have to deal with it. So, we'll train now, and later I'll discuss with the Imaginists what a good meeting time would be," Kafa said, smirking and shrugging.

"Okay. We should get going then," Joanne said.

Kafa nodded and opened the hatch, then helped them through it back into the tunnels. They walked to the arena where Kafa tossed them each a sword.

"Let's begin. First thing, do not ever let your eyes leave your opponent and their sword. One second...!" he said, suddenly whipping his sword out and pointing it at Rumple's neck, letting it prick the skin, when he saw Rumple was staring at a butterfly. Rumple looked down in surprise and jumped.

"What the-" he sputtered, but Kafa talked over him.

"…Is all it takes for your opponent to see that you are not focused. Then they will strike, and you will be dead," Kafa said, lowering his sword and sheathing it in one swift movement. Rumple felt his neck, a single drop of blood getting on his finger. He frowned at it.

Kafa continued.

"Always defend yourself, but also attack. If you only defend and never strike, then you will never win. If you only strike and never defend yourself, you will surely get hurt. I want you two to fight each other and see who wins. Whoever lands a successful blow on their opponent first will win. Begin!" Kafa said.

"You haven't even told us how to hold the sword yet!" Rumple said, his voice an octave higher than usual.

"Just go. You'll live. I hope," Kafa said, smirking and crossing his arms.

"What?!" Rumple shrieked. Joanne lunged at him; sword pointed at his chest. He yelled and dove to the side, almost stabbing himself with his own sword in the process. Rumple sprung up as Joanne lunged at him again, but this time he was ready. He blocked her sword with his own, trying to hold it as his feet slid back in the dirt from Joanne's strength. He pushed her back with a burst of strength smiled when she stumbled. He leaped towards her, about to push her to the ground.

"Don't forget to *imagine*, Joanne," said Kafa. "It's your best weapon."

Joanne's eyes widened and she shoved her hand out, a sudden powerful gust of wind crashing into Rumple and knocking him over.

"What the-" Rumple exclaimed as he crashed against the ground, bruising his back from the impact. He swore with gritted teeth in pain, but that didn't stop Joanne. She leaped down on him, bringing her sword down. Rumple squeezed his eyes shut but didn't feel anything. He cracked his eyes open and saw Joanne grinning triumphantly at him with her sword tip just a few inches above his chest. Rumple heard somebody start clapping. Rumple looked up and saw Kafa standing by his head, a smile slowly spreading across his face.

"Good job, Joanne! Nicely done!" he said. Joanne smiled back at him.

"Thank you!" she said.

"Wait one second! What the mess was that?" Rumple asked, wanting to sit up but staying on the ground because the sword was still too close for comfort.

"She imagined knocking you over with some wind and it happened. Remember, Rumple?" Kafa asked, his eyes sparkling with smugness. Rumple glared at him.

"But that's cheating!" he exclaimed.

"Whoever told you every fight was a fair one?" Kafa asked.

"Nobody, but that's really just not cool! I don't stand a chance against her if she uses her imagination! I don't think *you* could win against her if she used her imagination!" Rumple exclaimed. Kafa's eyes glittered dangerously.

"You think so? Joanne, how would you like to duel?" Kafa asked, turning to Joanne, his armor glinting in the light.

"I don't know…" Joanne said warily.

"Come on. You heard him. You have your imagination. I only have a sword. So, will you duel with me?" Kafa asked.

Joanne took a deep breath.

"Fine," she said.

A malicious smile spread across Kafa's face.

"Then let's begin," he said, and he and Joanne moved away from Rumple so they could duel.

Rumple breathed a sigh of relief now that the sword was gone. He sat up and began to watch the fight.

Joanne and Kafa stopped when they were about five yards away from each other.

"Are you ready?" Kafa asked, his eyes glinting.

Joanne began to feel less confident about agreeing, but she nodded anyways, trying to push her feelings of nervousness away. She waited for him to move, but he stayed where he was.

"You go first. I want to see what you do," Kafa said.

Joanne breathed deeply. *What could defeat him here and now?* Joanne wondered. She shot fire out of her palm at Kafa. His eyebrows raised in surprise, but he cartwheeled to the left and laughed as the fire hit nothing. Suddenly he was leaping towards her, sword slicing in an arc towards her arm. She dropped to the ground and he flew over her, landing in the dirt a few feet away in a crouch. She ran at him with her sword, aiming for his head, but he simply blocked her, shoving her sword to the side and punching her in the face. She stumbled back, not expecting him to have used his fists as blood poured from her nose.

"Don't worry, I didn't break it," Kafa said, then laughed. Joanne angrily wiped her nose and imagined a wave of water crashing over Kafa. And suddenly, there the wave was, rising up behind Joanne out of the dirt. She heard Rumple swear somewhere behind them. Kafa's eyes widened and the wave collided with him, water crashing onto the floor of the arena, soaking it and making it a muddy mess. Joanne sighed with relief, thinking he was defeated, when he suddenly leaped through the wave at Joanne, sword out and his eyes blazing. He tackled her to the ground, Joanne slipping in the mud so she fell over. She pushed at his chest, trying to imagine super strength, but imagining the wave had tired her, and she found that she didn't have it in her to imagine anything else. Kafa's knees straddled her hips, which made her feel sick. He pinned her arms to the ground and looked down at her with a victorious, criminal smile, his green eyes wild and his hair dripping water into Joanne's face.

"I win," he said, resting his sword against Joanne's throat. Joanne looked up at him, breathing hard. He plucked her sword out of his grip and got off her, standing up and brushing himself off, mud on his pants and shoes. Joanne got up, mud caking her back. She glanced over at Rumple, who was staring at them, open-mouthed. She looked back at Kafa, who was smirking.

"You know, maybe next time, y-" he started saying smugly, but suddenly a wave of white-hot rage shot through Joanne, and all she could think about was how badly she had wanted to win, and how sickened she had felt when Kafa was on top of her. Suddenly electricity shot out of her like a bullet from a gun, heading straight for Kafa. He only had a second to react, his eyes widening in fear as he raised his sword- and then it hit him, blots of white electricity branching all over him and into the ground, the damp ground making electricity crackle through it. The smell of burning hair rose into the air, and a scream wrenched itself out of Kafa's throat. Just as suddenly as the rage had come, it went away. Joanne stared at Kafa in horror as the lightning stopped and he crumpled to the ground, his eyes rolling back into his head.

"KAFA!" Rumple yelled, and suddenly Joanne saw him tearing towards Kafa, almost slipping in the mud once or twice. Joanne started running too, guilt already hitting her, her boots sliding a little in the mud. Rumple fell to his knees beside

Kafa and Joanne did the same. Kafa was laying on the ground so still that it made Joanne's blood run cold.

"He'll be okay, right?" Joanne asked frantically. Rumple looked at her, rage flaring in his eyes.

"Usually, yes. But since you're real, you can kill us! HE COULD DIE BECAUSE OF YOU!" Rumple shouted.

Joanne paled. She had forgotten that she and Kile were the only things that could kill imaginary friends. Rumple leaned over Kafa and checked his pulse, slumping in relief.

"Well, he's still alive. Come on, help me carry him," Rumple said, lifting up Kafa's arms. Joanne lifted up his feet, and they began to carry him to the Unavenged lobby. He was actually quite light for a full-grown man, around one hundred and fifty pounds. Joanne and Rumple strained to carry him through the tunnels, and they were about halfway back to the lobby when Rumple collapsed from exhaustion.

"I... I can't make... it. He's too... heavy," he panted.

Joanne set down Kafa's feet.

"Well, we have to make it back to the lobby so we can get help-"

"No! No. If we... drag him in there unconscious, he'll look weak to the Unavenged. Then they'll... challenge him and he'll be weak... and he'll lose..." Rumple said, trailing off.

"Why do you care if someone new takes over?" Joanne asked.

"If Kafa falls, there will be... a bloodbath... fighting for the position of king. The Unavenged... will be too busy fighting among... themselves... for them to help us defeat... Kile. Kafa is a strong leader. We... need him," Rumple explained, still breathing hard.

Joanne let his words sink in.

"I guess you're right. I might be able to imagine something..." Joanne said, then imagined a door way leading to Kafa's room. She was tired, but her fear for what might happen to Kafa gave her some energy. Suddenly, it was there. A doorway that showed Kafa's room.

"Come on. It's really tiring to hold this open," Joanne said, her face screwed up in concentration. Rumple grabbed Kafa and dragged him into his room. Joanne followed them and closed the door, sighing with relief.

"What are we gonna do? I don't know how to heal getting electrocuted," Rumple said, looking down at Kafa, whose breathing was still there, but shallow.

"I don't know. Maybe... maybe I could try and imagine something?" Joanne offered.

Rumple looked at her warily.

"Last time you did something to him he got electrocuted," Rumple said.

"I have to try! It's my fault he's like this!" Joanne exclaimed.

"I know. But do you think you have the energy in you for it?" Rumple asked.

"We'll see," Joanne said, then tried to imagine something that would heal him. An image came to mind, a soup that would help heal him. Joanne imagined it and almost fell over from the wave of tiredness that hit her as the bowl of soup appeared on the nightstand. Her knees buckled and she hit the floor as black spots danced across her vision.

"Joanne!" Rumple said, catching her before her head knocked against the floor.

"I'm okay. Just get the soup to Kafa," she said weakly.

"How do I feed soup to an unconscious person?" Rumple asked, looking slightly panicked that he didn't know what to do.

"Figure it out," Joanne said, and closed her eyes, darkness consuming her and sleep taking her in its warm embrace, the sound of Rumple's voice fading to a meaningless whisper.

~~

*Kafa stood there, looking distraught.*

*"Hey," Kile said softly, trying not to disturb him. He still blinked in surprise, turning to see who it was. A smile tugged at the corners of his mouth when he saw who it was.*

"Kile! I was wondering when you were going to show up!" he said, walking into the room and closing the door behind him.

"On time, obviously," Kile said. Kafa laughed his hyena sounding laugh that Kile found hilarious.

"Please. As if you're ever on time for anything," he said, chuckling. Kile shrugged.

"Well, maybe I realized that being on time is better than always being late," he said casually.

"Right. Why are you really here on time?" Kafa asked, peering at Kile with curiosity.

"Oh, well, I was nearby, and I thought, 'Why not catch him off guard by actually showing up on time?' So, here I am," Kile said, throwing his arms wide. Kafa grinned.

"I still don't buy it, but fine. I'm just glad you're here," he said, shaking his head.

"Good enough for me. What were you thinking about?" Kile asked.

"Hmm? Oh, I was just thinking about what I could do with this hotel," Kafa said, gesturing to the old hotel they were in.

"What do you want to do with it?" Kile asked, sitting down on Kafa's bed. Kafa blew out his cheeks.

"I don't know… I'd like to offer it for people to stay in if they need shelter," he said slowly. Kile smirked.

"Now you just sound like an Imaginist," he said. Kafa scoffed.

"Please. Imaginists don't care about the poor imaginary friends. They only care about looking good in front of the population of Imagine. They don't actually care about the citizens. Not like the citizens know that," Kafa said.

"Wow. You've gone into full 'former-Imaginist-who's-now-disgusted-with-them' mode," Kile said, chuckling.

Kafa looked at him dryly.

"In my defense, they weren't as bad when Imagine started as they are now," Kafa retorted, walking over to Kile and sitting beside him.

"I wouldn't know. I'm not old like you, so I only know the way the Imaginists are now," Kile said. Kafa looked at him, pretending to be offended.

"Umm, excuse me? I am not old, for your information. You are just very young and naïve. And you're still in play, so you're not as grouchy as most imaginary friends are," Kafa said, adding the last part after a moment.

"So, you admit you're grouchy!" Kile said, a triumphant smile on his face.

"I said no such thing," Kafa said, looking away so Kile couldn't see his grin.

"Mm-hmm. Right. Don't worry, I'll still be your friend. Even though you're old and grouchy," Kile said, trying to suppress a smile when he said the last part quietly. Kafa turned back to him, his eyes playfully annoyed.

"I'm still just the same as I was!" Kafa exclaimed.

"I don't believe you!" Kile sang. Kafa put his hands on Kile's shoulder and gave him a light shove.

"Well, you should," Kafa said, holding his nose high in the air.


Kile awoke with a start, looking around his room. Same place as he used to be. He wasn't at Kafa's, he was just in his own room. He put a hand to his chest, feeling his heart beat fast as it had that night.

*Why am I getting so worked up? I don't care what happens to Kafa anymore. I haven't cared since…* Kile thought, stopping himself from remembering. He took a deep breath before walking over to his window. He hadn't felt anything when he had threatened Kafa. He hadn't felt anything when he had watched Kafa get electrocuted from a distance. If he didn't feel anything then, why did old memories still make him care about his friend? He rubbed his eyes and looked down at the part of the view that overlooked a small fraction of the dark part of the City. From up where he was, he could see most of the good part of the City and only a small part of the dark areas. It hadn't been very convenient when he and Kafa *didn't* hate each other. He had to travel quite away to get to his house- err, hotel. He sighed, resting his forehead against the cool glass.

*You saw the light? You didn't see any light, you changed for the worse! There was never a moment when you improved!* Kile squeezed his eyes shut. *Maybe I did. But I wouldn't know. All I felt was sadness and despair for a long time. Then I just felt empty. I haven't felt anything in years. I'm starting to worry that I'm losing what once made me human... but what does it matter? After I finish my plan, I'll have power, more than Kafa ever had. Then they'll all bow down to me instead of their Creators. Creators will worship me, not the other way around. I will be invincible,* Kile thought. He looked down at his watch. It was around lunch. He walked across his room and picked up his cell phone. He dialed a number and held the phone to his ear. It picked up after the third ring.

"Dari, it's me, Kile. Hey...how would you like to be the queen of the Unavenged?"

# Chapter Nine

The world felt like it was spinning and was never going to stop, throwing Kafa every which way. His head throbbed, as if he had hit it on something hard. He felt something cold and hard in his mouth, then felt a cold liquid trickle down his throat. Kafa's eyes flew open and he sputtered, almost choking on the liquid.

"And the King wakes!" Rumple said dramatically, taking the spoon out of Kafa's mouth. Kafa sat up, wiping his mouth, which seemed to be covered in a pinkish liquid. It was also all over his chin from him spitting it out. He looked at the back of the hand disdainfully. He noticed that some of his hair was a little blackened on the ends. He felt it. The black parts were brittle and crunchy. Kafa inhaled sharply and looked at Rumple.

"Mind telling me what exactly happened?" he asked.

"Oh. Basically, Joanne got angry and electrocuted you," he said simply, plopping the spoon back in a bowl of the pink liquid. Kafa's eyebrows shot up.

"What?" he asked.

"Joanne got mad and electrocuted you," Rumple repeated. Kafa rifled through his memories. The last thing he remembered was turning his back on a defeated Joanne and walking away, then he had felt something sharp and hot, and it had felt like his nerves were on fire. Then blackness. Kafa's eyes narrowed.

"Joanne electrocuted me?" he asked slowly.

"I literally just said that. Yes, she electrocuted you. You want me to say it again?" Rumple said.

"No. Where is she now?" Kafa asked, looking around before he spotted her on the ground a few feet away, appearing to be asleep.

"Oh. Is she okay?" Kafa asked, reaching over and touching her shoulder.

"Very tired, but I think she's alright," Rumple said, glancing over at Joanne with brotherly affection. A small smile came to Kafa's face as he watched Rumple do so, memories of looking at his own Creator the same way years ago dancing through his head.

"You missed her a lot, didn't you?" Kafa asked.

"What?" Rumple asked, turning to face Kafa.

"You've really missed Joanne since you've been discarded, right?" Kafa said.

"Of course, I did. She's my Creator, and-"

"Not like that. You care for her. More than most imaginary friends care for their Creators," Kafa said, holding up a hand to silence him.

"Yeah, I guess so. How could I not? She's my sister," Rumple said. Kafa's face darkened.

"You don't have to love her just because she's your sister. I've seen siblings have no heart for one another. Blood means nothing sometimes," Kafa said.

"Well, I do care for her. We hung out basically every day for like, eight years. We were close, man. Real close," Rumple said, his voice softening as he glanced at Joanne.

"Then why did she discard you? You don't have to tell me if you don't want to. I know that it can be very personal," Kafa said. Rumple's eyes hardened.

"It's not like she had much of a choice. It wasn't her decision to get rid of me. We both knew the day would come, but we didn't know that it would come so... fast. We thought we had forever. I mean, heck, we planned to go to the same college and *share a dorm*. We were... great. It was her parents. She was a teenager and they thought she was just too old for me. They thought she didn't need me anymore. And I guess at that point, she *didn't* need me anymore. When she created me when she was five, she didn't have many friends and she wanted a brother. But then as the years went on, she got more friends, so using me wasn't really... necessary anymore. Her parents acted like it worried them to the point that they might send her to a place for crazy people one day if she didn't stop. So, she had to get rid of me. I had to leave. She discarded me because she didn't have a choice, not because she stopped caring like most people do. So, there's your answer. That's why," Rumple said, his voice flat. Kafa put a hand on Rumple's shoulder.

"I'm glad you told me. Was Joanne happy to see you?" Kafa asked.

"Well, no. Not at first. She completely flipped out and scared a poor guy away at Subway," Rumple said, chuckling. Kafa peered at him.

"Subway?" he asked.

"Oh. It's some sandwich place she really likes for some reason," Rumple explained.

"Ah. Why was she flipping out?" Kafa asked.

"I think she didn't want to believe I was back. I think she thought she was losing it," Rumple said. Kafa nodded, taking his hand back.

"That seems to make sense. But doesn't she have friends and family in the normal world?" Kafa asked.

"Umm, yeah. Duh. Why wouldn't she?" Rumple said.

~~

*"We still have no updates on the case of missing sixteen-year-old girl Joanne Raider. Her car was found at Watermore Mall, which has been closed for almost seven years, after she disappeared from Watermore High School at around eleven in the morning. Police have searched the mall for Joanne, but have found nothing except for some fresh footprints that do match the shoes she was wearing that day. The prints seem to disappear inside the mall. The last report of Joanne being actually seen was by a man who claims to have recalled eating near her at Subway around noon the day she left school. He says she was screaming but sitting alone, so he left. Security cameras have footage of this event,"* the reporter said.

The screen switched to the security footage.

> *"I'm sorry, but you come and tell me that the fate of the world rests on my shoulders and I'm supposed to not tell anyone and do nothing?" Joanne asked angrily. The man in the corner was now staring at Joanne, though she didn't seem to care. After a moment, she spoke again.*

> *"But why me? I don't want to get involved in this! I don't want to get involved with you again! When I said goodbye that night, I meant it!" She growled. The man in the corner grabbed their things and left hurriedly. Joanne stared the space in front of her in shock, and remained silent for another minute, looking as if she was listening to something.*

*"How much longer do you think the three realms have?"* she asked. It was a second before she spoke again.

*"Do you know where the Stone is?"* Joanne asked. Another beat of silence. *"Who stole it?"* Joanne asked. After a second, Joanne nodded and was quiet for a second.

*"Rumple, I'm really sorry, but I shouldn't get involved in this. I should live a normal life, without worrying about that... and without you,"* she said, biting her lip and staring at the space in front of her sadly. Suddenly, Joanne's eyes widened in concern and surprise.

*"Rumple, are yo-"* She started saying, but stopped, fear in her eyes. She jumped out of her chair and fell down on her knees to the floor.

*"Rumple! Oh my god, Rumple! Can you hear me? Are you okay? Rumple!"* She said, her voice frantic. She reached out as if to touch something, only for her to jerk her hand back in shock, her mouth wide open.

*"Are you-"* Joanne started, but stopped again, as if somebody had cut her off. She stared at the space in front of her for a few seconds, then she shut her eyes. Then she said something so softly, the cameras didn't pick it up. She opened her eyes and looked at nothing again, her gaze filled with determination.

*"I said I'll do it,"* she said loudly. Then she did something strange. It looked as if she was trying to hug air. She closed her eyes for a second, then opened them, looking annoyed but also amused.

*"Oh, shut up. You know I can't feel you, so I have no idea when you let go,"* Joanne said grumpily as she dropped her arms and stood up, but her eyes looked happy. Another moment of silence before her hand shot out as if to hit something. Then she started walking towards the door, smiling as she said,

*"Just be quiet!"*

The footage stopped there on the news channel. Lola stared at her TV for a second in shock before she jumped off her bed, shoving her shoes on.

*Rumple!? Oh, my god. What the heck is happening?* Lola thought as she raced out of her room. She sprinted down the hallway, grabbing her keys off the dining table.

"Lola McClain! Where do you think you're going?" Lola's mother's voice drifted from the kitchen.

"To find Joanne!" she said as she raced out the door, shutting it behind her and almost tripping over her cat as she stumbled down the steps. She threw open the gate that separated her house from her carport and got in her car, starting it and driving out of her driveway as fast as she could. She got out her phone and texted, *Schlotzsky's. Now.* She tossed her phone into the front seat.

The past two days had been chaos. Joanne had randomly run out of the school on Tuesday, then had texted around noon that she was at Subway. Lola had been so mad at Joanne she had handed the phone to Penny and not taken the opportunity to try to talk to Joanne at that moment. Now that Joanne was missing, Lola wished she had been nicer and said something else to her best friend when she had called. Lola had called Joanne fourteen times since she went missing, and she hadn't picked up since Subway on Tuesday. She hadn't been at school the next day and the school announced that Joanne had been reported missing by her parents. They said if anyone knew anything that might suggest where Joanne had gone, they should tell the police, which were waiting at the school. The entire groups of Joanne's close friends - Karrie, Lola, Penny, Alexa, Adele, and Asha - had rushed down to the office where the police were and told them everything, from the texts from the stranger, the way she had acted strangely, to the way she had hung up on them at Subway and hadn't picked up after that. Joanne's parents had already showed them the texts and were already scouring Joanne's social media for a potential stalker or kidnapper. The police hadn't released anything else of what they said.

Lola drove as close to the limit as she could without speeding all the way to Schlotzsky's, the place Joanne had been when she met the stranger. The police had scoured Schlotzsky's as well and had found some footage there, too, though they hadn't released it yet to the public. Schlotzsky's had been closed for a day when they searched the place for DNA, but they had only found Joanne's and not any other person's that appeared related, like someone that would had met her. Lola pulled into the parking lot, not caring that she parked over the line. She got out of her car and ran into Schlotzsky's. She looked around and saw Alexa was already there.

"What is it? Did you find something about Joanne?" she asked, standing up.

"Yes. I'll explain when the others get here," she said. A few seconds later, Penny ran in, her face flushed from the cold wind.

"Is it Joanne?" she asked.

"Yeah. I'll explain once Karrie, Asha, and Adele get here," Lola said, sitting down in the booth beside Alexa. Penny sat across from them. Before Joanne had gone missing, Penny and Lola had been arguing a lot, and Karrie and Adele had also been bickering. Then, Joanne had gone missing, and suddenly, the things they had argued about hadn't seemed so important anymore. They seemed small in comparison to Joanne being missing. Asha and Adele walked in a minute later, living so close to each other that they had just come together.

"It's Joanne, isn't it?" Adele asked.

"Yes, but let's wait until Karrie gets here," Lola said. Adele nodded and she and Asha sat down in the booth. About thirty seconds later, Karrie rushed in.

"Why am I always the last one to these things?" she muttered. "Is it news about Joanne?" she asked.

"Yes, come sit down," Lola said. Karrie sat down beside Adele.

"Okay. So, I saw something on the news. About Joanne," Lola said.

"We've all been watching the news, Lola. What did you see that was so weird?" Alexa asked.

"Hang on and let me talk. I was watching the news and they released the footage from Subway," Lola said. Everyone at the table either gasped or inhaled sharply.

"What was it?" Penny asked. Suddenly the manager, Cab, approached them. "You guys are Joanne's friends, right?" he asked.

"How did you know?" Karrie asked.

"I heard you talking about her. I have the news on a TV in the back if you want to see it," he offered.

"Yes, we'd like to see that," Penny said, standing up.

"Okay. Come on, then," he said, gesturing for them to follow. They all stood up so quickly the booths got pushed back, but they didn't care. They followed Cab back to the back, where there was a TV.

"I've been recording it," Cab said, then flicked it on. The girls huddled around the TV, eager to hear anything about their missing friend. Cab re-winded the recording to the beginning and pressed PLAY. It started where Lola had been listening. The same footage showed what Lola had seen. When she said Rumple, she could feel all of her friends stiffen. They all knew about Rumple, and they all knew that he had been gone for three years. They exchanged concerned and worried looks, then continued watching. The reporter continued after the footage, and Lola leaned forward, having not heard that part.

> *"Joanne Raider was last contacted at 12:31 PM eastern time through a FaceTime with her father. The FaceTime has not been released to the public yet, but an image from the FaceTime has been released," she said.*

The screen switched to a picture of an angry looking boy who looked to be about twelve with messy brown hair, blue green eyes, and a Batman hoodie. Karrie swore softly. Lola paled. Adele and Penny's mouths hung open. Alexa's eyes widened and she squinted at it.

"Isn't that what her imaginary brother used to look like?" said Asha. Before Lola knew what she was doing, she took out her phone and dialed Joanne's number for the fifteenth time in the past two days. All of Joanne's friends recognized the person on TV from the numerous drawings Joanne had done in the past.

"Yes, … it is," Lola said, after a moment of silence with the phone to her ear.

~~

"You can't just take a girl away from her friends and family! They'll think she was kidnapped!" Kafa exclaimed.

"I already took care of that," Rumple said casually.

*Oh, dear Jupiter,* Kafa thought.

"Rumple. What did you do?" Kafa asked, dreading the answer.

"Simple. Her dad FaceTime'd her, and he was yelling at her, so I took her phone away and let him see me," Rumple said nonchalantly. Kafa's eyes widened.

"You WHAT?" he shouted. Rumple flinched.

"Didn't you tell me that she used to draw you often – like, very vivid drawings of you, and hung them up on her wall? He could have seen the resemblance… and he could know who you are …or that you really *exist*, couldn't he?" Kafa asked, his voice suddenly a deadly calm.

"Well, yeah. And I literally said, 'You know who I am,' before I hung up." Rumple said. Kafa stared at him, open-mouthed.

"You… are so *stupid*! With technology these days, they're going to know where to look and they will discover us!" Kafa hissed. Rumple looked at him as if *he* were the dumb one, one eyebrow raised.

"Yeah, they'll totally know to look in some magical collection of three realms filled with inventions, characters, and imaginary friends for their missing child," Rumple said sarcastically. Kafa deflated a little, realizing the logic behind Rumple's words.

"Yes, but they'll think they've gone insane and their child is still *missing*!" Kafa exclaimed. Rumple shrugged.

"Yeah, well, we either have a savior for all imaginary friends and somebody has their child missing for a short period of time, *OR* **we** all die and humans are doomed, and one family keeps their child," Rumple said. Kafa opened his mouth, then closed it. He sighed.

"Fine. But it must be *very* chaotic in the normal world right now," Kafa said.

"I'm sure. Let's see how many calls she's missed!" Rumple said, then reached out and plucked Joanne's phone out of her pocket that she hadn't touched since they arrived in Imagine. He turned it on and whistled.

"What?" Kafa asked.

"Let's see… twenty missed calls from Mom, seventeen missed calls from Dad, fourteen from Lola, fifteen from Anna *somebody*… maybe her cousin?" sighing, and starting to sound exhausted by it, he continued … "six from Alexa, seven from Adele, six from Asha, ten from Karrie, twelve from Penny, and then a few from ….hmm…some other people. Then there are 102 unread texts. Dang. She's loved more than I thought," Rumple said.

Kafa rolled his eyes.

"What else did you expect? Nobody trying to contact her?" Kafa asked.

"Well no, but she's only been gone for like, two days," Rumple said.

"That's enough time for people to worry, especially when someone that looks creepily like the renderings of her former *imaginary brother* was the last face that they saw associated with her," Kafa said.

"I see that now," Rumple said. Kafa scoffed, shaking his head.

"You know what, just forget it. We'll deal with her family and friends when the time-" Kafa said, then stopped when her phone started to ring. The screen said, *Lola*.

Kafa picked the phone out of Rumple's grasp before Rumple could press ignore.

"Hey! What are you doing?" Rumple asked.

"I'm going to tell these people their daughter is safe, that's what I'm doing! Now shush!" Kafa said, then pressed answer. He heard a strange noise of excitement and the click of a button that signaled he was now on speaker phone.

"Joanne?! Joanne, is that you?!" a girl's voice shouted.

Kafa cleared his throat before he spoke.

"No, it's not. I'm-"

"WHERE'S JOANNE, YOU CREEP?" another girl's voice screamed.

"You don't need to worry, ladies, I have her with me," Kafa said calmly.

"What have you done with her?" a third girl's voice demanded.

"Nothing. I assure you, she's perfectly safe," Kafa said, trying to calm them down with using a soothing tone.

"Who are you, then? Is this… Rumple?" another girl said.

*How many girls are there in that room?* Kafa wondered.

"I am Kafa," Kafa said. There was a moment of confused silence, then he heard somebody quietly ask, "Did he say *coffee?*"

Kafa rolled his eyes.

"No, Kafa! Good Jupiter, you can't hear for the world, can you?" Kafa said dryly.

"Who's Jupiter?" the second girl asked. Kafa sighed, briefly shutting his eyes.

"The God I worship. I'm sure none of you do, but that's not important right now. I picked up because Rumple kept hanging up, and I thought you all deserved to know that Joanne was okay-"

"I want to talk to Joanne!" the first girl said.

"Well, she can't talk right now," Kafa said.

"I KNEW IT! YOU'RE A CREEPY KIDNAPPER AND YOU'VE HURT HER!" the second girl screeched. Kafa held the phone away from his ear, wincing.

"I didn't hurt her! She's just very, very tired, and she's sleeping right now," Kafa said.

"OH, MY GOD, HE *KILLED* HER!" the fourth girl yelled.

Another of the girls shouted, "WAKE HER UP!"

Kafa flinched.

"I'll try, but I can't make any promises," Kafa said, then went over to Joanne and gently shook her.

"Joanne, wake up. Come on, Joanne. Wake up please," Kafa said. Joanne stirred and cracked open her eyes.

"What?" she asked groggily.

"It's your friends. They want to talk to you," Kafa said. Joanne's eyebrows shot up and she grabbed the phone from Kafa, clicking the FaceTime button as she did so.

Six girls and a middle-aged man's faces filled the screen. The girls all screeched when they saw her face, asking questions all at once.

"One question at a time!" Joanne exclaimed.

Alexa spoke first.

"Who's this coffee guy we were just talking to?" she asked.

"Really? That's what you have to ask her?" Karrie muttered.

"Oh, that's Kafa. He's my… friend," Joanne said, turning the screen to face Kafa.

They all jumped.

"What the heck happened to him?" Lola asked, sounding disgusted.

"I got hit by lightning," Kafa said dryly before Joanne could say anything.

"Why are you wearing armor?" Penny asked.

Kafa ignored the question.

"Why did you kidnap Joanne?" Asha asked.

"He didn't kidnap me. I came willingly," Joanne said, rolling her eyes.

"Wait. We saw Rumple's face on the news. What is going on, Joanne?" Karrie asked.

"What do you mean?" Joanne asked. Rumple and Kafa gave her a weird look.

"You know, your imaginary brother from a long time ago – his face is on TV from your parents' phone and he's now wanted on the news because everyone is looking for you," Lola said.

"Is he?" Joanne asked. Lola turned the screen to show her a screenshot of the FaceTime between Rumple and Joanne's father on a TV. Joanne shot Rumple a glare. He gave her a sheepish look.

"Guys, you know Rumple's gone. I don't know where that came from, but-" Joanne started saying, but Lola cut her off.

"Um, yes you do! What is going on, Joanne? Where are you?" she asked. Joanne sighed.

"I can't tell you. But I'll be home in a few days. Okay? I'm okay, and I'll be back soon," Joanne said.

"Don't go!" her friends chorused.

"I have to. I'll see you guys later, okay? Goodbye," Joanne said, then hung up, her friends' cries of protest abruptly cut off.

"Why didn't you show them me?" Rumple asked.

"Because. Everybody knows about you. If they saw you, everyone would think that they had lost it. Nobody knows Kafa. I could show him and nobody would bat an eye," Joanne said.

"I guess that makes sense…" he said, trailing off.

"What did they mean, what happened to me?" Kafa asked, butting into the conversation. Rumple and Joanne looked over at him. Rumple winced.

"You might want to look in the mirror, dude," Rumple said. Kafa got up and walked into the bathroom, closing the door behind him.

"Ouch," he muttered when he saw his reflection. His eyeliner was smeared to the point where it looked like a child had gotten a hold of a black marker while he slept and his eyeshadow had halfway-washed off so it looked like he had been crying black tears. The tips of his hair were black, and the rest of it looked and felt fine, though it now was sticking out in more directions than it had been at the start of the day. With a sigh, Kafa wiped his makeup off and reapplied the eyeshadow and eyeliner, then got a pair of scissors and trimmed off the tips of his hair, making it so the black parts were gone. You couldn't even tell it had been trimmed. It looked just as long as it had before. With one last look in the mirror, he went back into his room. Joanne was holding the bowl of pink liquid.

"Do you need any more of this?" she asked.

"What even is that? I woke up to found Rumple feeding it to me and I almost wet myself from fear," Kafa said. A smile tugged at the corner of Joanne's mouth.

"It was a soup I imagined up to heal you. Are you okay? I'm really sorry I went all *Emperor Palpatine* on you," she said.

"Nerd," Rumple muttered, shaking his head.

"But I really don't know what happened. I was-" she said, but Kafa waved his hand dismissively.

"It doesn't matter. All that matters is, I'm okay, and you're okay. It's good you can do that. If you pulled something like that around Kile, he might not be expecting it and it could very well be the end of him," Kafa said. Joanne nodded, then looked at Rumple.

"What time is it?" she asked.

"Like, noon," he replied.

"Okay. I wasn't sleeping very long then," Joanne said.

"Nah, not really. Only like, half an hour," Rumple said.

"Good. Do you guys have lunch here?" Joanne asked. Rumple looked at her as if she was from another planet and Kafa just chuckled.

"Of course. Come on, let's go eat," Kafa said, offering Joanne a hand and helping her up. They left Kafa's room and walked down to the dining hall, imaginary friends bowing as they passed by.

When they entered the dining hall, the imaginary friends all stopped and echoed their hails to Kafa, and Kafa inclined his head in thanks.

"Thank you all. As you were," Kafa said, and the imaginary friends went back to eating. Kafa sat down in his seat at the head of the table, and Joanne sat on his right. The food today was hamburgers and hotdogs.

"Rumple! Come sit," Kafa said, patting the chair to his left. Rumple, a look of surprise on his face, walked over and sat down beside Kafa.
"I can't believe they all love you this much," Joanne muttered.

"Oh, I don't know if they love me. Fear keeps them in line. And some of them have nowhere else to go, so they'd have to be stupid to disobey me," Kafa said with a laugh. Joanne blinked in surprise at his bluntness.

"It's true," Kafa said, shrugging.

"Yeah, I guess so," Joanne said, then put a hotdog on her plate. Rumple grabbed a hamburger and Kafa did the same.

"Are you going to contact the Imaginists?" Rumple asked quietly so the other imaginary friends wouldn't hear.

"Yes, I will after we eat," he replied. Rumple nodded.

"Okay, cool," he said.

They ate in silence for a few minutes until Kafa spoke.

"So, do you still want me to try and train you two?" he asked.

"Yes, please," Joanne said.

"Very well, I will train you. But no electrocuting me with your Emperor-whatever powers. I like staying alive," Kafa said. A smile tugged at the corners of Joanne's mouth. She had only known Kafa for a little over a day, but she had begun to like him already.

*"Emperor Palpatine.* It's something from Star Wars," Rumple explained.

"Why are there wars in the stars? Why not down on Earth? Wait, since when can people even *go* to the stars?" Kafa asked. Rumple snickered, and Joanne smiled.

"It's a movie," she explained.

"Really?" he asked.

"Yup. It's like a forty-year-old movie," Rumple said. Kafa peered at them. "Does everybody like Star Wars?" he asked.

"No, some people like Star Trek," Rumple said.

"What's that? Is it like Star Wars?" Kafa asked. Rumple shrugged.

"I have no idea. I've never watched it," he said. Kafa nodded.

"I see," he muttered. Then they finished their hotdogs and Kafa led them back to the tunnels.

"Okay, no tricks this time please. I don't care for being fried," he said as they walked through the tunnels. As they walked, their footsteps soft in the dirt tunnels, Joanne spoke.

"How do you know Kile?" she asked. Kafa stumbled, catching himself before he could fall. A look of surprise crossed his face, but he covered it quickly.

"Oh, we were friends," he said.

"That's it? Friends?" Rumple asked.

"Yes, Rumple. You can stop that train right now," Kafa said.

"How did you meet him?" Joanne asked.

"Oh... I was still an Imaginist when I met him. He-"

"*You* were an *Imaginist*?" Rumple interrupted.

Kafa gave him a dry look.

"Yes. *Anyways*, he was a protester to a law the Imaginists had passed that I didn't really approve of either. He was a new imaginary friend, but he had been there long enough to know that the law wasn't right. I remember the other Imaginists sent me out to deal with them, and I don't know... he just looked different in the crowd. I quit the Imaginists about a week later and ran into him at a café a few days after that. He was wary of me at first, but we quickly became friends. There it is. Your story of the day," Kafa said.

"What was he like?" Joanne asked. Kafa looked uncomfortable.

"Let's discuss this some other time. For now, let's just train," Kafa said as they walked into the arena, the sun just starting to dry the damp dirt. They went over sword fighting tactics for the next five hours, sometimes dueling and occasionally taking breaks for water or the bathroom. The sun was low in the sky when they stopped, and they were all sweaty. Well, it was mainly Rumple and Joanne, who were practically drenched in it and were panting from exhaustion. Kafa just had a bead of sweat on his brow, his makeup not even affected by his tiny bit of sweat.

"Alright, let's head in and eat," he said cheerfully, as if five hours of intense sword fighting hadn't tired him at all.

"Can we… sit down?" Rumple asked, breathing hard, his clothes drenched with sweat and his hoodie tied around his waist.

"You can sit at the table. Come on," he said, then started walking towards the tunnels. Rumple and Joanne looked at each other, so tired that they couldn't say hardly anything. They trudged after Kafa, wanting to just sit down and drink some water.

Rumple slung his arm over Joanne's shoulders.

"Carry me the rest of the way, o powerful warrior," he said in a fake Scottish accent.

"What's the deal with the accent?" Joanne asked.

"I don't know. I just thought it sounded pretty legit," Rumple said, shrugging. Joanne rolled her eyes.

"Get off me," she said, pushing his arm off her shoulder. He pretended to be hurt.

"How dare thou? I was under the assumption that thou would-" Rumple started saying, going into full old-English mode, but Kafa talked over him.

"Please, don't. I used to know people who talked like that. They're all dead now," he said. That made Rumple shut up. Kafa sniffed the air and his nose wrinkled.

"You two need to bathe before tonight," he said.

"What's tonight?" Joanne asked. Rumple looked at her with a glint in his eyes.

"You'll see," he said mysteriously. She nodded.

"Okay, then," she said.

"Don't worry, it's loads of fun. Everyone enjoys it, so I'm sure you will too," Kafa said, glancing back at her and grinning.

"Alright," she said, and they were silent again for a few minutes.

"Kafa, why do you wear makeup?" Joanne suddenly asked. He looked surprised that she had asked that question, but he answered it anyways.

"Because I like it," he said simply.

"Why do you only put stuff around your eyes?" Joanne asked.

"It brings out the green in them. Make-up in any other place would look weird," Kafa said.

*It kind of already looks weird on you…* Joanne thought, but didn't say it out loud.

"Oh," Joanne said instead.

"If you ever need black or gold eyeshadow, feel free to drop by," he said cheerily.

"Umm, okay. Sure thing," Joanne said, then turned to Rumple and mouthed, *He has gold eyeshadow?* He nodded. *When does he use that?* Joanne mouthed.

*You'll see it tonight.* Rumple mouthed.

*What's tonight?* Joanne wondered.

They walked into the lobby, where Unavenged members were in a frenzy. There were about thirty of them, all running around doing the craziest things. They were spray painting on the walls, throwing toilet paper rolls, and shooting spray-foam every which way. Joanne had to duck to avoid getting hit with a roll of toilet paper. When the Unavenged saw Kafa, they all started to chant.

"The Unavenged will get their revenge!" they chanted. Kafa grinned evilly before he repeated the phrase, rousing wild cheers and hoots in the room.

"I ekdíkisi eínai dikí mas!" they said, Rumple and Kafa included. The Unavenged's smiles were contagious, and it wasn't long before Joanne felt herself start to smile, too. Kafa led them all to the dining hall, all of them cheering and chanting and howling. They sat down at the dining hall table.

"You may eat!" Kafa announced with a smile.

There were chicken legs, steak, and all different types of wine and beer. It almost seemed celebratory. But what they were celebrating, Joanne didn't know. Everyone drank, including Rumple. Joanne left her glass of wine alone. Most of the Unavenged grabbed chicken legs and ripped into them like animals. Joanne tried not to stare but wasn't successful. *They all look wild and crazy. As if they've completely lost their minds,* Joanne thought. She ate a chicken leg, though she didn't tear into it like everyone else seemed to.

"Come on, enjoy yourself, Joanne!" Kafa said at one point, lightly hitting her shoulder and sloshing his drink on the table, though he either didn't care or didn't notice.

When they were all done, Kafa began to speak.

"We meet in the lobby in one hour. Prepare yourselves, my Unavenged! Prepare yourselves for the Run!" he said. Then he turned to Joanne and Rumple, his eyes wild from wine and excitement.

"Go bathe, you two. Be here at the right time!" he said, then with a whisk of his cape, turned and strode towards his room. Rumple grabbed her wrist. He hadn't drunk much wine, but Joanne had seen him drink a little.

"Come on. You heard him. Let's get ready!" Rumple exclaimed, leading her to his room. They arrived at Rumple's room and he tossed her a bundle of clothes.

"You shower first. Change into that afterwards," he said. Joanne went to the restroom and stripped, grateful to get her dirty, sweaty clothes off. She stepped into the shower, letting the water run over her and wash her off. She scrubbed her hair with shampoo and then dried herself off with a towel. She unfolded the clothes Rumple had given here and stared at them. It was a tight black shirt, black leggings, and a gold jacket. She put it on and went back into the room. Rumple walked into the bathroom and showered as Joanne peered out of the window. There didn't appear to be anyone outside, though she couldn't really see due to the lack of lights. There were lights on the outside of the hotel, but none of them were turned on. Rumple walked out a few minutes later, dressed in an identical outfit and drying his hair with a towel.

"We have a few minutes," he said as he looked at the clock. "Come on, let's go to the lobby." Joanne followed him to the lobby and noticed that everybody seemed to be standing around the coffee table, staring at it as if something was about to happen, a stark contrast to the chaos that had been happening an hour ago. Joanne leaned over to Rumple to ask him a question.

"Why are they …?"

"Just watch," Rumple said, crossing his arms and grinning. Suddenly the doors in the direction of Kafa's room flew open, and Kafa strode out, cheers, hoots, howls, and hollers erupting so suddenly that Joanne had to cover her ears. Her eyes widened in surprise when she saw Kafa. He had glittery gold and glittery black eyeshadow with his eyeliner, making his eyelids sparkle in the dim light of the chandelier. He was wearing a sleeveless black shirt, black shorts that went down to his knees, a leather belt with his sword, tall black Roman-style sandals, golden shoulder plates, a golden chest plate, and a black velvet cape with raven feathers coating the back. A simple crown that was pitch black sat crooked atop his wild hair.

He leaped onto the coffee table and the noise died down until you could hear a pen drop. Kafa wore a maniacal grin and breathed in the silence before, to Joanne's surprise, he burst into song.

> *Silent in the dead of night, the Unavenged will make things right*
>
> *Might be considered a crime, but it is our time*
>
> *To rise, in our disguise*
>
> *And let the Unavenged, get their revenge*
>
> *Yes, the Unavenged will get their revenge*
>
> *Mightier than a lion's roar, upon darkness' wings we will soar*
>
> *Stronger than a pack of wolves, we glitter like jewels*
>
> *Tougher than a rhino's hide, tonight, the Unavenged will ride*
>
> *And let the Unavenged, get their revenge*
>
> *Yes, the Unavenged, will get their revenge*

Kafa sang, the Unavenged members joining in whenever Kafa hit the chorus. Everyone was really crazy now, jumping and making a wide variety of noises, some of them just shouting profanity.

"To the vehicles!" Kafa said, pointing to the doors, and everyone rushed out of the doors, acting as if they were all *hyped up* on something.

"Come on!" Rumple said, his eyes alight with excitement as he grabbed her wrist. They joined in with the wave of Unavenged, each one breaking off to load themselves into their vehicles. Rumple led Joanne into an old jeep. Joanne noticed that out of all the Unavenged, she was the only one who had buckled up. Kafa was on his horse's saddle.

"Let us ride!" he shouted, then kicked the horse and took off in the direction of the heart of the City. The Unavenged drove after him. When Rumple pressed on the gas, Joanne screamed.

"WHAT ARE YOU DOING?" she screeched.

"Driving!" he shouted over the noise of shouts.

"YOU'RE TWELVE!" Joanne shouted.

"For the record, I look younger than I actually am, honey. I'm fifteen, in case you've forgotten, so I can drive," he said.

"BUT NOT LEGALLY!" she yelled.

"Does *any* of this look legal to you?" Rumple asked, gesturing to the Unavenged around them. Joanne opened her mouth, but her words were lost in the wind as Rumple stepped on the gas. She screamed and held on to her seat, her knuckles going white. Rumple just laughed. The Unavenged drove recklessly through the streets, swerving onto curbs and hitting mailboxes, even crashing into a streetlight once. Kafa was leading them, his horse going impossibly fast as his raven feather cape streamed behind them. He glanced back once or twice, flashing them a malicious grin that made the Unavenged go crazy. The streetlights made bands of light run over the group, light revealing the cars for a moment before plunging them into darkness again. Most of the Unavenged were blasting the same alternative music station from their cars so the wild songs echoed throughout the City streets. They drove deep into the heart of the City, where most of the buildings were multiple stories or skyscrapers. There were some imaginary friends, all wearing designer clothes, who were walking on the sidewalks and ran away screaming something about the Unavenged when they spotted them. The reaction of the people seemed to get the Unavenged even more encouraged to shout and swerve.

Kafa led them down a road, and then he stopped. The cars all stopped as well. Kafa turned his horse to face the Unavenged. They seemed to be on a street of tall buildings.

"Alright, Unavenged. Go! Have fun!" he said, throwing his arms wide. The Unavenged killed their car engines and raced out on foot into the street until the streets were filled with Unavenged members, all of them pulling out weapons and looking excited. Joanne still didn't know what they were doing. Next thing she knew, Rumple was pressing a sword in her hand and telling her to get out of the car. Joanne obeyed, her shoes hitting the pavement road as she shut the door behind her. Then, they suddenly started racing into buildings, smashing through windows and picking locks, setting bushes on fire and throwing firecrackers into buildings. Joanne stared around in horror, while Rumple started running towards a big building that Kafa was going into. Joanne, not feeling safe by herself, ran in after them. They had blown up the door and the sound of fire alarms greeted Joanne. She almost reached up to plug her ears, but none of the other Unavenged were doing so, so Joanne kept her arms by her side. They looked like they were in a hallway with multiple expensive looking oil paintings, lights shining down on each one. Kafa was at the front of the group, pointing to some of them and waving away the others. The ones he waved away were spray painted on by Unavenged, while the ones he pointed at were brought back to the cars.

*So, this is how they have all of those expensive paintings. Interesting,* she thought. They burst into a main room that was filled with sculptures, jewelry, and lasers. Kafa put a finger to his lips, signaling for them to be quiet. He jumped and dodged through the lasers as gracefully as a dancer, not hitting one of them. He made it to a table with necklaces on display. He grabbed one with a yellow jewel and alarms started wailing, but the Unavenged just cheered and Kafa just smiled.

"Trash it," he said as he walked back into the hallway. As soon as the words left his mouth, Unavenged were tying strips of cloth to sculptures and lighting them on fire, then spray painting pictures all over them, and throwing firecrackers onto the rugs, making burn marks on the rugs. Joanne heard the wail of a siren.

"The I.P.O.s are coming! Everyone, move it!" Joanne heard Kafa yell from outside. The Unavenged raced out of the buildings, spilling back into the streets like water burst from a dam. Rumple was right in front of Joanne. She grabbed his arm.

"What's an I.P.O.?" she asked.

"Imaginary Police Officers," he replied as they walked back onto the street.

"Was that like a museum?" Joanne asked as the Unavenged gathered around Kafa sitting on his horse.

"Yeah," Rumple said, looking at her weird.

"So, we just stole all of that and ransacked it," Joanne said.

"All of those buildings too," Rumple said, gesturing to the entire street, which now looked like it had been through hell. The vegetation around the buildings were on fire, there was graffiti everywhere, windows were smashed, and firecrackers were being thrown about in fiery arcs. Joanne's mouth fell open.

"And you're all okay with that? Do you all just go around stealing and vandalizing?" Joanne asked.

"Yeah, that's what we do. This is what we call a Run, which we do about once a month," Rumple explained.

"I can't believe you would do this sort of thing," Joanne said, staring at Rumple. Hurt flashed across his face.

"Well, being discarded changes imaginary friends... sometimes for the worse," he said, and looked like he was about to say something else when Kafa's voice boomed through the street.

"My dear Unavenged, you've done well tonight. As you can hear, the I.P.O.'s are on their way. Feel free to leave firecrackers on the road behind us for them to run over. Now, let us head back to the Unavenged base, for we are clever, not cretins," he said, his gold eyeshadow glittering in the streetlights, then kicked his horse, and Kafa and his horse sped off into the night.

The Unavenged sprinted to their cars, jumping in and throwing firecrackers all around. Rumple ran off towards their jeep, and Joanne followed, still shocked that they had really just done all of that in just a few minutes. She got in the jeep and Rumple hit the gas so they weren't too far behind the other Unavenged members.

Joanne looked behind them and saw police cars swerving around the corner in pursuit.

"Are those I.P.O.s?" Joanne asked. Rumple glanced behind them and shouted obscenities.

"Rumple! When did you get such a mouth?" Joanne asked.

"When I met these people!" Rumple exclaimed. The wind was making Joanne's hair fly all around like a halo, and suddenly the I.P.O.s started firing some sort of guns. Rumple swore again.

"Trackers! Don't let them hit your cars!" he shouted, trying to get the other Unavenged to hear, though Joanne highly doubted they were even listening. The Unavenged sped up, pressing the gas pedals even more so they wouldn't be caught. Finally, Joanne saw the familiar turn of the road ahead that led to the dark part of the City. The Unavenged turned down it, and the I.P.O.s, to Joanne's surprise, didn't follow them. She was so relived she wasn't about to be arrested she actually laughed out loud. Rumple looked at her, grinning, as if he thought that she was having fun. Fun was the last way Joanne would describe any part of what they just did.

*Why do they even do this? How is this revenge? And what is this revenge for?* Joanne wondered as they turned a few more times to reach the hotel. They arrived, and everyone parked and got out of their cars, then gathered around Kafa, who was on his horse in the middle of the parking lot.

"Excellent job, all of you! We managed to get some nice trinkets," he said, holding up the necklace he stole, "and we all had fun. The City is much more beautiful now, with all that art on its buildings. Not to mention we attracted I.P.O.s! That is something that rarely happens, as those of you who have been in the Unavenged for a while know. We will strike again in approximately five weeks, this time the area by the Imaginist Office. Until then, rest and train, my Unavenged. But if you wish, you can join the victory celebration in the lobby tonight," he said, then gestured theatrically towards the doors. The Unavenged rushed towards it. Joanne didn't want to participate in any celebration of the crimes they had just committed, and all she wanted was to get back to Rumple's room and sleep, but Kafa called her out.

"Joanne! Join me, if you don't mind," he said, scooting back a little and patting the part of the saddle in front of him. Joanne tried not to sigh and put a genuine-looking smile on her face.

"Go," Rumple muttered, and gently pushed her in the direction of Kafa. She walked up to him and he offered her a hand. She hadn't gotten on a horse since she was six, which had been a very bad experience, so she eyed it warily and hesitated to take it.

"What, have you never ridden a horse before?" Kafa asked, smiling.

"Umm, not successfully," Joanne said. Kafa laughed.

"What do you mean by that?" he asked.

"I was six and it involved a lot of screaming and crying," Joanne said. Kafa laughed again.

"That's hilarious. But don't worry, Midnight will ride slow if that's what you're scared of," Kafa said, his face softening. Joanne breathed in deeply, then took his hand. He helped her onto the horse and she sat in front of him on the saddle. He gave the horse a prod with his sandal and it took off at a trot. Joanne inhaled sharply and held on tighter to the horse's mane. Kafa chuckled at her reaction. Once they had trotted away from the base and began trotting towards a road that led to the City, Kafa spoke.

"So, I asked you to come with me because I have some things to talk about with you, Joanne," Kafa said.

"Umm... okay," Joanne said, unsure of where this would even go.

"First thing, the Imaginists did *not* want to meet with me for some strange reason, so we will have to sneak into the ball tomorrow night," Kafa said. Joanne smirked.

"I wonder why. Wait, the ball is *tomorrow night*?" she asked.

"Yes, it is. *So* inconvenient, because that means we'll have to go get you a ball gown tomorrow before the ball," Kafa said. Joanne automatically thought of the Cinderella movie that had come out recently, and she tried to imagine herself in one of those ball gowns, but failed.

"Wait, like an actual ball gown?" Joanne asked.

"Yes," Kafa said slowly, looking at her weird.

"Is that what most people wear to these?" Joanne asked.

"Yes. They're not as big as you're probably thinking. You're probably thinking about the older ones. The ones ladies usually wear to these balls are smaller and easier to move in," Kafa said. Joanne sighed with relief.

"Wait, who's going to go?" Joanne asked.

"It'll be easier to get us in if it's just two of us, so you, because you are the key to the plan, and me, because I am the leader of the Unavenged," Kafa said.

"So, no Rumple?" Joanne asked.

"I'm afraid not. It's not like he hasn't gone to a ball before anyways. He attends to the Veteran one every year, so I think he'll live if he has to sit this one out," Kafa said.

"Rumple is *not* a veteran!" Joanne exclaimed, laughing at the thought of her cowardly little brother being a veteran, of all things.

"Not like that! Here in Imagine, if you're in play for over five years, you are considered Veteran status, which earns you a spot at that ball and it also gives you some discounts on things at some stores," Kafa explained.

"Wahoo, discounts," Joanne said flatly.

"Hey. Don't underestimate the power of discounts, Joanne," Kafa said.

"You sound like my grandparents," Joanne said, smirking. Kafa muttered something about not being *that* old, but he dropped it.

"So, yes, tomorrow, me and you will go dress shopping in the City," Kafa said.

"Oh, lord," Joanne muttered.

"Don't worry, I'm sure we'll have fun," Kafa assured her. Joanne tried to make it look like she believed him.

"Alright, on to the second thing. You didn't like that very much, did you?" Kafa asked.

"Like *what*?" Joanne asked, even though her thoughts immediately flew to the Run.

"The Run. I could tell on your face that you really didn't like it," Kafa said.

"Oh, that. Yeah, I didn't really like it that much…" Joanne said, trailing off.

"What part did you not like?" Kafa asked.

"Well… pretty much all of it," she said.

"Yeah, you seem to have better morals than all of us. Did you at least like the song?" Kafa asked.

"The song was pretty cool, actually. Who wrote it?" Joanne said.

"Me," Kafa said proudly.

"Good job," Joanne said.

"Thank you. Now, the third thing. I'm going to tell you as much as I know about Kile, because if you're going to face him, you're going to need some background information," Kafa said.

"Okay. I'm listening," Joanne said. And with that, Kafa began.

## Chapter Ten

"Alright. He's from around 1970, and his Creator was a little girl named Annie. She used him for about seven years, then discarded him when she was around ten. Before then, he was a really amazing guy. He was kind and caring, and he always thought of others before himself. He was smart and calculating, and could be cruel sometimes, though he didn't show it much. Kile and I were close. Very close. After I met him in that café, we continued to hang out and we became the best of friends. We planned on starting the Unavenged and everything. We did a lot together. We were... happy. Then he got discarded. He was down, *really* down, more than I've ever seen an imaginary friend down before. He wouldn't tell me exactly what happened, exactly what she said, but whatever it was, it changed him. He was also distant. Anything I did or said just seemed to bounce off him, as if he had lost his soul, lost his life. He didn't seem to want to be around me anymore like he used to. After a few weeks, he had begun to show emotions again. But they weren't the same as before. Now he was angry, he was cruel, and he was cold. He wasn't the man I used to know, the man that had been my best friend. We began to have arguments. He was now extremely power hungry, and he kept on blabbing about the Stone of Existence. I didn't think he was serious. I mean, how could he be? I was one of the imaginary friends that had helped put the Stone of Existence away for good! I didn't think he could ever get it. One day, I finally told him what I thought, and he got terribly angry with me. Then he left, and he never came back. I didn't see him again, until he blackmailed me yesterday. He is completely different. He is no longer the man he was. He has no heart now, and will destroy anything that gets in his way. I think he plans to use the Stone to rule over Imagine, but I'm not sure. Knowing the new him, he plans to rule more than that. We have to stop him. It all starts tomorrow, when we will meet with the Imaginists," Kafa said. Joanne nodded and was quiet for a moment.

"What do you think she said to him?" she asked.

"Something that he'll never forget," he said, a haunted look on his face as he seemed to remember Kile.

"Do you really think our plan will work?" Joanne asked.

"Maybe. It's definitely our best option and has a good chance of success. But we won't know until we do it," he said.

"Yeah," Joanne said.

"Alright, we should head back before the Unavenged start wondering where their king went," Kafa said.

"Probably," Joanne said, and with that, Kafa steered the horse back to the hotel.

"So, how did you like riding a horse?" Kafa asked as the hotel came into view. Joanne laughed.

"Umm, it was pretty good, actually," she said.

"Excellent. No screaming and crying this time, eh?" he said.

"Yeah, no screaming and crying this time," Joanne confirmed. They arrived at the hotel and he put Midnight in a stable Joanne hadn't noticed earlier, then helped Joanne off the horse.

"There. That wasn't so bad, now was it?" he said, smiling at her, his eyeshadow glittering in the light.

"Nope," Joanne said.

"Good. Now, do you want to come to the party, or would you rather not?" Kafa asked.

"Eh… I'd rather not," she said.

"Alright. I would escort you there, but if I'm gone any longer, then it would just look odd," Kafa said as they walked into the hotel.

"Yeah. I can make it to Rumple's room anyways," Joanne said. He gave her a small smile.

"I know you can," he said, and then the Unavenged saw Kafa and began cheering. Joanne waved at Kafa and began walking to Rumple's room. She walked down the hallway and froze. There was a girl standing in front of Rumple's door. She looked to be about twenty-one, and she was extremely pretty. She looked like a model that walked right out of her newspaper. She had tan skin, blond hair with some light brown streaks, and brown eyes so dark they looked black. She was wearing a jet-black dress that hugged her body, showing all of her curves. When she turned and saw Joanne, she smiled, her teeth needle-sharp. Joanne also noticed she had a pair of black wings sprouting from her back. Joanne tried not to flinch or run in the other direction. As Joanne drew closer to Rumple's room, the woman still didn't move.

"Umm, excuse me, but that's my room," Joanne said after she found the courage to speak to this scary-looking lady. The lady just laughed.

"Oh, my apologies. You are Joanne Raider, correct?" she asked, her voice silky and smooth. Joanne's eyes widened.

"Why, yes," Joanne said.

"Good. I'm Dari, a fellow Unavenged member. I saw how you defeated Barthemius in the arena. It was *very* impressive. Tell me, how did you manage to accomplish that?" she said, extending a hand. Joanne didn't want to be rude, so she shook it. Her skin was unnaturally hot, as if she was touching something that had sat out in the sun for a few hours. Joanne tried not to flinch away, but she did let go sooner than she probably had to.

"Umm, I don't know, honestly," Joanne said.

Irritation flashed across Dari's face.

"Really? Are you just naturally *that* athletic?" she said dryly.

"I guess so," Joanne said, and tried to step around Dari, but Dari blocked her.

"Tell me, Joanne, how would you like to be queen of the Unavenged?" Dari asked. Joanne's eyes widened.

"Umm, I don't want to be the queen," Joanne said.

"Are you sure?" Dari asked, positioning her body in a way that Joanne guessed was supposed to be seductive.

*Umm... does she think that pose is going to help her out or something?* Joanne wondered.

"Yes, I'm sure! Now goodnight!" Joanne exclaimed, ducking underneath Dari's arm and opening Rumple's door, then shutting it quickly behind her. She slumped in relief.

*Who the heck is she and why did she ask me those questions?* Joanne wondered, though she knew it wasn't good. Rumple wasn't in the room, so he was probably at the party with everyone else. Well, everyone else besides Dari. *What kind of person imagined her up anyways?* Joanne wondered as she kicked off her shoes and crawled into Rumple's old sleeping bag. She shut her eyes and quickly fell asleep, unaware that Dari was still outside of her door, calling someone.

~~

*He walked into the familiar café, the scent of coffee and pastries washing over him. Lucky's Café was a place Kafa had been going to for years to get coffee or just chill out. They did have the best coffee in Imagine, after all. He walked over to the counter and ordered a cup of black coffee. After it was given to him in all of its steamy goodness, he looked around for a place to sit. It was unusually busy that day, and every table was filled with imaginary friends. He sighed and was about to go drink it somewhere else when he saw a head of black hair. He squinted at them, trying to remember where he recognized them. Then it came to him. He was addressing some protesters, and there had been a man with black hair and intelligent looking gray eyes that had caught Kafa's eye. He walked over to the man and saw that he was reading a thick book, a cup of coffee beside him, though it was still full, as if he had gotten it but hadn't drank any of it.*

*"Do you mind if I sit here?" Kafa asked. The man looked up, his gray eyes flashing with recognition.*

*"Why would I let an Imaginist sit with me?" the man asked, a slight German accent with his words.*

*"Well, you see, I am no longer an Imaginist," Kafa said, gesturing to his chest, which didn't have the pendant on it that all Imaginists wore at all times. The man's eyes narrowed.*

*"Why did you quit?" he asked.*

*"They've become corrupt and are no longer worth my time," Kafa answered. The man seemed to like his answer. He nodded and said,*

*"Go ahead, then." Kafa sat across from the man.*

*"You're Kafa, right?" the man asked.*

*"You're correct. And you might be?" Kafa said.*

*"Kile," he said. Kafa smiled.*

*"That's a nice name. So, are you new to Imagine?" Kafa asked.*

*"I've been in play for about a month. How about you?" Kile replied.*

*"Oh, I've been discarded for a good... one thousand nine hundred years," Kafa said casually. Kile's eyebrows shot up, making Kafa smile again.*

*"Really?" he asked.*

*"Yes," Kafa said.*

*"So, you're like, one of the first imaginary friends," he said.*

*"Right again," Kafa said.*

*"Could you tell me about Imagine? I don't know much and I've gotten lost once or twice trying to find my way around," Kile said sheepishly. Kafa laughed, making some people whip their heads around and making Kile grin.*

*"Of course," he said.*

Kafa creaked open his eyes, his head pounding.

"Ouch," he muttered, gently touching his head with his fingertips. He fully opened his eyes and saw a blurry figure standing in front of him.

"Kile?" he muttered, reaching out to touch him.

"What? No! You must be drunker than I thought," a high-pitched boyish voice said. Kafa shook his head and the figure came into view. Rumple stood beside his bed, staring at him. Kafa jumped.

"Ah! Rumple! When did you get here?" he asked, looking around. He was in his room, but he had no memory of getting there.

"Oh, my god, I've *been* here. You've done this twice already! You've woken up, and then not made any sense," Rumple said, sounding annoyed.

"Wait... what happened?" Kafa asked. Rumple sighed.

"You drank way too much wine so I had to take you up to your room. You were *super* giggly and you kept trying to untie my shoes, so I had to spray you with a spray bottle. I also figured that you were drunk. No, I *prayed* you were drunk." Rumple said.

*I've never drank too much. I always control myself. Why did I get drunk this time?* Kafa frowned, wondering.

"Oh. I'm terribly sorry. I have no memory of that…" Kafa said, trailing off.

"The magic of alcohol," Rumple muttered. Kafa ignored the comment.

"What time is it?" he asked instead.

"Like, eleven thirty," Rumple answered, sounding very tired.

"Oh. I'm sorry. You should get back to Joanne," Kafa said, running a hand through his hair.

"Okay. Goodnight. Don't try to untie anyone else's shoes, please," Rumple said as he walked towards the door. Kafa almost smiled.

"I won't. And thank you, Rumple," Kafa said as he grabbed the knob. Rumple turned and gave him a smile.

"Sure thing," he said, then walked out, shutting the door behind him.

Kafa looked up at the ceiling, slightly embarrassed that he had tried to untie Rumple's shoes. But he closed his eyes and fell asleep anyways, unaware of a black-haired, gray-eyed figure opening the balcony door. He walked into Kafa's room, sat down in a chair and watched him sleep for a little while, and then left just as silently as he had come.

The next morning Kafa woke up to sunlight streaming through the windows, the light turning the insides of his eyelids an orange color. He opened his and sat up. Everything looked normal. He reached over and checked the time on his cell phone. His eyebrows shot up. *Nine already? Shoot!* He thought as he leaped out of bed, almost tripping, and raced towards the door. Then he stopped, realizing that he was still in his Run outfit. With an impatient sigh, he threw open his closet doors and selected his usual outfit. He threw it on and went into the bathroom, wiping off his makeup and putting on eyeliner and black eyeshadow. He set his crown down on the counter and rushed out of his room. He walked over to Rumple's room and knocked on the door. A few seconds later, Joanne opened it. She was already dressed.

"Are you ready to go dress shopping?" Kafa asked.

"Yeah. Rumple's sleeping, so let me go leave him a note," Joanne whispered, and then she disappeared back inside. She came back out a few moments later.

"Okay, let's go," Joanne said. They walked down the hallway and down into the lobby, then outside. Joanne started to walk towards the stables but stopped when she saw Kafa walking towards the cars.

"Aren't we taking Midnight?" Joanne asked.

"Nope. The traffic is too much to handle for Midnight on a weekday during the day. So, we're taking my car instead," Kafa said. Joanne's eyes widened when she saw him get into a black Ferrari F12.

"You have a Ferrari F12?" she asked in awe.

"Umm… yes," he said, acting as if it wasn't a big deal.

"How did you afford that?" she asked.

"You forget that I am king. I can afford a lot of things," he said as Joanne got inside.

"Do you even drive this?" Joanne asked.

"Sometimes," he said, shrugging.

"*Sometimes?*" Joanne said indecorously, unbelieving that he didn't drive his expensive car around that much.

"Yes," he said as he started the engine and pulled out of the parking lot. Joanne just looked at him, but he didn't notice since he was now focused on the road.

"Okay, so there are three different places in the City that sell gowns. Well, good places. The rest are… trash. Anyways, they all have variations, from really fancy to relatively simple, and all different styles and colors, too. I'm sure we'll find something by the end of the day. Oh, and I was thinking that we could stop by Lucky's Café for lunch whenever you get hungry," Kafa said.

"What's Lucky's Café?" Joanne asked.

"Only the best café in all of Imagine! They have pastries, sandwiches, and the *best* coffee!" Kafa said.

"Even better than Starbucks?" Joanne asked. Kafa scoffed.

"Please, Starbucks is a place for people who want dessert with their breakfast. It shouldn't even be called a coffee place," he said, rolling his eyes. Joanne laughed.

"It's true!" he exclaimed.

"Yeah, it kind of is," Joanne agreed.

"Okay, so the first place is *Deborah's*. It's right around here…" Kafa said as they entered the heart of City. He suddenly turned sharply to the left, making Joanne slam against the door. Then he stopped the car.

"Okay, we're here!" he exclaimed, getting out. Joanne got out after him and they walked into the shop.

"Hello, and welcome to *Deborah's*! Let me know if I can help you with anything!" a lady that was standing behind the checkout counter said.

"Alright, thank you!" Kafa said. *Deborah's* had hard wood floors and dim lights over some dresses on display. Most of them were relatively simple, but some were extravagant.

"Alright, go try on some dresses and then come back out and let me see if any of them are ball-worthy," Kafa said, sitting down on a bench outside of the dressing rooms and taking out his cell phone.

"Umm, okay," Joanne said, then, taking a deep breath, plunged herself into the jungle of dresses.

~~

It had been about a day since Joanne had FaceTime'd them, but everyone was still in a frenzy. There had been a man named Kafa that had looked insane with Joanne, and she had dodged all questions about Rumple, even though her father's FaceTime showed Rumple, there and solid, as if he was real, which was impossible. She had said that she had come willingly and she couldn't tell them what she was doing, but she would be back in a few days. Karrie had filmed the entire FaceTime on her phone. The police had tried tracking where Joanne's phone was, but for some reason, it read that she was in New York, then Los Angeles, and then San Francisco, all in a matter of minutes, which was also impossible. Joanne's face was all over the news, due to how strange her disappearance was. Some people thought she was kidnapped, some thought she had gone insane, and some even thought that something greater was at hand. She had looked insane in the Subway and Schlotzsky's security footage, but she had looked perfectly fine when she FaceTime'd them. It had looked like she was in a hotel room of sorts, but that wasn't anything they could track her down with. The police had searched records for a man named Kafa, and had tried using his face to track him down, but they had come up empty-handed, as if nobody like that existed. But they had to... right?

Everyone was at Alexa's house a day later after having spent the night, eating ice cream from her mom and scheming about possibilities on Alexa's bedroom floor. They had a list tacked to the wall of possibilities:

- *Kidnapped*
- *Lost it/gone insane*
- *Taken into sex trafficking*
- *Ran away*
- *Gone to meet someone*
- *Went "off the grid"*
- *Something else*

Either way, they didn't have much. Joanne didn't seem like the type to just randomly run away, she probably didn't know how to go off the grid (why would she want to anyways?), and none of her texts had people telling her to meet them places. Even if she was kidnapped, gone insane, or taken into sex trafficking, it still didn't explain how her location was jumping all over the world map. It didn't explain really *anything*.

And then there was that other option, sarcastically suggested by Alexa at 1 A.M.. *Something else.* Something strange. Something *otherworldly*. They had all thought something like that was impossible, but the facts that had been presented about Joanne's case were impossible.

"Okay, so we've got: *Her imaginary brother came to life and kidnapped her, she can teleport,* or s*ome creeper hacked into her phone and is making us see stuff,*" Alexa said.

"I think the last one is the most likely," Karrie said.

"Yeah, but how can you put something like that in a FaceTime?" Penny asked.

"You can't. I mean, I don't think you can," Adele said.

"I don't think you can either," Alexa said thoughtfully.

"Then *what?* What happened to our friend? She says she's okay, and maybe she is, but that still doesn't explain what happened or where she is!" Asha said, then plopped her face into her pillow.

"I don't know! I mean, there's some things that make it seem like we've got it figured out, and then something is revealed that screws that theory over!" Karrie exclaimed.

"Well, why don't we try calling her again?" Alexa suggested.

"We've already tried seven times since she hung up yesterday," Lola moaned before eating a spoonful of ice cream.

"It wouldn't hurt to try again," Adele said.

"Okay, fine," Lola said. Alexa took out her phone and pressed the FaceTime button for Joanne. The next moment, the screen lit up and Joanne's face appeared.

"Joanne!" Alexa exclaimed. Alexa's friends immediately scampered over to the phone.

"Oh, hey, guys!" Joanne said, a smile breaking over her face.

"Okay. Where the heck *are* you?" Alexa asked.

Joanne seemed to hesitate.

"I'm in a dress shop. See?" she said.  Then she moved the camera around so they could see racks of dresses all around her.

"Why are you in a dress shop, Joanne?" Penny asked.

"Kafa is insisting that I get a dress for a ball tonight," Joanne said, glancing over in the direction Alexa assumed Kafa was in.

The girls stared in confusion.

"Ball?" they asked, almost in unison.

"Oh, yeah. Some politicians wouldn't agree to meet with me and Kafa, so we're going to sneak into their ball tonight and meet them there," Joanne said casually, as if it was something she did every day. Her friends gaped at her.

"What the heck are you talking about?! Hold on. You're *sneaking into* to a *ball* and you're going to *meet politicians*?!" Lola asked.

"Yes," Joanne responded.

"What politicians?" Penny asked.

"What do you mean?" Joanne asked, her brow furrowing.

"Like, politicians of where?" Penny elaborated.

"Umm, I can't really tell you that," Joanne said sheepishly.

"So, you *can't* tell us where you are?" Asha asked. "Your parents and everyone else in Watermore are freaking out looking for you!"

"I know, but I will be back in a few days, okay? I should go now-"

"Wait!" Alexa said. Joanne stopped talking and looked at Alexa in surprise.

"*Something else*," Alexa said.

"What?" Joanne asked, her brow creasing.

"Something else. That's what happened to you, right? Not kidnapping, not running away, not going off the grid, not going to meet someone, not getting taken up into sex trafficking, not going insane… it's something else, right? Something impossible?" Alexa said. Joanne looked at them for another second before she said,

"Yes, something else has happened to me." Then, before her friends could ask her any more questions, she hung up. Her friends closed their mouths immediately, stopping the questions they were about to pepper Joanne with from leaving their mouths.

"I knew it. It is something else. But what is something else?" Alexa asked, but the only thing that answered her was stunned silence.

# Chapter Eleven

Joanne slipped her phone into her pocket, worrying that she had said too much. But she pushed thoughts of her friends away as she looked up and down the racks of dresses. She found a few that looked like they might be bearable, so she took them to the dressing room. One was a dark green that was really just a sundress that went down to below her knees with wide straps. Another was a light pink that flowed down into a large, silky skirt that had lace sleeves. The last one was a dark red that's straps were on her shoulders that had a deep, plunging neckline while the skirt went down to just above her knees that was more of a thicker fabric. She put on the dark green and walked outside to Kafa. He looked up from his phone, but didn't seem impressed.

"Too simple. The color doesn't really go with your blue eyes anyways," he said dismissively, then went back to his phone. Joanne sighed, and went back into the dressing room. She took off the green sundress and wriggled into the pink one. The skirt fanned out too much for Joanne's liking. It seemed like something that would be hard to do much in. She walked outside and Kafa looked her up and down.

"Hmm… I guess it's good, but it's a bit *too* fancy. Besides, I can tell you don't care for it much at all," he said thoughtfully.

"Yeah, I don't. I'll try the next one," Joanne said, going back in the dressing room, the fabrics of her skirt rustling as she did so. She got out of the pink one and into the red one and went back outside.

His eyes trailed over her.

"It's good, it's just… the ball requires dancing. I don't know how much you'll be able to dance without showing… too much," Kafa said, his gaze lingering on her chest for a second before going back to her face.

"Well, these were the best dresses here," Joanne said.

"Okay. Let's go to another shop then. Well, lunch first, since it's almost time. Then we'll check out the other two," Kafa said.

"Alright. I'll go change," Joanne said. Kafa nodded, and she went back into the dressing room, slipping out of the dress and back into her usual clothes. She walked out and they went back to the car. Kafa drove a little bit before he pulled over at a small, cheerful looking building called Lucky's Café. They got out of the car and Kafa led Joanne inside, the aroma of coffee and pastries hitting her the moment she stepped inside. It was a little small, filled with round wooden tables that had red and white checkered tablecloths. There was a chalkboard above the ordering counter, a bookshelf against one wall, and music playing in the background. There were also some windows that let light pour into the café, rendering some small lights on the ceiling useless.

"What do you want?" Kafa asked.

"What do they have?" Joanne asked.

"Well… look at the menu, for Jupiter's sake!" he said, gesturing to the huge chalkboard over the counter. There was a huge selection of coffees and sandwiches. Joanne's eyes scanned the menu until her eyes found something familiar.

"I'll just have a ham and cheese sandwich," Joanne said. Kafa gave her a strange look, as if she had said something quite ridiculous.

"What?" Joanne asked.

"There's all of these options for sandwiches here and you choose ham and cheese?" he asked.

"Yes," Joanne said.

"Okay," he muttered, then walked up to the counter and ordered their sandwiches and bottles of water for the two of them. Then he led them over to a table for two near the middle of the café. He looked at the seat Joanne sat at with a sad expression, as if somebody had sat there once that no longer did.

"What is it?" Joanne asked.

Kafa shook his head, a casual looking smile on his face.

"Nothing, Joanne. Just thinking about if we'll find you a dress at these other two shops," he lied.

*That's not why you're sad,* Joanne thought, though she didn't say it.

"Oh. I'm sure we will," Joanne said.

"Yes, it is likely. Don't worry, we'll find something before it starts," Kafa said.

"When does it start?" Joanne asked.

"Starts at six, ends at nine," he replied. Her eyebrows shot up.

"A three-hour ball?" she asked.

"The Imaginists don't throw their balls lightly, Joanne. I would know. I used to be in charge of them. When I was in charge, they were more extravagant, more impressive, showing the cultures of Imagine. But now... now they put somebody else in charge and they're poor quality," Kafa said sourly.

Joanne laughed at his tone.

"It's true! They're so... dull, now," he said distastefully. Joanne just shook her head and smiled. A waitress delivered their food. Kafa had gotten some Roman thing, while Joanne just ate her simple ham and cheese.

"Do you ever miss Rome?" she asked.

"Hmm? Oh, yes. All the time. Rome was... glorious. It was powerful, it was civilized... it was just remarkable, Joanne. You should have seen it," he said, a small smile on his face and a twinkle in his eyes as he stared off into the distance.

"If you don't mind me asking, who was your Creator?" Joanne asked.

His smile grew.

"It was a little boy by the name of Linus. His parents died when he was young, so he imagined someone that was like a father to him. Me. I ended up being more like a mentor than a father, but he loved me to death, and I loved him like a son. Then..." Kafa said, trailing off. His smile faded, but he continued.

"Then the City was attacked by some barbaric tribe. Linus... Linus didn't make it. Poor boy. He was only about fourteen. They tied him up and- set him on fire, as they did with many other children to get the City to surrender. He spent his last moments... he spent them screaming and crying for- *me*. But I couldn't save him. I couldn't save my little Creator..." Kafa said, looking somber as he looked down at the table. Joanne reached out and put a hand on his shoulder.

"I'm sorry," she said quietly. He looked up; his expression less blue.

"It's alright. There's nothing for you to be sorry for. He died; he's been dead for years... the pain *has* faded over the years. The loss never truly goes away, but it does get easier to deal with over time. It's okay, though. He had a happy life," Kafa said, shrugging.

"You shouldn't have had to watch that though," Joanne said.

"You're right. No imaginary friend should have to watch their Creator die, but some do. It usually tears them apart with grief, makes them soulless. I've heard stories of little kids who have gotten kidnapped, and right before they get brutally murdered, since their parents don't answer their screams for help, they imagine their imaginary friend. So, their imaginary friends' face is the last thing they see, not their murderers'. Same thing with kids in a car accident. Just... it is a terrible thing, watching your Creator die and not being able to help, but it happens to some," Kafa said sadly. Joanne suddenly felt sick. Whenever a kid went missing and they found their body later, if they had an imaginary friend, was that the last face they saw? Was that their last shred of comfort? The face of someone that didn't even truly exist? Joanne shivered, trying to chase those thoughts away.

"Can you feel it when your Creator dies?" Joanne asked.

"Well, most imaginary friends do. It depends on how much their Creator loved them. For those who do, it's suddenly like a part of your soul is gone, as if you had it, and you thought it was all yours, but once they die, it is as if half of it disappeared. It's almost like you can feel a hole, a void in your chest, sucking up things. Some things you used to like to do that your Creator did will make you suddenly feel empty, as if you never enjoyed it and never will. For those who don't, the air might feel a bit off one day, but they never think anything of it," Kafa said slowly. Joanne nodded.

*That's how I felt for a little while after Rumple left. As if some things I used to do with him were no longer fun. As if there was a hole in me that couldn't be filled,* Joanne thought darkly. Kafa looked at her, a smile on his face.

"But, we're not here to get sad, now are we? Come on, let's finish our food so we can go get you a dress," Kafa said.

"Okay," Joanne said, trying to push memories of Rumple being gone away. *He's here again, and that's all that matters,* Joanne thought. They finished their food and walked out to the car.

"Hey Kafa, why'd you look at the chair I was sitting in so weirdly?" Joanne asked as they got in the car. He looked taken aback by this, as if he hadn't expected her to notice the way he looked at the chair.

"Oh! Umm, I met somebody there," he said.

*I ran into him at a café a few days after that,* Joanne remembered.

"Was it Kile?" she asked. He looked at her, an unreadable expression on his face.

"Yes, it was," he said after a long pause.

Then they drove to the second dress shop, called *Tiffany's*. The exterior was hot pink, and the dresses in the windows were all shades of pink.

"Umm, I don't really know if I'll find something here," Joanne said.

Kafa eyed the shop warily.

"Oh, I'm sure it'll be fine," he said dismissively. Yet as soon as they walked in, he swore, getting some rude stares from some women in there.

"This place is *pink*!" Kafa whispered. It was. Everything was a shade of pink, from the floor to the ceiling. Pastel pink, sunset pink, tickled pink, hot pink, cotton candy pink, you name it. It was all there.

"Umm, I don't think I'm going to find a dress here," Joanne muttered. Some of the women, who were all obviously girly girls, were staring at Kafa as if he was something that had crawled out from under a rug. Joanne didn't blame them. With his eyeshadow and wild hair, he didn't exactly look normal. He didn't deserve the looks the women were giving him, but still. Kafa nodded.

"We should go," he said under his breath, and with that, they walked right back out of the stores.

"I don't like the way they were looking at you," Joanne said as they opened the car doors. He shrugged.

"I've had worse. Besides, if they knew who I was, they would faint," Kafa said confidently.

"Faint? That might be pushing it," Joanne said, smiling. Kafa shrugged.

"For your information, I have had a grand total of one lady faint in my presence," Kafa said proudly.

"From fear?" Joanne asked. Kafa laughed.

"I think so," he said, which made Joanne laugh.

"Well, did you even catch her?" Joanne asked as they started driving to the third shop.

"Umm... well, no. I wasn't expecting it, so she just fell... into a river," Kafa said slowly, looking slightly embarrassed as he told the story. Joanne looked at him with a wide smile on her face.

"Wait, she fell into a river?" she asked, trying not to laugh at the story. Kafa scratched the back of his head sheepishly.

"Umm, yes. But don't worry, she was fine. Some dolphin threw her out of the river," he said, acting as if the whole thing wasn't a big deal. Joanne's brow furrowed.

"What was a dolphin doing in a river?" she asked.

"It's Imagine, remember? A lot of things happen here that don't happen elsewhere, in case you've forgotten," he said. She nodded, still smiling at the story. He drove to the third shop, which looked pretty promising compared to the other two. It was called, *The Best Gowns in Town!* Joanne didn't know if that was true, but they went inside anyways. The variety of dresses was much wider here.

"Go do your thing," Kafa said, waving a hand and sitting on a bench. Joanne walked into the dresses, her eyes scanning them for the perfect one. Then she saw it. It was pure white at the top and sleeveless, but when it got to the skirt, it began to fade to blue until the very bottom of the dress was aquamarine blue. The skirt wasn't too flowy and big, nor was it too simple. It was perfect. Joanne put it on in the dressing room and walked out to Kafa. He looked up lazily from his phone, as if he was expecting something else. But when his eyes rested on Joanne, they widened, his mouth even opening slightly in surprise.

"What do you think?" Joanne asked when he didn't say anything.

"You... look flawless. It looks perfect on you, Joanne. The white goes great against your skin and the blue helps bring out your eyes..." he said, trailing off. A small smile broke out on Joanne's face at his words. He stood up and walked over to Joanne. She didn't move, unsure of what he was doing. He reached over and fluffed her hair, then the skirt of her dress. He took a step back and admired his handiwork.

"It's great. Let's buy it," he said. Joanne smiled. She changed out of it and they bought it. They walked out of the store, Joanne grinning like a child.

"Excellent! We've found you a dress with about… three hours until we need to get ready," Kafa said.

"Three hours? It starts at six!" Joanne exclaimed.

"Well, we need a little bit to do makeup and stuff. Don't worry, I'll do your make-up. It'll look great! Everyone goes overboard with make-up at these things, so it takes a little bit of time to get to that level," Kafa said. Joanne looked over at Kafa, suddenly concerned for her face's welfare.

"Kafa, what are you planning to do?" she asked. They both got in the car. He grinned mysteriously at her.

"You'll see," he said.

"Should I be worried?" Joanne asked.

"I don't think so," he said.

"Think so?" she asked, her eyebrows raised.

"Correct," he said as they pulled out of the parking lot and began driving back to the hotel.

"Oh, dear lord," Joanne muttered, causing Kafa to laugh. They suddenly drove past some I.P.O. cars in front of a building that looked like it had a bomb dropped on it, the walls crumbled or scorched badly. They were standing outside of it and searching the inside, as if they were looking for something… or someone.

"What's going on over there?" Joanne asked. Kafa's face darkened.

"By Jupiter," he whispered. Then he shook his head.

"My guess is that that right there is the work of Kile. That is an imaginary friend's home, though who lived there or what he wanted with them is beyond my understanding," he said. She looked at him in surprise.

"You think *Kile* did this?" she asked.

"No doubt. He probably did it last night during the Run so nobody would notice until the next day. Smart," he replied.

"It's more dangerous to have a smart enemy than a powerful one, isn't it?" Joanne asked.

"Sometimes. This is one of those times," Kafa said as he turned into the dark part of the City.

"Do you think he…"

"Killed them?" Kafa asked, then laughed mirthlessly.

"No doubt, Joanne. And I'm sure this is just the first of many killings. This is the first time he's killed since… well, I guess since he stole the Stone, ten or eleven days ago," Kafa said as they turned down a beat-up road. They pulled into the hotel parking lot.

"Well, somebody's got to stop him!" she exclaimed.

"Yes, somebody does have to stop him. The only problem is that it's going to take a few days for us to do so. He might actually strike again tonight because of the ball going on, though I don't know who he's targeting now," Kafa said as they got out of the car, Joanne grabbing her dress before she shut her door.

"It can't be random people; it's got to be certain people. Right?" Joanne said, her brow creased in thought.

"If he just wanted to do mass murders, he would have blown up a store or something. So, you're correct. I believe he is targeting certain people that will make it easier to carry out his plan… whatever that is," Kafa said as he held open the door. As soon as they walked into the lobby, a wave of panicked Unavenged surged towards them.

"King Kafa! Did you hear? Kelly Bram, supervisor of the East Wall, has been killed! We all think Kile killed her, but we're not sure," an imaginary friend said that was right in front of Kafa. His eyes widened a fraction.

"Kelly Bram? Are you sure?" he asked.

"Yes!" she said.

"Hmm. I want everyone to just stay calm for the moment. Don't go outside alone after dark, and double check the locks on your doors. Okay? I highly doubt Kile is going to target us," Kafa said calmly.

"But what if he does?" one imaginary friend asked.

"Then we'll fight him as Unavenged do. But for now, just keep to those safety precautions. Everyone, just stay calm. There's really nothing to worry about right now," Kafa said. One by one, the imaginary friends left the room, all whispering to each other about who Kile would kill next.

"What's the East Wall?" Joanne asked Kafa once they had all left.

"It's the border that separates us and characters from Create. If he killed her, that means that his plan probably has something to do with the East Wall. Either way, it can't be good," Kafa said.

"Nothing about his plan seems good," Joanne muttered. Kafa let out a short laugh that had no mirth.

"You're right about that, Joanne. Now, we still have almost three hours, so you can just go hang out with Rumple or something. I'll call you to my room when it's time," he said.

"Okay," Joanne said. Kafa turned and walked away to his room. Joanne, having nothing else to do, went to Rumple's room. Thankfully, Dari wasn't there this time. Where Dari had gone, Joanne didn't know, but she was just glad that she didn't have to deal with her again. Rumple was sitting on the bed, playing some game on an Xbox he had hooked up to the TV. He looked up when she walked in.

"Joanne! Oh, thank goodness! I was so worried when I heard somebody had been killed! I thought it might have been you..." he said, leaping off the bed and giving Joanne a hug. Joanne, surprised for a second, hugged him back. She could feel him. He was there.

*This is the first time I've really hugged my little brother,* Joanne thought, but he quickly stepped back, looking embarrassed.

"You're taller than you used to be. Shoot," he said. Joanne laughed. Rumple had always been shorter than her, but not by much. Now that she was sixteen and he still had the body of a twelve-year-old, she really was taller.

"Yeah, I've grown. But you..."

"Have stayed exactly the same. Benefits of being imaginary, am I right?" he said dryly. Joanne shook her head as she smiled.

"Yup. I would so love to stay at the same height forever," she said sarcastically. Rumple snickered.

"Trust me, honey, it isn't so great once it happens to you," he said, then noticed the dress slung over her shoulder.

"Ooh, nice, your dress! Can I see it?" he asked.

"Sure," Joanne said, handing the dress bag to him. He unzipped it and whistled.

"Nice," he muttered.

"I know, right?" Joanne said.

"Hmm. Some of the blue matches your eyes," Rumple observed, glancing at Joanne's face.

"Yeah, that's what Kafa said," Joanne said. Rumple handed the dress back to her.

"Well, Kafa knows what he's talking about. Most days. Anyways, how long until you have to get ready for the ball?" Rumple said.

"Like, almost three hours," Joanne said.

"Hmm. You shouldn't train because then you'd get smelly… how about we watch a movie?" Rumple suggested.

"Okay. What did you have in mind?" Joanne asked. Before Joanne knew it, they were both sitting down on the bed with a bucket of popcorn between them as they watched the Lego Movie. Rumple was screaming *Everything is Awesome* by the end of the movie, making Joanne laugh and throw popcorn kernels at him.

"Okay… you've got like, ten minutes, so he should be calling you pretty soon," Rumple said, looking at the clock on the wall.

"Yeah, probably. I wonder what he's wearing…" Joanne said, trailing off.

"Oh. Knowing Kafa, it's probably something super shiny to make all the ladies go crazy," he said casually. Joanne laughed. Her phone rang a few minutes later.

"Come on, Joanne. Bring your dress and I'll help you get ready," Kafa said as soon as she picked up before he hung up, giving her no time to respond.

"Umm. Okay. I guess I'm going to Kafa's room now. I'll see you afterwards, Rumple," Joanne said as she grabbed the dress and walked out of the room.

"Buh-bye!" he said as he tossed popcorn into his mouth. Joanne walked down the hallway and then up the stairs. She knocked on Kafa's door and he flung it open, already dressed himself. He was wearing a shiny gold long-sleeved shirt underneath a black suit. He was also wearing black earrings and black boots. His make-up was gold eyeshadow that faded out to nothing and black eyeliner. When he blinked, Joanne saw that there were little Greek letters in eyeliner on the gold eyeshadow.

"Come on, let's get you ready," he said, grabbing Joanne's shoulder and yanking her inside. He shut the door behind them and turned to Joanne.

"Go put that on in the bathroom and then come back out," he instructed, then went over a mirror that hadn't been on the wall before and started applying some glittery highlighter to his face. Joanne walked into the bathroom, shutting the door behind her. She stripped down and put on the dress, zipping it up to her neck. Then she walked back out into the room. Kafa also now had on glittery highlighter and black lipstick. He looked her up and down before pointing to a chair.

"Sit there," he instructed before he walked into the bathroom. He came back out a few moments later with a lot of make-up in his hands. Joanne's eyebrows shot up. "Okay, while I apply all of this, you're going to have to be still. No talking, no facial expressions, none of that. Also, if you have your eyes open, please don't use them to stare into mine, alright? It's weird whenever people do that. Okay? Now, let's get to work," he said. First, he put some foundation on her face. Then he applied some light pink blush and some glittery highlighter, the feel of the brush making Joanne want to laugh, but she bit her tongue so she wouldn't smile or bust out laughing.

"Now, just close your eyes. And do *not* open them until I say," Kafa said. Joanne was suddenly concerned about what he might do, but she obeyed. For about the next fifteen minutes, she felt the tickle and prickle of different makeup supplies on her face. Some of them were extremely pokey, making Joanne want to flinch away. But she worried Kafa would get angry with her, so she didn't. Joanne was relieved when he said he was done. She opened her eyes, her eyelashes sticking together for a moment from the mascara Kafa had applied at one point.

"Okay, now pucker your lips," he said. Joanne did so, and he put a light blue lipstick on her lips. Then he quickly painted her nails an alternating white and light blue.

"Okay. Hmm. Stay here, I'll be right back," he said, then went back into the bathroom. He returned about a minute or two later with some strange bottles. He squeezed out some white soap-looking liquid and rubbed it on his hands. Then he ran his hands over Joanne's hair from her chin down. Joanne wanted to ask what he was doing but decided against it. Then he squeezed out the other bottle, which had a similar substance inside, only this one was blue. He put it on his fingertips, running them through her hair. Then he took a step back and looked at her.

"I think... we're done," he said slowly.

"Can I look in the mirror?" Joanne asked.

"Feel free," he said. Joanne walked into the bathroom and gasped. She looked completely different. Her face was a little sparkly from the highlighter, her lips were a light blue, and her mascara was black with blue mascara at the tips. How he had managed that, Joanne didn't know. Her eyeshadow was the real star, though. It started at a darker blue and faded to a lighter blue until it became white before it faded into nothing. He had somehow used a white something to draw little snowflakes on her blue eyelids before they branched out around her eyes like a little snow flurry. Her hair had faded from blond to white once it reached just below her chin, and there were light blue streaks through her hair, becoming darker at the tips of her hair. She turned to Kafa, who was standing with his arms crossed in the doorway, a triumphant smirk on his face.

"I look..." she said, trailing off.

"Extraordinary," he finished for her.

"Thank you so much! I look better than I ever have before!" she exclaimed.
"Sure thing. After all, you have to look good for tonight, otherwise the Imaginists won't pay you any attention when we talk to them. Also, you'll blend in looking like this," Kafa said, smiling at her.

"Can I give you a hug?" Joanne asked, since she was somebody who liked to give people hugs.

"Mm... after the ball when we don't need your face looking perfect anymore. I wouldn't want to risk messing up any of your makeup," he said.

"Okay. Wait, can I take a picture of myself and send it to my friends?" Joanne asked.

"Just don't tell them where you are," Kafa said. Joanne took out her phone and took a picture of herself, something she rarely did.

She sent it to her friends and said, *I'm about to go to the ball!*

Lola responded almost immediately: *OH, MY GOD, WHO DID YOUR MAKEUP?!*

Joanne laughed and typed out, *Kafa.* Then she quickly put her phone back on her pile of clothes she had changed out of.

"Okay, I think we're ready. Oh look, we only have about seven minutes until we leave. So, I'm going to go over etiquette with you. First off, no elbows on the table. Second off, a salad fork has three tines while a meat fork has-" he started saying, but Joanne cut him off.

"I already know all of that," she said. His eyebrows shot up.

"Really?" he asked.

"Yeah. I learned it in a special class at my school," Joanne explained.

"Wow. That's impressive. Well, do you know how to Waltz? Because that's a dance we'll most definitely be doing," he said.

"Yup, I learned that too," Joanne said.

"You must have gone to a really good school," he muttered.

"I did. I do," Joanne said, correcting herself.

"That's good that they teach that in case some of you ever need to know etiquette in your future," Kafa said approvingly.

"Yeah, it is," Joanne agreed. He looked at his cell phone screen to see the time again.

"You know what, we're close enough. Let's go," he said.

"Don't they have reserved seats at the ball?" Joanne asked as they left his room.

"Yes. I'm afraid we'll have to jump someone and take their place," Kafa said casually, as if it were no big deal.

"*Jump someone*? Are you serious?" Joanne asked, her eyebrows raised.

"But of course. I don't usually joke about those kinds of things," he said seriously.

"I'm suddenly second-guessing our plan," Joanne muttered.

"Well, it's the best way to get the Imaginists to work with us against Kile," Kafa said. Joanne sighed.

"Yes, but jumping someone? Don't you think that's a little much?" Joanne asked.

"Well, I doubt they would *agree* to let us take their place!" Kafa exclaimed.

"Fine. But if it comes down to it, I'm not hurting them," she said.

"I never said we were hurting them," Kafa said.

"But-"

"I mean we're simply going to tie them up somewhere and release them afterwards," Kafa said simply.

"That's still basically kidnapping them!" Joanne exclaimed.

"You don't have to come if you don't want to, but the Imaginists won't believe me if you aren't there," Kafa said. Joanne huffed.

"Fine! Fine, I'll go and I'll help you kidnap *innocents*!" she exclaimed, clearly uncomfortable with the idea. Kafa gave her a smile.

"Now that's the spirit!" he said cheerfully, so much so that Joanne wanted to hit him for it. They walked out of the hotel and got into the Ferrari again, because according to Kafa, arriving by horseback would look weird. They drove in silence until Kafa broke it.

"I mean, who knows, maybe we'll find a pair that doesn't want to go," he said. Joanne just gave him a look.

"Look, Joanne, I'm sorry that we're going to kidnap people, but it's the only way," Kafa said apologetically. She sighed and looked out the window.

"No, it's fine. I know it's our best option," she said, her voice dead of any emotion. A huge building loomed in the distance.

"What's that?" Joanne asked.

"The Imaginists Palace. That's where we're headed," Kafa said. It was a beautiful structure, with domed roofs and lots of stained-glass windows. There was a line of people in cars waiting to get inside.

"This is where you drive and I go kidnap people," Kafa said, getting out.

"Wait, what?" Joanne asked, hoping that she had heard him wrong.

"I'll be back!" he said, ignoring her question as he closed the door. So, Joanne crawled over into the driver's seat and waited. About ten minutes later, she was almost in the castle. Suddenly the front seat door opened and Kafa slid in.

"There. Now we're good to go," Kafa said, a triumphant grin on his face. They pulled in through the gates and parked in a huge parking lot. Kafa got out and offered Joanne his arm. She gave him a quizzical look.

"Just take it. Most pairs of men and women are dating or together, so it would look strange if we were just walking side by side," he said quietly, so nobody else could hear. Joanne nodded and took his arm, feeling very awkward, though Kafa didn't seem bothered. They walked up to a pair of huge wrought-iron gates, where some I.P.O.s were asking for imaginary friends' names and then checking them off a list.

"Our names are Charlotte and Michael Forefair," Kafa muttered to her, leaning close so she could hear. Joanne nodded, burning the name into her brain. There were a lot of other imaginary friends pouring into the gates, all of them dressed just as exquisitely as Kafa and Joanne.

"Names, please," the I.P.O. said when they got to the gate.

"Charlotte and Michael Forefair," Kafa said with a genuine-looking smile. His eyes trailed down the list before he crossed out two names.

"Alright, move along," he said, waving them away.

"Not so hard, was it?" Kafa muttered as Kafa and Joanne walked into the gates.

"Yeah. It was easy," Joanne said, then thought, *Too easy.*

# Chapter Twelve

Joanne and Kafa walked down a sidewalk that had hedges shaped like animals all around them. There was also a tunnel made of glass beside the sidewalk that was filled with water that had the occasional siren, mermaid, or merman swim through it to the palace. The sidewalk itself was cobblestone that shimmered in the light of the setting sun. The Imaginists Palace was even more grand up close. The stained-glass windows glittered in the light, depicting scenes of the beginning of the three realms. The palace itself was white with dark green domes and trim. The imaginary friends all around Joanne were pretty things to look at. Obviously, not all of them were human, which Joanne was still taking some getting used to. She could see some fairies, identifiable by the plants woven through their hair and their pastel colored hair. There were also other creatures she didn't recognize. Kafa pointed them out to her as they walked. There were nymphs and elves, satyrs and spirits. And then the ones Joanne knew what they looked like, such as fairies, werewolves, and vampires. She shied away from the vampires, knowing that two vampires had kidnapped her just a few days ago. There was a set of huge, dark green double doors, carved with scenes from the three realms history that were open, allowing the guests inside, light pouring from them.

"How is the light not hurting the vampires?" Joanne asked.

"Oh. They're special lights. Doesn't look any different, doesn't feel any different, but it has something in it that isn't harmful to the vampires," Kafa explained. Joanne nodded, still staring at some vampires, recognizable by their extremely pale skin and dark eyes. Kafa and Joanne walked into the Imaginists Palace, and Joanne's breath caught in her throat. There had to be at least ten chandeliers in the room, all glittering with diamonds. There were multiple round tables around the room, each one with snow-white tablecloths and dark green velvet chairs. The floor was white marble with swirls of gold and emerald in it, the emerald and gold shining when the light hit it the right way, looking a little bit like the northern lights Joanne had seen pictures of. There were huge windows with dark green velvet curtains overlooking Imagine, providing a breathtaking view. There were also huge oil paintings of some of the Imaginists on the wall, each one different from the last. There were marble pillars around the perimeter, and a huge mural of different places in Imagine on the ceiling. Kafa looked at her and smiled at her expression.

"Extraordinary, isn't it?" he said.

"Yes," Joanne breathed.

"Come. Let's go find our seats before it starts," Kafa said, and with that, they set off towards the tables, their eyes scanning for place cards that said their "names". After a few minutes of searching, they found them and they sat down at the table. There were six seats at each table, and two other imaginary friends were already sitting there. One of them was a blue giraffe wearing a tuxedo, while the other was a purple gazelle. Joanne tried not to stare. They were talking with one another, but stopped when Joanne and Kafa sat down at their seats. They both smiled at them and the giraffe spoke.

"Well, hello there! I'm Blue and this is Marissa!" he said, extending a hoof. Joanne wasn't sure what to do, so thankfully, Kafa handled it for her. He reached over and shook the giraffe's hoof as if it was a completely normal thing to do and smoothly said with a charming smile,

"Michael and Charlotte Forefair. A pleasure to meet the both of you."

"The pleasure is all ours! Are you two from here?" Blue said cheerfully.

"Why, yes. Are you two from the Desert?" he asked.

"Yes, indeed. Me and Marissa were just talking about that terrible event that went on here last night!" Blue said, the smile leaving his face.

"Oh, the death of Kelly Bram?" Kafa asked, his smile also disappearing.

"Oh, no, not that. That was bad, of course, but we were talking about that horrible little group that came through here last night!" Blue said. Kafa's brow furrowed in confusion.

"My apologies, I'm afraid you've lost me. What group?" Kafa asked.

"Well, the one from here! What are they called, Marissa? Something weird… the Una-something?" Blue said, his brow furrowing as he tried to remember. Joanne felt Kafa let out a huff that Joanne assumed was a held back laugh.

"The Unavenged?" he said innocently.

"Oh, yes, them! Yeah, we were just talking about how they came through part of the City last night with all of their hooting and hollering! They stole quite a bit and almost destroyed the road they raided!" Blue said.

"Yes, we heard it was terrifying! I heard a rumor that their leader is a past Imaginist! Can you believe that? I just can't imagine an Imaginist doing all the horrible things that man does! Can you?" Marissa said, shaking her head. Joanne could tell Kafa was trying really hard not to smile or laugh, since both things would blow their cover, or at least arouse suspicion.

"No. I mean, he must be a monster if he can do all that and the I.P.O.s not catch him!" Kafa said with fake horror.

"I know! I mean, I've seen pictures of him before from some security footage. He looks mad! I've never seen anyone look so insane! He wears this crazy get-up and he always wears make-up, which is strange. He's not even that tall either! He's such a little thing! Hmm. Sort of like you," Marissa exclaimed. Joanne could tell Kafa was no longer trying to suppress a smile.

"I mean, it's a miracle nobody's walked all over him yet! I'm surprised nothing's flattened him into an evil pancake!" Blue said, and he and Marissa laughed.

Kafa curled his hands into fists.

"He really can't help that he's short, you know. It's just how he was imagined," Kafa said, his voice trembling with effort to keep calm.

"Yes, I'm sure. But I'm also sure he has his men *stand up for him* all the time!" Blue said, then burst into wild laughter, Marissa joining him a second later. Kafa suddenly shot up out of his seat, his fists slamming on the table and making the glasses on the table shake. Blue and Marissa stopped laughing abruptly, looks of surprise on their faces. Kafa's eyes were wide and wild with rage, his fists so tight his knuckles were white, and his mouth was set in an angry line.

"If you could excuse me for a moment!" he said with a deadly calm before stalking off to what Joanne assumed was the bathroom.

"What did I say?" Blue asked after Kafa had left.

"Too much," a cold voice with a slight German accent said from behind Joanne. Joanne turned her head and saw a man standing behind her. He had jet-black hair and intelligent looking gray eyes. He had on some light silver eyeshadow, as if he hadn't wanted to put any on but had done it simply to fit in with the crowd. He was wearing a simple black and white suit, so nothing fancy like some of the men were wearing.

"Come on, you two. You know that you *really* shouldn't make fun of an imaginary friends' appearance. It's not their fault at all and they can't change it," the man said. Blue looked sheepish.

"Sorry. I don't know why he got mad, though. It's not like we were teasing him," Marissa said. The man sighed.

"He wasn't exactly tall, you know," he said. Marissa and Blue had the decency to look ashamed.

"Oh," Marissa said quietly.

"Yeah, "oh" is right. I don't want you two saying anything similar to what you just said to him, understand?" he said in a dangerously calm tone. Marissa and Blue nodded, looking slightly scared of this man.

"Good," he said, then turned on his heel and walked away. Joanne stared at him for a second before deciding to follow him. He weaved and ducked through the crowd until Joanne caught his sleeve. He whirled around; eyebrows raised.

"Yes?" he said.

"Umm. That was really nice of you. What you did back there to defend Michael," she said. He shrugged.

"It's what should have been done in the first place. Who might you be?" he said, peering at her.

"J… Charlotte," Joanne stuttered. Something flashed across his face, though only for a second. Joanne couldn't identify it, though it didn't look very friendly to Joanne. It made her want to take a step back from her.

"J'charlotte! What a pleasant name! Tell me, how creative was your Creator to come up with that?" he said, smiling like a wolf.

"Oh! They were just little, so I don't think they said Charlotte right. What's your name?" Joanne asked.

"Daswars. It's German," he said when he noticed her confused face.

"Oh," Joanne said.

"Somebody's looking for you," Daswars said, something strange in his eyes as he pointed. Joanne turned and saw Kafa making his way towards her through the crowd, looking around as if he hadn't seen her yet. His eyes finally found her, and he walked towards her.

"Joanne! What are you doing out here in the middle of the dance floor?" he asked.

"Oh! I was talking to Daswars!" Joanne said. Kafa peered at her, his brow creased.

"Who?" he asked.

"Daswars. Look, he's right-" Joanne began, then stopped when she realized Daswars was no longer behind her.

"Right where?" Kafa asked.

"He was right here!" Joanne exclaimed.

"Well, he's not anymore. Why were you talking to him?" Kafa asked.

"Well, he was defending you to Blue and Marissa, and then he started walking away, so I followed him and we talked a little," Joanne said.

"Hmm. Say his name again," Kafa said.

"Daswars," Joanne said.

"Now say it slowly," Kafa said.

"Daswars," Joanne repeated, slower that time.

"It's German for something. I just can't remember what…" Kafa said, trailing off.

"The guy did have a German accent," Joanne said. Kafa's eyes widened.

"What did he look like?" he asked.

"Umm… he had black hair, gray eyes, and he was wearing a suit," Joanne said. Kafa paled considerably.

"What?" Joanne asked, dread beginning to pool in her stomach.

"Daswars. Daswars is German for Kile," he said slowly. Joanne felt her breath catch.

"Kile?" she asked.

"Yes. I never showed you what he looked like, did I?" Kafa asked fearfully. Joanne shook her head and Kafa swore softly. He took out his phone and scrolled through his gallery. Then he showed Joanne a picture from it. It was a picture of Kafa leaning against a wall, watching a man that was beside him as he appeared to be acting out something. The man had the same black hair and gray eyes. Joanne's throat suddenly felt very dry; her pulse faster than it should have been.

"That's him," she said, her voice barely above a whisper.

"Then Kile is here," Kafa said.

"What is he going to do?" Joanne asked, fear in her eyes.

"Nothing good, I'm sure. Did you see which way he went?" Kafa asked, barely contained emotion in his voice.

"No," Joanne said. Kafa groaned.

"Perfect, we have no idea where he is, only that he's here," Kafa said.

"We could look for him," Joanne suggested.

"No, we shouldn't. The food is about to be served, so we need to get back to our seats," Kafa said dismissively, then took Joanne's wrist and pulled her gently back to their table, which now had two fairies at it as well, both discussing the lack of flowers for decoration in the ball. Kafa and Joanne sat down, both of them scanning the crowds for Kile, but it looked as if he had just disappeared off the face of Imagine. Suddenly waiters came out carrying bowls of some kind of soup and water goblets. Each guest had a bowl set in front of them and a water goblet filled to the brim with, well, water. Joanne and Kafa sipped their Tomato Basil soup as the two fairies and Blue and Marissa made conversation. Kafa would have joined in had his mind not been so preoccupied with thoughts of Kile.

*Where is he? Why is he here? What does he want? Or rather, who does he want?* Kafa's thoughts raced through his head. *Did he come for me? Or Joanne? Did he even know we would be here? Or is he here to kill someone?* Kafa wondered, his face darkening. He finished his soup just as the music for the first Waltz began.

Most of the guests got up to dance, so Kafa turned to Joanne for a dance.

"Dance?"

She nodded. He stood up and offered her his hand. She took it and he led her out onto the dance floor.

"Keep an eye out for him," Kafa muttered as they began to waltz to the sound of classical music.

"Okay," Joanne whispered. Kafa's eyes scanned the surging crowd of people, looking for the familiar head of black hair. Most of the people that were dancing were talking or laughing, as if they didn't have a care in the world. Kafa wished he could say the same. He had been able to say that, once upon a time. But not anymore.

"Did you see him?" Kafa asked Joanne, as they ended the dance.

"No. Did you?" she asked. He shook his head. They went back to their seats and sat down just as the fruit course was getting served.

"We can't forget what we came here for. We will approach the Imaginists during the main course," Kafa whispered to her as they shoveled assorted fruits into their mouths.

"Alright," she said, then ate a large strawberry. A few minutes later, music for some dance that neither Kafa nor Joanne knew began, so they stayed in their seats and just looked at the other tables and the crowd for Kile, but they were just as unsuccessful as they had been during the Waltz. Finally, the main course was

served. Kafa jerked his head in the direction of the table of Imaginists, and Joanne nodded. They started to get up when suddenly all of the chandeliers turned off at once, dousing everyone in darkness. A great collection of screams rose up from surprised and frightened guests, sounding like something from a horror movie. Suddenly, a flashlight turned on, held by a figure that was perched on one of the chandeliers like Spiderman or something. He had black hair and gray eyes, the look of them so familiar that it raised goosebumps on Kafa's arms.

"Quiet!" he shouted, his voice echoing throughout the space. The screams stopped. Kafa could see the Stone of Existence glinting in the light on a chain around his neck.

"As some of you may know, the Stone of Existence is missing, and Imagine shall collapse in approximately two to three weeks. For those of you who don't know, I am Kile, the bringer of the New Age. I will tell you now, bad things happen to those who go against me. Take this Imaginist here, for example. He is against me. So, I shall dispose of him properly," Kile said, lifting up a man with unnatural strength that Kafa recognized as Wilbur, an Imaginist that had been there when Kafa had been one. Suddenly, Kile let go of him. There was a collective gasp from the crowd as Wilbur streaked to the ground, screaming the entire way. His screams were abruptly cut off when he hit the ground, a loud thud and the crunch of breaking bones silencing him. Everyone stared at his lifeless body in horror, too shocked to move. Then Kile spoke again.

"I want you all to stand with me when I carry out my plan. Or else you'll have the same fate as that idiot. So, unless you want that, gather at the square on Sunday at noon. I will leave you to make up your minds. Have fun finding your way out in the dark!" he said, then turned off the flashlight, plunging the room into complete darkness again. While people began to scream, Kafa found himself tearing towards the exit. There was only one exit leading outside, so if Kile went anywhere, it was probably that way. He raced outside, shoving open the doors, just to see Kile disappear around the corner. Kafa leaped up into a nearby tree and swung through the treetops. Kile was walking towards a car, the I.P.O.s by the gate unconscious. Kafa swung himself into one last tree before he flung himself down. He hit the ground, rolled, and sprung up a few feet in front of Kile. Kile stopped, his eyes widening a fraction in surprise.

"Kafa! I was wondering if I would run into you!" he said, sounding pleased.

"Why. Why are you doing this?" Kafa asked slowly. Kile's eyes looked sad and his face hardened.

"It's the only way, Kafa. There's not a better option," Kile said sadly. Kafa took a step towards Kile.

"Yes, there is. You can stop now. I'll hide you in the Unavenged and you can put the Stone back. We can all forget this all ever happened. We can go back to the way things used to be," Kafa said gently, taking another step. The sadness in Kile's eyes increased.

"Oh, if only we could go back to the way things used to be," he said, his voice filled with despair. His eyes traced across Kafa's face.

"You are still the same person that you used to be. Me leaving didn't change you one bit," he said softly.

"Of course, I didn't change. I had to keep moving, Kile," Kafa said.

"Oh, of course you did. You were always so emotionally strong. But you never stopped caring about me, did you?" Kile said, looking at Kafa with interest, as if he didn't know how he would react.

"Of course, I didn't," Kafa said, his voice barely above a whisper.

"You should have stopped," Kile said, then reached over and gently touched Kafa's shoulder. Kafa found that he was in too much shock to move away. Then, just as suddenly, he pulled his hand away.

"I'm sorry you were unfortunate enough to care for me," Kile whispered, then suddenly disappeared, as if he had never been there at all. Kafa whirled around, but Kile was gone. Kafa slowly reached up and touched his shoulder where Kile had touched it.

"But you were always the *only* best friend for me," Kafa whispered, but nobody was around to hear him except for the wind.

## Chapter Thirteen

Joanne ran outside to find Kafa standing in the middle of the sidewalk, his hand touching his shoulder as he stared out at nothing.

"What happened? Where'd Kile go?" Joanne asked, jogging up to Kafa before stopping as she looked around wildly. He took a moment to respond, as if he had been deep in thought about something.

"He's… gone. I don't know where he went. One moment he was standing in front of me, the next moment, he's gone," Kafa said, sounding hollow.

"He just disappeared?" Joanne asked.

"Yes," Kafa answered.

"Great. We're not going to be able to talk to the Imaginists now, with everyone in the chaotic mess everyone's in and- wait, are you okay? You look like you had some ice cream and it just melted in your hand," Joanne said, suddenly looking at Kafa with concerned eyes.

"What? Oh, I'm… I'm fine," he said, even though he didn't look fine.

"What did Kile do?" she asked softly.

"He didn't do anything! He just… it's what he *doesn't* do anymore," Kafa said, his voice starting out as a shout and slowly getting quieter.

"Kafa, if I'm going to understand, I'm going to have to know what happened," Joanne said. He laughed a sad laugh.

"Believe me when I say you don't *want* to understand," Kafa said, sounding very tired. Joanne stared at him. The only other time he had acted this defeated was when he had coughed blood onto his hand.

"What happened? What was he to you in the past?" Joanne asked. Kafa shook his head.

"I'll tell you some other time. For now, let's just get back to the Unavenged before somebody recognizes me," Kafa said, and with that, turned on his heel and walked towards the Ferrari. Joanne followed him got in.

"Was he your friend?"

He looked at her for a moment.

"The best of friends," he said.

"Do you think he'll ever go back to the way he was?" Joanne asked. Kafa let out a slow breath.

"I don't know, Joanne. I don't know," he said, sounding defeated again. Joanne decided to change the subject.

"Do you think the others will join Kile?" Joanne asked.

"Perhaps, but it's hard to tell," Kafa said slowly.

"On one hand, you've got the fact that he's killed quite a few of your own, but on the other, he'll kill you too if you don't cooperate, and I think fear is what is going to get people to join him," he said. Joanne nodded.

"Fear is a good motivator," she said. He laughed, though it sounded dangerous, not full of mirth like a laugh should sound.

"Yes, it is," he said. They drove the rest of the way in silence. Just as they pulled in, Joanne's phone rang. She looked at the screen. It was Rumple.

"Yes?" she said.

"Oh, thank god! You need to quit being in places where people die and nobody's sure who died! You're starting to scare the crap out of me!" Rumple exclaimed, yet relief was clear in his tone.

"Oh. Yes, I'm fine, but somebody did die at the ball," Joanne said, shuddering as she remembered the noise the man's bones had made when he hit the floor like a rag doll.

"Who?" Rumple asked, tension in his voice.

"Some Imaginist named Wilbur," Joanne said.

"Oh. What exactly happened?" Rumple asked.

"Well, me and Kafa were about to go talk to the Imaginists, and the lights went off, and suddenly everyone saw him on a chandelier, and he dropped the Imaginist and threatened the imaginary friends in the room, and then Kafa chased him but he got away," Joanne said in one breath. There was silence for a second before Rumple swore softly.

"Well, you guys should get inside. The Unavenged are a mess right now," he said.

"We're parking now. I'll see you in a sec," Joanne said.

"Okay. See you then," he said, then hung up.

"Rumple?" Kafa asked as they got out.

"Yeah," Joanne confirmed.

"Hmm. I figured he'd be concerned after news got out about what happened," Kafa said.

"Any sane person would," Joanne said.

"No. Any person with feelings would," Kafa corrected, something strange in his tone that suggested he had seen too much in his long life. Joanne had a feeling that very soon, she would be able to say that too.

~~

Kile glanced lazily at the TV. *Kile strikes again, this time at the Imaginists!* the headline read. Kile smiled, though it was the cold and cruel kind you wouldn't want to see on a person's face. He tugged off the pieces of his suit. They reeked of cologne. Then he went in the restroom and scrubbed the eyeshadow off his face as quickly as he could. The eyeshadow reminded him too much of Kafa. He put it away in the locked box that had other things in there. They were simple things, really. A pallet of silver eyeshadow. A bookmark. A receipt from Lucky's Café. A sock. And a picture. Kile took it out and stared at it. In the picture, he was grinning as he acted something out as Kafa watched him, a growing smirk on his face. They were both in their sock feet. It had been the day they had gone horse riding together, so their hair was a little messy. Well, Kafa's was always wild looking, so you couldn't tell, but Kile's was out of its usual stylish wave. Kile sighed a sad sigh.

*I'm sorry you were unfortunate enough to care for me,* he thought. Kile ran a hand through his hair. Kafa had said in all the one thousand and nine hundred years he had lived, he had never had a true best friend; and the closest thing he would ever find would be Kile. Kile had been around for almost fifty years, and Kafa had been the only person he had ever cared for that wasn't Annie. Until he got discarded. Until that horrible night… Kile quickly shoved the photo back into the box, shutting it closed and putting it back in its place on the bathroom counter. He walked back over to his bed, where he collapsed onto it.

He remembered watching Kafa the night before, watching him sleep before he had left. Kafa didn't even know. He just continued sleeping. One thing that Kile had heard though, was Kafa muttering in his sleep.

*"Kile. Why did you change?"* Kafa reached his hand out as if trying to grab something before it dropped back onto the pillow. Kile had patted it, trying to give him a sense of comfort. Kile slept too while there and then had woken up early, as he always did. He had looked at Kafa one last time before disappearing through the balcony, going the way he had come the night before.

*I left him for the good of things. We're both better off this way. I did it because he didn't deserve the monster I had become. He deserved to be allowed to move on. Every time I looked at him it hurt, and I knew it hurt him, until I had to leave,* Kile thought. Then he closed his eyes and despite trying to stay awake, sleep pulled him into its warm grasp anyways.

*"I hate stormy days,"* Kafa muttered as they sat on the edge of his balcony, *the rain pouring down in the space right in front of them.*

*"You're just saying that because you never had them in Rome,"* Kile said, *smirking.*

*"We did have storms! Just… not as much as this. So- Ahh!"* Kafa yelped as *lightning struck in the distance, flinching up against Kile. Kile laughed and patted Kafa on the head.*

*"Aww, it's just a storm. But does Kafa need to go inside? Is lightning too much for you?"* Kile asked in a baby voice. Kafa swatted away his hand and *leaned away from him, brushing off his shoulders.*

*"Oh, shut up. You know I don't like storms,"* Kafa said. Kile laughed.

*"Believe me, I know. Last week it was raining and you refused to go outside, saying that if you did the sky's tears were so big, they would drown you,"* Kile said.

*"I did not say that!"* Kafa exclaimed.

*"Umm, yes you did. That was the day you were so tired you just crashed at my place," Kile said, smiling at the memory. Kafa frowned.*

*"When did that happen?" he asked.*

*"Like, two weeks ago," Kile replied. Kafa opened his mouth, then shut it, looking very confused.*

*"Oh, I remember that now. Whoopsies," Kafa said sheepishly. Kile laughed again, then turned to look at Kafa, who was facing him. Kile looked over at a storm cloud over Kafa's shoulder, but when he looked back, Kafa was looking at the storm anxiously.*

*"Can we please go somewhere away from the window?" he asked. Kile laughed, his laughter echoing before it warbled into nothing as the scenery and Kafa faded away.*

Kile's eyes snapped open. He looked around. It was dark outside, the clock saying that it was past midnight. He could almost feel Kafa sitting beside him.

*No. Why do I keep dreaming about my memories with Kafa. I don't care what happens to him anymore… right?*

~~

Rumple stared at the doors, and just as Joanne said, a few moments later, she and Kafa walked in, both of them looking terribly tired. He leaped up from the couch and gave her a hug.

"Don't do that again," he said.

"Do what?" Joanne asked as she awkwardly patted his back.

"Just… you know!"

"Be in the wrong place at the wrong time?" Joanne asked dryly.

"Yes, that!" Rumple exclaimed. Joanne laughed, but Rumple rolled his eyes.

"I'm serious!" he insisted. She just patted his head and said something to Kafa.

"Frickin' still treating me like I'm twelve," Rumple muttered, crossing his arms.

"You both need to get some rest. Tomorrow… well, I don't know what'll happen tomorrow, but we'll figure it out. Goodnight," Kafa said, then turned on his heel and walked to his room.

"Come on," Joanne said, jerking her head in the direction of Rumple's room, though it was beginning to become their room. They walked to it and went inside, Rumple locking the door behind him.

"So… is that all that happened?" Rumple asked.

"Well, that's all that I saw. But I think Kile said something to Kafa that… ruffled him," Joanne said slowly.

"What is their deal? Were they like best friends or something?" Rumple asked. Joanne breathed in deeply.

"Yeah, they were," Joanne said. Rumple nodded.

"Why do you think so? I have just a wild guess," Rumple said.

"Because the way Kafa's talked about Kile sometimes. Kafa even told me they were like best friends," Joanne said.

"Wait, when did he tell you that?" Rumple asked, confusion across his face.

"Earlier. Do you know of any other friendships Kafa's had before? Heck, do you know if he's ever been in a romantic relationship before?" Joanne asked.

"I mean… no," he said,

"Are you sure?" Joanne asked.

"Pretty sure!" Rumple exclaimed. She stared at him, unbelieving that in almost two thousand years, Kafa hadn't had another friend or been in a relationship.

"It's true! You can ask him yourself! He seems kind of lonely sometimes…" Rumple said, trailing off. Joanne nodded.

"Okay. He does seem kind of distant sometimes. But anyways, I'm just… tired. I'm just going to go to bed," she said, sighing and running a hand through her hair, which was still a little peculiarly colored from the ball.

"Yeah, we should both get some rest," Rumple said tiredly.

"Yeah. I'm going to go change out of… this," Joanne said, then disappeared into the bathroom to change. Rumple sat on the edge of the bed and sighed. *What is*

*Imagine coming to? One bad guy shows up and suddenly everyone I care about is in danger, and things I thought I knew aren't so true anymore.* He thought, running a hand through his messy hair. Joanne emerged a few minutes later in pajamas, the complicated-looking makeup washed off her face. She walked over and crawled into the sleeping bag.

"Goodnight, Rumple," she said.

"Goodnight," he said back, flicking off the lights and lying down in his bed. He could hear her breathing even out, and he knew she had fallen asleep. The thought brought him sleep as well, and soon he was drifting off into sleep's dark peace.

"Come on, hurry!" Joanne's voice cut into Rumple's dream, which had been about singing tacos for some reason.

"But they were about to hit the chorus!" he groaned as he sat up. She stared at him weirdly.

"What, no! Come on, something's happening in the dining hall!" Joanne exclaimed, then rushed out of the room. Rumple leaped out of bed, throwing on his shoes and racing after her.

"What... exactly... is happening here?" he asked, panting from running halfway across a hotel.

"It's Dari," Joanne said darkly as they rounded the corner. Sure enough, Dari was standing on the Unavenged table, looking at Kafa with an evil grin that made Rumple feel terrified for some reason. Kafa was looking at her expectantly, probably because she was standing on his table.

"Now that a lot of you are here, I will make my announcement. I, Dari, challenge King Kafa for role of the leader of the Unavenged," she said. The quiet murmurs suddenly died.

Then came an uproar. Cries of, "What!" and, "You can't do that!" and, "Who do you think you are?" rang out through the dining hall. Rumple's mouth fell open. Nobody had challenged Kafa in about seven years. It was something that only an idiot would do. Everyone knew how strong Kafa was. Anybody that challenged that was *asking* for a beating.

"Quiet!" Kafa shouted, and the protests stopped just as suddenly as they had begun.

"You dare challenge me?" Kafa asked, a dangerous glint in his eye. Dari just smiled at him, her pointed teeth glinting in the light of chandeliers.

"You heard me, Kafa," she said. A sharp inhale went through the crowd. Only Kafa's closest men and women were allowed to address him without his title in front of his name. His jaw set.

"Well, you all know the rule. You are allowed to challenge me and fight for the position, but you must also know that losing means getting banished from the Unavenged," he said. Dari laughed.

"I know, and I keep to my challenge. Do you accept?" she asked.

"Yes. We shall fight at noon," he said.

"Very good," Dari said, then flapped her wings, making glasses fall over and people's hair fly before she flew over Rumple and Joanne's heads out of the room. Everyone watched her go in shock, but Kafa seemed unbothered by it. Everyone's heads slowly turned towards Kafa. He looked at them back.

"What? Go back to eating, all of you!" he ordered, and everyone obeyed. Joanne and Rumple sat by Kafa.

"How are you not concerned about this?" Joanne asked as soon as she sat down.

"Because I've faced multiple challengers and I've held my position for twenty years. One measly challenger doesn't intimidate me," Kafa said, shrugging.

"Has one of them been a very hot demon-lady?" Rumple asked. Joanne shot him a glare, but Kafa laughed.

"She's a succubus, for the record," he said.

"What's that?" Rumple asked.

"A demon that takes the form of an attractive woman to seduce weak-willed men," Kafa said.

"I wonder what kind of weirdo imagined her up," Rumple muttered. Kafa laughed.

"Probably some pervert. But to answer your question, I've never had a succubus challenge me before," Kafa said. Rumple nodded.

"Well, *I* think you should be concerned," Joanne said.

"Why is that?" Kafa asked. She bit her lip.

"Because she came to me about two nights ago asking me if I wanted to be Queen of the Unavenged," she said.

"Oh. Yes, people try and build little groups against me. It's quite annoying, actually," Kafa said, frowning.

"But I think she like… knows. She asked me how I did what I did to Barthemius in the arena. It's almost like she knows about my secret," Joanne said, her voice dropping to a whisper.

"Hmm. That's something to be concerned about. But really, Joanne, I think I can handle one rogue succubus," Kafa said.

"Okay," she said. They finished their breakfast and Kafa told them he was going to train in the arena beforehand, so Rumple and Joanne went to their room. They sat on the edge of Rumple's bed. Rumple could practically feel the unease coming off of Joanne in waves.

"Are you that worried?" Rumple asked.

"Yes! I don't know why, she just… she creeps me out! And I feel like she's got something else up her sleeve…" Joanne said, trailing off.

"It's possible, but you have to remember that Kafa's very capable," Rumple said.

"Are you sure?" Joanne asked.

"Bro, you're talking about the guy that jumped from a running horse onto a van going about forty miles per hour like it was no big deal. He's probably going to be fine," he said dismissively. Joanne nodded, though she still looked unconvinced.

"Hey, it'll be okay. Kafa will win, and then that Dari chick will be gone," he said, putting a hand on Joanne's shoulder.

"Yeah, you're probably right," Joanne said.

"Honey, I know I'm right," Rumple said, making Joanne laugh.


About five hours later, it was time. All of the Unavenged were walking towards the arena stands, eager to watch their King and his challenger fight. Joanne and Rumple found a spot relatively close to the front and they sat down.

"I think it's about to start," Rumple said to Joanne. She nodded, and about two minutes later, Kafa and Dari walked out on opposite sides of the arena.

"Ladies and gentlemen, silence, please! Let the fight between King Kafa and Dari commence!" an announcer said. Then the fight began. Kafa and Dari were circling each other, slowly getting closer to one another. Kafa looked concentrated, while Dari just looked like she was having fun. Suddenly, she lashed out with her whip, and it flew through the air towards Kafa's face. Kafa ducked and brought his sword up so the whip wrapped around it. He yanked it down, making the whip get pulled from her grip. Then he danced back a few steps, unwinding the whip from the sword until it was free. Now Kafa had two weapons. A sword and a whip.

Dari's eyes narrowed, but she simply pulled a dagger out of her boot and held it out, as if she hoped to fend Kafa off with it. Kafa leaped at her, sword swinging and whip flying. She suddenly did a flip backwards, dodging both, and brought her dagger up, cutting his leg as he flew over her. He rolled to the ground and got to his feet, blood trailing down the side of his leg from the cut. It didn't look deep, but Joanne couldn't tell from where she was. There was some pain in his eyes, but mainly determination and fury. She lunged forward with the dagger, but Kafa flicked the whip out with his wrist, and it wrapped around Dari's hand holding the dagger, cutting into it. She screamed, though it hardly sounded human as she dropped it.

Then Kafa reached up and slashed down with his sword, letting it make a shallow cut across her shoulder. She cried out, but somehow managed to wrench the whip out of Kafa's grip and back into her own. Her hand was now dripping smoking black blood onto the arena floor, staining it drop by drop. She lashed out with her whip, and Kafa tried to block it but only succeeded in getting his sword jerked out of his grip. He looked surprised, as if nobody had managed to do that before.

Grinning manically, Dari lunged towards him, sword and whip extended. Kafa brought up his arms in an X in front of him, and the sword clanged off his metal arm gauntlets, the whip wrapping uselessly around one of them. Then with a yell, he brought his arms down, pulling Dari towards him. He brought one of his arms up and he struck her across the face with his metal wrist gauntlet, the noise echoing hollowly through the arena. Dari flew back, her nose streaming black blood and both weapons flying out of her grip as she slid through the dirt, finally coming to a stop a few feet away.

Kafa snatched his sword off the ground and chopped her whip in half before he approached her. He walked up to her, moving his sword to point it at her throat, when she suddenly leaped up, doing a flip and kicking Kafa to the ground, the sword spinning out of his grip. Rumple swore, as did many others around him. She caught the sword and landed on Kafa's chest, making him gasp for air as it was knocked out of him. She pointed it at his chest, a triumphant smile on her face.

"I win," she said. Kafa, breathing hard, looked up at her in shock. The arena was filled with stunned silence until the stuttering, surprised announcer said, "Dari has won against King Kafa and he will now hand over the role of leader to her."

"Go on, say it," Dari said, her eyes glinting with twisted glee. Kafa looked up at her furiously, still pinned below her.

He then almost robotically began a speech Rumple suspected he had written long ago.

"I, King Kafa, officially hand over my role of leader of the Unavenged to Dari. I shall be gone by sunset, and then Queen Dari's rule shall begin. Hail... hail Queen Dari," he said slowly, sounding as if each word was killing him to say.

"Hail, Queen Dari," a shocked crowd of Unavenged echoed back.

Joanne and Rumple just stared with their mouths open at the events unfolding beneath them.

"Kafa lost. Oh, my god, Kafa lost," Joanne said in shock. Rumple remembered something Kafa had once said to him. *Nothing lasts forever, and that includes me. One day I shall fall, and when I do, the Unavenged will crumble.*

"Kile says 'Hi'," Dari whispered as she leaned down close to Kafa's ear.

Then she stepped off him, walking to the Unavenged hotel, which he supposed she now ruled. The Unavenged slowly filed out of the arena, most in shock. Kafa closed his eyes and stayed there, wishing he could just disappear and never reappear.

*Kile says 'Hi'?* Kafa thought, but he was too humiliated to connect the dots. Suddenly he heard somebody walk up to him.

"Kafa?" Rumple's voice asked. Kafa opened his eyes.

"Yes?" he asked.

"We can't let her be Queen! There must be a way-" Joanne started saying, but Kafa cut her off.

"No, Joanne. I made the rule that the King or Queen could be overthrown. I'm not going to go back on my word now. Now, if you'll excuse me, I'm going to go pack up my things and head out before sunset," Kafa said, getting up and walking past them, not waiting to see what they said. He heard Joanne start to follow him.

"Don't. He needs some time," Rumple said to Joanne.

Kafa walked through the hallways, the Unavenged now eyeing him with something that was no longer the respect it once was. Now it was something else. Fear. Fear of what Dari could do to them, now that she had defeated Kafa. He walked up to his room and unlocked it. Everything looked the same, only now everything was different. He opened his closet and his eyes fell on the faded gold and black backpack he had used before he started the Unavenged. He took it out and looked around, deciding what was important enough to pack and what he had to leave behind. He put his eyeliner and eyeshadow in there first, then his hairbrush for his unruly hair. Just because he was overthrown didn't mean he needed to start looking awful. He put some food in his backpack, then started putting his raven feather cape inside when he heard somebody clear their throat behind him. He whirled around and inhaled sharply. Kile was sitting on the edge of his bed, watching him with something like sadness.

"I'm sorry things had to go that way for you. I wouldn't have asked Dari, you know, if you had kept your word. I only asked her to challenge you because you told Joanne and her little brother about what I had told you, which I told you not to do. So, instead of burning the hotel, I just did something that would kill your pride. I took your Unavenged away from you," he said, smirking now, the sadness gone. Kafa tried to glare at him but found that he couldn't and busied his hands by going back to packing up his cape.

"You're not going to try and kill me?" Kile asked in surprise after a moment of silence.

"Nope," Kafa said.

"Why not?" Kile asked as Kafa crossed the room to put a blanket in his backpack as well.

"Well, let me think. I'm tired, I don't feel like it, and I'm sure you would kill me, so, it's quite pointless," Kafa explained, ticking off each reason on his fingers.

"But I just took everything away from you," Kile said, sounding lost.

"Not everything," Kafa said, looking up at Kile for a second before crossing the room again to get to a drawer. Kile slid off the bed and walked over to Kafa.

"Did she hurt you?" he asked gently. Kafa gave him a look.

"What does it matter to you?" he asked coldly. Kile flinched at his tone.

"You may not think I still care about your well-being, but I do," Kile said. Kafa gave a short, cold, laugh.

"Oh, I'm sure," he said, walking over to his bed and crouching down beside it.

Kile sighed and walked to him, forcing him to meet his gaze as Kafa stood up.

"You can join me, you know. When I carry out my plan, you can join me and we can rule. Together. Like our old plans," Kile offered. Kafa just looked at him sadly.

"What is it?" Kile asked, some concern and curiosity in his voice.

"The *old* you didn't want that much power. Besides, all I ever wanted to rule was the Unavenged. Not… *whatever* you're planning," Kafa said.

"Such a pity. I wanted you beside me. I still do. If you want to join me, you know where to find me," Kile said, getting up.

"Wait!" Kafa said, grabbing Kile's sleeve. Kile turned and looked at him expectantly. Kafa took it out from under the bed, the thing he only looked at sometimes. It was a photo album, filled with pictures of them. Kile and Kafa.

Kafa held up the photo album and Kile stiffened.

"Why did you keep that? I left. You should have thrown it away," he said, his voice unreadable.

"I know, but I didn't because you are still my best friend. Even after you got discarded, I still cared. I still do. Please, Kile. Come back," Kafa said, his voice filled with emotion. Kile looked down at him with something that looked like agony.

"I... I can't. I'm sorry," he said, trying to pull away, but Kafa held onto his sleeve and stood up until he was face-to-face with Kile. Or rather, almost face-to-face, since Kile was much taller than Kafa.

"Yes, you can. Just let me help you," he said.

"How could you possibly help me?" Kile asked, his voice barely above a whisper.

"With the same friendship I used to give you," Kafa said. Kile stared at him for a moment, looking as if he might agree, might give in. Then Kile suddenly wrenched himself away from Kafa, as if he couldn't stand to be touching him for another second.

"Kafa, I'm sorry. I can't do this right now. You know where to find me. Goodbye," Kile said, then sprinted to the balcony and leaped off it.

Kafa went to the edge of the balcony and looked around, but Kile had disappeared. Again. Kafa slumped against the railing, looking down in despair.

*Stupid! Why did I do that? I was getting to him, I could tell. I shouldn't have rushed him,* Kafa thought hopelessly before he trudged back to his backpack. He picked up the photo album. It held memories he and Kile had shared over the seven years they had been friends. They had been some of the best years of Kafa's life. He had been happy, so happy when he hung out with Kile. Then Kile got discarded, and he changed and left. He flipped through it, seeing pictures of Kile, pictures of himself and pictures of the two of them. He closed it and put it in the backpack. Then he picked up his black, simple crown and put it inside, too. He looked around his room one last time. The room he had for about forty years. Then, with one last sigh, he turned on his heel and began to leave. He walked into the lobby and his eyes widened in surprise. There were about thirty Unavenged members there, all looking at him sadly.

"Hail, King Kafa, forever leader of the Unavenged," they said in unison. Kafa looked around in awe.

"You saved us, King Kafa," one of them came forward and said. You gave us a home and a purpose. For that, we are forever grateful, so we have come to thank you and say goodbye." One by one, the Unavenged members came up to him and gave him a hug and thanked him. Once they were all done, they again chanted hails to Kafa.

Then, with one last look around the hotel had ruled, he walked outside of the doors of the Unavenged hotel, surprised to find that his eyes were growing wet. He walked up to his horse and climbed onto it. He took one last look at the hotel, memories racing through his mind, then kicked his horse in the side, and they took off into the unknown, never looking back.

## Chapter Fourteen

"I can't believe he's gone," Joanne said, still in shock of the past events.

"Well, he is," Rumple said, his voice sounding flat and dead.

"I know that," Joanne sighed. They had both checked his room about an hour after the fight had ended, but he was already gone. Rumple had tried calling him, but he hadn't picked up. Some Unavenged members had said goodbye to him, apparently, and then he had taken off on his black horse. It was almost time for dinner, though nobody had much of an appetite left.

"I'm going to check his room again," Joanne said, getting up from Rumple's sleeping bag.

"He's not coming back," Rumple said blankly.

"I know. Do you want to call him again?" Joanne said, her shoulders slumping.

"No. If he's not picking up, he doesn't want to be bothered right now. Maybe tomorrow we'll try again," Rumple said. They were silent for a few more moments.

"Rumple, how are we going to defeat Kile now? Without the help of the Imaginists or the Unavenged, how do we stand a chance?" Joanne asked.

"I don't know, Joanne. I don't know," Rumple said quietly.

"How much time do we have left?" Joanne asked.

"Sixteen days," Rumple replied. Joanne shivered. That meant that there wasn't much time left for them to defeat Kile.

"Rumple, what's happening? Why is everything falling apart?" Joanne asked.

"Not everything is falling apart. You've still got me. Hold on to me, and you'll be fine. We'll be fine," Rumple said. Joanne reached over and grabbed his hand, feeling as if everything was slowly dying and cracking open.

They sat there for a few minutes in silence and holding hands.

"Dinner's starting soon. We should go," Rumple suddenly said. Joanne nodded and they left the room, heading down to the dining hall. It was strange, without

Kafa there. They walked in and just heard silence other than the clinking of silverware.

Joanne and Rumple saw Dari sitting at the head of the table, tearing into some raw meat as the other Unavenged uncomfortably ate some kind of mushy soup. Rumple and Joanne joined them, sitting as far away from Dari as they could. They ate in silence, afraid to break it. Once they were done, they got up and left hurriedly. When they got back to the room, they did a lot of staring at the walls and thinking about Kafa and trying to call Kafa. Eventually, they just went to bed, the shock of the day letting them fall asleep relatively quickly. They slept peacefully until suddenly a loud noise jostled Joanne out of her dreams. She opened her eyes a crack and saw two dark figures standing over her.

"RUMPLE!" Joanne screeched.

"What? Oh, my god, where is it? Who took it? Wait. WHO THE MESS ARE THESE GUYS?" Rumple said sleepily, suddenly yelling as he saw the figures. The two figures leaped into action, swinging swords at them. Joanne scrambled back until she hit the wall, screaming all the while. Rumple leaped out of bed and swore as a sword arced through the air towards his head. He ducked, rolling, and got back up, sprinting over to Joanne. Then he swore again as he realized that they were now in a corner and the two figures were blocking the exit on the other side of the room.

"WHY THE HECK ARE THERE ALWAYS TWO? WHY NOT ONE? WHY TWO?!" Rumple screeched, his voice jumping an octave.

"We're trapped!" Joanne exclaimed.

"Well, I always knew I would die young. Too bad my body still looks like I'm frickin' twelve. The ladies won't swoon over my coffin if I'm only twelve," Rumple said sarcastically.

"As if any ladies would ever swoon over your dead body ever!" Joanne exclaimed.

"Um, excuse me? I'm sure I look very good dead and- wow, that is something I thought I would never say," Rumple said, suddenly looking surprised with himself.

"Why do they always have to block the exit? Wait. Unless…" Joanne said, trailing off.

"Unless wh- OH, MY GOD, THEY HAVE *KNIVES*!" Rumple whispered.

"How did you *just* realize that?" Joanne asked, exasperated.

"BECAUSE, I'M TIRED AND IT'S BEEN A REALLY LONG DAY!" Rumple shouted.

"Well, hold on to me," Joanne said, suddenly grabbing Rumple's hand and pushing against the wall. It fell right out as if it were a piece to a dollhouse. She leaped out into the open air below even though they were a story up and both had no idea how to break a fall that big.

"WAIT! OH, MY GOD, YOU'RE SUICIDAL! I KNEW IT! I'M GONNA DIE NOW!" Rumple said, his voice getting higher and higher pitched with each word. Joanne, her brow furrowed in concentration, imagined a big, beautiful something swooping down and rescuing them- though Rumple screaming was making it very difficult. His screaming reminded Joanne of the viral video of a goat screaming. Suddenly something caught them, and Joanne's face was pressed against warm fur. Rumple's screams suddenly stopped.

"Wow. Okay, I must be dead now, because there's no way an angel came and rescued me from my insane sister. I must be like a force ghost or something, because- what the *frick*. Why are *we* on a *goat*? With *wings*?" he said, suddenly stopping, his voice now very confused. Joanne cracked her eyes open. The fur her face was buried in was white. She was sitting on whatever it was. She could feel wings flapping from the animal. She opened her eyes fully and jumped. Sure enough, they were flying on a white goat with stubby little horns and blue eyes that had a pair of white wings. Joanne just stared at it, mouth open.

"Why the heck are we on a goat?" Rumple asked.

"Your screaming distracted me... so it made a goat with wings instead of a horse with wings," Joanne said slowly.

"How the crap did my screams make you think of a *goat*?" Rumple asked.

"I don't know! Your screams were just reminding me of the goat for some reason, so when I imagined it, it was a goat, okay! It's really not-"

"Umm, excuse me. You're both talking about me like I'm not here. Might I remind you, you're on my back. And I'm flying you over a bunch of weird houses. So, maybe be a little nicer when you talk about me," a deep voice interrupted Joanne. Joanne and Rumple looked at each other open-mouthed.

"Rumple. Please tell me you hit puberty just now," Joanne said slowly.

"I think I still sound like a *tween*ager going through some puberty," Rumple said.

"You two must be really dull if you can't tell that I'm the one talking. I mean, really, there's nobody else here but me and you two idiots. Did you two go to school?" the deep voice said again.

"Oh, my god we're on a talking, flying goat," Rumple whimpered, suddenly looking very scared for his life.

"I can't believe you just now realized that. You two must be stupider than I thought. Were either of you dropped as a child?" the goat said, turning his head so one blue eye peered at them.

"I don't think so, but I don't know because I never knew my parents," Rumple said.

"Oh. Such a shame. Some kids were abandoned in the pen, though it didn't happen too much. My mom always told me I was special, but I don't know why your parents would tell you two that," the goat said.

*Did a goat just offend me? What the heck?* Joanne wondered.

"Yeah, my parents didn't love me. They just left me in a carriage and I never saw them again," Rumple said casually.

"Oh. You must have been the runt then. You look like the runt," the goat said, looking Rumple up and down. Rumple's mouth hung open.

"I will have you know, sir, that just because I'm a little on the small side does not mean that I was a runt," he said. The goat kind of shrugged.

"Yeah, well, the truth is hard to accept for some of us. Anyways, what are you two idiots' names?" he said.

"Okay, I'm not an idiot, sir. But my name is Rumple and her name is Joanne," Rumple said. The goat let out a series of quick breaths that Joanne only assumed was a laugh.

"Rumple? As in a rumple in clothing? Humans are terrible at names," the goat chuckled.

"It is not my legitimate name! It's a nickname! And you never told us what your name was, sir. What is it? Binky? Snowflake?" Rumple huffed.

"It's Harold, actually," he said dryly. Joanne and Rumple just stared at him.

"Did you seriously just imagine this guy up?" Rumple asked.

"No, I already existed, sadly. I was just randomly summoned here where you two landed on my back. How rude. I wasn't even given time to brace myself for how heavy you two were," Harold said.

"Oh, I'm sure it's all her," Rumple said. Joanne looked at him, open-mouthed.

"Excuse me?" she said.

"Oh! Umm, that's not what I meant!" Rumple stuttered, his face going red.

"Ah, lover's quarrel. A problem I never had, thankfully," Harold said.

"We are *not* lovers!" Rumple and Joanne said in unison.

"That's what they all say," he muttered.

"We're siblings, man!" Rumple exclaimed.

"Oh! Well, that changes things. Siblings quarrel then," he said. Joanne suddenly had the urge to whap this goat upside the head. But then she realized that they were currently flying about four stories off the ground, so doing so would be really stupid.

"Now, where do you want to go?" Harold asked, sounding very bored.

"What do you mean?" Joanne asked.

"You summoned me. I fly you somewhere. End of story," he said.

"Can you take us to Kafa?" she asked.

"Do I look like a hound dog to you? I can't track down imaginary friends just like that! Could you tell me what he looks like?" Harold said grumpily.

"Umm… black eyeshadow, green eyes, crazy brown hair, wearing armor, riding a black horse…" Joanne said, trailing off.

"Oh, yes, him. I saw him earlier on my way here. I will take you to where I saw him," Harold said, then suddenly steered to the left. Joanne's legs tightened around him, her grip on his fur tightening as well.

"Chill out, Joaquina, I've been flying people around for a few years. I've never dropped someone. Well, I did once, but that was because they kicked me. Their fault. But anyways, why are you guys so intent in finding this Kafa guy? Is he a friend of yours?" Harold asked.

*I'm not Joaquina,* Joanne thought, but she answered him anyway.

"He is a friend," Joanne said.

"Then couldn't you just meet with him somewhere instead of dragging me around Imagine?" Harold asked dryly.

"Well, he hasn't been answering his phone," Joanne explained.

"You guys seem like you're all great friends then," Harold said sarcastically.

"We are," Rumple said, ignoring the sarcasm in Harold's voice. They flew in silence for a few minutes before Rumple asked,

"Where exactly did you see him?"

"Oh, he was just at a house," Harold said casually.

"Do you know whose house?" Joanne asked.

"I'm not a stalker. But I do happen to know. It's the house of that crazy man that's going around killing imaginary friends," Harold said simply, as if this weren't a big deal at all. Joanne's eyes widened.

"Who?" she asked.

"Oh, you know. What's his name? Kile?"

~~~

Kafa slid the keys into the lock, unlocking the door for the first time in about thirty years. It opened without a sound. He stepped inside, closing the door behind him. He looked around. It was the same as it had always been. Modern and spacey. Kafa walked over to the table and pulled the letter out of his pocket, setting the sealed envelope on the table. Then he lifted the crown he no longer deserved off his head and set it down on top of the letter, the black metal glinting. He took out a piece of paper and wrote,

> *Read this letter if you are ready. Here's the crown I guess I don't deserve anymore because of you.*

Then Kafa backed away from the table, going back out into the chilly night, the door swinging shut behind him. He walked along the side of the road until he found his horse, Midnight.

"Come on. We have to go find shelter now, and not here," he said, casting a glance at Kile's house. He swung himself up onto his horse and was about to take off when he saw something hurling towards him out of the sky. He heard a high-pitched voice screaming,

"TURN! FRIKIN' TURN, GOAT! OH, MY GOD!"

*That voice sounds awfully familiar.* Kafa thought. He jerked his horse to the side, and a second later, something with great white wings and two people on its' back crashed to the ground where Kafa and his horse had been moments before.

"For the record, my name is Harold, not *goat*," a deep voice said. Kafa stared in surprise at the winged animal. It was a white goat with stubby horns, blue eyes, and *wings*. A *goat*. With *wings*. Kafa recognized the two passengers as Rumple and Joanne, both looking as if they had just seen their lives flash before their eyes.

"Kafa! Hi!" Joanne exclaimed, her voice a little higher than usual. All he could do was blink at them.

"What in the name of Jupiter are you two and a *flying goat* doing here?" Kafa asked, his eyebrows raised.

"My name is Harold," the goat said. Kafa nodded.

"My apologies, Harold," he said.

"Oh, you're fine. At least you're better than these two," Harold said, jerking his head in the direction of Rumple and Joanne. Kafa noticed that Rumple was wearing Batman pajamas.

"Again, I ask what is happening here," Kafa said.

"Oh! Well, we were in the hotel and then some weird figures were trying to kidnap or kill us in our sleep, so I imagined our way out and I was trying to imagine a Pegasus as we fell through the wall, but Rumple's screams reminded me of a goat, and here we are," Joanne explained.

Kafa just stared at them, at loss for words.

"Umm. Why are you *here*? With me? How did you even find me?" Kafa asked, still thoroughly confused.

"Oh, we told the goat -," Rumple began.

"*Harold*," Harold corrected. Rumple gave him and annoyed look.

"We told *Harold* to take us to you, and he knew where to find you because he saw you earlier. Speaking of where we are, *why* are you at *Kile's* house?" he said, his brow creasing a little.

"Oh, I left him a letter. But we need to go because he'll be back soon," Kafa said.

"Why don't we just fight him now if we know he'll be back?" Rumple asked.

"Because we're not ready and there's not enough of us. We would all surely die," Kafa explained.

"Oh, yeah," Rumple muttered.

"But who were those two figures?" Kafa asked.

"We don't know," Joanne said.

"Probably work for Kile. Then again, Dari works for Kile, so the Unavenged is basically under Kile's control now, which is… very bad," Kafa said.

"So, you think it was just two Unavenged?" Rumple asked.

"That's my theory," Kafa said.

There was silence for a moment before Rumple spoke up.

"Wait. If you know where Kile lives, then couldn't you tell the Imaginists or something?"

Kafa considered it for a moment.

"I could. But then they'd rush in underprepared, and then they'd all die. So, probably shouldn't. Now, we really must get going, before Kile gets here," Kafa said, then nudged his horse so it took off at a light trot.

"Umm, could you follow him?" Rumple asked Harold. Harold sighed.

*Goats can sigh? That's different,* Kafa thought. Suddenly he saw Joanne, Harold, and Rumple trotting beside him, Joanne and Rumple's heads much shorter than Kafa's, since Kafa was on a horse and they were on a goat.

"Where are we going?" Joanne asked.

"Well… somewhere to stay," Kafa said.

"Where is that?" Rumple asked.

"We're about to find out," Kafa said, and with that, they set off into the City in hopes of finding a place to stay.

~~~

Kile walked up his sidewalk to his door and unlocked it, slipping inside his house quickly in order to not be spotted and recognized. He hung his cape up on a rack he used for capes that he rarely used. He walked over to the fridge, looking for something to eat. He selected some leftover spaghetti from a restaurant and started walking over to the table when he froze, dropping his spaghetti to the floor. It clattered when it hit the ground, the only noise in the quiet house.

He approached the table slowly as one might do when approaching a wild animal. He couldn't believe his eyes. A black, simple crown sat on the table, looking lethal in the dim light of the still-open fridge. He walked up and touched it. It even felt the same as it used to when Kile would take it off Kafa's head. Cold, and smooth. There was a note beside it. Kile strained to read it in the dim light, but he could read it all the same.

> *Read this letter if you are ready. Here's the crown I guess I don't deserve anymore because of you.*

He looked back down and noticed a sealed envelope on the table beneath the crown. He slowly reached down and slid it out from underneath the crown. It felt heavy in his hand, as if a heavy-duty or expensive paper had been used. The envelope looked plain and was addressed, *Kile* in the handwriting Kile would recognize anywhere. His hands shook as he held it and just stared down at it.

*Am I ready? Am I ready to read this? To hear what Kafa has to say?* Kile wondered. Taking a deep breath, he opened the letter and took it out. It was written on expensive, heavy paper, just as Kile had first thought. It *was* a letter, somewhat short. Kile walked over to the fridge, and by the light of it, began to read.

*Dear Kile,*

*I honestly didn't think I'd give this to you. I told myself I would one day if I ever saw you again. I must have, if you're the one reading this and not some nosey member of the Unavenged. I want you to know that I'm sorry. So sorry. I think I pushed you too hard after you were discarded. I was too pushy about what happened, forgetting what it was like to be discarded myself, since the years have worn down my feelings about it. I don't know what she said, but I want you to know that you are just as important as you were before. You're still the same. Nothing she said should have changed that.*

*I don't know why you left either. Probably because of the reasons I mentioned earlier. I just want you to know that even though you might act a little different now, be a little sadder, I can help you through it if you just let me. I can help you. Because I still care. In the almost two thousand years I've been alive, Kile, you're the only one I've ever truly worried and cared about. If you don't care what happens to me anymore, fine. But I will always be here, whether you care about me or hate me. It's not too late.*

*Kafa*

Kile read the letter two more times, letting the words sink in.

*It's never too late,* Kile re-read as he shook his head.

"Yes, it is," he muttered. He folded the letter back up and placed it on the table, not wanting to throw it away. He felt sick.

"How could you still care?" Kile muttered as he put his face in his hands.

*I still worry about you. I still care about you. But I just don't care about what has happened to me. Who I have become?* he thought. He reached over to put the paper back in the envelope when something fluttered out of it. Kile snatched it up and stared at it. It was a photo of the two of them, Kile reading while Kafa made a face behind him. Kile remembered that it had been the first time Kafa had ever been at his house. Back when they were beginning to become great friends. Kile set the photo back down on top of the letter and sunk into his chair, head in his hands.

*I can't go back. I'm sorry.*

~~~

Kafa led them down a street and then down two more streets before he stopped in front of an apartment. He led his horse around to the side of the building, then walked back to the door. He reached in his pocket and unlocked the door. Dust flew at him when he opened it. He coughed and swatted at it, but with watery eyes managed to say,

"Welcome to my old house!" They all walked in, their shoes making footprints in the dust. It was old and decorated like most homes had been in the sixties. Rumple whistled.

"This place is old," he said.

"I know. I haven't been here in around fifty years. There's a guest bedroom, and a nice rug if you're interested, Harold. I'm going to bed now. Good-night," Kafa said, going down the hallway into his bedroom. He closed the door behind him and laid down on the bed and fell asleep almost immediately, drifting into sleep.

*He was lounging at a restaurant, watching the sun set as chariots raced around the dirt roads. He sipped his posca and sighed.* Today has been a nice day, *Kafa thought happily. He had gone around town and picked out a horse at a stable. Due to its jet-black color, he had named it Midnight. Midnight was currently eating a bucket of oats beside Kafa. And then just like that, he felt the tug an imaginary friend had whenever they were being imagined, and had just enough time to set his posca down before he was whisked away to the normal world. He popped up on the road beside Linus's house. The full moon hung above Kafa in the sky, shining down on the City. Kafa peered into the window of Linus's home but saw that it was empty. Kafa checked again just to be sure.*

Where is Linus and what is he doing imagining me in the middle of the night? *Kafa wondered. Suddenly, Kafa could hear screams and shouts in the distance. He looked around wildly, knowing that nobody should be making those noises at night. Then he spotted them up ahead. There were people chasing after Romans, firing arrows at them. Something was terribly wrong. Kafa suddenly smelled something burning. It smelled like burning flesh. Kafa's eyes widened.*

We're under attack! *He thought as he rushed towards the crowd of people.*

*"Linus! Linus! Where are you? Linus!" Kafa called as he passed through the crowd, scanning for his Creator.*

*Kafa listened and didn't hear anyone for a moment.*

*"Kafa! Kafa! Help me!" he heard. Kafa ran through the crowd, his feet kicking up dust as he tried to get to the front, where he had heard Linus's voice.*

*"Linus! Linus, I'm coming!" Kafa shouted, though nobody but Linus could hear him. The crowd was going towards the center of the City. The trees were already filled with two dozen Romans, all of them swaying in the breeze as they hung from ropes wrapped around their necks. Kafa's mouth fell open and he stared in horror at the hanging people, trying not to be sick. He recognized some of them as Linus's friends and neighbors. The crowd had reached the center now, and Kafa gasped in horror of what he saw. The pillars in the middle of the City had people tied to them, all of them children,*

all of them screaming and crying. Kafa ran faster towards the front to get to Linus.

"Linus! LINUS!" Kafa shouted when he saw Linus up ahead, tied up to one of the pillars with rope. Linus's eyes found Kafa's, the green meeting the brown.

"KAFA! HELP ME!" he screeched; his face streaked with tears.

"I'M COMING!" Kafa called, running as fast as he could, trying not to trip on the ground. Suddenly, the people that weren't Romans began to set sticks and hay beneath the children on fire. There were screams of horror from the crowd as the fires began to catch the children's clothes on fire.

"SURRENDER, ROMANS!" the people shouted. Linus's toga began to catch fire. His screams for Kafa intensified.

"I'M COMING!" Kafa called, pushing through the last of the crowd and sprinting up to Linus, whose entire toga was now burning, lighting Linus on fire, too.

"KAFA!" Linus screamed in agony.

"I've got you!" Kafa said, reaching out for the ropes, only for his hands to pass right through them. He looked at his hands in horror before trying again. He got the same result and looked up at Linus, who was now on fire like a piece of tinder. The smell of burning flesh was so strong it made Kafa want to gag. Linus stopped screaming and looked at Kafa sadly, though Kafa could see the agony and pain in Linus's eyes.

"You can't help me, can you?" he asked quietly. Tears had begun to gather in Kafa's eyes. He shook his head.

"I'm so sorry, Linus. I'm- so, so- sorry," he said, his voice breaking. Linus just looked at him sadly.

"It's not your fault," he said, tears streaming down his cheeks.

"I wish I could do something," Kafa said.

"You can. Go. And never come back," Linus said. Kafa looked at him, feeling heartbroken.

"I don't want to leave you," Kafa said. Linus was looking at him, but he seemed to be focused on something else entirely.

"I don't have much longer anyways. And Kafa…" Linus said, his voice laced with pain, his breaths beginning to weaken.

"Yes, Linus?" Kafa asked.

"I love you. You were like the family I never had," he said quietly, then took one last shuddering breath. His eyes suddenly became unfocused and glassy, staring at nothing.

"Linus? LINUS?" Kafa yelled, reaching out to touch him as his hair caught fire as well. Then, he felt himself getting sucked back to Imagine. For good. He reached out, trying to hold on to Linus, but it was already too late for both of them.

Kafa was discarded.

And Linus was dead.

# Chapter Fifteen

Kafa began to mutter wildly in his sleep, saying the name Linus over and over again, tossing and turning, kicking the sheets of the bed around.

Kile sighed and walked over to Kafa. He used to occasionally have nightmares about Linus's death, and he'd always wake up screaming his name. Kile would have to calm him down and remind him that he wasn't still there in that City, that he was safe now. It hadn't been very hard to get into Kafa's house. After reading his letter that he so obviously wrote a long time ago, he had to see where Kafa went. He told himself he'd visit Kafa as he slept one last time. After tonight, it'd be too late. His plan would be too far to drag Kafa into it if he wasn't on his side. Of course, Kafa went to his old house.

Kile had slipped in the door, the girl in the guest bedroom and the goat on the rug not stirring at all when he crept into the main room to find Kafa's room. It hadn't been hard, since he had heard his muttering. Kafa calmed a little, but not by much. A single tear leaked from Kafa's eyes, trailing down his cheek and making a little wet circle on the pillowcase. Kafa's eyes snapped open and he sat up, looking around the room wildly, though based off the slightly unfocused look to his eyes, he was half-asleep.

Kile froze, fearing for the worst. Kafa just looked at him, and blinked.

"Why are you here?" he asked slowly, his speech a little slurred from sleep.

"I was just sleeping and you woke me up from your nightmare," Kile lied, hoping that Kafa was too asleep to notice that it was Kile there. He looked confused for a second, then looked sheepish.

"Oh. Sorry, I didn't mean to wake you," he said.

"It's fine. You know I'm a light sleeper," Kile said, shrugging.

"Yeah, I know," Kafa said.

"It's fine. Just go back to sleep," he said.

"Okay," Kafa said sleepily, yawning. He laid back down, closing his eyes and falling asleep.

*He must be even more tired than I thought,* Kile got off the bed and sat down in a chair in the corner, quickly dozing off. The next morning, he woke up to sunlight streaming through the windows. Ice cold fear laced through him for a second, afraid that Kafa had woken up and discovered him, but one glance showed that Kafa was still sleeping peacefully.

Kile slowly got up and opened the door. Kafa stirred, but he didn't awake. Kile cast one last look at him before he turned and quietly left the room. He moved soundlessly down the hallway and slipped out the front door, touching the Stone around his neck and suddenly popping up in his own home. He looked around and let out a sigh of relief.

*That was the last time that will ever happen. The last time he'll ever look at me without hatred,* Kile thought sadly, then shook his head, putting up his emotional wall. The wall that let no emotion penetrate it, the one that let him do terrible things and feel nothing.

*The time draws nearer for my plan to spring into action. Then, everything will change, and I will rule.*

~~~

Harold woke up with a yawn, opening his bright pink mouth wide. He licked his lips and looked around. It didn't sound like anyone else was up, nor look like it. He looked down at the rug he had slept on. At first, he had been insulted that this random guy dared to suggest that he would sleep on a rug! But Harold had been tired, and the rug had been very soft. Probably too soft for the rug's sake, since it now had a chunk of it missing from Harold wanting a three A.M. snack.

Harold hoped Kafa wouldn't be mad, but Harold decided quickly that he didn't care about what Kafa felt. It was his fault for letting Harold sleep on it. He got up, stretching his stubby legs, before he went over to the refrigerator. He opened it with his nose and peered inside. There was nothing in there but a weird smell.

Harold shut it with an annoyed grunt before walking to Kafa's room, deciding he could ask him about food. He trotted over to the door Kafa had gone in and nudged it open with his nose. He looked in and he froze.

*What in Billy's name?* he thought. There was Kile! Kile was sleeping in a chair in the corner of the room and Kafa was sleeping in his bed.

*Hmm. Maybe I should come back later,* Harold thought, then got back on all fours and trotted back to the rug. He shut his eyes and fell asleep again. He woke up to a noise later. He opened his eyes and saw Rumple and Joanne standing by the fridge, whispering.

"Ah, good job, you woke him up!" Joanne said, gesturing towards Harold. Rumple sighed.

"Oh, well, I'm sorry. It's not my fault that I'm just trying to get some food and there's a goat in the middle of the frickin' floor!" Rumple exclaimed.

"You know I can hear you, right?" Harold asked grumpily as he got up off the floor and trotted up to Joanne and Rumple, his hooves making clicking sounds on the tile.

"Oh, I know by now. You can talk and you can hear and you can fly. Good job, I'm sure that'll get you a job at Goats-R-Us," Rumple said sarcastically.

"That's not a thing, dummy," Harold said. Rumple gave him a sour look.

"I *know.* It's called a *joke,* something *you* can't seem to make," Rumple said dryly.

"I have one. The sun disappeared. Guess who died?" Harold said.

"Umm, everyone," Rumple said.

"Nope. The giant squids lived for a little bit longer than everything else," Harold said cheerfully. Rumple and Joanne just stared at him.

"It's what my mom told me as comfort when I was sure the sun would explode," Harold explained.

"How is *that* a comfort?" Rumple asked.

"Well, it's nice to know that the squids got a longer life," Harold said. Rumple and Joanne just stared at him again.

"What kind of mom did you have?" Rumple asked.

"A realistic one," Harold answered.

"She sounds like a terrible mom," Rumple said.

"Well, she's better than *yours*. My mom didn't abandon *me*," Harold said. Joanne chuckled, which she tried to turn into a cough, and Rumple's mouth fell open.

"Hey! That is *not* funny!" Rumple exclaimed. Harold smiled.

"She thought it was," he said, pointing a hoof at Joanne. Rumple glared at him.

"Well… she has a cruel sense of humor," he said.

"I'm sure you just don't want to admit that I'm hilarious," Harold said.

"A joke about everything except for squids *dying* is *not* hilarious!" Rumple exclaimed.

"No, but the one about your horrible mom was," Harold said. Joanne snorted and Rumple shot her another glare, as if he was insulted that she was laughing at Harold's jokes. Kafa walked into the room, rubbing his eyes.

"What time is it?" he asked.

"Like, eight," Rumple replied. He blinked sleepily.

"Really? I must've slept…" Kafa said, trailing off and suddenly looking quite puzzled.

"What?" Joanne asked, curiosity creeping into her voice.

"I… I could have sworn… I was dreaming about- about Linus, and I woke up, and something… it seemed like a dream. I don't remember…" Kafa said, trailing off.

"Remember what?" Rumple asked.

"I was tired. Something… I woke up- or I think I woke up; I could have just been dreaming. And something… something oddly comforting was there, I just don't remember what. After that, I slept fine…" Kafa said, his words dying in his throat.

"What?" Rumple said, sounding just as confused as Harold felt.

*This Kafa guy isn't making any sense,* Harold thought.

"I- something was there, probably someone. They told me just to go back to sleep; that I had just woken up from a nightmare. Was that one of you?" Kafa asked.

"Umm, hate to break it to you, bro, but I don't usually watch people while they sleep and then tell them to go back to sleep if they have a nightmare. I'm sorry, but I'm not that kind of guy," Rumple said.

"Was it either of you by any chance?" Kafa asked, looking at Joanne and Harold.

"Uhm, no," Joanne said. Harold shook his head.

Kafa shook his head, a smile coming to his face.

"I must've been dreaming then-"

"Was it *him*?" Harold asked. Kafa stopped talking abruptly and looked at Harold with something like dread in his eyes.

"Was it *who*?" Kafa asked.

"The man that was in your room," Harold replied.

"*What* man?" Kafa demanded, paling a little.

"Umm. Surely you would know who was in your room," Harold said. Rumple and Joanne's mouths fell open.

"Wait, what-" Rumple started saying, but Kafa held up a hand to silence him, looking slightly embarrassed.

"Do you know the name of this man?" he asked.

"Oh, yeah. The one that you were visiting yesterday. The crazy one. What's he called? *Kile*?..." Harold said, searching his memory for the man's name.

"Kile," Kafa said quietly, paling.

At one point, Rumple had started sipping water, which he spat out at that moment, spraying Joanne with water. Joanne glared at him through her now damp hair, beads of water trailing down it or soaking in it.

"Really?" Joanne asked, annoyed.

"Boy, did you hear what he just said!" Rumple said loudly, gesturing towards Kafa.

"Yes, but you didn't have to *spit water on me*!" Joanne exclaimed. He held up his hands in the air.

"Look, I'm sorry. Can we just listen to Kafa and his theories on how Kile got in here in the first place?" Rumple asked.

"Fine. If it was him, how did he get in here? The door was locked, right?" Joanne asked, turning to Kile and putting her damp hair behind her ear.

"Yes, it was. I have no idea how he even got in here…" Kafa said again, trailing off.

"Wait, so just for the record, you two had some sort of lose relationship in the past, right?" Rumple asked. Kafa, Harold, and Joanne looked at him as if he were stupid.

"Even *I* picked up on that, stupid," Harold said.

"Yes, it did. We were best friends," Kafa said shortly.

"Ah, okay. Continue, please," Rumple said, leaning back against the counter, his brown hair sticking in different directions from sleep. Kafa sighed and then started talking again.

"If he got in here, then we really can't stay here. He knows we're here. It's very likely he wants Joanne dead. We have to leave," he said.

"Then let's leave," Harold said.

"Okay, let's get our crap," Rumple said, turning to go to the guest bedroom before he turned back around, looking sheepish.

"I forgot me and Joanne didn't bring anything," he said, scratching the back of his head.

Kafa rolled his eyes.

"Let me get my bag and then we'll leave," Kafa said.

"But what about breakfast?" Rumple whined.

"We'll figure it out!" Kafa said, then went to his room, coming back with a bag slung over his shoulder.

"Let's go," he said, walking towards the door.

"Where?" Joanne asked. He grabbed the doorknob and took a second to respond.

"I don't know," he said softly, as if not wanting to believe it. He swung open the door and walked out, not looking back once. Rumple and Joanne looked at each other before following him, Harold falling into step behind them. Kafa went around the side of the building and came back on top of his horse.

"Okay, Joanne, get on Midnight. Rumple, get on Harold. Let's go try and find a breakfast place," Kafa said. Joanne took his hand and he helped her onto Midnight, and Rumple looked down at Harold.

"Umm. Can I get on your back?" Rumple asked.

"I don't think I can say no," Harold said flatly.

"Umm, okay," Rumple said, then got onto Harold's back, making Harold grunt.

"Follow me!" Kafa said, nudging Midnight's side so he set off at a trot. The morning was warm as the sun peeked above the skyscrapers in the distance, its gentle light reflecting off Kafa's armor and making Harold want to shut his eyes. Kafa led them down a few roads until they were only a few blocks away from the Imaginists Palace, which had practically been on lockdown since Kile crashed the ball. The streets weren't as crowded as they had been before the ball either.

News of what Kile had said and the fact that he had killed an Imaginist had spread through Imagine like wildfire, and now most imaginary friends didn't want to leave their homes. Kafa led them over to a small, friendly-looking place called Lucky's Café. He tied his horse to a post and then helped Joanne down. Rumple quickly got off Harold, just as relieved as he was that he was no longer riding on Harold's back.

"We'll eat breakfast in here," Kafa said, holding open the door to the café. Rumple, Joanne, and Harold followed him inside. They sat down at a table as Kafa ordered them food. He came back with some bagels, which they passed around.

"As we all know, Kile told everyone to meet at noon on the square on Sunday. I'm afraid that most imaginary friends will be there, due to fear. I believe he's going to do something, and it will not be good when it happens. I don't know what, but whatever it is, we must stop him. Otherwise... we might as well have already given up," Kafa said.

"What are we going to do?" Rumple asked, chewing on a bit of bagel. Harold sniffed his and took a nibble, then regretted it, spitting it out.

"Well, we have to try and stop him," Kafa said.

"From what?" Harold asked.

"From doing something bad," Kafa said.

"Do you know exactly what he's going to do?" Harold asked.

"Well… no," Kafa said.

"Then how are we going to stop him?" Harold asked, raising an eyebrow.

"I'm not entirely sure yet, but-"

"In case you've forgotten, Sunday is tomorrow, idiots. We don't have much time to figure this out," Harold said, cutting off Kafa.

"Wait, you're helping us?" Rumple asked, looking surprised.

"I've got nothing better to do this weekend," Harold said, shrugging.

"Nice," Rumple muttered.

"*Anyways*, if everyone gathers in the square, we could slip into the crowd, and if he gets close enough, Joanne could kill him," Kafa said simply, as if he was telling a toddler how to use the toaster.

"Wait, I'm *killing* him?" Joanne asked, sounding surprised.

"What else did you think would happen?" Kafa asked, his brow slightly furrowed.

"Well… I don't know. I thought maybe you didn't want him to die, so we'd find an alternative," Joanne said slowly. A look of sadness crossed Kafa's face, but he quickly covered it up.

"I don't *want* him to die, but he's too dangerous to live," he said, looking down at the table.

"How come *she* gets to kill this guy?" Harold asked.

"Because she's the only one that can," Kafa replied. Harold stared at him in confusion.

"Why?" he asked.

"Oh, well. She's… special," Kafa said.

"She doesn't look special," Harold said, glancing at Joanne.

"Thanks," Joanne muttered as Rumple snickered, earning an elbow between the ribs from Joanne.

"Well, she is," Kafa said.

Harold nodded slowly in acceptance.

"Right," he muttered, receiving a dry look from Joanne.

"Anyway, we have to figure out a way to get close enough to where we he won't notice us until it's too late. Not getting noticed is the tricky part," Kafa said, brow furrowed in thought.

"Can't we just go to his house and kill him? Or at least capture him?" Harold asked.

"That doesn't sound like a bad idea," Rumple said, shrugging.

"Well… we could, I guess, but if it fails, then…" Kafa said, trailing off.

"Then what?" Joanne asked.

"He could probably kill all of us where we stand. Versus if we do it in a crowd, they might join in and it'll be harder for him to kill us," Kafa said.

"Could we try?" Rumple asked.

"I mean… we could, but I don't think it'll work," Kafa replied, shrugging.

"Why?" Rumple probed.

"He'll be ready for something like that. He'll be expecting us to do something like that, and he *will* kill us where we stand," Kafa said.

"Then why didn't he kill us last night? He could have done so easily," Joanne asked, looking very confused.

"I have no idea," Kafa said, looking down at the table, his face unreadable.

"Do you think he wants us alive?" Rumple asked.

"Why would he want us alive?" Harold asked.

"I don't know! Maybe he needs us for something…" Rumple said, trailing off.

"For what? Some crazy ritual?" Joanne asked sarcastically.

"Maybe," Kafa said.

"What kind of ritual would he need us for?" Joanne asked.

"I don't think he needs us. I think he might need *you*," Kafa said. Joanne looked at him in surprise.

"What? Why?" she asked.

"Think about it. You're re- special. You're special, so he probably needs you for something. The rest of us, he might use as leverage," Kafa explained.

"Leverage against me?" Joanne asked, her eyebrows raised.

"Yes," Kafa replied.

"But why wouldn't he capture us last night?" Rumple asked.

"I don't know, but I feel like he's got a plan. And it's not going to be good," Kafa said as he finished his bagel.

"But what kind of plan? What's his- what the frick is that?" Rumple started saying, then stopped when a tiny TV on the wall suddenly glitched from the news to a dark room. Everyone's heads whipped towards the TV; confusion written all over their faces.

> *"Hello, citizens of Imagine. Don't forget, meet at the square at noon tomorrow, or all of Imagine will suffer. Do not bring weapons, for they will do you no good. Do not try and stop me, for I will slaughter you all. Stand with me when the borders fall, and you might live. Bring Joanne Raider to me before the sun sets, and I won't let Imagine feel my wrath. Drop her off at the Imaginists Palace, tied up and with no weapons. For those of you who don't know what Joanne looks like, here's a nice picture," Kile said, suddenly coming into view before a picture of Joanne in the Unavenged hotel flickered onto the screen.*

> *"She is with former king of the Unavenged, Kafa, and her brother, Rumple. Bring her to me, and you will all walk away unharmed. If I were you, I would consider this offer and take it seriously. See you at noon tomorrow!"*

Images of Kafa and Rumple also popped up on the screen. Then it glitched back to the news, the news reporters pale with their mouths open. Kafa, Rumple, Joanne, and Harold looked at one another in shock.

"We have to go," Kafa whispered, getting up so fast the table rattled. Rumple and Joanne quickly followed suit.

"THERE SHE IS! JOANNE RADIER!" a shrill voice suddenly rang out from the other side of the café.

Joanne swore under her breath as Kafa shoved them towards the doors as the people in the café shot out of their seats and started surging towards them in a wave. Kafa whipped out his sword in an effort to keep them back, but there were so many, Harold knew that they wouldn't be able to fend them off. They rushed outside, trying not to trip over the sidewalk.

"Joanne, get on Harold! Rumple, get on Midnight! We'll lead them away from her!" Kafa instructed, sprinting towards his horse.

"Ahh, great, I'm a diversion! These things never work in movies!" Rumple exclaimed as he followed Kafa.

Harold stopped for a moment, almost tripping Joanne.

"Get on my back now!" he ordered. Joanne obeyed without hesitation, and with one strong flap of his wings, they shot up into the sky, leaving the angry crowd behind them on the ground. The cold wind made Harold's white fur stream behind him as Joanne clutched it as if it was the only thing keeping her from falling to her death.

*Well, I guess it is the only thing keeping her from falling to her death,* Harold thought as they soared up into the clouds, Joanne screaming all the while. Harold glanced down and saw Kafa and Rumple climbing onto the horse as the angry crowd approached them.

"Where are we going?" Joanne asked over the howl of the wind.

"I have no idea, kid," Harold answered.

"Well, where are they going?" Joanne asked, jutting her chin in the direction of Kafa and Rumple on the ground, who were now taking off on the horse.

"I don't know! But I'll follow them anyways so we don't get split up," Harold said, steering so that way they flew above Kafa and Rumple.

"It's so pretty up here," Joanne breathed, staring down at the City below. Harold glanced down, unimpressed by the City.

"It's okay. I liked the farm better," he said, shrugging. Joanne laughed, for some reason, though it sounded half-terrified.

"What? Are you scared of heights?" Harold asked.

"A little bit," Joanne squeaked.

"Oh, well. Don't worry, I'm a good pilot. You'll be fine," Harold said reassuringly.

"Okay," Joanne said, though she didn't sound fully convinced. Suddenly, Joanne's phone rang. She picked it up and groaned.

"I'm sorry, but now is not a good time," she said into the phone as she answered it and then hung up.

"What kind of conversation was that?" Harold asked.

"A short one," Joanne replied.

"Kids these days," Harold muttered, shaking his head. Joanne sighed then gasped.

"What are they doing?" she muttered. Harold looked down and saw Kafa and Rumple suddenly drive Midnight into a glass building.

"They're idiots," Harold mumbled.

~~~

"Wait, *what* do you want us to do?" Rumple asked shrilly, his voice an octave higher than usual.

"We're going to break through the glass!" Kafa repeated, glancing back at some imaginary friends that were still following them.

"You're frickin' crazy!" Rumple exclaimed.

"I've done worse! Now, cover your face!" Kafa exclaimed, then steered Midnight so they crashed into a glass building. The sound was loud and made Rumple want to cover his ears as the glass rained down on them like really sharp hail. Rumple heard Kafa swear at the exact moment that Rumple did. Midnight landed on the tile floor, his hooves making a loud noise in the office. Imaginary friends screamed and ran out of the way, papers from printers soaring through the air. Midnight was somehow unharmed from smashing through glass, while Kafa had a cut on the side of his face, blood trailing down his neck and staining his black shirt even darker. Midnight charged through the office, sending people ducking for cover. They crashed through the glass again on the other side, emerging on a different road, cars swerving in order to not hit them, their horns blaring angrily at Kafa and Rumple. Rumple suddenly heard the wail of I.P.O.s' cars behind them. He looked behind him and saw them at the other side of the block.

"I.P.O.s?" Kafa asked, too focused on steering Midnight around obstacles to glance back in fears of them crashing.

"Yup. Ride faster, please!" Rumple said.

"Midnight is going as fast as he can!" Kafa exclaimed. Rumple was shouting obscenities out of fear and anger. Kafa turned Midnight to the right into an alleyway, Midnight almost falling over from how sharp the turn was. Kafa swore and tried to turn around when he saw the alley ended in a dead end, but the I.P.O.s were getting louder and Rumple could see their red and blue lights flashing on the road.

"Aww, man, this is like a really bad movie," Rumple whined. Kafa leaped off Midnight and grabbed Rumple's hand, yanking him down with him. Kafa used his sword to pry open a sewer grate, the lid moving aside after it popped out of place.

"Get in!" Kafa exclaimed.

"Are you kidding? That hole smells like crap-"

"Just get in!" Kafa ordered, shoving him in. Rumple fell down into the sewer, landing on damp, slimy concrete a few feet below.

"Ooooww!" Rumple exclaimed just as Kafa dropped down beside him, the sewer lid going back into place, dousing Kafa and Rumple in darkness.

"Why is it dark?" Rumple asked, then realized how stupid the question was. He could practically hear Harold calling him an idiot. Kafa sighed.

"One second," he said. Suddenly, light filled the space, illuminating the sewer better than before. Rumple still had some battery left on an old flashlight. There was a small, shallow channel of sewer water, but it was mostly dry. The sewer was made of bricks that had their color washed away with time that also smelled, except for the ground, which was just concrete.

"Oh, my god, it's so disgusting in here!" Rumple said, springing off the filthy ground.

"It's a sewer," Kafa said dryly.

"I know! But it's… way dirtier than it is in the movies," Rumple said with disgust, looking around. Kafa rolled his eyes as the I.P.O. sirens could be heard above them.

"We need to get going," Kafa said, then started walking along the side of the sewer.

"Wait. Where's Midnight?" Rumple asked, remembering Kafa's horse.

"Oh. He couldn't fit, so I told him to run," Kafa said, sounding a little down. Rumple jogged to catch up with Kafa.

"Oh. Do you think he'll be okay?" Rumple asked.

"Hmm? Oh, yes, I'm sure he'll be fine," Kafa said dismissively, though Rumple could detect a note of doubt in Kafa's usually confident voice. Suddenly there was the sound of the sewer grate moving, and Kafa sped up to a sprint.

"They're coming! Hurry!" he hissed. Rumple ran after him, suddenly motivated to get away from the grate. Rumple could hear thuds and splashes of I.P.O.s landing on the sewer floor, some of them swearing in disgust when they did so. Kafa and Rumple ran down the sewer, trying to be as quiet as possible. The sound of quick footsteps suddenly broke the silence. Kafa swore under his breath.

*This is it. I'm gonna get caught by the frickin' I.P.O.s,* Rumple thought glumly as he almost tripped over a stick on the ground. Suddenly a figure dropped to the ground in front of Kafa. Kafa skidded to a stop, Rumple slamming into his back. The figure put a finger to his lips, and jerked away their flashlight, turning it off quickly.

"Shhh, follow me," the figure said, nudging Kafa and Rumple's shoulders and dragging them to the side of the sewer.

"What the-" Rumple started saying, but Kafa slapped a hand over his mouth, silencing him. Suddenly Rumple felt cold for a second, as if somebody had dumped ice water on him, but it was gone in a moment. Suddenly, a light ignited. The figure was holding a torch, but the fire was white with blue and purple tongues of flame. The torch itself was black as ebony, carved with some strange language. The man was extremely pale, almost paper white, with eyes such a dark blue that it was hard to tell they were even blue and not a shade of purple or black. He had ears that were a little longer than most people's that were pointed. His hair was silver that shone in the light of the torch. He looked to be about sixteen or seventeen, his face still youthful. He wore a dark blue robe that was decorated with silvery stars the same color as his hair.

*He's an elf,* Rumple thought.

The boy eyed them for a moment.

"Come. Follow me if you don't wish to be caught," the young elf said. Then he turned on his heel and strode off into the darkness, leaving Kafa and Rumple no choice but to follow.

"Who the heck is this guy?" Rumple whispered.

"I have no idea, but he's our best option right now," Kafa whispered back. They followed the boy in silence until he suddenly stopped.

"Watch your step," he said, then started up a stairway that Rumple hadn't noticed until that moment. To Rumple's surprise, he hadn't heard any I.P.O.s since the strange, cold feeling had come over him. Kafa and Rumple looked at one another before following him up.

The boy paused for a moment, unlocking something, and suddenly, a hatch opened up, letting light spill into the sewer. The boy gestured for them to follow and climbed out of the hatch. Kafa and Rumple stepped up onto the last stair and hauled themselves up onto… grass? Rumple peered at the blades of vegetation that were by his face in confusion. They felt like grass and they looked like grass- well, they were the wrong color, but other than that, it seemed to be grass. Instead of a vibrant green or dead yellow that grass should be, this grass was a light purple and light blue color.

"What the actual crap…?" Rumple muttered; his brow furrowed. He lifted his head and looked around, his eyebrows flying up in amazement. They appeared to be in a sort of clearing in the middle of some trees. There was a light dusting of snow on the ground on top of the grass that sparkled in the moonlight. The grass was all purples and blues under the white dusting of snow. The sky was black with streaks of purple, dots of stars throughout it as the two moons hung in the sky. The trees were all black, the leaves on them pastel colors.

*Wait… why the frick' is it night?* Rumple wondered as he looked up at the moons.

"Umm. Where are we?" Rumple asked as he got to his feet.

"Welcome to the Forest," the boy said, gesturing to the scenery around them.

"The Forest looks like this?" Rumple asked, puzzlement written on his features.

"These parts of the Forest do. We are in the Eternal Night part of the Forest. If you can't decipher what that means, we are in a part of the Forest where 'tis always night," the boy said, looking around fondly. Rumple just stared at him.

*Who says 'tis?* Rumple wondered.

"Umm. Who the crap *are* you?" Rumple asked, cocking his head to the side like a dog.

The boy sighed theatrically and rolled his eyes.

"My name is Edmund Hayes. Who might you be?" he said.

"Rumple," Rumple replied. Kafa sat up behind Rumple.

"Oh. Hello. I'm Kafa-"

"I'm well aware who thou are, but I am afraid I had no knowledge of who *he* is," Edmund said, cutting Kafa off as he pointed to Rumple.

"Oh. Umm, okay. Why did you save us back there?" Kafa asked, shaking his head.

"Oh! Yes, that. Well, you two seemed as if you were in a bit of a jam, so I came to your rescue," he said casually, as if it was no big deal.

"No other reason?" Kafa asked suspiciously.

"My apologies if I come off as rude, but why *else* would I take you to safety?" Edmund asked.

"Umm, no reason," Rumple said.

"If you don't mind me asking, why were the force of government soldiers pursuing you?" Edmund asked, looking at them with curiosity.

"Well, we're sort of wanted by some evil supervillain, so they're trying to get us so they can hand us over to him, that way they don't die," Rumple explained. Kafa looked at Rumple indecorously.

"Did you really just-" he hissed, but was cut off by Edmund's laugh that sounded like a bell.

"Oh, you all amuse me terribly! Word travels quickly through the ranks of the Elves, so I am already aware of this news. But you two do not look like a blond sixteen-year old female," he said, smiling at them, his teeth pearly white.

Kafa slumped behind Rumple with obvious relief.

"Don't worry, we aren't," Kafa said with a relieved laugh.

"But you *are* her friends," Edmund said, still smiling.

Kafa stopped laughing.

"Umm…" Rumple said, trailing off.

"Don't get yourselves all worried now. I have no intention of turning you two over. Or her, wherever she might be," Edmund said with a small laugh.

"How can we trust you?" Rumple asked.

"Well, the fact that I haven't called down other elves down upon thou yet should be enough," Edmund said, his eyes glittering.

"So, this is a 'blind leap of faith' thing?" Rumple asked.

"Thou art correct," Edmund said happily, seeming quite pleased by the fact. Kafa and Rumple looked at each other.

"We have to find Joanne," Rumple said. Kafa nodded in agreement.

"Yes, we do. Sorry, but we really have to find our friend-"

"Then phone her," Edmund said, cutting Kafa off again.

"Umm, okay. Call her, Rumple," Kafa said.

"Will do," Rumple said, taking out his phone and dialing Joanne's phone number.

~~~

"Where did they go?" Joanne asked, peering down at the City below them and trying not to be sick all over Harold's fur. She hated heights. Harold sighed.

"I already told you, I don't know! They went down that alley and then they were gone!" he exclaimed, annoyance creeping into his voice.

"Are you sure? They couldn't have just disappeared!" Joanne scoffed.

"Well, they did," Harold said. Suddenly, Joanne's phone rang. She picked it up, expecting to see her friends again, but instead saw Rumple's number.

"Where are you guys?" Joanne demanded.

"We're in the Eternal Night part of the Forest with Mr. 'I say "thou"'!" Rumple's voice said with false enthusiasm.

"Mr.- what?" Joanne asked, her brow furrowed in confusion.

"Mr. 'I say "thou".' It's a long story. Well, not really, but kind of. Anyways, where are you?" Rumple said dismissively.

"Umm, I'm flying on Harold's back over the City," Joanne said, glancing down before quickly looking back at Harold's fur, trying to ignore the feeling of her wrenching gut when she saw how high they were.

"Like, where in the City?" Rumple asked, sounding a little impatient.

"Umm... do you know what part of the City we're in, Harold?" Joanne asked.

"Nope," Harold replied.

*Thanks for being helpful,* Joanne thought sarcastically.

"Well, we don't know," Joanne said.

"Then come to us," Rumple said.

"But I don't know where the Forest is!" Joanne exclaimed.

"Well... Harold probably knows," Rumple said.

"I do know where the Forest is. Is that where they went?" Harold asked.

"Yes, actually," Joanne said.

"Okay, hold on," Harold said, sounding very bored.

"Wait, why-" Joanne started saying, but her voice died in her throat and a scream rose out of it when Harold suddenly shot forward like a bullet, leaving Joanne clinging to him for dear life. She held her phone so tightly in her hand in fear of losing it that her knuckles were white as she buried her face in Harold's neck, trying not to focus on the fact that they were going *really* fast through the air stories above the ground.

About twenty seconds later, Harold slowed back to the speed he was flying at earlier. Joanne slowly cracked open her eyes and her mouth fell open. They were now soaring over a magnificent forest, the trees stories tall and the vegetation varied and beautiful. The City was nowhere in sight, as if it had completely disappeared off the face of Imagine.

"Now, what part of the Forest did they say they were in?" Harold asked.

"Eternal Night, or something like that," Rumple's voice said through Joanne's phone.

"Hmm. I think I know where that is…" Harold said, turning a little to the right.

"Hurry up, please, I don't know how much longer I can stand this guy," Rumple begged.

"We're on our way. See you in a second," Joanne said, then hung up.

~~~

"Hmm. Most curious. Where did he go? And, where is she?" Kile muttered, leaning closer to the screen showing security camera footage. He was watching pieces of Rumple and Kafa riding Midnight around the City before they went into an alley and disappeared. The last footage of Joanne was of her right outside of Lucky's Café, where she got on a white, fluffy something. Then there was a blur of white and suddenly she was gone.

*What the heck was that?* Kile had wondered after the first time he watched it. After watching it a few more times, he made a theory.

*She probably got on that goat and flew away while Kafa and Rumple were a distraction. Smart, Kafa. But not smart enough. The only question is, where did both pairs go?* Kile thought, his brow creased in thought. He got up from his desk and imagined he looked different. His black hair lightened until it was brown, his face thinning a bit, and his eyes turning to yellow-brown. He tucked the Stone inside his shirt so his true identity would be protected. He then walked out of his house, looking around and sighing with relief when he saw that nobody gave him a second glance. He got into his truck and drove down to the last place that Kafa and Rumple were seen.

The alley looked normal, though it was now blocked off with I.P.O. tape. There were two I.P.O.s standing around something on the ground.

*I need to get closer,* Kile thought, then imagined himself invisible. He silently walked over to them and noticed they were standing over a sewer grate. Kile looked at them, double-checking that they couldn't see him before he slipped into the grate, landing on the sewer floor below in a crouch. He looked around, grunting in disgust at the sour smell of the sewer. There were I.P.O.s here too, though they didn't seem to know where they were going or what they were doing.

"I know they went down there; I just don't know which way they went," one of them was saying, scratching his head.

"Well, I don't know, Carl. We've gotta find her or else that Kile guy's gonna do some bad things," another one said.

"I know, I know. Who the heck is he anyway? I've never even heard of him and he suddenly steals the Stone and shows us all how he can kill us in an instant. Like, what's his deal?" the first one asked. Kile gritted his teeth and his hands curled into fists.

"I don't know. It almost seems like one of those stories from Create," the second one said.

"Yeah... how ironic," the first one said. Kile, growing tired of their meaningless talk about him, slipped past them. His gaze slid over the sewer tunnels, searching for where Kafa and Rumple might have gone. Finding nothing, he blew out his cheeks in frustration.

*Where could they have gone?* he wondered, but nothing answered him but empty silence.

# Chapter Sixteen

"When might this lady be arriving?" Edmund asked, examining his naturally perfect nails.

"However fast Harold can fly," Rumple said. Edmund gave him a slightly puzzled look but decided not to press the matter.

"Once she arrives, we must go inside," Edmund said, his eyes tracing the skies for threats.

"Why?" Rumple and Kafa asked in unison.

"'Tis not safe for people here," Edmund said.

"Wait, what do you mean?" Rumple asked.

"The Eternal Night is a dark place, Rumple. Human imaginary friends do not live here for good reasons," Edmund said darkly.

"Wait, what *does* live here?" Rumple asked, his eyes widening a fraction in fear.

"Vampires, werewolves, Dark Elves and Dark Fairies, Sirens, Goblins... nothing you want to deal with, Rumple," Kafa said before Edmund could respond.

"Wait, you're a Dark Elf?" Rumple asked, turning to look at Edmund with something like uncertainty.

"What gave it away? My dark eyes and light hair?" Edmund asked dryly.

"Wait... you don't make any sense," Kafa said, peering at Edmund.

"Whatever do you mean?" Edmund asked.

"Dark Elves have dark hair and dark eyes, while Light elves have light hair and light eyes. You seem to be..." Kafa said, trailing off.

"A mixture. My Creator imagined me to be half Dark Elf and half Light Elf, which is why I can leave and go to other places in the daytime," Edmund explained, sounding very bored as he did so.

"Oh. That makes sense," Rumple said, then leaned over to Kafa and whispered,

"Not really."

Edmund, with his excellent elf-hearing, heard him, but simply rolled his eyes, deciding that the words of a twelve-year-old boy were not his concern. Suddenly he spotted movement out of the corner of his eye. He whipped his head to the side, scanning for the threat. Then he spotted it again. Something in the underbrush, something moving, something coming... Edmund ran his hands over his torch until he found the right switch. He flicked it and his torch lengthened and became a bow. He reached down and took an arrow made of unicorn bone from his boot.

"Hide, now!" he hissed to Kafa and Rumple. They got the message and hid behind a tree, having nowhere else to hide. A figure emerged from the trees. She was a little large for a woman, but she gave off an aurora of power. Her hair was a curly honey brown that spilled down to her waist. Her eyes were such a shocking blue they looked alive with electricity, and her lips were a plum color. She wore a black dress with long black lace sleeves, lace up black boots, and a velvety black cape. The odd thing about her was that she had a pair of horns on the side of her head that were the color of fresh acorns in the fall. She eyed Edmund with something like disgust and anger blended together.

"Edmund! Why are you still here?" she asked, her voice a deadly calm.

"She. I am here because... 'tis my home, dear lady," he said. She sighed and rolled her eyes.

"It might have been once, but it is no longer. You have no place with the Dark Elves here. You're ... Light. Too pure. Too untainted. The Dark Elf Senate already banished you and gave you a month to get out. Yet, here you are, *two months* after the Dark Elf Senate made their decision. You know what the punishment was if you returned. Do you want me to call upon the Darkness? Or would you rather leave while you still can?" she said, her voice cold. Edmund's eyes narrowed to angry slits. One thing Edmund absolutely hated was being threatened.

"I would rather have a fight, a fair one, mind you! 'Tis not my fault that I was imagined this way! Every imaginary friend is unique in their own way, and the

Dark Elf Senate failed to see that! You, of all imaginary friends should know that!" Edmund said, his voice rising with irritation. She sighed with annoyance.

"I know, Edmund, but this is the way of the Dark Elf Senate. You don't get a say in this! In fact, it would be better off if you just went to the Light Elves! I'm sure they'd-"

"They would not welcome me! They did not welcome me when I tried, for the same reasons that the Dark Elf Senate has! I shan't go to the Light Elves because I cannot, She. Half of the Forest is ruled by the Dark Elves and the other half by the Light Elves. I belong in the Forest, but all of the elves are trying to chase me out! I shan't go and live in the City or any other part of Imagine, for the Forest is my home, nowhere else," Edmund exclaimed. He suddenly heard applause break out from behind him. It stopped abruptly and Edmund could hear Kafa scolding Rumple. Edmund rolled his eyes and turned back to She.

"Who's back there?" she asked, her eyes narrowed in suspicion; her body tense, ready for a fight.

"Nobody," Edmund said smoothly. She gave him a look.

"Edmund, who did you bring with you?" she asked, dread written all over her face.

"Not a soul," he said. Elves were excellent liars, but She had always been frustratingly good at being able to pick out whenever he wasn't telling the truth. She raised an eyebrow at him.

"I don't believe you," she said, then set off towards the tree Kafa and Rumple were hiding behind at a fast pace. Edmund mouthed a curse and leaped in front of her.

"Edmund! Move!" She demanded, trying to duck under his arms, which he was moving around so wildly that he looked like a car dealership balloon.

"Trust me, you do not want to go near that tree, dear lady!" Edmund said. She looked at him, confusion written all over her face.

"Why is that?" she asked.

"Because... 'tis a diseased tree! Full of nasty things ready to infect a lady such as yourself!" Edmund said, praying that it was believable, though he knew that it probably wasn't. He could hear Rumple slap his hand to his forehead behind him. She looked at him, unconvinced.

"Right," she said, then ducked under his arm and leaped towards the tree, landing on its trunk and peering over the other side of it in just a few moments. Suddenly Edmund heard a high-pitched,

"HI-*YAAH*!" and suddenly She went flying away from the tree, landing on her back in the grass. She let out a grunt as the air was knocked from her lungs. A very triumphant and surprised looking Rumple stood atop one of the branches. "Ha-ha! I have defeated you, evil horn lady!" he said, then lost his balance and fell off the branch and onto the ground, landing on his bottom. Edmund heard Kafa sigh before he also came into view.

"Good job, Rumple. Smooth, as always," Kafa said sarcastically. A smile quirked the corners of Edmund's mouth that quickly disappeared when he heard She get to her feet behind him.

"What kind of sorcery was that?" she asked breathlessly, looking at Rumple with a mix of wonder and… admiration?

"That was Kung-Fu," Rumple said proudly. Kafa rolled his eyes behind Rumple, who was currently picking himself up off the ground.

"What's that?" She asked, intrigued by Rumple's ability to take her down.

"A form of fighting," Rumple replied.

"Where did you learn it?" she asked.

"The *Karate Kid*," Rumple said.

"Who's that?" She asked.

"The kid that can do some serious karate," Rumple answered, smiling to himself and nodding slowly. She was just staring at Rumple as if he was an angel come down from heaven to tell her that she had won the lottery. Kafa rolled his eyes again.

"It's actually a movie" he muttered, but She didn't seem to notice.

"Who are you two?" she asked.

"I'm Rumple and this is Kafa," Rumple said, giving a small, theatrical bow.

"Pleasure to meet you. Might I ask what the two of you are doing hanging around *Edmund*?" She asked, jerking a thumb in the direction of Edmund as she emphasized his name with repulsion. Edmund sighed at her tone.

*Half-demons don't ever get over grudges,* he thought tiredly.

"We just kind of ran into him, and... yeah," Rumple said in one breath. She looked at him skeptically.

"Hmm. Right. Edmund, how did you pick up these two and why did you bring them here?" She asked.

"They were in a bit of a jam, you see; so, I brought them here," Edmund explained, leaving out some important details.

"What kind of a jam?" She asked, one eyebrow raised as a gentle wind blew the skirts of her dress to the side so it whispered over the grass.

"Strawberry," Rumple randomly said. Everybody turned and stared at him.

"What? Sorry, I just kind of started listening just now. I wasn't paying attention because I was staring at that and thinking, 'Dang. What the heck is that?'" he explained, then pointed behind them. Kafa, She, and Edmund turned. Kafa whistled, She swore, and Edmund groaned. At the other edge of the clearing, there were about ten horses, all of them pitch-black. The riders atop them looked equally ominous. They were all Dark Elves; since Dark Elves ruled the Eternal Night part of the Forest. Everything else that lived there was supposed to obey the wishes of the Dark Elves or be banished.

"Is that the Darkness?" Kafa muttered in Edmund's ear.

"Some of them," he whispered back. Kafa nodded and eyed the Darkness members warily. Kafa suddenly sunk down to one knee, She following. Edmund also kneeled, yanking Rumple down with him, who didn't seem to realize that the custom was to kneel in the presence of the Darkness or the royal Dark Elves.

"Edmund of the Dark Elves! Kafa of the Unavenged! She of the Half-Ones! And... boy," the one in the front said, looking at Rumple in confusion on who the heck he was.

"The name's Rumple," Rumple said dryly.

"And Rumple of the..."

"Unavenged," Rumple muttered.

"And Rumple of the Unavenged! You have all been found with a lying half-Light Elf! Him being here is breaking the law; you being with him is considered betrayal! What do you have to say for yourselves?" the front one accused. The front elf had hair such a dark blue it looked black and had dark yellow eyes. She gasped and Edmund internally groaned.

*This is what happens when I save people. Why must I bother?* Edmund wondered.

"I swear I didn't do anything! I was taking a walk and I heard voices, so I investigated and it was Edmund with these two!" She said, pointing to them.

"Why were you so close to the border of the Eternal Night and Eternal Day?" the front one asked after a moment.

"I was just taking a walk around Eternal Night!" She said frantically.

"Is that so?" the front one asked.

"Yes!" She exclaimed.

"Hmm. What are you doing here, Edmund?" he asked, turning to look at Edmund. "I was not here at first, sire. See, I was wandering around the sewers since I prefer the darkness, and I saw that these two were lost. So, I brought them to the nearest exit, here," Edmund explained. It wasn't a total lie. More of a half-truth.

"Hmm. Tell me, Kafa, how did you and… *Rumple*… get lost in the sewers?" the front one asked.

"We were walking and somebody forgot to put the grate back, so he fell and I went back in after him, but we couldn't get back up, so we thought we could find another exit, and then we got lost in the process," Kafa lied. The front one nodded once.

"Normally, I would believe you, but I have met you before, Kafa, and I know that you would be too smart to simply get lost in a sewer system. Since you have decided to lie to me, we must take you all in to the Grove for questioning," the front one said, shaking his head.

"What? How dare you! I am-" Kafa started saying, but the front one cut him off.

"You *were* king. Don't think we don't know. Word travels fast among the elves. And besides, you're on Dark Elf territory without permission. That alone is something not done," the front one said coldly. Kafa closed his mouth and glared at the ground, curling his fists.

"Now. Come with us, or suffer the wrath of the Darkness," the front one said. She was the first to get back up, followed by Edmund and Rumple, and last, with a nudge from Rumple, Kafa. They trudged over to the Darkness, where they chained them up with thick silvery vines and tied them to the horses. She looked angry and was glaring dagger-eyes at Edmund. Kafa looked greatly insulted, and Rumple just looked exasperated.

Edmund felt a sinking feeling in his stomach. If he was being taken to the Grove, he would get in serious trouble for returning after banishment. As in, imprisonment. For the rest of eternity. *Then again, with this* Kile *fellow running around, eternity might not be much longer,* Edmund thought, then scolded himself for thinking such thoughts.

The Darkness members forced them onto the backs of their horses, and then they took off, galloping through the forest so fast that it made Edmund's stomach clench. The trees flew past them, never touching the Darkness members or their horses, even when they should have. The vegetation around them was a pallet of cool colors, making Edmund dizzy if he stared at it for too long. They rode in silence, never talking due to how the Darkness members might react. The tension was thick in the air, so much so that Edmund could've sworn that he could actually feel it.

After about ten minutes, the Grove loomed in front of him. Nobody knew why it was called the Grove, it simply was. The Grove was the castle for the royal Dark Elves. It was pitch-black with tall, pointed towers that seemed to pierce the sky; made of the darkest stone in all of Imagine, so dark that it seemed like a void, ready to consume any wanderers without a second's hesitation. It didn't get many visitors for that reason. The gates were woven with silver and iron in order to keep away an attack from werewolves or dark fairies, and there was a moat of holy water to stop vampires from doing the same. The drawbridge was lowered over the moat so they could cross.

The Darkness members didn't hesitate, crossing over the drawbridge onto the other side and into the courtyard. Edmund noticed She shiver when they crossed over the moat. *Must be her demon blood,* Edmund thought. When he and She were friends, he had learned quite a bit about the Half-Ones. Their demon blood made them vulnerable to certain things, but it also made them quite powerful. Even though all imaginary friends were supposed to be considered equal, it didn't really work that way, especially in the Forest. In the Forest, Dark and Light Elves were considered above everything else in the Forest, even if they were criminals.

The drawbridge raised once they had crossed over into the courtyard. The Darkness members got off their horses and yanked on the prisoners' vines, forcing them to follow the Darkness members into the Grove. They passed through the ginormous black double doors carved with scenes of Dark Elf victories, cold air rushing at them from inside. It didn't bother Edmund due to his Dark Elf blood, but he could see the others shiver. The doors closed behind them with a thud, and at that moment, the reality that he was now in the Grove settled on Edmund's shoulders.

*Well, I am in a bit of a jam myself, now. Good job, Edmund. Good job,* Edmund scolded himself. They walked through the hallways, the only sound their footsteps on the cold marble floors. They arrived at the throne room and Edmund tried to ignore the sick feeling in his stomach. Last time he had been there, he had been banished from the Eternal Night part of the Forest. He glanced over and saw that She was close to tears as she stared at the ground. Guilt began to gnaw away at Edmund.

*Oh, dear me. 'Tis my fault that this poor lady is even in this situation. I must have to attempt to get her and the others out of it,* Edmund thought guiltily.

The front Darkness member rapped on the door. A moment later, a cold, silky voice answered.

"Come in," the Queen of the Dark Elves said. The Darkness member opened the door and led them all inside. The Queen's eyes ran over them as they entered, the guards shutting the doors when they were all through. The front Darkness member bowed.

"My dearest Queen, I present to you Edmund of the Dark Elves, Kafa of the Unavenged, Rumple of the Unavenged, and She of the Half-Ones. We found them lurking on Eternal Night land; Edmund being banished should not have been there in the first place. We have brought them here for questioning and punishment." The Queen inclined her head to him.

"Thank you, Alexai. I will take it from here. Your men may go, but you should stay," she purred. The Queen was a beautiful elf. She had pitch black hair that spilled over her shoulders in glossy locks that shone in the light of the chandelier in the room. Her skin was terribly pale, so much so that it was frightening. Her eyes were a deep, twinkling violet one might find on a jungle flower but nowhere else with long, curling eyelashes that cast shadows on her cheeks. Her lips were a pale pink that were as soft as a rose petal that looked full and perfect. She wore a gown that was black with blue and purple woven through it in a design of flowers and vines that hugged her torso to show all her curves before flowering out into a large skirt. Her crown was a ring of thorns with shimmering silvery blossoms woven through it. Somehow, the thorns never harmed her. Legend was that if anybody unworthy tried to wear the Queen's crown, it would cut into them and they would bleed forever, even if they took it off. Nobody had ever tried it because of that. She turned her violet gaze on Edmund and the others. The Queen seemed annoyed, as if they were all nuisances.

"I will start with you," the Queen said, pointing a nailed finger at Edmund. The vines that bound him suddenly dropped to the ground. Edmund swallowed and stepped forward before dropping down into a kneel.

"Edmund, why are you here in the Eternal Night, yet again?" she asked.

"Well, you see, my lady, I was helping out Kafa and Rumple, and when I led them to the nearest exit, it dumped us out in the Forest," Edmund explained.

"Where were you that had an exit that dumped out into the Forest?" she asked, eyes narrowed.

"The sewer system," Edmund replied. She gave him an odd look.

"And why were you in the sewer system?" she asked.

"Because… I had no place else to stay," he answered, a note of sadness in his voice.

"Hmm. You say that you were helping out Kafa and Rumple. What were you helping them out with?" she probed.

"They were running," Edmund replied, not wanting to give away the doings of Kafa and Rumple.

"From?" the queen said, raising an eyebrow. Edmund swallowed. *I do not wish to betray them; yet how might I avoid telling her the truth?* He wondered. Edmund was silent as he stared down at the ground.

"Answer me, Edmund," the Queen commanded. He forced himself to look back up at her, his throat dry.

"I shan't tell you," he said. The Queen looked at him in shock and ice-cold anger that he dared to disobey her before she struck him across the face, the surprising strength of the blow sending him sprawling.

"Hey! You leave him alone!" Rumple exclaimed angrily. Edmund groaned and looked up. Rumple was struggling against his restraints, and almost like magic, Alexai had appeared behind him, holding a sharp black blade against his throat. Kafa was looking at them with his eyebrows raised, as if he couldn't believe how fast Alexai had gotten there. Then he shook his head and stepped forward.

"Enough of this! I will tell you what you want to know," Kafa said. The Queen smiled.

"What were you and Rumple running from?" she asked.

"The I.P.O.s. They were chasing us and Edmund led us away from them," Kafa said.

"And why were the I.P.O.s chasing you?" the Queen asked, looking pleased that Kafa was talking. Rumple's struggling increased.

"No! Kafa! Don't-" he started saying, but stopped, wincing when Alexai pressed the blade harder against his throat, making a bead of blood trickle down and stain his clothes.

"Rumple, stop. It's not worth it. They were chasing us because we are associated with a wanted person," Kafa said, turning to Rumple before turning back to face the Queen.

"And who is this wanted person?" she asked, looking interested.

Kafa sighed sadly, as if it hurt him to answer her. After a beat of silence, he spoke.

"Joanne Raider," he said quietly. Her eyebrows flew up in surprise. Edmund suppressed a gasp.

*Joanne Raider? They were with her?* Edmund wondered, slightly shocked.

"Joanne Raider! What an interesting girl to be running around with! Tell me, where is she? Why isn't she here?" the Queen questioned, her eyes looking hungry and deadly.

"Because we split up. We split up, and she ran another direction," Kafa said.

"Do you know where she is?" the Queen asked, leaning forward.

"I'm afraid I don't," Kafa replied, not pretending to be sorry that he couldn't tell her Joanne's whereabouts. The Queen's eyes narrowed into aggravated slits.

"He's not lying. Half-One! What is your role in all of this?" the Queen asked, her gaze sliding over to She. She trembled under the gaze of the Queen.

"I-I was just walking in the woods, my Queen, and I found Edmund talking with Kafa and Rumple. I started telling him that he shouldn't be in the Forest anymore, and then the Darkness showed up. They didn't believe me when I told them my story," She explained. The Queen regarded her through her long eyelashes.

"Hmm… I cannot tell when Half-Ones lie. Though your story does *sound* believable, I don't think I can trust you. You were all found with Edmund on Dark Elf ground. Kafa and Rumple were also trespassing. Since Kafa is no longer king of the Unavenged, then no Unavenged members will storm the Eternal Night if we imprison him. Alexai, arrest them all, and arrange a whipping for Edmund," the Queen said casually before she started examining her nails, as if she had nothing else better to do. Edmund paled.

"No! You can't do this!" Rumple exclaimed. The Queen laughed, but it was cold and mean.

"I am Queen, boy. I can do *whatever* I want," she said.

"Wait! I beg of you, do not lock them up! They have not done a sinful thing! I led them astray. 'Tis wrong for them to all be punished when 'tis my fault. Punish me, but let them go free! Please," Edmund exclaimed as he leaped up and landed on his feet in front of the Queen. She eyed him; her gaze unreadable.

"Let this be a lesson to you, Edmund. A lesson that when you do wrong, you are not the only one that will suffer," she said after a moment. Edmund felt rough hands grabbing his arms and tying his hands together as they yanked him to face away from the Queen. Darkness members poured into the room and escorted Kafa, Rumple, She, and Edmund out of the throne room, down towards the dungeons. Down towards imprisonment. All Edmund could do was hang his head in guilt as they walked, each echoing footstep seeming like another nail in his coffin.

~~~

Harold peered down at the Forest below them.

"Do you see them?" Joanne asked. Harold sighed in annoyance.

"No, I don't! For the last time- wait. Hang on. That kind of looks like those two idiots," Harold said, peering down at something down on the ground. Harold felt Joanne shift on his back so she could also look down.

"Is that them?" Joanne asked.

"I don't know. If it is, they're in deep hay," Harold said.

"What do you mean?" Joanne asked, nervousness creeping into her voice.

"Well, it looks like they're being led by Darkness members towards the Grove, which is where the rude Dark Elf Queen lives. If they're going there, they're in trouble," Harold explained, not sounding concerned at all.

"What? Are we sure that's *them*?" Joanne asked, her voice rising an octave.

"Who else has hair like that Kafa guy?" Harold asked. Joanne opened her mouth, then shut it.

"How are we going to get them out?" Joanne asked after a moment.

"Whoever said *we* were getting them out?" Harold asked. Joanne looked at him in surprise.

"Umm, aren't we getting them out?" she asked, eyebrows raised.

"You have to realize that the Grove is a very guarded place. Trying to break them out will be almost impossible," Harold said.

"It is possible!" Joanne exclaimed.

"Really? How?" Harold asked.

"Because! I can do it!" Joanne said. Harold started steering them back.

"Where are we going? They're that way!" Joanne said, pointing at the Grove behind them.

"I know," Harold said.

"Then turn back around!" Joanne exclaimed.

"Listen, kid, you can't get them out. You'll just get yourself caught. It's not worth it. Trust me on that one," he said, sighing.

"Yes, I can!" Joanne exclaimed.

"Really? What can *one* imaginary friend do against the power of the Grove?" Harold asked, one eyebrow raised.

"I am *not* imaginary!" Joanne exclaimed. Harold stiffened in surprise and they dropped a few feet from him missing flapping his wings for a few seconds.

*What did she say?* he thought.

"What did you say?" Harold asked, turning his head to look at Joanne, searching for some clue that he might be joking.

"I am not imaginary. I am *real*, and I am here to save all of you from Kile. I can imagine things and they come true here. I *can* get them out," Joanne said. Harold just stared at her.

"Prove it," he finally said.

"Fine. Tell me something that you would not expect to see at this moment," Joanne said, sounding very sure of herself.

"Okay... a phoenix," Harold said after giving it some thought. Suddenly a phoenix in all of its' fiery glory swooped up in front of Harold, shooting into the sky, its' wings leaving fiery trails in the sky. Harold gaped up at it, forcing his wings to continue moving up and down despite his shock. He looked back at Joanne after it had disappeared from sight. She had her arms crossed and an eyebrow raised; the wind making her hair blow out behind her.

"Do you believe me now?" Joanne asked.

Harold nodded.

"Good. Then let's go to the Grove," she commanded. Without another word, Harold turned them towards the Grove, its black towers looming in the distance.

"Grove, here we come," he muttered. The wind was cold and the night around them was dark. Things in the Forest chirped and hooted beneath them, a choir of sounds in the Eternal Night. Once they were close enough, Harold swooped low to the ground, landing gently on his hooves on the Forest floor.

"Okay, how are we going to get in?" Harold asked, looking at Joanne expectantly. She blew out her cheeks and ran a hand through her hair.

"Well… what goes in the Grove?" Joanne asked.

"Dark Elves. Darkness members, Dark Elves that work in the palace… all of them," Harold answered.

"Hmm. What do they look like?" Joanne asked.

"Uhm… what are you planning?" Harold asked, suddenly concerned on why Joanne was wondering what Dark Elves looked like.

"Well, it's simple. I imagine myself to look like a Dark Elf, and I imagine you to look like… one of the horses they ride. Then we sneak in there, and I get us out by breaking a wall or something," Joanne explained.

"Umm, no," Harold said.

"What? Why? Is that a bad plan?" she asked, cocking her head to the side.

"No, it's just dangerous. And, anyway, I don't want to be a horse. They're too cocky," Harold said grumpily.

Joanne rolled her eyes.

"Really, Harold? Yes, it's dangerous, but it's worth a shot," Joanne said.

"I still don't want to do it," Harold said crossly, negative thoughts of horses running through his head.

"Come on! Please, Harold!" Joanne begged.

He obviously dreaded it but finally sighed in agreement.

"Fine. I'll do it to get those idiots out of there. But you'd better give me a lot of carrots and lettuce afterwards," Harold huffed.

"Okay. I can get you carrots and lettuce. But really, what do Dark Elves look like?" Joanne asked.

"You'll see once we get close enough," Harold said, then set off towards the Grove, the tall vegetation brushing along Harold's neck and on Joanne's knees as she followed him. When they reached the edge of the vegetation, Harold stopped and turned to Joanne. He jerked his head in the direction of the Grove.

"Look at them. That's what they look like," he said.

Joanne peered at the Dark Elf guards, and a second later, her features began to change. Her hair became a pitch black, darkening from the roots down like a wave of ink. Her eyes went from icy blue to an aquamarine, and her skin paled considerably. Her features sharpened, the softness going away, and her ears stretched until they were pointed. Her clothes also changed, the jacket, shirt, and pants morphing into a Dark Elf-looking dress that was silver.

"Okay. Your turn," she said, sounding a little breathless. Suddenly Harold felt hot all over, as if he was standing in a ring of fire. He could feel his legs and face getting longer, his horns shrinking back into his head and his tail lengthening as his hair darkened and shortened from its usual long, white fluffy locks. After a few seconds, it was over. Harold looked down at himself.

"Oh, dear, Billy," he muttered.

Joanne clapped her hands and grinned.

"Perfect! Okay, please don't try and throw me off," she said.

Harold sighed.

"Let's just get this over with," he said. She climbed onto his back with surprising grace, as if she had climbed onto the back of a horse a thousand times before.

"Lead the way," she said, and Harold set off at a trot, almost stumbling at first since he was not used to his long legs. They broke out of the vegetation and into the clearing with the Grove in it. The guards stared at Joanne and Harold as they entered the clearing. Harold couldn't help but start panicking inside a bit, but Joanne seemed calm and collected, as if this entire thing didn't faze her. Harold stopped at the gate. A guard approached them warily, looking uneasy.

"Name and business," he said.

"Evangeline Dim. I am here to fill the role of the sick handmaiden," Joanne said smoothly.

*Hmm. She's a good liar. But will the Dark Elf be able to tell she's lying?* Harold thought.

"Oh, yes! Her! Please, follow me," the guard said, giving Joanne a smile and opening up the gate. He led them across the drawbridge and into the Grove. Harold shuddered when they entered the Grove, but the temperature didn't seem to bother Joanne. He led them down a hallway, then another, and another. When he stopped in front of a door and began to speak, Joanne suddenly leaped off the horse and kicked him in the face, sending him flying. He smacked against the opposite wall and slumped down.

*Ahh, perfect. She just knocked a guy out,* Harold thought as she landed nimbly on her feet.

"What was that for?" Harold asked.

"Oh. He was going out figure out sooner or later that I made up the sick handmaiden story. So. Also, we need to get to wherever the others are being held. Where do you think they are?" Joanne explained.

"Well, they're probably in the dungeons," Harold said.

"That makes sense. Wait. Where are the dungeons?" Joanne asked.

"I don't know, kid! I don't work here!" Harold exclaimed.

"Well, I guess we'll have to go find them," Joanne said, sighing, before setting off down a hallway. Harold trotted after her, his hooves echoing on the hard, cold floors.

"Don't worry, we'll find them," Joanne said when she glanced back at Harold.

*I hope so. I hope nobody else finds us first,* Harold thought darkly.

~~~

Alexai sighed, trying to ignore the almost silent sobs of the Half-One behind him. He whirled around, his eyes flashing with annoyance.

"Will you just be quiet?" he demanded. She glared at him.

"No. I should not be in here. I won't stop until I'm let go," She said defiantly.

Alexai sighed.

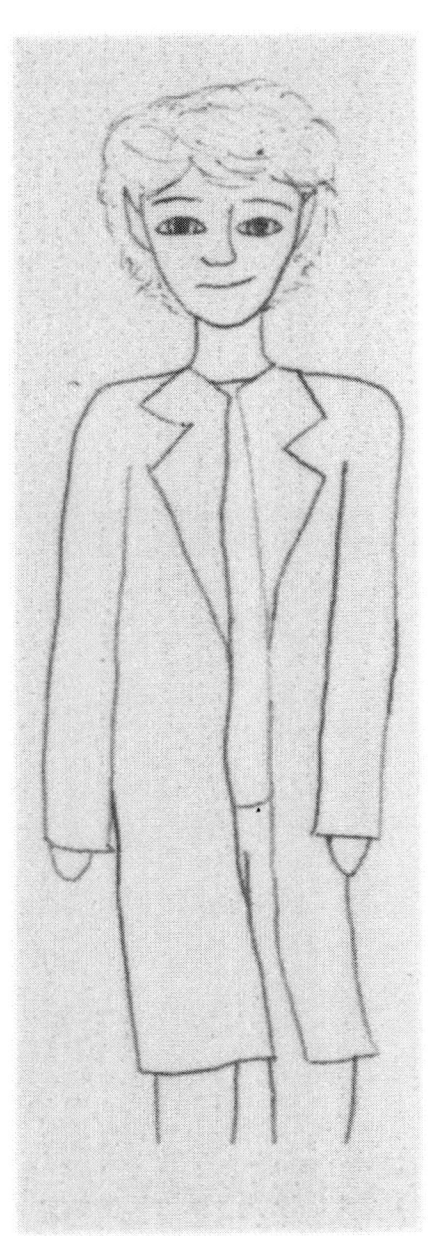

"Whoever told you that you were going to be let go?" he asked.

She paled.

"I- I-," she started.

"Exactly. Now, do shut up. It's quite annoying," Alexai said, then turned back around. He heard her sniffle behind him, but after that, she was silent. Alexai sighed.

*I need to go to the restroom,* he thought. He looked around, making sure that the prisoners were all locked up before he left the dungeons at a brisk pace, climbing the stairs as gracefully as a cat to get to the first floor of the Grove. He walked to the restroom and took care of his business, then started going back to the dungeons when he noticed a Dark Elf girl with a horse trailing behind her. Alexai's eyes ran right past her before he looked back, his brow furrowed.

*I don't recognize her... who is she?* he wondered. She had silky black hair that fell to her shoulders that shone in the light of the chandeliers. Her eyes were an aquamarine blue that sparkled as if she had a secret that only she knew. She wore a dress that fanned around her like silver petals, making it look as if she was some sort of exotic flower. She seemed to be looking for something as she peered around the Grove. He redirected his footsteps so he was walking towards her. She noticed he was walking towards her and she froze before she regained her composure, tucking a strand of hair behind her ear.

"Hello. Might I ask what you're looking for?" Alexai asked, as he stopped when he was a few feet in front of her.

"Oh! Umm, I was just looking for ... a restroom. I've gotten lost since it's my first day here... I'm just a bit of a mess," she rambled, looking nervous for some reason. Despite his suspicion, he forced a small smile onto his face.

"That's quite alright. I remember somehow winding up in the kitchen when I was going for the throne room on my first day. I still don't know how I managed to do that. But the bathroom is right over... there," Alexai said, chuckling as he pointed to the bathroom. The girl laughed.

"Thank you," she said. He inclined his head towards her.

"But of course," he said politely. The girl gave him one last smile before walking into the bathroom.

Alexai watched her go, his eyes narrowing and his smile dropping.

*She's up to something... I just don't know what. I can't really hang around without arousing her suspicion. I should go back to the prisoners and maybe report her to a guard if I see one,* he thought, then spun on his heel and began walking back to the dungeons, feeling a little down that he had to leave the Dark Elf girl behind. He was turning to go down the hallway that held the stairs to the dungeons when he heard light footsteps and a horse's hooves behind him. He glanced over his shoulder and saw the girl and her horse.

"Wait!" she said. Alexai stopped in surprise. She jogged up to him and then stopped.

"The Queen dismissed me for today. Are you off?" she said, something like hopefulness on her face.

"Oh! Umm, I- I am not off, *but* you can come with me. The prisoners won't care if a lady is there too," Alexai said, forcing a smile again.

"Prisoners?" she asked curiously, something flashing through her eyes.

"Yes, I am leader of the Darkness, so I watch over the prisoners most days," Alexai said.

"You are? Oh, I'm so sorry, I didn't-" she started saying, looking embarrassed as she sunk down into a curtsey, but Alexai put a hand on her shoulder.

"It's quite alright. Curtseying is unnecessary anyway," he said dismissively. She stood back up, looking a little more relaxed. He gently took her hand and kissed it.

"I'm Alexai. What's your name?" he said, looking up at her.

Joanne was blushing a little, as if flattered by the gesture. Behind her, it looked like her horse rolled its eyes. Alexai peered at it for a moment before deciding that he probably imagined it.

"I'm Evangeline," Joanne said, a small smile on her lips.

"That's a nice name. Now, come with me," he said, offering her his arm, which she took after a moment of her looking surprised. He led her down the hallway and then down the stairs. He felt her stiffen when she saw the prisoners. He glanced at her, slightly confused as his suspicion grew, but he didn't say anything. He led her over to the wall and they leaned against it.

"How was your first day of being a handmaiden?" Alexai asked as he watched her horse slowly step down the stairs into the dungeon.

"Oh! Umm… it was good. The Queen is really…" she said, trailing off.

"Intense?" Alexai offered.

"Yes! Yes, she's kind of intense. But she's also really pretty," Evangeline said, looking slightly relieved.

By now they were near where Kafa, Rumple, She and Edmund were being held. Alexai noticed out of the corner of his eye that Rumple was staring at them very intently, as if he was trying to figure something out. Alexai decided to ignore him.

"She's that too. I mean- she *is* Queen of the Dark Elves. What did you expect?" Alexai asked.

"I wasn't sure what to expect, honestly and- why does he keep staring at us?" she asked, peering at a prisoner behind him. Alexai turned and saw that Rumple was still staring at them.

"What are you looking at?" Alexai asked, looking at Rumple unexpectedly.

"What? Oh, uh, nothing. Nothing at all… sir," he said, adding the last part after a moment of silence.

"Right," Alexai said, his eyes narrowed and feeling unconvinced, when Evangeline walked up to the bars of Rumple's cell.

"Evangeline! I don't think that's such a-" he started saying, but suddenly he had ropes around his wrists and ankles and a gag formed around his mouth. He grunted in surprise as he fell to the ground, landing on his side.

"I'm sorry," Evangeline said sadly, looking down at Alexai. Then Evangeline spread her arms wide, and then squeezed her eyes shut. Alexai looked at her with his brow furrowed, very confused about what was happening. Suddenly all of the doors swung open at once, their unison sending chills through Alexai.

"Let's GO!" Evangeline yelled. Suddenly her features began to change. Her hair lightened to a platinum blond and her eyes faded to an icy blue. Her dress shimmered before it changed to a t-shirt, jeans, and an army green denim jacket. Alexai just watched with as much of an open mouth as he could get. The prisoners rushed out in a wave, heading for the exits. Alexai tried in vain to sit up, but he wasn't successful.

"Joanne! How the frick-?" Rumple started saying as he rushed out, giving her a quick hug, but she gently pushed him away.

*Joanne? Wait...it's Joanne Raider. It's Joanne Raider!* Alexai thought, his eyes widening.

"Another time, Rumple. Not now. We have to go," Joanne said, looking around.

"Well, no, duh. Otherwise… we are screwed," Rumple said.

"Come on! Kafa, where- there you are! Come on, let's go!" Joanne said as Kafa jogged towards them.

"We have to get Edmund!" Rumple said.

"Who?" Joanne asked, looking slightly confused.

"Edmund!" Rumple exclaimed, gesturing towards one of the cells. Edmund suddenly stumbled out of his cell, looking sheepish.

"Pardon? My deepest apologies, I am afraid I did not-" he started saying, but broke off when Joanne grabbed his arm and started yanking him towards the staircase.

"Who might you be?" he asked Joanne.

"I'm the person saving all of you right now! Come on, you three, let's go!" she said, waving Kafa, Rumple, and a white goat that was once her horse over to her. Everyone scurried towards the staircase, not caring about who they shoved or where they were stepping. Alexai got stepped on a grand total of seven times, each of his cries muffled by his gag.

"Wait! She! Come on!" Edmund called, wrenching himself out of Joanne's grasp and rushing towards a cell. She was sitting in the corner of her cell, looking defeated. Edmund stopped in front of her and offered her his hand. She glared up at him.

"Why would I go with you?" She asked, her tone full of loathing.

"Because perhaps you wish to survive tonight," he said. She huffed and got up herself.

"Who is she?" Joanne asked.

"A friend!" Edmund exclaimed as he and She rushed over to the goat, Joanne, Rumple, and Kafa.

"I am *not* your friend!" She said angrily, but Edmund ignored her. Meanwhile, Alexai wriggled on the floor to avoid a centaur's hooves.

"Come on, let's *go*!" Rumple exclaimed, but Joanne was looking back at Alexai and worrying her lower lip.

"Joanne, *come on*!" Rumple said, grabbing her arm. But she wasn't fully listening to him. She twisted her arm out of his grip and sprinted over to Alexai. She landed on her knees beside him and the gag in his mouth disappeared.

"What will they do to you?" she asked. He stared up at her in confusion and surprise.

"What?" he asked, his brow creased.

"I said, what will they do to you once all the prisoners are gone?" Joanne asked.

"Oh. Easy. I'll be punished since I failed to do my job," Alexai said, paling a little as thoughts of what they might do raced through his head.

"Do you want to come with us?" she asked.

"You want me to come with you?" he asked, disbelief coloring his tone as his eyebrows shot up.

"If you want to come, yeah," she said, shrugging.

"Yes, please," he said. She grabbed his bound wrists and yanked him up.

"I'm not unbounding you until we're safely away. For now, just follow us," Joanne said, jogging back over to the others. The bounds on his ankles disappeared so he could move after them.

"Woah, this isn't babysitting service!" Rumple exclaimed when he noticed Alexai following Joanne.

"Umm, I am older than you, so you can shush," Alexai said, sounding slightly annoyed at Rumple's comment. Rumple shot him a glare as Joanne spoke.

"Shut up, both of you! Just follow me!" she exclaimed, then turned and began taking the stairs two at a time. They all looked at one another before following her, Kafa behind Alexai to make sure he didn't try and run away.

Alexai had met Kafa years ago, back when Kafa had been king of the Unavenged. He had seemed like a good leader of an alliance when he spoke to the Dark Elf Queen. Alexai knew of Joanne Raider and her brother, Rumple, from the news that traveled like wildfire around the Forest. But he had no idea where the goat had come from, or why they had decided to take Edmund and She with them. Alexai thought, his thoughts blowing through his mind like leaves in the fall on a windy day:

> *Evangeline ... or... Joanne changed, and so did the horse. And my bounds. Nothing can do that... unless... no. She can't be- yet she obviously is ...real. But how? How did she even - her brother. Her brother! He must have brought her here, yes, that's it, in hopes of saving Imagine! But will their plan succeed? That is the better question. Another matter: why did she want to bring me along? What use am I to her? Dear me, I hope I'm not to be used as a hostage. On second thought, that is too unlikely. Hmm. I don't know if I understand her motives. I am concerned now...*

They raced up the staircase, Alexai trying very hard not to trip on his long black cloak that flew out behind him. They burst out into the Grove, the prisoners zigzagging in every direction in hopes of finding an exit. Joanne, on the other hand, seemed to know exactly what she was doing.

*At least she seems to have a clue what she is doing,* Alexai thought with false cheeriness as she led their little group through the many freezing hallways towards the doors. They burst into the main hallway to find the exit guarded by Darkness members, most of whom were already fighting escaped prisoners. Alexai recognized each of them, of course. They were his men, after all. He stumbled when he saw one getting stabbed with a sword, and because his hands were still tied, he fell to the ground, unable to balance himself. He squeezed his eyes shut, bracing himself for impact, but was relieved to find that no impact came. Instead, two hands grabbed him by the shoulders and yanked him upwards. His eyes flew open to see Kafa holding his shoulders and gently pushing him forward.

"Come on, we don't have all day! Try to stay on your feet, please. It'll slow us down if you go down," he said, not unkindly. Alexai could only nod, not sure that he could do much else. The Darkness members that tried to attack their group as they ran through them would suddenly freeze, suspended in midair.

*It must be Joanne,* Alexai thought as they shoved open the doors and ran out into the courtyard, the warmer air of the Forest slapping against their faces. The drawbridge was not lowered, which changed in a second. One moment it was up, blocking their escape, the next it was down, letting them cross over the moat. Alexai noticed prisoners behind them also running over the drawbridge, a few Darkness members catching some of the slower ones. They burst into the vegetation, the Grove getting smaller and smaller behind them as they leaped over roots and ducked under branches, trying to put as much space as possible between themselves and the Grove.

Suddenly Joanne stopped, making the others stop as well. They all stood there, breathing heavily, until She started to speak.

"Well... today has been- interesting. It started off normally, then I ran into Edmund, got arrested, got questioned, got imprisoned, and now I'm running from Darkness members with the most wanted person in Imagine! How could this day get any more... strange?" She said tiredly, plopping down on a root.

"Wait, she's the most wanted?" Kafa asked, turning to She. He sounded genuinely surprised, though Alexai had no idea why.

"Yes, she is, since that weirdo Kile wants her and he's threatening everyone. You were number one, but then you lost your position and nobody cares anymore what happens to you," She said as she examined her dark red nails with disinterest. Kafa opened his mouth as if he was going to say something before he shut it, as if he thought better of what words were about to leave his mouth.

"She's not wrong," the goat said, shrugging.

Alexai found himself fixated on the goat.

*Since when can goats shrug? Or talk?* he wondered. He had known many creatures in the forest, but they mostly resembled something human, such as himself. He had never met a talking animal imaginary friend, though he knew they were extremely common in the Eternal Day part of the Forest and some of the other sections of Imagine. Kafa gave the goat a look.

"Thank you for the input, Harold-"

"Anytime," Harold said, though he sounded sarcastic about it. Kafa gave him the same dry look before he sighed and continued.

"But we are currently in the middle of the Eternal Night part of the Forest, a place that we shouldn't be. We are trespassing and we all just escaped Dark Elf prison.

So, I was saying that maybe we should get out of here before something finds us," Kafa said, pacing back and forth on the mossy Forest floor.

"He is probably right, you know. It would not be smart to stay here. Only a fool would. But I have no clue how we shall get out of here," Edmund said thoughtfully as he leaned against a tree as far away as possible from She.

"Hmm. That is the real problem. Joanne!" Kafa said. Joanne jumped, as if she had been lost in her thoughts.
"Y-yes?" she asked, looking like an unprepared student that was called on by a teacher to answer a math question.

"Do you think you could imagine us a way out of here?" Kafa asked.

Joanne sighed, her eyes looking tired.

"Yeah, probably," she said.

"Perfect. When do you think you could do it?" Kafa asked, looking at her with something close to concern.

"Now would be great," Harold said.

Kafa sighed impatiently and looked at Harold with annoyance.

"She gets tired from imagining things, Harold. It drains her energy. If she doesn't have enough energy, she will just sort of pass out and then we're really in trouble. So, if you could just wait a minute that way, she doesn't exhaust herself and pass out if we are flying in the air or something, that would be perfect. So, unless you have anything helpful to say, then please, be quiet," Kafa said, sounding aggravated.

"I was just gonna say that now would be great because they're right there," Harold said, sounding very bored as he jerked his horned head in the direction of the Grove. Everyone's heads whipped around. Sure enough, trees could be seen shaking and shouts of Darkness members could be heard from the direction of the Grove. Rumple and Kafa started swearing and suddenly changed their sense of urgency.

"Okay, Joanne, can you please conjure something up now?" Kafa asked, looking slightly alarmed. Even though she looked tired, she breathed deeply, shutting her eyes, before opening them.

"Yes. Yes, I can. Okay, everyone, brace yourselves," she said.

Rumple looked at her, clearly confused.

"Like, hold on to something, 'because I don't know-"

"No! Just… be ready," Joanne said, shooting him a look like he was stupid.

*Hmm. Sibling quarrels. I'm sure this isn't even the worst. Good thing I never had a sibling,* Alexai thought, a smile tugging at his mouth despite the circumstances. Suddenly Alexai felt something underneath him, and he was shooting, soaring up into the night sky. He heard She and Rumple scream, though everyone else just gasped or did nothing. He looked down and his eyebrows raised in surprise. He was riding on some sort of black and yellow dragon that swooped through the air quite smoothly with its leathery wings. Kafa sat in front of him, holding onto reins of some sort. Alexai didn't know that you could put reins on a dragon until that moment. He looked around. Joanne and Rumple were riding on a silver Pegasus, while Edmund and She were riding on a calico hippogriff that cawed like a parrot every ten seconds. Harold was just flying himself using his wings. Alexai could hear Rumple complaining about their Pegasus.

"This is so not fair! Why the crap am *I* on the *My Little Pony* ride? Why couldn't I be on the *How to Train Your Dragon* one? Or even the *Harry Potter* one?" he whined. Joanne sighed and rolled her eyes.

"It's *not* My Little Pony! It's just a Pegasus. There's a difference," Joanne protested, sounding very tired.

"Oh, yeah, right. The difference is that *this one* doesn't talk. Oh wait, maybe it's a little surprise like frickin' Harold over there and it talks! Do you talk?" Rumple said, looking at the Pegasus expectantly. The Pegasus said nothing.

"Of course, it doesn't talk, idiot. If it did, it would have thrown you off by now for calling it My Little Pony and then laughed about it," Harold said, flying up until he was beside Joanne and Rumple. Rumple eyed him with annoyance. Meanwhile, Alexai could hear She and Edmund whispering about what My Little Pony was.

"What's My Little Pony?" Alexai asked Kafa.

"I have no clue," Kafa said, shrugging. Then he glanced over at Joanne and a crease appeared between his brows.

"Joanne, are you okay?" he asked, concern in his voice. Alexai looked over and saw why Kafa had asked. Joanne was extremely pale and looked sick.

"I... I'm fine," she said, though she didn't sound fine.

"Hmm. Harold, how much longer until we reach the City?" Kafa asked.

"Uh... maybe a mile or two. So... maybe five more minutes?" Harold replied.

"Can you make it five minutes, Joanne?" Kafa asked.

"I think so," she said weakly.

"Okay," Kafa said, though he still sounded worried.

"She's real, isn't she?" Alexai asked Kafa.

Kafa looked at him, slightly surprised.

"Yes. How did you- wait. Never mind. That whole break-out-of-the-Grove thing made it pretty obvious, huh?" Kafa said.

"It did make it obvious," Alexai confirmed.

"Do you think everyone knows now?" Kafa asked.

"Yes. The Dark Elves will check footage and figure it out. Soon, all the Dark Elves will know, and rumors will begin to spread. Everyone will know that Joanne is real very soon. It's only a matter of time," Alexai said, nodding. Kafa looked grim.

"What time is it? I can't tell because the sun is gone," he asked.

"Hmm. I'd say it's around one in the afternoon," Alexai answered.

"Mm. Kile wants Joanne by sundown," Kafa muttered.

"Imaginary friends will get more desperate as each hour passes. We will probably have to hide somewhere, otherwise we will be found and she will be handed over," Alexai thought aloud.

"You're right about that," Kafa said.

*Why does he want her? She is real, that is all that is special about her. But if he is real because of the Stone, doesn't that mean that only something real can stop him? Oh. Of course! He wants to eliminate her before she can eliminate him! He is threatening Imagine and it is working because he is real, but nobody knows that*

*Joanne is real! Nobody knows that they're handing over their only hope,* Alexai thought.

"Wait! Nobody knows she's real except for us, correct?" Alexai suddenly blurted.

"Correct. Why?" Kafa asked.

"Well, think about it. If she's real, she is the *only thing* that can defeat Kile. Kile wants her in order to destroy her. But nobody else knows she's real. She is their *only hope*, and they don't even realize it. If they knew that Joanne was real, maybe they wouldn't be trying to hand her over to Kile, because they would know that she could save them. If we make it known that she's real, then they won't try and catch her! If anything, they'll rally up with her *against* Kile!" Alexai explained. Kafa stared at him for a second.

"You know, I know why you are leader of the Darkness now. You, Alexai, are a genius! I never would've thought of that! You're absolutely right! All we have to do is make it known that Joanne is real, and maybe they'll all rise up against Kile! It is a perfect plan! We must get to the Imaginists, they know how to spread news the fastest," Kafa said, a grin slowly spreading across his face.

"Only one problem about your plan. The girl's passed out," Harold said, suddenly flying beside them. Sure enough, Joanne, as pale as computer paper, slumped against the Pegasus, which disappeared a second later. Then the dragon and the hippogriff disappeared, and suddenly, they were all suspended in midair. Then, just as quickly, they all began to plummet towards the ground, their screams and yells lost in the howl of the cold night wind.

# Chapter Seventeen

She screamed. There was nothing else she could do, really. One moment she had been riding above the Forest on a hippogriff with *Edmund*, of all elves, and the next moment, it disappeared, letting them all free-fall towards the ground.

His blue robe billowed around him in the wind, showing his black pants he wore beneath it. He looked surprised and frightened as he flailed his arms and legs in the air.

She looked over and saw Rumple holding Joanne's hand as they fell. He was screaming something at her, looking terrified, but Joanne wasn't responding at all. Dread pooled in She's stomach.

*Nothing is going to stop us. Nothing will stop me from hitting the ground,* She thought, feeling sick. She looked around again and spotted Kafa and Alexai a little bit above them, the only ones that looked slightly calm. Alexai and Kafa looked as if they were just standing in the air and dropping straight down, holding their arms out as if to keep balance.

Alexai suddenly crossed his arms, making him fall even faster to the point where he shot down past She and Edmund so he was even with Joanne and Rumple. He said something to Rumple when he was right above them, who after a moment, reluctantly let go of Joanne's hand. Alexai grabbed onto it and suddenly spread his arms wide so quickly that his cloak billowed out, making a sort of parachute, slowing he and Joanne's descent considerably.

Edmund, after a moment, grabbed She's hand and opened his robe, letting it do the same parachute affect. Her screaming stopped. She looked up at Edmund, thankful and surprised. Rumple and Kafa, on the other hand, were still falling, Rumple much faster than Kafa.

Suddenly a white blur came across She's vison, and after a moment, she realized it was the oddly grouchy goat, Harold, that had wings and could talk for some reason. Harold caught Rumple on his back, then flew up and caught Kafa as well, though he looked terribly weighted down. They all floated down to the ground, except for Harold, who flew Rumple and Kafa down. They landed on the Forest floor and all looked at one another, surprised that they were still alive. Rumple leaped off Harold and rushed over to Joanne, whom Alexai had set down gently.

"Joanne! Joanne, are you okay? Say something, Joanne, please! Joanne!" Rumple said desperately, giving Joanne a little shake. There was dread and wild fear in his eyes, fear of losing his sister and dread of what might happen without her. She saw that Joanne didn't look well. Her skin had taken on a grayish tinge, her breaths were shallow, and her eyes were closed. Kafa ran up to them, looking concerned.

"This is what I was afraid of. She needs medical attention. Harold! How far away are we from the City?" he said, turning to Harold, who didn't look bored for once.

"Oh, uhm… maybe a mile? Probably a little less," Harold said.

Kafa turned to the rest of them.

"Okay. Let's go," he said, then bent down, picking up Joanne and slinging her over his shoulder with a small grunt of effort. He began walking the way they had been flying; west. Rumple began to follow, then Harold, Alexai, Edmund, and She. They hiked through the Forest, glancing behind them every now and then to make sure they weren't being followed. After about twenty minutes, the trees and plants began to thin, revealing the City.

"Our goal is to get to the Imaginists Palace. Nobody knows that Joanne is real, so they're still looking for her. They will recognize me or Rumple, and maybe even Harold, so the imaginary friend with her needs to be one of you," Kafa said, pointing to Edmund and She.

"What about him?" Harold asked, pointing to Alexai.

"You've only just met me. I don't seem very trustworthy to you, which is fine, I would do the same if I were you. I shouldn't be trusted with the only hope," Alexai explained before Kafa could.

"He's right. It should be Edmund or She, even though we met them recently too," Kafa said, frowning as he realized that Edmund or She were probably not much better than Alexai as far as trusting them went.

"I can do it," She said, stepping forward.

"Are you sure? You know where the Imaginists Palace is, right?" Kafa asked.

"I'm sure. And yes, I do. I've visited the City before, despite what you may think," She said, looking determined.

"Okay," Kafa said, then put two fingers in his mouth and whistled loudly. A few seconds later, a pitch-black horse galloped up to them. Kafa grinned.

"Midnight!" he said happily, stroking its' muzzle for a moment before he slung Joanne over the back of the horse.

"Before you go, let's explain the events of the past few days so you know what to say to the Imaginists," Kafa said, then he and Rumple told her everything that had happened. When they were done, She climbed on in front of Joanne, and Kafa adjusted Joanne to make it look like she was holding onto She.

"Take care of her," Rumple said.

"I will," she said, as her features softened.

"Okay, we'll meet you up there. For now, go!" Kafa said, then gave Midnight a pat, and with that, Midnight took off like a bullet, shooting out of the greenery and into the streets. She gasped and held on a little tighter to Midnight's reins, putting a hand on Joanne's back to make sure she was still there and stayed there. She steered Midnight through the maze of streets and roads towards the center of it. Towards the Imaginists Palace. Suddenly, She heard the wail of a siren. She glanced behind her and saw a lone I.P.O. car take off after them.

"Crap!" She muttered before prodding Midnight's side, urging him to go faster. He increased speed a little, but not by much.

*He can't go any faster! No, no, no! Come on!* She thought desperately. The I.P.O. was getting closer. She looked up and spotted the Imaginists Palace a few blocks ahead of her. *We'll never make it! Unless… time to improvise, I guess. Goodness, what did I get myself into?* She thought, then suddenly jerked the reins to the left. Midnight jumped straight over a moving car and landed on the sidewalk like it was nothing. The I.P.O. car swerved to keep up with them. She steered Midnight to go behind a building and into another road, making unsuspecting imaginary friends scatter in all directions. The I.P.O. hit another car when they came out into the road. She sighed in relief and kept riding. They made it to the gates, where guards pointed rifles at She and Joanne.

"Name and business!" one of them barked.

"She! I bring you Joanne Raider. Let me in," She said, her voice never wavering despite the wave of nervousness she felt. They peered around her and their eyes widened when they saw Joanne.

"Give her to us," one of them said.

"No! *I* am bringing her in. Otherwise, you will not get her," She said, her voice rising. They exchanged a glance before opening up the gate.

"I want to bring her to the Imaginists myself," She said.

"We will escort you to the Discussion Room, then leave you there," one of them said. She nodded. They led her into the Imaginists Palace, which took her breath away. It was just so beautiful, such a blend of cultures from times and places, some of them lost forever except there. The rugs on the marble floors were elaborately woven with gorgeous designs that caught one's eye. The ceiling was painted with scenes of the start of Imagine, with chandeliers that gave off soft white glows. The walls were adorned with portraits of Imaginists and tapestries just as elegant as the rugs. There were huge windows with gold frames that let light spill into the Palace, though it was hardly necessary with the chandeliers.

The guard led her down the hallway and into another one before he stopped at a pair of doors. She could hear arguing voices on the other side of them.

"In you go," he said, before he turned and walked back down the hallway. She took a deep breath and slowly opened the door. The arguments abruptly stopped as She walked inside the room, Midnight and Joanne trailing behind her.

"I present to you Joanne Raider," She said.

They all stared at her and then turned to look at Joanne in shocked silence.

"How did you...?" a girl with green hair finally asked.

"Get the medics. Now," She said.

"What? Why?" A boy with brown hair asked, looking very confused.

"She's hurt. Get a medic in here now!" She commanded, meeting their confused gazes with her own resolute one. The Imaginists looked at one another before one stepped forward.

"I'm a medic," he said.

"Good. Get over here to her," She said, waving the medic over.

"What happened?" he asked as he bent down beside her.

"She used up too much energy imagining things, so she passed out…" She started to explain.

They all stared at her.

"What do you mean, she used too much energy imagining things?" one of them asked.

"Please don't interrupt me, because I'm about to explain," She said as she sighed. "We all know that Kile stole the Stone of Existence and is now real. We also know that since he is real, he cannot be injured or killed by an imaginary friend. Only by somebody that is real. So, Rumple, Joanne's discarded imaginary friend, went through one of the holes at the exterior of Imagine and explained everything to her. She decided to help out, so she came back and went to the Unavenged with Rumple, since he was a member at the time. Kafa was able to figure out that she was real, so Rumple and Joanne had to explain everything to him. Kile found Kafa while he was alone, threatened to take Kafa's life and told him to bring him Joanne or he would kill him. Kafa told Joanne and Rumple of Kile's plans anyway, so he started to try and prepare her for an encounter with Kile. Kile has eyes everywhere and gave Dari, an Unavenged member, the assistance needed to overthrow Kafa. So then when Kafa had to leave, Joanne and Rumple were attacked, making them flee. Somewhere they met up with Harold, a flying, talking goat, for assistance," she said, showing on her face that she could hear how ridiculous that part may sound.

"After he was overthrown, Joanne, Rumple and Harold the goat found Kafa and went out in search of a place to stay, but then Kile's broadcast came on and everyone began chasing them. They got split up but all ended up in the Forest, where Rumple and Kafa were captured by Dark Elves and imprisoned for trespassing. Joanne got wind of this, so she and Harold came in and rescued them, also picking up Edmund who is a mixed Elf; myself, a Half-One; and Alexai, the leader of the Darkness whom Joanne tricked to get to where he was holding them. Alexai then pointed out something… *nobody else knows* that Joanne is real. If the public knew Joanne was real, they wouldn't be hunting her. If anything, they would stand by her, if they just knew. Unfortunately, Joanne passed out from over-imagining herself as we escaped the Forest. So, we decided to bring her here in hopes of getting help from you, one for medical attention, the other in hopes of getting help to stop Kile," She said.

They all looked at her, deep in thought. Finally, a man stood up.

"I do suppose that you are right… though it won't do you much good at all," he said slowly as he walked toward She. She squinted at him.

*He looks familiar,* She thought.

"Why do you say that?" She asked.

"Because. You really think that Kile would tell the finder of Joanne Raider to drop her off at the Imaginists Palace if he didn't have control over them? Ha! Ha-ha!" he said, a maniacal grin splitting his face. In a split second, something small and shiny darted out and sunk into She's side. She gasped in pain, crumpling to the ground as blood began to pool on the ground around her.

*Kile. It's Kile,* She thought.

"Stupid Half-One. Your friends will have a little surprise waiting for them once they get here. I know they're on their way. Kafa would not let you do this alone. No, he is coming. When he does… it will be quick. For him. For the others, it will be quite slow. As yours will be now. Night-night!" he said, then brought the sole of his shoe down on her side. She screeched in pain; so much of it that it was blinding. Then she started to slip into darkness.

~~~

Kafa sighed as they ducked behind yet another trash can.

"How much more of this madness must we do? I am beginning to grow tired of hiding behind waste bins," Edmund whined.

"Shut up. We are running around the City in secret and we don't need to hear your complaining, okay?" Rumple said, sounding very on edge. Edmund sighed theatrically.

"Very well. Though thou may regret silencing me later," he said.

"Mm-hmm. *Right,*" Rumple said sarcastically, sounding unconvinced.

*They bicker like two children,* Kafa thought.

"Will you two just be quiet? Unlike some of us, I am trying to stay quiet so we *don't* get caught," Kafa hissed. Edmund and Rumple both huffed but said nothing.

"This way," Kafa whispered, and they slinked behind a building and onto another road. The Imaginists Palace loomed in front of them; only a block or two away.

"How are we going to get in?" Harold asked.

"The gate," Rumple replied.

Alexai's brow furrowed and he gave Rumple a disapproving look.

"Uhm, no. We are not going through the gate. We will take another route. A window, perhaps. Look at all of the skylights they have. Harold could fly us up, one by one, and then we descend into the Palace. After that, we walk around until we find She, Joanne, and the Imaginists. Or we could take the sewer route-"

"No more sewers! Jeez, what is it with you people and hanging out in sewers?" Rumple said in disgust, cutting off Alexai. Alexai glared at him.

"Fine. We take the skylight route," he said.

"*Or* we could just take the *gate*, like a normal person!" Rumple said, giving Alexai an exasperated look.

Alexai sighed, sounding annoyed.

"First off, I am not a person, I am a Dark Elf. Remember that. Second, I am anything but normal. Third, they might be expecting us to go through the gate, where they then capture us," he said, ticking each thing off on his fingers.

"*Why* would *they* capture us!?" Rumple said, growing agitated.

Kafa threw Rumple a look of displeasure at his stubbornness.

"Unless they're just stubborn ...*biscuits*... who refuse to listen, why would *they* capture us?" Rumple asked, rephrasing the question.

"Well, Rumple, you haven't seemed to consider all the possibilities. For all we know, they are working with Kile, or they have Kile hanging over their heads, forcing them to capture us and imprison or kill us," Alexai said.

Everyone let his words sink in.

*That actually sounds possible,* Kafa thought.

"You could be right, Alexai," Kafa said after a moment, looking thoughtful.

"I don't think he is," Rumple said, shaking his head.

"And why is that? Please give me a good answer, as we really don't have time for naivety," Alexai said, looking genuinely interested.

"Because. If we were gonna get captured, that means that we're walking into a trap, and I don't want to live *Return of the Jedi*, okay? *'It's a trap!'* Yeah, no, that's not gonna happen to me. It also means that Joanne and She are captured, and I don't really think they'd do that to them," Rumple said.

"You think so?" Alexai asked, eyebrows raised.

"Yes," Rumple said confidently.

"Okay. But if we get caught and we all die, my last thought will be, *I was right, and the stubborn nerdy twelve-year-old was wrong,*" Alexai said casually, shrugging.

"I'm flattered your last thought will be of me. Really, it makes me feel all warm and fuzzy inside, like I just ate a hamster or something," Rumple said with a false smile and equally false cheeriness.

"You eat hamsters?" Harold asked.

"In my spare time," Rumple said sarcastically.

Harold looked disturbed.

Kafa rolled his eyes.

"Enough, you two! We're almost there. Are we going to take the skylight or the gate?" Kafa asked.

"Gate," Harold, Edmund, and Rumple said.

"Skylight," Alexai simultaneously said.

Kafa sighed.

"I don't care," he said, sounding and feeling tired as he ran his hand down his face.

"Harold, will you take me to the skylight?" Alexai asked.

"Umm, we don't trust you enough to split up!" Rumple said.

"But you trust a goat?" Alexai asked, eyebrows raised.

"Let me think, I've known him a good almost twelve hours, and you for one or two. So, yes, I do," Rumple said with mock consideration.

Alexai sighed.

"Just let him go! If he wants to go on the roof, let him go on the roof. Harold, bring him up there, then come down to the gate with us," Kafa ordered.

"Fine," Harold muttered, then looked at Alexai expectantly. After a moment, Alexai got on Harold's back. Harold grunted from the weight and then flapped his wings and they soared up into the sky, high above the roof of the Imaginists Palace.

"I really hope he doesn't pull one of those only-seen-in-movies kind of betrayals," Rumple said as he, Edmund, and Kafa watched them go up.

"I don't think he will," Kafa said, sounding confident of his opinion. Harold swooped back down and landed beside them.

"Let's move it, girls," he said, trotting towards the gates. Kafa almost smiled at the comment, while Rumple looked annoyed and Edmund looked confused.

"Where are the girls? I don't see any," Edmund asked, looking suddenly very interested as he gazed around in search of non-existent girls.

"It's an expression," Rumple said as they walked.

"Really? Was he calling *us* girls?" Edmund asked.

"Yup," Rumple replied.

"But I am no girl!" Edmund exclaimed, putting a hand on his chest.

"We know that, it just means… never mind," Rumple said, sighing.

"But what does it *mean*?" Edmund asked, his brow furrowed as he tried to piece it together.

*I swear. 1600's imaginary friends understand nothing. How is it that I was created far before that, and I am able to keep up with the times, but them? Learn to do the same already,* Kafa thought, rolling his eyes.

They arrived at the gate, so Rumple stopped talking to Edmund about the girl's expression, as they approached a few guards.

"Names and business!" one of them said.

"Kafa, Harold, Edmund, and Rumple. We are with Joanne Raider and She. Please take us to them," Kafa said. The guards exchanged a look, one that Kafa couldn't read, despite his almost two thousand years of being around imaginary friends.

"Follow us," they said, then opened the gates and began walking towards the Imaginists Palace. Kafa and Harold looked at one another as Rumple quietly tried to explain to Edmund what an expression was.

"Did you notice…?" Harold said lowly, so only he and Kafa could hear.

Kafa nodded.

"Keep your sword close," Harold muttered.

"I always do," Kafa whispered, a small smile on his face. The guards led them inside down hallways that Edmund, Harold, and Rumple gaped at while Kafa just casually eyed them. He had worked there once and seen the same paintings and tapestries every day. None of it was new to him. They led them to the Discussion Room, where the guards closed the doors behind them. They looked around, Kafa recognizing most of the faces sitting in the chairs.

"Where's Joanne?" Rumple asked. The Imaginists were silent. They seemed to be looking fearfully at something behind them.

Kafa turned and almost jumped. Kile stood behind them, still as a statue.

"Hello, Kafa. I liked your note. Very… touching," he said, taking it out of his pocket. He blew on it, and it burst into flames. The pieces of charred paper fluttered down to the ground, their edges glowing. Only a few words were still distinguishable, none of them part of the same sentence.

Kafa looked up from the paper back at Kile.

"You were stupid to come here. Now, you will all suffer," Kile said with an evil grin. A second later, something shiny and sharp whipped out towards Kafa. He could hear Rumple screaming his name, but all he could do was just look at Kile and wonder at what point his best friend had been lost.

~~~

Alexai stepped along the roof.

"Which room are they in?" he muttered as he peered down into what had to be the seventh skylight. He sighed in annoyance and continued walking. It was windy up on the roof, and hotter than he was used to. The Eternal Night was always cool or cold or freezing. Never warm, hot, or humid. There were a few birds up on the roof that flapped off whenever he got near enough to them. He continued walking on the roof, careful to not step on a skylight. He looked down and tried to see what was going on inside. Suddenly, he saw them.

"I knew it!" he shouted triumphantly, probably a little too loudly, but nobody was around to hear him. Inside, the Imaginists were watching a scene unfold in horror. On the other side of the room, Kafa, Rumple, Harold, and Edmund had been cornered by Kile, who was currently holding up a knife against Kafa's throat. There was quite a big bloodstain on the floor. Alexai squinted at it and recognized the strange mixture of normal red blood and black demon blood as the blood of a Half-One.

*It's She's blood. It must be. But if that's her blood, where is she?* Alexai wondered.

Kile was saying something, but Alexai couldn't hear him through the glass. It was clear that he was making a threat, though nothing more was clear to Alexai. Kile gestured to the knife he was holding against Kafa's throat, and then to something else. They all turned and paled. Alexai leaned over the glass to see what was the big deal. She and Joanne were tied to a post in the corner, dry plants beneath them. They were both unconscious. She was bleeding from a wound in her side based off the tear in her dress and the black and red blood oozing from it. Alexai could see Rumple mouth Joanne's name and start to move towards her, but Kile said something and pressed the blade harder against Kafa's throat, making Rumple back up. It looked as though it made him sick to not go to Joanne.

*Hmm. What can I do to get them out of there? I am one Dark Elf, and there's six of them… I must be very careful about how I do this… I just have no idea how I'm going to do it,* Alexai thought.

He backed away from the skylight, making sure to remember where it was, before he ran over to a different skylight. He looked into the room, and there didn't appear to be anyone in that room. Alexai smashed his boot through the glass, letting shards of it fall to the ground. He smashed his boot through it again and again, three or four more times so that there was a hole big enough for him to slip through. Taking a deep breath, he jumped through, throwing his arms wide so his cloak would billow out, slowing his fall. When he hit the ground, he rolled and landed in a crouch. He brushed himself off, feeling very pleased with himself. He was in some sort of pantry. He took a bag of flour and put it on his back with his arrows and bow. He walked over to the door and opened it slowly, looking down the hallway to make sure that nobody was there. Seeing no one, he took off at a light run to the right; the direction of where the others were seen. The bag of flour was heavy as it continued to bang against his back, but he knew that for his plan to work, he'd need a distraction. Flour seemed like the best available option.

He walked down a hallway and saw the room. He went up to the handles and saw that they were locked… from the outside, meaning that whoever was in the room was trapped there. He unlocked the doors and opened one just a crack. Kile had moved himself and Kafa over to where Joanne and She were. Rumple, Edmund, and Harold were standing right by the door where Alexai was slipping in. Kile seemed to be more focused on Kafa and the terrified looking Imaginists than Harold, Edmund, and Rumple. Probably because he thought the door was locked. He slid the sack of flour off his back and took out an arrow. He ran a slit down the side of it with the point of his arrow so some flour would fall out when necessary.

Harold, Rumple and Edmund had not yet noticed him as he whispered to them.

"Harold, don't turn around. I am going to slide this flour to you. Put it on your back and fly up so it creates a fog. Then I want you all to run." Harold slowly nodded once to show that he understood. Alexai opened the door a little more and slid the flour to Harold, who used his back legs and wings to nudge it up onto is back.

Alexai shut the door a little bit so he could see but you couldn't tell it was open unless you really stared. Harold shook his head and suddenly shot up towards the ceiling, making the flour fly out of the sack and down below. Harold flew back and forth until the bag was empty and the air was thick with foggy flour, so much of it that it was hard to breathe. Screams and coughs exploded.

"RUN!" Alexai shouted as he threw open the doors and ran in.

Imaginists flew out of their seats and flocked towards the doors. Rumple and Edmund moved out of the way in order not to get trampled while Alexai moved across the room.

"I was right," he muttered to Rumple as he went past him.

Rumple gave him a glare, as if saying, *how could you possibly be thinking about that right now?* but he said nothing, looking a little grateful for the help.

Edmund whipped out his bow and arrow and began firing at the skylights, letting glass rain down into the room before he began shooting at Kile, who was just barely distinguishable through the flour-fog. He still had Kafa and was standing in front of Joanne and She.

"EVERYBODY STOP SHOOTING OR THEY ALL DIE!" Kile shouted.

Alexai had been pulling out an arrow and froze, as did Edmund and Rumple. All of the Imaginists had left already, probably running out into the City for safety.

"Thank you. Very clever, you. Makes sense that you would be the leader of the Darkness," Kile said, smiling at Alexai approvingly, something Alexai wasn't sure how to feel about. Disgusted or horrified? Flattered or sickened?

"Nice little trick with the flour. Smart, I'll give you that, but not enough to defeat me. In case you remember, *you* are imaginary. Therefore, you cannot even hurt me, while I can kill you. You see how stupid it was, charging in here like you had the *Darkness* behind you? So stupid. Now, you have a choice. The door is right there. I won't be able to stop all of you from escaping. So, I will offer you this. I will let all of you go except for Joanne, but *only* if one of you stays and if some of you give me some of your blood. I don't need a Half-One's blood, as I already have hers. But I want the blood of elves. And an animal. Also, a nymph and a vampire. I've got the rest from the Imaginists. So, if the goat and the Light Elf-Dark Elf will step forward, then the rest of you - except for *one* - is home free," Kile said, giving the Stone a little shake.

Edmund, Harold, Rumple, Kafa, and Alexai all looked at one another. Rumple started to open his mouth when Kafa saw what he was about to do.

"No, Rumple. Don't. It's me he wants to stay. I'll stay. The rest of you go," Kafa said.

"But-" Rumple started saying, but Kafa shook his head.

"I've lived for almost two thousand years. You've only lived for fifteen. It's my time, Rumple," Kafa said, a note of sadness in voice. Rumple stared at him, a torn look on his face.

"Kafa, n-"

"Rumple. Go. There's nothing left you can do," he said, finality in his voice. Rumple slowly turned to Joanne, looking like leaving her was the last thing he wanted to do.

"Come on, we don't have all day. Goat and elf, come on," Kile said impatiently. Harold and Edmund stepped forward, Edmund looking a little frightened, while Harold just looked like he hated Kile with every fiber in his body.

"I should have headbutted you in the crotch when I had the chance," Harold said. Kile's eyes flashed.

"Well, good thing you didn't, or we'd have a little dead goat on our hands," he said before taking out another knife. He took Harold's hoof and made a small cut right above it. Blood began to run from it, and Kile collected the drops on the Stone. They dissolved as soon as they touched the smooth surface of the Stone. Then Kile took Edmund's hand and made a cut across his palm. Dark blue Dark Elf blood and light-yellow Light Elf blood swelled up onto his palm. Kile pressed the Stone against it so it collected the blood before he took a step back. His eyes glittered with glee.

"You're all free to go. Have fun!" he said, an evil grin on his face as he waved goodbye.

"Come on," Alexai whispered to Rumple, who had a shattered look in his eyes. Kile snapped his fingers and the bounds around She disappeared, letting her fall to the floor.

"There's that. Now leave," he said dismissively. Edmund walked up to She and threw her over his shoulder. Then he turned and walked out, Alexai following him and then Harold following Alexai. After a few moments and one last glance at his sister, Rumple turned and left, not bothering to shut the doors behind him. They walked out of the Imaginists Palace and into the street, feeling shocked and sad.

"What do you think you'll do to them?" Edmund asked. Nobody wanted to answer him, so all he got was silence.

"Where are we going?" Edmund asked, after he realized nobody was going to say anything. Surprisingly, it was Harold that answered him.

"I don't know, kid. I don't know."

# Chapter Eighteen

Her head throbbed, and every inch of her felt sore. She opened her eyes to light that felt like a sharp jab to her head. She winced and forced them all the way open. She looked around, thoroughly confused. She was in a lavishly furnished room with about thirty chairs, but all of them were empty except for one. In it sat Kile, who was watching her, looking very bored. She flinched, not expecting him to be there.

"Look who's finally awake," Kile said, twirling the chain with the Stone of Existence around his fingers.

"What? How…?" Joanne said in confusion. The last thing she remembered was flying on a Pegasus, then everything had suddenly gone black and she had felt like she was falling… somebody had been screaming her name, but who? She couldn't remember…

"Ask him. I only know part of the story," Kile said, gesturing towards the other side of the room. Joanne turned her head and saw Kafa sitting in the corner of the room, staring out a window and looking somber. Kafa didn't even glance their way when Kile mentioned him. Joanne sat up.

"Kafa! Where are the others? What happened?" Joanne asked, getting up and trying to walk over to him, only to find her ankle jerked back, making her fall to the ground with a surprised grunt.

"What the?" Joanne muttered, twisting to see what had jerked her back. Her ankle had a chain around it that was a strange dark red color that seemed to shimmer in the light.

"Do that again and it might give you a little shock," Kile said as he lightly touched the Stone, the threat he was making clear to Joanne. She crawled backwards so the chain was not pulled taunt.

"Please, don't hurt her," Kafa said, not looking away from the window.

"I can't make any promises if she tries to escape," Kile said, shrugging. Kafa shot him a glare, the first time Joanne saw him look away from the window.

"What happened? Where am I, and why is he here?" Joanne asked, still very puzzled about what was happening.

"He is here because he decided to be here," Kile said. Joanne's confusion shot up a level.

"What do you mean, he decided-"

"I did not decide! I stayed because I wanted nobody else to have to stay!" Kafa exclaimed angrily.

"You still chose to stay instead of letting somebody else do it," Kile said, his face smooth and clear of any emotion.

"Because I have lived far longer than anyone else. If you were going to kill the one that stayed, I would it rather have been me than one of them," Kafa said.

Kile looked at Kafa with something Joanne couldn't read.

"You were willing to give yourself up for people you've only just met," he said in wonder.

"I've known Rumple for three years, and I've met Alexai before. But yes, I was. Because that is what true leaders do, Kile. They are ready to protect those that follow them," Kafa said seriously. Despite his words, Kile looked unimpressed.

"Hmm. How touching. But that won't get you out of here. You two will watch my plan unfold with front seat views. I do need your blood, though, at one point. But that will come later. If I use it now, well, then it will run out of power too soon. I'll collect it later," Kile said, glancing lazily at Joanne.

"You need my blood?" Joanne asked in alarm as she spotted a blood stain on the floor.

"Yes," Kile replied.

"Wait, what happened to our friends?" Joanne asked.

"Tell her, Kafa," Kile said.

"I don't have to do what you say," Kafa said, going back to staring out of the window. Kile raised his eyebrows at his defiance.

"Really? You don't have to, huh?" he said, looking at Kafa with something like amusement.

"I don't," Kafa said, shaking his head.

"We'll see about that," Kile said, then rubbed his fingers together. Kafa screamed in pain, dropping to the floor, before he stopped, breathing hard.

"Don't forget about that little trinket, Kafa," Kile said. Joanne peered at Kafa and noticed a metal collar around his neck. Joanne's eyes widened in anger and disgust as she whipped her head around to face Kile.

"You put a *collar* on him?" she asked, fury in her voice.

"Yes, I did. One must control their animals," Kile said, smiling as if it was something pleasant.

"He is not your *animal*!" Joanne exclaimed angrily.

"Joanne, please. Don't encourage him," Kafa said tiredly. Joanne shut her mouth, despite wanting to leap at Kile and do something to him, like claw his eyes out.

"So, basically, you passed out and we knew that we had to tell people you were real if they were going to stop hunting you, because then they would maybe follow you instead of Kile. So, She took you to the Imaginists Palace on Midnight because you didn't look well and she told them everything. Kile was there, and he stabbed She. Then we arrived, and Alexai went on the roof due to paranoia while we took the gates. We walked inside of this room, and Kile cornered us and showed us you and She, both unconscious. Kile held a knife against my throat and threatened to kill me if they tried anything, and then Alexai came in and created a diversion. The Imaginists were able to get away, but we were not. Kile said he would let us all go except for you if one more of us stayed, and if Harold and Edmund gave some of their blood to Kile. I volunteered to stay, and Harold and Edmund gave some blood. Then they left. Now, you finally woke up, so, here we are. I'm sorry, Joanne. We walked right into a trap and we didn't know… we couldn't get you out. I'm so sorry. So, so sorry," Kafa said, hanging his head at the end of his story.

"Aww, how touching. But yes, everything he said was true. Your friends, your brother, left you. You and Kafa are mine now," Kile said, sounding delighted with it all.

*Rumple left me?* Joanne thought in disbelief. It just seemed so unlike him to just give up and leave like that.

"Good. I wouldn't have wanted them to stay," Joanne said, even though she felt a pang when he mentioned Rumple leaving her.

"You know Rumple wanted to be the one that stayed, but I didn't let him. Leaving you was the last thing he wanted to do," Kafa said.

"Ah, who cares? You two are here now, and you will attend the ceremony tomorrow, where everyone will meet me in the square and watch as I unravel the very strands of Imagine. It will go down in every history book, every record, everything. And I will forever rule and forever be praised," Kile said, a look of greed and crazed excitement in his eyes.

Kafa looked sad as he shook his head.

"What happened? I don't understand what broke you so badly that you want to rule everything, that you want to be so cruel… I just don't understand, Kile. I don't get it," Kafa said, whirling around from the window and staring at Kile with a look of desire to want to understand. Kile sighed.

"*Nothing*, Kafa. Please stop asking me about it. And that's not a request, by the way," Kile said, closing his eyes and leaning back against the chair.

Kafa looked at Kile with a look of giving up before he sat down beside the window, also closing his eyes.

Kile opened his eye after a moment.

"I'm going to go make preparations for tomorrow. If either of you tries anything, I will know and there *will* be consequences," Kile said, standing up. Joanne and Kafa watched him leave in silence. As soon as the door clicked shut behind him, Kafa rushed over to Joanne.

"Are you alright? How do you feel?" Kafa asked worriedly.

"I feel fine. What about you?" Joanne asked.

"Well, I was just shocked like a dog, but other than that, I'm fine," Kafa said, shrugging as he winced at the memory.

"Thank you," Joanne said.

"For…" Kafa trailed off, looking confused.

"For staying instead of Rumple," Joanne said. His confusion disappeared and changed into a small, sad smile.

"Of course. Like I said, he's younger. He deserves to live longer. I am old. If one of us is to die… I would rather it be me than any of them," Kafa said.

"How do you know you're going to die?" Joanne asked.

"I don't know. That's actually the funny thing about this entire thing. Each one of us imaginary friends thought that we would live forever. That we would always exist. We never considered death, because we thought that for us, it was impossible. Oh, how wrong we were. But if death has finally come to grab me after almost two thousand years, so be it. Real humans usually live less than one hundred, so I feel as if maybe I have cheated death. So, if I die, it will be just and it will be my time. If I am to die to… get you out of here, don't hesitate. Do not mourn me. If you do, do it later. Because it is Rumple's fault you are here and my fault that I let you stay. Our goal is to get you out, because I really don't know what Kile wants you for. Your blood, obviously. But I feel as if he wants you for something more… not to frighten you, but it is likely that he will try and kill you-"

"Then I won't let him," Joanne said, her eyes blazing with determination. A small smile tugged at the corners of Kafa's mouth.

"That's the spirit, Joanne. Don't let him. Fight with everything you've- AH!" Kafa said, suddenly breaking off into a cry before he collapsed to the floor again.

"Kafa!" Joanne exclaimed. The doors swung open and Kile walked into the room. He held out a hand.

"Don't help him. You two were plotting to overthrow me, now he must suffer," he said. When he saw that Joanne wasn't moving away, he sighed impatiently and flicked a finger in her direction, making an invisible force pick her up and hurl her against the wall. She cried out when she hit the wall, the force of it causing severe pain in her back, before she slid down to the ground.

"Obey me and things like this won't happen," Kile said as he stepped over Kafa, who was breathing weakly on the floor.

"Don't you care?" Joanne shot at him. He turned his head to look at her, an eyebrow raised.

"About?"

"About Kafa! You two were best friends! How can you just- how can you hurt him like this?" she exclaimed, gesturing and glancing at Kafa.

"I gave him his chance to join me. I was going to offer him another chance, but it's clear that he won't join me at this point," Kile said coldly.

"I mean, if you two were friends, how can you just shock him? How do you have it in you?" Joanne asked, shaking her head and looking at Kile with curiosity and pity.

*What happened to him to make him this way? What did he have to go through?* Joanne wondered.

"Because I know when to focus on my plan. This plan is all I have left. Everything in my way will suffer. Because if I don't have this plan, if it doesn't work… then I might as well have never been created in the first place," Kile said, his voice rising with emotion before it softened to just above a whisper.

"Because *you* made it this way. *You* built up *your* walls. *You* pushed *everyone* away. That's why the *only* thing you have left is this plan. Because *you* made it that way. It's *your* fault, *not* anybody else's," Joanne said angrily. Kile's eyes glittered dangerously.

"Perhaps. But all of the imaginary friends will love me, praise me, when I am finished. Including Kafa. And everyone that is real will cower in fear. Including you," Kile said, his tone a deadly calm.

"I will *never* cower in front of you, you bas-" Joanne's face was suddenly slung back so it slammed against the wall.

"Do not call your king names, Joanne. It isn't good for your health. Do it again and your face might not be as pretty as it once was," Kile drawled.

Something in his pocket buzzed. He took a phone out of his pocket and answered it.

"I'll be back soon. You know not to do anything," he said to the caller. He got up and walked out of the room.

Joanne rubbed the back of her head when suddenly her own phone began vibrating. She took it out of her pocket, surprised it had survived this much. It did have a crack on the screen that wasn't there before, but everything else about it seemed fine. Besides the battery. Joanne winced when she saw the 10%. The call was coming from Adele. Joanne looked around before she picked up. All of her friends were on screen, all of them looking worried.

Before they could explode at her, Joanne quickly spoke as quietly as she could to them.

"Be quiet. I- I'm in trouble. I need help. I'm going to... I think he's going to kill me." Her friends' mouths fell open.

"Is it Kafa?" Penny asked.

"No. No, it's somebody worse. Either way, I could die soon, and I just want you to know that I love all you guys and you- you were the best friends ever. Tell my family- tell them that I love them," Joanne said, her voice breaking and her vison growing blurry.

"Who has you? Who's going to kill you? What's happening, Joanne?" Adele asked, concern all over her face. All of her friends saw her tears and looked scared now. Scared for her.

"You won't be able to find him. You won't be able to find me. We're somewhere else. Something else is happening to me, but I can't tell you. This guy that has me is bad and he's planning to destroy so much... and I think it will affect you. All of you. I think he'll kill me because I could stop him. Only I have the ability, but he already has captured me," Joanne said, shaking her head as she tried not to start crying.

"Who is he? Joanne, we need to know," Alexa said.

"Annie, born in 1967. She's German. That was his Creator. Find her. Find her, because you won't find him. You won't find Kile," Joanne said, shaking her head.

"Kile?" Asha asked.

"Yes," Joanne replied.

"Where can we find you, Joanne? Where are you?" Lola asked.

"You don't want to come here. You really don't," Joanne said, shaking her head again. The door swung open.

"I'm back- what are you doing?" Kile said, walking in, looking at Joanne with lethal eyes.

"N-nothing," Joanne said, covering her phone with her hand.

"Really? Are you sure it's nothing?" Kile asked, narrowing his eyes at her as she slowly began to lift in the air. His eyes began to glow a soft red.

"Yes!" Joanne exclaimed fearfully, careful not to drop her phone.

"Is that so?" Kile asked. Suddenly Joanne felt pressure on her windpipe. She couldn't breathe. He was choking her.

"WATERMORE MALL! THE COMPASS! IT'S ON PURPOSE! IMAGINE! INNOVATE! NO-" Joanne shouted, then suddenly felt a burning, searing sensation across her face, from her temple to her jaw. She screeched in pain, her phone dropping from her hand onto the floor. Joanne could hear her friends, concerned, worried calls from the phone.

"What's this?" Kile asked, bending down and swiping the phone up from the floor. He looked at the screen of Joanne's friends and smiled wickedly.

"Oh, look at this! Friends. How nice," Kile said.

"WHAT DID YOU DO TO HER?" Lola demanded. Kile's smile disappeared, revealing a curled lip and angry eyes.

"This is what happens when you cross me!" he said through gritted teeth before turning the phone to face Joanne. Joanne saw her friends' faces of terror when they saw her and heard their horrified screams. Joanne's face throbbed painfully, as if somebody was pressing a red-hot iron across her face. She sobbed, but her tears didn't help cool the pain.

"You are all out of my reach for now, but not for long. Soon I will be coming, and this will be you! All real people will suffer! All of you will pay for how you treated us! Your fragments of imagination are coming back to haunt you! I shall rule over you all! I am coming. I am Kile," Kile shouted, then the phone crumbled like paper with a sickening crunch as tendrils of red energy attacked it. The phone dropped to the ground, now in unrecognizable pieces. Joanne screamed in anguish on the wall, tears and blood streaming down her face in a waterfall, staining her white shirt. Kile looked at her and smiled.

"You see what happens when you go behind my back? It will no-" he started saying, but broke off, his eyes widening in surprise, when Kafa suddenly tackled him to the floor. Kile fell forward, his hands landing on the sharp shards of phone. They sliced through his palms, but he just regarded them distastefully. Kafa had his arms wrapped around Kile's neck, cutting off airflow. There was a look of rage in

Kafa's eyes, so intense that one would think he was insane. Joanne dropped to the floor and her face stopped burning; Kile's concentration on her lost. Kile tried in vain to throw Kafa off, but was not successful.

"Say it! Say that you'll stop hurting her!" Kafa shouted. Slowly, Kile began to laugh.

"Fine, I'll stop," Kile said, seeming unaffected by the pressure on his windpipe. Kafa released his grip on Kile, rolling off him and landing in a crouch on the ground. Kafa and Kile stared at one another, Kafa breathing hard.

"How- how bold. You never changed much, did you, Kafa? Almost never doing the safest option? I do admire you for your bravery… or stupidity, depends how you look at it. That is the only reason I'm not about to shock the lights out of you. You also forget that since you are imaginary, you cannot touch me. So, that whole attack was pointless. But really, attack me again and you can say goodbye," Kile said, the pieces of phone dropping from his hands and he stood up and brushed himself off. The cuts on his hands were gone, as if they had never happened.

"But one must still learn a lesson. Sweet dreams, both of you," Kile said, then suddenly raised his hands and dropped them. A wave of darkness and tiredness overcame Joanne, and she found herself drifting off to sleep before she could do anything to stop it.

~~~

"Oh, my god! Oh, my god! What the *frick* was that?" Alexa said as everyone else freaked out around her.

"Did you see that? She was bleeding across her face, like a line of blood, like there was a cut… and she was levitating," Karrie said worriedly, adding the last part as a second thought.

"Who was he? What did he do to her?" Penny rambled.

"Everyone needs to calm down! Yes, I know Joanne just told us some very disturbing things, but we need to focus. She said to find her at Watermore Mall. Which is where she was last seen," Adele said calmly.

The cries and screams of her friends died down.

"But the police have looked all through the mall! They didn't find anything!" Asha pointed out.

"Yeah, well, if Joanne told us to go there, she's trying to tell us something. She needs us to find something," Adele said.

"But what is there to find?" Asha asked.

"Um… she said something about the compass. Do any of you guys know about a compass in Watermore Mall?" Alexa asked.

"There was a compass on the floor. It was like a tile design, but it was roped off, like we weren't allowed to get too close to it," Lola said.

"Do you think that's what she was talking about?" Asha asked.

"It could be," Alexa said thoughtfully.

"I mean, I don't know of any other compasses in there," Lola said, shrugging.

"Then we should go now," Penny said.

"Why now?" Adele asked.

"Because she said she thought somebody was going to *kill* her. We have to hurry!" Lola exclaimed. Everyone had been sitting on the floor, but at that moment they hastily got up.

"Come on, let's go!" Adele said, throwing open her bedroom door and racing out into the hallway as she tugged on a pair of shoes. Everyone threw on their shoes and jackets before running after her. They sprinted outside, almost forgetting to close the door behind them. They piled into Lola's car, leaving only one seat empty; the one that Joanne usually sat in. Seeing this sent a pang through Asha.

*We're coming, Joanne. Hold on,* Asha thought as she buckled up. Lola put the keys in the ignition and the engine roared to life. She pulled out of the driveway and then they were off, shooting through the streets of Watermore to the mall.

"Slow down! Jeez, we're gonna get pulled over!" Alexa said from the front seat, clutching her seatbelt like it was a life line.

"Joanne could die! Explain that to the cops if we get pulled over!" Lola exclaimed, yanking the wheel to the right, making skid marks on the road. They sped out of the busy, bustling part of Watermore and into the outskirts by the highway. The mall had police tape strung all throughout it and the amount of police cars had died down the past few days. There were about two police cars at the mall now, though everyone knew they had scoured the mall and found nothing that pointed to where Joanne went. Lola turned the car into the parking lot, killing the engine and leaping out of the car before the others even had time to unbuckle their seatbelts. They filed out of the car and started jogging towards the mall. There was a police officer standing near the door who saw them and sighed. She had been one of the police officers that was on the case and was determined to solve it. She had dark skin and curly black hair that was tied back in a bun.

"Girls, for the last time, we haven't found anything," she said, shaking her head.

"But we *did*!" Adele said fiercely as they stopped in front of her.

"What did you find?" the police officer asked, genuine curiosity in her voice.

"She said to go to the compass," Lola said.

"Compass?" the police officer asked.

"The one on the floor in the center of the mall!" Lola said.

"When did she tell you this?" the officer asked.

"We called her, and she picked up, and she said she was in trouble, and that she thinks somebody is going to kill her and we're all in danger! Then some guy took her phone and- I don't know what he did, but then she had a long cut across her face that was bleeding, and she screamed at us to go to the compass at the mall, and then it just cut off into static after the guy said some stuff," Lola said, only taking a breath once or twice.

"What did he say?" the officer asked, looking concerned now as she took out a notepad and began jotting stuff down.

"He said, '*You are all out of my reach for now, but not for long. Soon I will be coming, and this will be you! All real people will suffer! All of you will pay for how you treated us! Your fragments of imagination are coming back to haunt you! I shall rule over you all! I am coming. I am Kile.*' And then it just went black and staticky," Karrie quoted, sounding haunted. The officer finished writing down things on her notepad and she opened the mall door.

"Come on," she said.

"Do you know what he meant?" Penny asked.

"I don't know… all real people will suffer; your fragments of imagination are coming back to haunt you… he sounds insane to me. It just doesn't really make sense, that's all," the officer said, shrugging.

"I know. That's what makes me worried," Karrie said. The officer nodded. "Have any of you ever heard of this Kile guy?" she asked. They all shook their heads.

As they walked towards the middle of the mall to get to the compass, the officer talked to them with skepticism.

"Well, he could be somebody that she met online, or somebody that she met somewhere else… I'm not really sure what to tell you, girls. We've never had a case like this before," the officer said.

"She meets with somebody but there's no trace of them anywhere, on the cameras or DNA-wise. The next day she seems distressed and then leaves school, going to a fast food place, where she appears to be talking to somebody that's not there. Then her dad calls her where according to her parents and you guys, her old *imaginary* brother takes the phone and starts talking. Then later, you guys call her and she brushes off comments of her imaginary brother and then is showing somebody new that none of us have ever seen or heard of before. She says that she is not in danger. Then she picks up again and she's in some sort of dress shop and again denies any danger. Then, according to you, she answered again today and she started talking about how she was in trouble and none of us were safe. Then the phone gets taken from her and some guy starts talking after showing her on the phone with a bloody face. Then he says that confusing bit and the call disconnects. Every time we try to track her, it shows that she's in different places around the world within seconds, and even if she's in the same place long enough, once police forces get there, she's not actually there, even though her location says that she's there. We searched all of her social media and she never once talked to strangers. We've checked her texts, her browser history… none of it makes sense. None of it. Joanne Raider has baffled police, FBI… even her parents have been interrogated. But nothing has turned up that even points a finger in the direction she went, or where she is. Or the bigger question, what happened. If we find anything, we'll let you guys know, but at this rate, I don't know if we'll find anything," the officer concluded.

They all nodded. They had all been expecting this, but they had just hoped that it wouldn't happen. That they would find something. But they hadn't. They approached the compass and stopped just outside the rope.

"Screw the ole' mall rules," Alexa muttered before she ducked underneath it, the others quickly following suit. They stared at the compass expectantly, as if they expected something to leap out from it. It looked like just a normal compass that was made of beige, faded green, and faded red triangles in a beige circle that was inside of a red circle that was inside of a green circle.

"The letters are wrong," Alexa said in the silence.
"What?" they all said, staring at her.

"Look, the letters. Look at them. They don't stand for North, East, South, and West. They're something else. Look. Im, In, No, Cr," Alexa said, pointing to each one.

"That's… weird. You think they made a design flaw?" the officer asked, peering at it.

*It's on purpose. Imagine, Innovate, No-* Asha remembered.

"No. They didn't. After Joanne said the compass at the mall, she said '*it's on purpose.*' She might've meant the letters," she said, shaking her head.

"Yeah. I mean, remember what she said? Imagine, Innovate, and then she started to say something else," Penny said.

"Im and In. I guess she started to say whatever No was, but then she got cut off," Karrie said, her chin in her hand.

"But what do the words Imagine and Innovate have to do with this?" Lola asked.

"Hmm. I mean, they're both things that you can do. When you imagine something, you're forming a mental image or concept. When somebody innovates, they're like, inventing something or making something new. But I don't know what No or Cr would be," the officer said, looking as though she was trying to solve a riddle.

"Maybe they are all things you do. Things you create. You know what I mean?" Lola said, as she stepped closer to the compass.

"Maybe," Alexa said, thoughtfully.

Lola stepped onto the compass design and gasped.

"What?" Everyone asked.

"I feel something… like there's a current underneath here or something," Lola said.

"Of water?" Adele asked.

"No, but yeah. You know when you stand in a river and you can feel the current around you? It's like that," Lola said as most of them nodded.

"Like… air instead of water?" Karrie asked.

"More like energy," Lola said.

"I want to see this," Alexa said and stepped onto the compass. Out of curiosity, the others also stepped forward. Everyone looked at Lola in confusion except for Karrie and the officer.

"Oh, my god, I feel it!" Karrie said.

"I *do* feel something…" the officer said in amazement.

"I don't feel anything," Asha said, looking down at the compass beneath her shoes in confusion.

"I don't either," Penny said, her brow furrowed.

"Neither do I," Alexa said as she squinted down at the compass.

"I don't feel anything, guys," Adele said, shrugging.

"Why do we all feel something but you guys don't?" Karrie asked.

"Use your imagination," Alexa said sarcastically, doing little jazz hands in the air.

Lola snapped her fingers.

"That's it! I knew it! I knew it had something to do with imagination! Alexa, you're a genius!" she said, a look of wonder dawning on her face.

"Yeah, I know," Alexa said, trying to toss her hair, but it was so short that it didn't really work.

"Think about it. Kile said that our fragments of imagination were coming to haunt us. One of the letters represents Imagine. We saw Joanne's imaginary friend on the FaceTime. What if it has something to do with imagination?" Lola asked.

"Alexa is one of the most imaginative people here, so why can't she feel it?" Asha asked.

"Hmm. What if it has something to do with imaginary *friends*? I had one when I was little. What about you two?" Lola asked, turning to the officer and Karrie.

"I had a few imaginary friends," Karrie said.

"I had one when I was a little girl," the officer said.

"Then what if it has something to do with imaginary friends?" Lola suggested.

"But that's impossible, there's no w-" Alexa started saying, but Adele talked over her.

"Is it, Alexa? Think about this whole thing. Most of it hasn't been even close to possible. Seeing Joanne's old imaginary friend on a FaceTime, seeing random people Joanne should've had no way of knowing, Joanne's location jumping all over the map, and Joanne floating in that last FaceTime. None of it is normal or possible, I'm telling you. Something else, guys. Joanne said it herself. This is something else. Something big," Adele said. There was silence as everyone took in the information.

"Yeah... but what's the big thing?" Alexa asked.

"Nothing good. Whatever it is, it's big, and it's bad, and it's coming," Asha said.

# Chapter Nineteen

At some point they wound up in a café, and a cup of coffee was slapped onto the table in front of Rumple, but it might as well have never been there for the amount of attention he paid it. Edmund and She were having a conversation about… something. They had found some clothing to bandage up her wounds, so for now, She was doing alright.

Rumple found himself slipping away, losing focus. They had been walking aimlessly down the streets of the City, not going anywhere in particular, before Alexai had basically told them that they needed to focus on the problem at hand and had dragged them into a coffee shop in hopes of bursting their energy and their spirits. Alexai seemed lost in thought as Edmund and She talked, while Rumple just stared at nothing, his coffee growing cold. Alexai sipped his occasionally, though not enough, so it went cold on him, too. She had drained hers almost as soon as she got it, and Edmund had ordered her a second one. Edmund had taken small, polite sips, though Rumple knew that he didn't like it.

Harold had flown off to go see if there were any potential break-in points in the Imaginists Palace.

"Rumple! Goodness, you've been staring at nothing and drooling everywhere for the past five minutes! I *said*, is there anything you know about Kile that we could use as an advantage?" Alexai said, looking slightly annoyed, but mostly solemn.

"What? Oh. Umm… his Creator was a little girl named Annie… she said something to him that crushed him and, according to Kafa, made him an entirely different person. That's kind of *it*… Kafa didn't really mention anything else that I feel like we could use," Rumple said, racking his memory for information about Kile.

"Hmm… when did Annie say this thing to Kile?" Alexai asked, his brow furrowed in concentration.

"When he was discarded," Rumple replied.

Alexai nodded thoughtfully.

"Maybe he's doing all of this to prove something… to show something," he said slowly.

"I guess so? But what?" Rumple asked.

"I have no idea… there aren't that many things that can destroy a man mentally, but whatever she said must have been… somewhat Earth-shattering for him," Alexai said, thoughtfully.

"Yeah, I guess," Rumple said. Then Alexai was silent as he sipped his coffee again, his dark yellow eyes unfocused as his thoughts flew elsewhere.

*It's all my fault. Alexai was right. It was a trap and we should've all taken the skylight. If I hadn't been so stubborn, so stupid, then maybe Joanne would be okay right now. She could die, and it'll be all my fault. All my fault,* Rumple thought guiltily, his thoughts spiraling down into self-blame.

She was sitting there, listening to the two of them, and seemed to have noticed Rumple's face and guessed what he was thinking. She reached over and put a hand on his back. Rumple looked up at her. Her face was soft and her eyes comforting.

"Hey. It'll be okay. We'll get them back. Just you see," She said softly, quiet enthusiasm in her voice. Rumple tried to give her a smile, but it felt forced and unnatural. It twitched on his lips before his lower lip trembled and it jerked down at the corners. He felt his face grow warm with embarrassment as hot tears began to gather in his eyes. She's face contorted in pity and sadness, and she reached over and wrapped her arms around him, pulling him into a comforting hug.

"It's okay. You can cry," She said gently in his ear, and despite trying to keep a shred of what was left of his pride, tears began to run down his face and into the fabric of her dress. Because heck, he was a kid, and his only family had just been snatched away from him into the hands of a person who might kill them. When Rumple stopped crying, she gently pulled away and put her hands on his shoulders and looked at him kindly.

"Better?" she asked. Rumple nodded, wiping his nose as he sniffed.

"Thanks," he said. She gave him a small smile.

"Of course," she said, then let go of him and sipped her second coffee. The door of the café swung open and Rumple heard the clacks of hooves on wood flooring as Harold trotted up to them. Alexai turned and looked at him.

"Well?" he said.

"No way in but the skylights, which are now barred up, thanks to you. The best bet would be to try and rescue them tomorrow during this little meet at noon," Harold said, shaking his head.

"The query is, shall they be there or elsewhere?" Edmund asked.

"I have no idea," Harold said.

"Well, the advantage would be to show how much power he has. How much he's accomplished. The disadvantage would be that they'd be out in the open, so it would be harder to protect them from potential rescuers. The advantage of leaving them there is that they will be out of the way. The disadvantage is that somebody could come and rescue him without him knowing until later," Alexai said, using his hands to show the advantages and disadvantages of both cases.

"So, which one do you think he'll take?" Rumple asked.

"Hmm. He's smart, I'll give him that, but *new* leaders like to show off their power when they attain it. Makes people want to follow them, either out of respect or fear. In this case, it would be fear. I think he'll take them with him, which could make a rescue plan a little harder," Alexai said after a few beats of silence.

"And how might we come to their aid?" Edmund asked.

"Well, that's the hard part, since we don't know what he is going to do at the meeting. I would say that we could make a distraction, maybe, and then one or two of us rescue them while he is occupied. The plan is unlikely to work, though. I would prefer to know more. Then I could make a more foolproof plan," Alexai said uncertainly.

"Well, we don't know anything else," Harold said.

"Hmm. Do you think there is a way we could find out more? Any way at all?" Alexai asked hopefully.

"I mean, we'd have to spy on Kile or something like that to find anything, and I don't know how we'd do that without him knowing," She said, shaking her head.

"Hmm. How unfortunate," Alexai muttered.

"Are we going to save them? Or at least try?" Rumple asked.

"We have to try; we don't really have any other hope against Kile except for Joanne. This is one of those situations where we succeed or we die. It's that simple," Alexai said.

"Do we have a plan?" Harold asked.

"Give me time. Let's go somewhere more… private. Come, I know just the place," Alexai said, sliding off the stool he had been sitting on as he slapped down a twenty on the table.

"Keep the change," he called as he walked out of the door. The others followed him, none of them knowing where they were actually going. He led them down the roads of the City, the traffic a little lighter than other times of the day. It was what imaginary friends called the "shush hour", where imaginary friends on one side of the world were being told goodnight and imaginary friends on the other side were about to be used with their almost-awake Creators. The sidewalks were scarce with imaginary friends as some left their shops and businesses and the night shift imaginary friends came in after them. About ninety percent of public places in Imagine were open all the time due to imaginary friends being used around the clock based off where their Creators lived. They had been walking for almost twenty minutes when Harold complained had had enough.

"Are we almost there? My hooves are going to fall off if we don't get there soon," he said.

"Don't worry, we're almost there," Alexai said as he glanced at him.

A huge building loomed in the distance. It had twenty stories and was filled with thousands of shelves, each of those shelves with books crammed on them. It was called the Imagine Library, a place where Imaginary friends went if they wanted to check out books. It had every finished story, even stories that people had made but never shown to anyone else.

"The Library? Why are we headed there?" Edmund asked.

"Because almost nobody is here right now. Besides, they have records here of every imaginary friend ever. We might find something on Kile here," Alexai said, not looking back at Edmund as he spoke. Edmund nodded.

The library was gently lit, enough to read, but not too much to where the brightness would be uncomfortable. It was filled with couches and chairs, tables and cushions. It was about as good as you were going to get as far as libraries went. There were sections for different languages, and different genres. There was even a section of languages that only ancient imaginary friends could read because people in the real world had long forgotten how to read the languages. Rumple couldn't help but feel a pang as he remembered how much Joanne loved libraries; how she had always treated them like holy ground. Alexai led them over to one of the many huge oak desks that had librarians positioned at them.

"Hello. What can I help you with?" an elderly librarian wearing ninja clothes at the desk asked.

*What the actual crap?* Rumple wondered. As he looked around, he noticed that all of the librarians were dressed that way; like ninjas.

"Why are they all ninjas?" Rumple whispered to Alexai. Alexai ignored him. She sighed.

"Haven't you ever been in this library before?" She asked.

"No..." Rumple said.

"All of the librarians are ninjas. Or wizards. But the wizards usually take the day shift," She informed him.

"Umm, okay. That's *totally* not weird," Rumple said.

"You live in Imagine. None of this should be weird to you," She said.

"Yeah, well, I didn't get out of the Unavenged much," Rumple said. She rolled her eyes again.

"Obviously," She muttered. Rumple was about to make a smart remark when Alexai answered the librarian.

"We're looking for information on an imaginary friend," Alexai said.

"Oh, okay. Which one, dear?" she asked.

"Kile. K-i-l-e. He was created around 1970; his Creator was a girl named Annie," Alexai said. She typed in something at the computer she was at and then a manila folder appeared out of thin air. It floated down to the desk and the librarian grabbed it with a grace that shouldn't have been possible at her age. She handed it to them with a sweet smile.

"There you go, hon. Have fun!" she said, then went back to the computer. Alexai took it and led them over to a round table with velvety chairs. They sat down and he opened the folder, spreading the contents on the desk. There were pictures and clips of things, and a page with information. There were seven pictures of a girl, the first one when she was three, the last one when she was ten. She was blond with curly hair and bright blue eyes, grinning ear to ear in every picture. There was also a picture of Kile. He was smiling with mirth, not with the cruelty that Rumple had seen him smile with. His eyes looked brighter and happy, something that Kile hadn't had ever since Rumple had met him. There were clips of magazines and photos that Rumple guessed Annie had taken and cut out. One was a picture of an empty field with Kile in it, while another was Annie on a swing and Kile on the one next to her.

Rumple looked over at the information page.

**KILE ALTER**

**CREATED: APRIL 29, 1970**

**IMAGINED AGE: TWENTY-EIGHT**

**CREATOR: ANNIE ALTER, AGE 3 YEARS AND 10 MONTHS AT CREATION**

**KNOWN RELATIONS: KAFA DUX (FRIEND), DARI HELLFIRE (ASSOCIATE), AND BUSINESS ASSOCIATES**

**BUSINESS: UNKNOWN**

**DISCARDED: AUGUST 21, 1977**

**ADDRESS: 219 BIKER ROAD, IMAGINE**

Alexai turned it over.

"I guess that's it," he said.

"Do you think he has something at his house?" Harold asked.

"It's possible, but I'm not sure if he would have anything we could actually use against him. We already know that Annie basically destroyed him and that he and Kafa used to be close. He seems like he keeps to himself a lot," Alexai said.

"Kafa's last name is Dux?" Rumple said in disbelief.

"Yes. Why?" Alexai said.

"Nothing. I just didn't know his last name," Rumple said, shrugging.

Alexai gave him an exasperated look before he turned back to the folder.

"Hmm. I'm not really seeing anything that would help us out," Alexai said.

"So, what are we going to do?" Rumple asked.

"We rescue them," Alexai said as he stood up.

"How?" Edmund asked. Alexai gave him a wry smile.

"With our guns blazing."

~~~

Joanne opened her eyes slowly. She was on hard ground that was soft at places but rough at others. She looked around. She was in the middle of a group of trees; lying on the ground. She got up; looking around in confusion.

*How did I get here? Where are the others?* she wondered. She looked down and noticed that she was wearing an old jacket from four years ago. *Weird,* she thought. Everything had a strange lighting to it, as if she was viewing her surroundings through a camera filter. She started walking around.

"Kafa? Rumple! Edmund? She? Alexai? Harold?" she called. She heard a noise behind her.

"Kafa?" she asked, turning around. But it wasn't Kafa behind her. It was Kile. She opened her mouth to scream his name, but no sound came out. She tried to run, but she was frozen in place as Kile reached towards her, his eyes glittering.

"All of the real ones will pay," he said angrily.

She woke up with a start, breathing hard and looking around anxiously. She saw Kile sitting in one of the chairs near a still-unconscious Kafa. He was looking at him tenderly as he leaned towards him and was whispering something. Joanne strained and managed to hear what he was saying.

"I'm sure you hate me. I hate myself. For hurting you, for taking your dreams and plans away from you. But it was all necessary. All of it. You'll see. Then you'll be glad, and we can go back to the way things used to be. Two friends against the world. Best friends. I won't have to hurt you, and you won't have to hate me. We'll be happy again," he said gently. *"I hate myself."*

Joanne stood up.

"Then why?" she asked. Kile whirled around, his face showing surprise for a second before he recovered from it, putting on his cruel sneer Joanne was already so used to.

"If you know he hates you and you hate yourself so much, then why do you do it? What could possibly be worth you doing this?" she reasoned.

"Revenge, Joanne. Revenge and the need to explain, the need to prove, the need to show... I don't expect you to understand. You were never discarded. You don't know what it's like, and you never will," he said, acid in his tone. Joanne felt a rush of fury as she thought of Rumple and Kafa being perfectly fine; how they had never done things as destructive as Kile and kept their cool.

"No, I just don't think you could handle it. Every other imaginary friend has gotten over it, and has pressed on. *You* never did. *You* are *weak*," Joanne growled.

Kile looked at her in surprise, as if he hadn't been expecting her to say something like that. Then his face contorted in rage.

"How *dare* you! I am anything *but* weak! I have *power*! I *rule* over Imagine and soon, I will rule over *your* world!" Kile ranted on, even insulting her with profanities.

"You will never amount to *anything*! You *will* die tomorrow, and it will be for a show of power! Your death will be *useless* and will mean *nothing*! Just like you do now. They're not coming to rescue you, you know. They've given up on you. Even your precious little brother that you missed *so* much after you discarded him. Why? Because you are like any other teenage girl. You are not special, and you never will be. You are expendable. There will always be more teenage girls that have no special skills with stupid dreams. You are *weak*. You can't even do anything right now. *I* have power. *I* am strong. *Not you*," Kile shouted, raising his hand and making Joanne shoot up straight in the air, her ankle getting painfully jerked by the chain when she went as high as it would let her. He levitated up to her and took out a ruby red whip as he yelled again and again.

"YOU ARE NOTHING!" he repeated.

Joanne squirmed, her eyes widening in fear. She struggled, trying to get out of Kile's invisible grip. He turned her around so her back faced him and invisible hands took her jacket off, leaving just her shirt. He reached back and brought the whip down across her back, making her screech in pain. It felt as if lines of fire and white-hot energy were racing up and down her face as the whip connected with her back again and again, droplets of her blood flying and splattering on the walls each time he brought it back. Finally, he stopped once Joanne's throat felt raw from screaming and her face was slick with tears. He floated down to the ground and he let her drop. She felt the force of it shake her bones as she hit the ground, but he was already upon her, shoving her back against the wall so she cried out.

"This is what happens to idiots like you who challenge other's authority. It's not good, is it?" he whispered in her ear. He got off her and pointed at the ground in front of him.

"Kneel before your king like a good girl," he said. Joanne hesitated and his hand flew to the whip. She quickly dropped down into a kneel, biting her lip hard enough to draw blood as she tried to keep herself from yelling when she moved and her back throbbed. He smiled, the evilness of it making Joanne shudder. There was a crazy look in his eyes, the one a man would wear after killing everyone he knew and cared for.

*What kind of person were you before, that Kafa cared for? And what happened to change you this much?* Joanne wondered as she tried not to sob. She was alone.

## Chapter Twenty

They settled down in the library behind some couches, hoping that the ninja librarians wouldn't find them and chase them out. It was really the only place that they had to stay. They couldn't go back to the Forest in fears of the Dark Elves finding them, they couldn't go back to the Unavenged because Rumple had been kicked out, and Harold said he couldn't take them to his pen because his mom would get mad at him for bringing strangers into her home. So, they laid down in the library, using some cushions from the couches as pillows. They planned to head to a weapon shop the next morning and get as many weapons as they could before they would head to the square where they hoped to blend in with the crowd so they could get close enough to Kile to find Joanne and Kafa. Rumple had taken the biggest cushion and insisted that he needed his beauty sleep, so everyone else had tiny cushions. They all closed their eyes except for Harold, who wasn't tired. Once his friends' breathing had evened out, he got up from his miserable little spot on the floor and trotted outside. His mother had always told him that going outside was good for a goat and would help clear your thoughts. He sat outside on the sidewalk and sighed as he gazed up at the moon.

*I must be crazy. Why have I stayed with these idiots who think that rushing at Kile is a good idea? Mom wouldn't approve. She'd say that I'd lost it and that I better not get myself killed because she'd have to pay for my funeral. I love my mom,* Harold thought.

Suddenly Harold heard shouts and cries of protest and his friends being kicked out of the library. Like, literally kicked. The ninja librarians didn't mess around.

"Ouch! You hit my-" Rumple started saying, but a tired and annoyed looking Alexai talked over him.

"We don't need to know, Rumple. Has anyone seen Harold?" Harold sighed before he got up and trotted over to them.

"I'm right here," he said.

"Why were you outside, man? Like, what the crap, we were all in there, and then a ninja librarian woke us up and kicked us out, only for us to figure out that you weren't even there," Rumple said.

"I went outside for some air. Why did they kick you out?" Harold asked.

"Apparently they don't want people using the library as a place for sleeping," Alexai said.

"Well, where else have we to go?" Edmund asked.

Slowly, everyone turned their heads to look at Harold.

"What? You're not suggesting… we can't go to my place," Harold said, shaking his head.

"Why not?" She asked.

"Because my mom won't want strangers in our pen," Harold said.

"We're not strangers. You know us," Rumple said.

"I've known you for about a day and the rest of them for about twelve hours," Harold said.

"Yeah, well, at least you sort of know us," Rumple said, shrugging.

"*Sort* of," Harold muttered.

"It's enough. Right?" Rumple said, looking at Harold expectantly. Harold shifted uneasily.

"Well…" he trailed off.

"Well, what?" Alexai asked.

"She just won't let you guys in and she'll look at me disapprovingly," Harold said.

"What if the mother does let us inside?" Edmund asked.

"Then, you're …inside." Harold said blankly.

"I meant; do you believe that there is a miniscule chance she shall let us in?" Edmund asked.

"It's possible," Harold said, eyeing them warily.

"Then let's go. I am quite ready to sleep somewhere," Alexai said, putting his cloak hood up. Harold sighed, knowing he wasn't going to get out of it no matter how hard he tried.

"Fine. Come on," he said tiredly, setting off for the Forest.

"Wait, we have to go back there again?" Rumple whined as they approached the line of trees.

"Yeah, but I live in the Eternal Day part of the Forest. We'll be fine," he said as he walked along the edge of the trees until the leaves went from cool colors to warm ones. The trees were light browns and whites, and the leaves were light yellows, pinks, and oranges. Everything seemed to sparkle, including the sky. Harold led them down a small dirt road through the middle of the trees for about two miles before the trees began to thin and they found themselves in a clearing with a small stream. There was a tiny farmhouse with a huge barn in the middle of the clearing. The barn had once been painted light yellow and the farmhouse had been light purple. Harold took a deep breath before he trotted up to the barn, rapping his hoof on the wooden door that had just a tint of the light yellow it once was. The door swung open just an inch and a goat peered out suspiciously. The graying fur and yellow eyes were just as familiar to Harold as his own face was. He swallowed before he spoke.

"Hi, mom," he said.

~~~

He coughed and groaned as he sat up, peering around, his sight still a little blurry from sleep. Joanne lay on the ground a few feet away, looking like she was asleep. She had the cut across her face that Kile had given her earlier and her jacket was on the floor a few feet away. He squinted at her but noticed out of the corner of his eye that Kile was sitting on a chair right beside Kafa. Kafa didn't flinch, but merely looked up at him.

"What do you want?" Kafa asked. Kile's eyebrows raised a fraction.

"What do you mean?" he asked.

"You're watching me. What do you want?" Kafa repeated.

"I want to explain," Kile said.

"Explain what?" Kafa asked.

Kile swallowed.

"Everything. Why I left. Why I'm doing this. You of all imaginary friends deserves to know," Kile said.

Kafa narrowed his eyes at him suspiciously.

"Go on." Kafa said.

Kile took a deep breath.

"So, I'll start with the beginning. Why I left. I was summoned to- Annie for the last time. She was standing in a meadow, wearing her favorite dress. She said that she wanted to talk to me. I thought she'd just talk about something with me. Like, something that was worrying her. But- but she wasn't. She looked at me and said- said that her parents had forced her to get rid of me. That-" he started saying, but Kafa held up a hand.

"I've always been able to tell when you're lying and you're doing it now. What did she actually tell you?" he asked, his eyes alight with curiosity and slight disappointment that Kile had even tried to lie to him. Kile looked at him and then gave him a knowing but sad smile.

"You're right. I am lying. Fine. You really want to know what tore me apart, what changed me, I'll tell you. She was standing there and she told me it was time for me to leave. I was surprised, and I didn't understand. I asked her why, and she said because- she said that people were going to think she was weird at school if she had an imaginary friend in fifth grade. She said that she wanted to get some new friends, some better friends, ones that she could touch. Ones that were real. She told me that I wasn't good enough. She told me that I was just a fragment of her imagination and she was silly to ever talk to me in the first place. She told me how she didn't enjoy my company anymore, how I was just annoying and embarrassing now. Then she turned and looked at me over her shoulder one last time and said, 'Goodbye Kile.' And I was discarded, just like that. And I was wrecked. My Creator had told me that I *wasn't good enough*. That I wasn't enough because I wasn't *real*. Do you have any idea how much that *hurts*? DO YOU? No, you don't. Linus died. He didn't say something to you that felt like knives to your heart," Kile said, his voice shaky as he shook his head and his eyes grew misty.

"Yes, he did. There's nothing worse than watching your Creator die and them acknowledging that you can't do anything to help them, anything to save them. You just have to watch until their last breath. *That* is knives to the heart, Kile. I have felt pain, too, you just seemed to have forgotten it," Kafa said angrily, memories of that fiery night springing to his mind as he tried to viciously shove them away.

"At least he didn't throw you aside like a toy. At least he didn't abandon you," Kile said.

"At least you didn't have to watch Annie *burn*! Watch her hair go up in flames, watch her clothes burn away and her skin sizzle. You didn't have to see that. I did, and I will never forget it," Kafa said, his voice echoing with pain.

"No. But at least you knew that Linus loved you till his last breath. You had something I didn't. Love from your Creator," Kile said quietly.

Kafa looked over at Kile, pity lacing through him. He had just wanted to be cared about. He had just wanted to be enough, just wanted to be special.

"Kile-"

"Don't. Just let me finish," Kile said, then inhaled shakily.

"I knew I was different. I was empty, so empty. I felt nothing for weeks. Nothing for you, nothing for anything. Then just sadness, which transformed into anger. Anger at Annie for just throwing me aside like that, like our past seven years had meant *nothing* to her. I wanted to do something. But first I had to leave you. I knew you'd never want revenge. You'd never want power, at least not that much of it. I knew that I didn't, before I was discarded. I knew I had changed, and I hated myself for it. *So much*. Every time I looked at you and you tried to make a conversation with me, I just saw *disappointment*. Disappointment that I was no longer the person I used to be. I couldn't take it, seeing that pain in your eyes *every day*, every time you tried to help me, to fix me. But I can't be fixed. Don't you see that? Not anymore. It's too late now to mend me. So, for your sake and mine, I left. I left and I began creating my plan. I would get the Stone of Existence, then use it to take over Imagine and then make an army and take over the real world. I'd find Annie and I'd show her. I'd show her that I'm enough now, and that she'll never be able to just toss me away ever again. Never. And then, once I rule over the real world, we can be friends again. And we'll be happy," Kile said, looking at Kafa hopefully, once he was finished.

Kafa looked at the ground as he took it all in.

*He's hurt. He wants to prove to her that he's worth something. That's why. That's the reason for all of this. Because he was hurt,* Kafa thought. After a minute or two of silence, Kafa looked up at Kile.

"Kile, I'm sorry. If I had known-"

"Then you would have hated my plans," he said sourly.

"No, I would have helped you. I still can, if you just-"

"Help me? Please. I already told you, I can no longer be fixed. I'm broken, Kafa. Shattered. I'm in too deep of this mess. I can't stop what's happening tomorrow, now," he said, shaking his head.

"What's happening tomorrow?" Kafa asked. Dread began to pool in his stomach.

"I can't tell you. But you'll see. I'll let you watch me talk in front of all those people before the next step of the plan is carried out," Kile said, smiling to himself.

"Kile. Please. It's really not too late. If you go back now-"

"Then they'll lock me up forever. I know what happens to guys like me. You know what, they might even use the Stone on me just to make sure I never do something like this again. I'd die. Fade away. Who knows, it might be fun. Peaceful. Free. How come is it that we don't die when our Creators do? How come we live on and we get to see them all die when we just watch? It's not fair, Kafa. IT'S NOT FAIR! I WANT TO ESCAPE BUT I CAN'T!" Kile said, suddenly shouting as tears gathered in his eyes. He slunk down out of his chair and hit the ground beside Kafa. Kafa just stared at him with a slightly open mouth, not sure what to do.

"I want to die," Kile whispered.

"Kile-"

"I'm already dying. Did you know that? The Stone of Existence is draining me, Kafa. Imaginary friends weren't made to hold the power of the Stone. I will die within the next ten years. It will be slow and it will be painful. But then I'll finally get to say goodbye. I'll finally get to be free," Kile said, his voice getting softer as he talked.

*He wants to die. He thinks he's in too deep and he can't get out. Jupiter, I want to help. But how can I help someone that doesn't want to be helped?* Kafa wondered. So, instead he leaned over and wrapped his arms around Kile in a hug.

"It'll be okay, Kile. It'll be okay," Kafa said, trying to keep his voice steady. Kafa could feel his heart hurting for Kile. He had cared about Kile in the past, and he still did. To know Kile's true wishes seemed shocking to Kafa, but it also made sense. What did Kile have to lose? If he got defeated, he got death, which was something he wanted desperately. If he won, he'd get to take over the real world, something the imaginary friends had tried to protect for centuries. Who knew that their biggest threat would be one of their own?

After a moment, Kile hugged Kafa back.

"No, it won't. But that's fine. Don't worry yourself over it. I know you're just trying to make me feel better, but there's no *feeling better* for me anymore. Nothing you say will stop my pain. But I guess that's what friends are for, right? Trying to help even when they know it's a lost cause," Kile whispered as he dropped his arms and stood up, forcing Kafa to let go.

"You're not a lost cause-"

"But the man you became friends with years ago no longer exists. I'm sorry, Kafa. I really am. You keep trying to get the old Kile back, and that, *that* is a lost cause," Kile said, then turned on his heel and left the room, his face emotionless, no more tears in his eyes. Kafa watched him leave before he looked down at himself.

*He's really gone. He changed so much. The old Kile loved life. He never wanted to die. Where did I go wrong? When was I not enough to keep him centered? Jupiter, what am I to do?* Kafa thought, running his hand through his hair and sighing. *What can I do?*

~~~

She stared at the goat as she was greeted by Harold. It looked like a normal goat. It sounded cranky, but it didn't have wings or anything like Harold did. *Are all goats cranky? Because Harold sure is.* She wondered.

"Harold? What the hay are you doing here?" Harold's mom asked.

"Can I spend the night, mom?" Harold asked.

"Umm... who're they?" his mom asked, peering at She and the others behind Harold.

"They're my- friends," Harold said, hesitating as if he couldn't think of how to describe them.

"Gee, what an honor," Rumple muttered, rolling his eyes and crossing his arms.

"Really? Since when do you have friends?" Harold's mom asked disbelievingly.

"Uhm... since a while ago," Harold answered.

"Hmm. I did not know that. Well, if they're your friends, come on in! I have cookies and plenty of extra pens!" Harold's mom said cheerfully as she opened the barn door all the way. Inside was a wood floor covered with hay with a coffee table in the middle of the space. There was a vintage lamp duct taped to the ceiling upside down to offer lighting. There were about ten pens around the sides of the barn. There was a small dog bath in one corner, and a small doggy door that led outside.

"It's glorious," Rumple muttered as he looked around, unimpressed. There were three pens that looked decorated. The first one had a faded pink blanket on the ground and a small pile of dolls. There was also a tiny desk that was crammed with pictures of goats. She recognized Harold in a few of them. The next one had heavy metal rock bands and *Grumpy Cat* posters all over the wall behind it. There was a blue blanket and a small desk that instead of pictures had something on it that was covered by a blanket. The other pen was messy with things strewn all over the floor. It smelled, too. There was a blanket... somewhere.

"Is that your pen?" Rumple asked, pointing at the one in the middle with the covered-up desk.

"Yeah. Home, sweet home," Harold said.

"Nice. What's this?" Rumple asked, taking the blanket off the desk.

"Wait, don't! Aww, too late," Harold said, hanging his head. Rumple busted out laughing in his strange shrill boy laugh.

"What the crap is *this*? Wait, why do you even *have* these?" Rumple asked, gesturing to the things on top of the desk. She tried to suppress a smile. On top of Harold's desk was a collection of Disney character china. There were characters from Mickey Mouse to Elsa, all of them smiling and polished and perfect.

"They're collectables," Harold muttered, looking embarrassed.

Rumple chuckled.

"Right," he said, sounding unconvinced.

"I do not see what is the matter. What is the issue with Harold having possession of a few statues?" Edmund asked, tilting his head to the side in confusion.

"They're not just statues. They're *Disney characters*," Rumple said, trying not to laugh again.

Edmund looked at him in confusion.

"Who?" he asked. Rumple sighed, the almost-laughing look leaving his face.

"Never mind. Dear god, people from the 1600's know nothing," Rumple muttered. Edmund huffed but didn't say anything back. Alexai had a small smirk on his face at the situation, but nothing more than that, as if he found it mildly amusing. She still felt uncomfortable around Alexai, despite him helping rescue her and the others. He had locked her up in the Grove only hours before. She was still a little mad at Edmund, too, for helping her get locked up in the Grove in the first place. He had tried to make conversation since then, which was mainly him apologizing. She had ignored him at first, though as the day wore on, she had begun to talk to him a little. They had been friends in the past, after all. It shouldn't be too hard to become friends again. Right?

"Alright, you guys just make yourselves at home and have fun! I'll be sleeping in my pen," Harold's mom said as she trotted over to her pen and laid down on her blanket. She nodded and looked back at Harold.

"Okay. Go find a pen and shut up. Goodnight," Harold said grumpily before he walked over to his pen and laid down on his blanket, shutting his eyes.

"Do we just lay down on the hay?" Rumple asked, his eyebrows raised.

"Yes. Now shut up," Harold said without opening his eyes. Rumple looked at the pens and then back at the others.

"I am *not* sleeping on that," he said.

"Well, I guess you'll have to stay awake then," Alexai said as he walked over to a pen and laid down. Rumple glared at him before he looked at one of the pens distastefully and slowly walked over to it before laying down, a pout on his face.

Edmund shrugged and went over to his own pen before he settled down in a pile of hay and quickly fell asleep. She sighed and told herself that at least she had a place to sleep before she went to a pen as far away from Edmund's as possible and went to sleep.

*There was darkness and nothingness. After all, it had nothing to sense with, therefore he sensed and felt nothing. It was simply a possibility, one that she might not even take. Then, there it was. A light. A warmth. Something. It didn't feel surprised because he didn't have emotions either. It didn't have any thoughts either to ponder what this light was and why it was seeing it, and why it knew what light was at all. One moment it had known nothing, the next it suddenly knew what light was. The light grew brighter and bigger until it enveloped it. Suddenly it felt. It had something. A body. And it was somewhere. And it could see. Sight was so beautiful and unexpected that it took its breath away. The newfound breath hitched in surprise.* I'm… breathing. *It thought, then blinked in surprise at its own ability to think. There was something around it. It was lying on the ground, green blades of grass in its face and poking at its back. It blinked again and looked down at itself. It was wearing all black, and its skin was pale. It somehow suddenly knew that he was a male human. Before, he hadn't known what anything was, but now he seemed to know what everything was. And then his eyes saw the pair of tiny white shoes. He looked up and saw her. She was about three with curly blond hair and bright blue eyes. She was wearing a red dress and chewing on her fingernails as if she was nervous. Her hair was pulled pack in a ponytail and she was sniffling, tear tracks on her face.* She's crying. *He thought, and suddenly felt an unexplainable urge to make her feel better.*

*They stared at each other for a second before he spoke to her.*

*"Why are you sad?" he said.*

*She looked at him and took a deep, shaky breath.*

*"My friend said she doesn't want to play with me anymore. She said I was a dummy," she said, her lower lip trembling.*

*He sat up.*

*"You're not a dummy. They are for calling you that," he said.*

*Her sniffling stopped.*

*"You think so?" she asked. He nodded. A small smile spread across her soft featured face.*

*"I'm Annie. What's your name?" she asked.*

*"I..." he said, trailing off, for he did not know his name.*

*"Do you have one?" Annie asked.*

*"I don't think so," he said, his brow furrowed as he racked his brain for one.*

*"Then I'll give you a name. Hmm... Kile. Your name is Kile," Annie declared, grinning from ear to ear.*

*"Kile. I like that name," Kile said, smiling at the sound of it.*

*"Do you want to play?" Annie asked.*

*"Play what?" Kile asked.*

*"House," Annie said.*

*"What's that?" Kile asked.*

*"We pretend that we live in a house," Annie explained.*

*"Umm, okay!" Kile said, the smile returning to his face. Annie clapped her hands and giggled in delight.*

*"Come on, I can do the dishes and you can walk the doggie..." Annie said, her voice fading away as the scene changed to something else.*

*They were in a meadow and she was years older. She saw him and turned, a grim look on her face.*

*"Kile, we have to talk," she said, and concern laced through Kile, not fear. Why would he be scared? He and Annie had been best friends for seven years. He had nothing to worry about. Something in the back of his mind suddenly seemed to wake up. An uneasy feeling washed over him and he squinted. For some reason he felt like he had been in this situation before. No, he was being silly. Right?*

*"What is it?" Kile asked, walking towards Annie. She took a deep breath, closing her eyes, before opening them.*

*"Kile... you have to leave," she said, her voice stone-cold and steady. Kile felt like the ground was being ripped out from underneath his feet. Cold shock crashed down on him like a wave.*

Suddenly she disappeared, cold hitting Kile like a winter wind as he sat up so fast that he almost hit his head on the bedframe. He looked around wildly, breathing hard and fast. His sheets were a tangled mess around his legs from what Kile guessed had been him turning and tossing. There was nobody in the room with him. No Annie or anyone else. Just memories. His memories. His ghosts, his demons. He swung his legs over the edge of the bed and let his feet hit the rug. He walked over to the window, throwing open the curtains to reveal the morning sky. Kile glanced over at the clock on the wall. It was 8 a.m.

*Four hours until showtime. Four hours before phase two begins,* he thought as he shut the curtain. He stretched, his bare legs and chest receiving a slight chill from the temperature of the room. He strolled over to the closet that wasn't his and opened the door. His eyes scanned over the clothes before he found the plain black shirt and black pants he was looking for. He slipped them on and left the room, heading down the hallway to the Discussion room. He opened the door just a crack to see Joanne with her jacket tied around her sliced up back sleeping peacefully on some cushions from some of the chairs. Kafa was sleeping nearby, his head lolling forward onto his chest since he slept sitting up against a chair. Kile walked silently over to Kafa and knelt down beside him.

"You just couldn't resist helping out Joanne, could you? Oh, Kafa. You never changed. If only I hadn't either. If only you ... but you'll see. Once it's all done. You'll spend the last years of my life by my side and we will finally be great friends again," Kile murmured, not daring to touch Kafa in fears of waking him up. Then, just as silently as he came, he left without anyone knowing, just like a ghost.

~~~

"Get your lazy butts up! Come on, people, it is 10:30! We need to *move*!" Rumple's voice cut into Alexai's dream, ending his visions of him riding upon his horse through the Eternal Night.

"10:30?" She asked with alarm. Alexai forced his eyes open and sat up, hay stuck in his hair and clinging to his cloak. She was sitting up while Rumple and Harold were already up, standing outside of their pens. Edmund was rubbing his eyes as he sat up. Alexai looked for Kafa and Joanne for a moment before he remembered that they weren't there. He shook his head and stood up, attempting to brush the hay off his cloak.

"Yes, 10:30, and the little performance starts at twelve. It'll take us like, forty minutes to even get to the square. So, we have an hour and a half to mentally prepare ourselves and fifty minutes until we really need to leave," Rumple said.

"Are we to charge into battle without any weapons?" Edmund asked.

"Bro, you have a bow," Rumple said, glancing at Edmund's bow.

"I have one, too, though I don't know if the rest of you have any weapons," Alexai said.

"I don't have anything," She said, throwing her hands up in the air.

"Me neither," Rumple said. Everyone looked at Harold, who stared back at them.

"What? Do you think that *I* have a weapon on me? Come on, idiots, I'm a *goat*! How would I even *use* a weapon?" Harold asked indecorously.

"I don't know, maybe your eyes shoot lasers or something," Rumple said, scratching the back of his head. Harold just stared at him.

"*If* I had any, you'd be toast right now," he said after a moment.

"Never mind then," Rumple muttered.

"Well, we shan't go into battle with no weapons upon ourselves! We must go and search for them on our journey to rescue the others!" Edmund declared, standing up, a small shower of hay raining down from his robe.

"Where exactly would we get weapons? You guys seem to keep forgetting about that tiny detail," She asked, her chin resting atop her fist.

"Umm... that is a good question," Rumple said. After a moment of silence, Rumple snapped his fingers, a grin on his face which seemed to quickly fade away.

"What?" She asked.

"Umm... this might not work. So. But I'll say it anyways. You know what has a bunch of weapons that's not a weapons shop?" Rumple asked, looking as if he dreaded his own answer.

"No," Harold said. Alexai's brow furrowed and his eyes closed as his mind raced around, trying to determine any possibilities.

*Hmm. Where would Rumple know that we wouldn't? Where has he been? The City. It must be in the City, though that is very broad. Who did he hang around with and where in the City? Kafa. It's Kafa, and he was... It's the Unavenged,* Alexai thought, his eyes snapping open.

"The Unavenged!" he blurted out. Everyone stared at him.

"Good job. Yeah, that's right. The Unavenged," Rumple said. She sighed, rolling her eyes.

"Must we really go there? That petty little group wouldn't be very happy if we did," She said. Rumple looked offended.

"*Petty*? What're you calling petty, Ms. I-cry-when-I-get-arrested-because-I-have-no-positivity?" Rumple asked somewhat angrily, a hand on his chest. She's eyes blazed.

"Really? Well, let me start. The Unavenged are a band of worthless idiots-"

"Will everyone shut up? We just all slept in my mom's barn together and you people are arguing about what might be our best option," Harold complained. Rumple crossed his arms and She huffed.

"Fine," Rumple muttered.

"So, you are suggesting that we all run along to the Unavenged?" Edmund asked.

"Yes," Rumple said.

They looked at one another.

"It's probably our best option. Now come. If we are to make it to the Unavenged and then the square in time, then we must leave now," Alexai said, leaping over the gate of his pen and pulling his cloak close as he strode over to the barn doors.

"You heard him. Let's move, peeps," Rumple said, awkwardly half-leaping over a hay bale. She sighed while Edmund sprung up and over his pen gate cheerily. Harold called out and said goodbye over his shoulder to his somehow still sleeping mom.  He walked up to the barn doors and butted them open with his horns. They filed out, She the last one to do so.

"Okay, let's move," Rumple said, pointing towards the direction of the City. The outline of skyscrapers could just barely be seen over the tall trees despite how close they were to the City. They set off through the Forest, Harold leading the way. They walked the same path they did yesterday, the amount of light the exact same since night never fell in the Eternal Day. The grass and greenery brushed against Alexai's cloak, though he paid it no attention. It might as well be nothing for how much Alexai cared about it. They made it to the edge of the Forest and walked out onto a sidewalk. The City was eerily quiet. There were almost no cars on the roads and only a handful of imaginary friends could be seen walking around. Those who were kept their heads down and looked somewhat frightened and on edge, as if they expected to be jumped at any moment. Almost all of the shops were closed as well, which never happened in Imagine. They all stared at it.

"Everyone's scared. They think that Kile's going to hurt them," She said, half to herself.

"He probably will," Rumple said. They were silent at his words for a few seconds before Alexai spoke.

"Then it's our job to stop him," he said, then set off down the sidewalk in the direction of the Unavenged.

"Wait, how do you know which way it is?" Rumple asked as he jogged to catch up with him.

"I've seen maps before. Despite what you may think, I am not a cretin," Alexai said.

"A what?" Rumple asked. Alexai waved his hand dismissively.

"Forget it," he said, sighing.

Harold trotted to Alexai and the others fell in line behind him.

"They seem to think that Kile is going to attack them when they go out. No, he won't do that, but he will strike at the meeting that I'm sure most imaginary friends will attend, including us. I don't know if he'll strike at them or something else… his motives are still a bit unclear to me," Alexai said thoughtfully, mostly to himself.

"Just a bit?" Rumple asked dryly.

"Yes," Alexai said.

"So, you don't know what he's planning?" Rumple asked.

"No, I don't know. I'm not a genius, Rumple, though I'd like to think I'm pretty smart. Considering he and Kafa's past friendship, it's likely that Kafa knows the plan by now, whether Kile told him or he simply figured it out," Alexai said.

"Why do you think that?" Rumple asked.

"I don't know, it's just probable. Now shut up, I'm thinking," Alexai said, slapping a hand over Rumple's mouth and silencing any remarks he would have had. In reality, he wasn't thinking, but he needed everyone to be quiet. Their constant pointless blabbing was beginning to wear on Alexai's nerves. They walked the streets, not having to worry about looking both ways since practically nobody was out and about anyways. Slowly, the quality of the buildings got worse and worse, the sidewalks became cracked, the parked cars became broken-down, and the few people looked dangerous and shady.

Thankfully, nobody approached them, they just eyed them strangely. Alexai didn't blame them. After all, they were a strange crowd of people. One Dark Elf, which was strange because they rarely left the Eternal Night, one Half-One, also weird because they also infrequently left the Eternal Night, a goat with wings, which was just plain odd, a half Light Elf and half Dark Elf was just unheard of, and then there was a seemingly normal looking twelve year old boy, which made it peculiar because he was traveling with such an odd crowd. Alexai suddenly stopped, causing Rumple to crash into him. Alexai resisted the urge to roll his eyes.

"Why did we stop?" Edmund asked.

"Because now we are fairly deep into the dark part of the City, and the Unavenged hotel is not on a map, so I don't know which way to go. Rumple, lead the way,"

Alexai said, throwing his arm out and gesturing to the buildings, streets, and the occasional vegetation around them.

"Gladly," Rumple said, before ducking underneath Alexai's arm and setting off towards the road that went to the right. They walked down it for a few minutes before Rumple suddenly veered to the left off the road between two buildings. Everyone followed him, curious to see the Unavenged hotel. The grass crunched underneath their shoes, the sound of it seeming terribly loud in the silence. Alexai noticed that the ground was slowly going downhill, towards a building at the center of a shallow valley. There was a road leading away from it into another part of the dark part of the City, but there was no road from the direction they were coming from. When they were a couple of yards away, Rumple stopped.

"Okay, last time I was here, Kafa got overthrown and then I was attacked. So. We should probably be careful," he said.

"No dip, Sherlock. Yeah, and then I came in and saved your life," Harold muttered.

"How did you even know to come and save us?" Rumple asked.

"I'm a goat taxi. I feel when people are falling, and I catch them. The end," Harold explained, shrugging.

Rumple stared at him.

"That's weird, but okay," he said before turning back around and walking towards the hotel. There didn't seem to be anyone outside, but Alexai kept one hand near his bow just in case. As they grew closer, the features of the hotel revealed itself to Alexai. There was some graffiti on it from Unavenged members and some of the windows were broken out, but other than that, it looked okay. There was an empty stable nearby and something that looked like an arena behind the hotel.

"The Unavenged will get their revenge," Rumple said as he went up to the door. Then he pulled on the door, as if he expected it to open, but nothing happened. Rumple looked at the door in confusion.

"What is it?" She asked.

"Umm. The password didn't work," Rumple said, still staring at the door as if he thought it was still going to spring open any second.

"Really?" Harold asked.

"The new leader probably changed it. Who did you say was the new leader?" Alexai said, looking over at Rumple.

"Umm, Dari," Rumple answered.

"Hmm. Yes, she works for Kile. It is likely that she changed it. But to what?" Alexai said to himself.

"Perhaps 'tis something to do with her own name," Edmund said.

"What, you think she just says her name and it opens up? That'd be really dumb of her to do," Rumple said, rolling his eyes. Suddenly Alexai's elf ears picked up the sound of grass crunching behind him.

"Somebody's coming," he and Edmund said at the same time, Edmund's ears having picked up the same thing.

"Where?" Rumple asked, looking around. Suddenly a voice came behind them.

"What the- Rumple? What the hell are you doing here?" a voice asked. Everyone whirled around in surprise as icy fear laced through their stomachs. A man in his late teens stood behind them. He was wearing bleached jeans, a faded black t-shirt, a faded flannel jacket, and black shoes. He had hair such a light blond it was almost white, and he had black eyes that seemed to stare into Alexai's soul. His skin was alarmingly pale, though he didn't look sick.

"Phoenix! Um, hey! What are you doing here?" Rumple asked, trying to casually lean against the hotel wall, though it failed miserably.

"Uhm, I'm a member here, remember? Like you. Where were you?" Phoenix asked, peering at Rumple.

"What do you mean?" Rumple asked, his voice rising in pitch.

"You disappeared for a few days, and now you show up with these clearly not-Unavenged people that I've never seen before," Phoenix said, gesturing towards Alexai and the others.

"Well, they're my friends," Rumple said before letting out a nervous peal of laughter.

"I'm flattered," Harold muttered.

Phoenix stared at Rumple.

"Last time I checked, I was your *only* friend," he said.

"Yeah, well, you're still my best friend. These suckers are just… people. And elves. And a goat! Goats are really nice, you know-"

"Rumple, what's going on?" Phoenix asked, cutting him off.

"Umm. We kind of need inside," Rumple said sheepishly.

"But you're a member of the Unavenged. Surely you know the new password…" Phoenix said, trailing off when he realized that Rumple did not know the password he spoke of.

"I don't," Rumple said.

"But Dari told everyone, how do you not know?" Phoenix asked.

"Well I was sort of away, and, um, yeah, I didn't hear it," Rumple said, scratching the back of his neck.

"It's, '*Fear the new leader'*," Phoenix said.

"What, is Dari talking about herself or something?" Rumple asked.

"With all this Kile stuff going on, I don't know," Phoenix said, shrugging.

"Hmm. Well, thanks buddy! You're the best!" Rumple said, turning back to the door.

"Fear the new leader," Rumple said, and the door swung open. Rumple did a small fist pump before Phoenix spoke again.

"Wait, were you one of the people Dari kicked out?" he asked. Rumple froze, paling slightly.

"Umm… what makes you say that?" Rumple asked.

"Oh, my grave, you were," Phoenix said, running a hand down his face.

"Oh, my grave? That's different," Harold muttered.

"He's a vampire, obviously. He can't say god," Alexai said.

"Oh," Harold said.

"But if he were a vampire, wouldn't he be burning up?" She asked.

Phoenix glanced at them.

"I was imagined to be half human so I don't burn in the sun," he explained.

"Well, so what if I was? All that matters is that I need to get back in and then I'll leave," Rumple said.

"Why do you need to get in?" Phoenix asked.

"To get weapons," Rumple said.

"For what?" Phoenix asked.

"That ceremony thing Kile's holding. We're going to go crash it," Rumple said casually. Phoenix's almost invisible eyebrows raised.

"You can't be serious, Rumple," Phoenix said.

"I am. Kile's got my Creator," Rumple said, sadness flickering across his face.

"Rumple!" Edmund hissed.

"No point in hiding it now. Everyone's gonna know soon," Rumple said, shrugging.

"Joanne Raider is your- wait. Joanne Raider *is* your Creator. I knew that her name sounded familiar! But she's real. How did she get here?" Phoenix asked, confusion written all over his face.

"I'll explain some other time. Thanks for letting us in, Phoenix. Hope to see you later!" Rumple said, before ducking into the Unavenged hotel. Everyone followed, including Phoenix.

"Hang on, you're going to crash the ceremony?" he asked.

"Yes," Rumple said as he walked towards the tunnel entrance.

"You're going to try and stop him?" Phoenix asked, sounding surprised.

"Oh, my god, yes! I already said that," Rumple said, sighing as they descended into the tunnels.

"I want to join in," Phoenix said.

"You wish to help us and our cause?" Edmund asked.

"Yeah," Phoenix said.

"Are you sure, man?" Rumple asked, glancing at Phoenix.

"Yeah, I'm sure," he said.

"You could die," Rumple said.

"Well, a lot of people are going to if I don't, so… who cares? I've lived pretty long anyways," Phoenix said, shrugging.

"Okay, man. Welcome to the team. Follow me," Rumple said before he sat off into the tunnels, the others following him without hesitation.

"I'm Edmund," Edmund said to Phoenix as they walked, extending his hand to him. Phoenix took it and shook it, giving him a warm smile.

"Phoenix," he said.

"Your name is Phoenix, and you're a vampire?" Harold asked.

"Yeah. Is that weird?" Phoenix asked, swiveling his head around and looking down to face Harold.

"Not really. You *are* talking to a speaking goat with wings, so you know. I'm Harold by the way," Harold said, once again somehow shrugging his shoulders. Phoenix nodded again, smiling.

"I'm She, since everyone seems to be introducing themselves," She said, glancing over at Phoenix.

"Alexai," Alexai said, lost in thought and not looking at Phoenix.

Phoenix nodded.

"Well, it's nice to meet you all," he said.

"Mm-hmm. I know," Harold said.

Phoenix looked at him with a strange expression but didn't say anything. They arrived at the weapons room that was beneath the arena. Edmund and Alexai got more arrows for their bows while everyone else browsed the tables and shelves for their perfect weapon. Rumple grabbed a silver pistol and put it in a holster with such grace that Alexai wondered if Rumple had used pistols before. Harold chose a strange kind of rocket thing that he strapped to his back while She picked a small dagger. Phoenix just grabbed a sleek black gun and clipped it to his belt casually, though Alexai knew that with his vampire senses and strength, he probably wouldn't even need the gun.

"All right, let's move. What time is it?" Rumple asked as he turned back towards the tunnels.

"About 11:25," Phoenix said.

"Crap, we've got to *move* or else we're not gonna make it on-time," Rumple said, then set off into the tunnels at a brisk pace. Everyone hurried after him, the little time left motivating them to move faster.

"We're going to have to run or something, because I don't know how we're going to make it otherwise," Rumple said.

"We can take my van," Phoenix offered.

"You have a van?" She asked, looking interested.

"Yeah," Phoenix answered.

"We are now taking the van instead of running, thank goodness," Rumple announced.

"Does it have room for all of us?" She asked.

"Yeah," Phoenix replied. They broke out of the tunnels and into the Unavenged lobby, which still looked the same except for the Greek signs being gone. They raced out into the parking lot, Phoenix steering the group towards a black van with white graffiti for heavy metal bands on the side. Phoenix got in the driver's seat.

"I CALL SHOTGUN!" Rumple screamed as he got in the front, before anybody could stop him. Harold didn't want to sit in the back and insisted on hogging all the seats in the middle, so She, Edmund, and Alexai were crammed together in the back, Alexai in between Edmund and She to make sure they didn't argue.

"I am getting into the van of a vampire I just met. Mom wouldn't approve," Harold said.

"Well, you can trust me. I'm a good driver, if I do say so myself," Phoenix said, flashing a grin at Harold. His fang teeth were a little sharper than a normal person's, though not by much.

"Do you drink blood?" Harold asked as Phoenix began to back out.

"What? Oh, yeah, I do. Don't worry, I only drink animal blood," he said casually, then noticed Harold's panicked face.

"Oh, sorry. I meant not you. Like… already dead animals," Phoenix said, looking sheepish.

"This is Imagine. Where do you *get* dead animals?" She asked, paling a little.

"Uhm… there are vampire hotspots throughout the City. They serve dead animals there. They also serve blood," Phoenix explained, not looking bothered by this. Everyone else looked disturbed except for Alexai and Rumple, who were both acting as if it was completely normal.

"But, anyways, this whole thing is happening at the square, right?" Phoenix asked.

"Yeah," Rumple said. Phoenix turned down a road and they began driving towards the square. Towards Joanne and Kafa.

# Chapter Twenty-One

Joanne woke up to her back still throbbing and feeling a little light-headed, but she still felt better than she had earlier. She opened her eyes and saw Kafa watching her from beside her.

"Joanne! You're awake! How do you feel?" Kafa asked gently, leaning towards her a bit, concern and something else in his eyes.

"Like my back got used for target practice," Joanne said. Her voice sounded rough and croaky and hurt a little when she talked from all the screaming that she had done the day before. Kafa's face hardened.

"Did Kile whip you?" he asked seriously. Joanne nodded. Anger and something like defeat flickered through his eyes. He hung his head, looking ashamed.

"How could he... I didn't know that he'd ever go that far. I'm so sorry Joanne. I'm so sorry that I couldn't stop him-"

"It's not your fault. You were unconscious. I started saying things he didn't want to hear. I was the one making him mad and I knew it. I did this to myself. There's nothing you could have done, Kafa," Joanne said, shaking her head. He sighed.

"I know. But I can't help feeling bad. Just because I knew him in the past. Maybe if I had done more, he wouldn't be the way he is now. Or maybe nothing I could have done would have prevented this. I guess I'll never find out," Kafa said, staring off into the distance as he remembered Kile in the past.

"I guess not," Joanne said. They were silent for a minute or two until Joanne talked.

"Kafa?" she said.

"Hmm?" he said, still staring at the wall. She swallowed.

"Do you think Kile will kill us today?" she asked.

Kafa looked a little surprised, then a little sad.

"Do you want me to be honest with you?" he asked, not meeting her gaze. She nodded gravely.

"I think that there is a very high chance that we won't make it out alive today," he said slowly. Joanne nodded, the tiny flicker of hope she had extinguishing.

"I should have never let you stay in Imagine," Kafa said guiltily, shaking his head.

"Saying sorry or regretting it isn't going to change anything. I wanted to stay anyways. I had to try and stop him-" Joanne said, her voice cracking. Kafa put a hand on her arm since her back was still in pain.

"It'll be okay, Joanne. Don't worry. We'll be fine," he soothed, trying to sound convincing.

"I know. It's everything else I'm worried about," Joanne said quietly. Kafa looked grim.

"Me, too, Joanne. Me, too," he said just as the door swung open and Kile stepped in, dressed in all black with Kafa's old crown atop his head. He grinned evilly.

"You two ready to start the show?" he said, a broken, crazed look in his eyes. Kafa and Joanne looked at each other and then back at Kile. One thing was for sure. It would be hard to make it out alive, but they would try together until the end.

~~~

Phoenix swerved onto another road at the last possible second, almost hitting a blue giraffe, with Rumple randomly screaming in his ear.

"GO RIGHT!" shouted Rumple. Phoenix wasn't sure his hearing would ever recover.

"I almost hit that guy!" he exclaimed, looking at Rumple like he was crazy.

"Yeah, I know. Good job on not doing that, by the way," Rumple said, giving Phoenix a not-so-reassuring pat on the shoulder.

Phoenix sighed and turned his attention back to the road.

"You're going to be the death of me," Phoenix muttered.

"If this goes wrong, Kile will be the death of you, not *that* idiot," Harold said from the back.

"Yeah, I guess you're right," Phoenix said as he snorted from laughter.

"Of course, I'm right. Kids these days don't even know what they're talking about half the time," Harold said.

"He's kind of cranky," Rumple whispered.

"No kidding," Phoenix muttered. Phoenix heard Alexai exhale what was a held-back laugh behind him.

*Elf ears probably heard me,* Phoenix thought.

Phoenix had decided to leave the Unavenged and go with Rumple and the random imaginary friends, because they were honestly his best bet. The Unavenged had become corrupted and just terrible, really, the past few days that Kafa had been gone. Kafa had run the Unavenged smoothly and always made it perfect for everyone and tried to fix problems if any arose. Dari, on the other hand, didn't seem to care about anything but herself. She was a horrible leader, not breaking up fights or trying to keep order in the Unavenged. Phoenix was honestly about to quit when Rumple had showed up, who was Phoenix's best friend. They had been friends since before Rumple even got discarded. Then when he was discarded, they decided to join the Unavenged together. They had been friends so long, hanging out in each other's hotel rooms late into the nights, until almost a week ago when Rumple had started acting really strange. Then he suddenly just disappeared for a few days. Well, not disappeared, but whenever Phoenix tried to get over to him, he'd be gone before he arrived, always with some blond girl.

When Kile hacked the news system, he recognized her as Joanne Raider, a girl that Kile wanted for some reason. He hadn't really thought of it much, her face and name tugging at his mind but never telling him anything. Then Rumple had said they had his Creator, and everything came together. But there was still the matter on why Joanne was in Imagine and how she even got there, something that Phoenix was sure had to do with Rumple.

Phoenix turned down a few more roads before he had to stop. There was a long line of cars and they were at the back of it. Phoenix sighed and hit his palm against his leg in frustration. He turned to Rumple.

"Now that we're in traffic, spill it. What happened with Joanne? How did she get here, why is she here, the entire enchilada?" he said, then looked at Rumple expectantly, ready for some stupid story or some amazing one.

"Umm, okay. So, basically, the Stone was stolen, and I knew only somebody real could defeat the guy who stole it. So, I slipped through the growing holes in Imagine's fabric and told Joanne everything, persuading her to come with me. I took her to the Unavenged and she joined, and then Kafa figured out she was real and he decided to help us. Well, some crap that I'm not gonna explain happened, and Kafa got overthrown and me and Joanne were basically kicked out because Dari works with Kile. Then we ran around and got captured and met some peeps and Joanne rescued us but then she wasn't okay, so we took her to the Imaginists because everyone was hunting her and we thought if we made it known she was real, people would join her and not Kile. But then Kile was there and he captured her, so yeah. Now we're going to rescue her and Kafa at the ceremony thing. That's what is going down. And we're going to get them back and maybe fight, but we'll probably just end up running," Rumple explained, the imaginary friends in the van listening as well.

"You left a lot out," She said.

"I covered the main bullet points," Rumple shrugged, nonchalantly.

She sighed and rolled her eyes.

"Umm. Wow. Okay. That's actually pretty weird," Phoenix said slowly.

"What did you think I was going to say?" Rumple asked.

"I had no idea," Phoenix said honestly.

"Well, now you know what kind of crap we're in. And now you're in it, too. So, welcome to the group of stupidly brave people!" Rumple said with false cheeriness.

"Whoopee," Phoenix muttered.

"I know, right? It's just great," Rumple said, sarcasm practically dripping from his words. Phoenix looked back at the road. They hadn't moved an inch since a few minutes earlier.

"What is going on?" Phoenix muttered. Sure, there was traffic in the City, but it was never *this* bad, even this close to the square.

"I have no idea," Harold said.

Phoenix sighed, since it had kind of been a rhetorical question.

"Everyone is going to the square at once. This is your result," Alexai said, gesturing out towards the traffic in front of them.

*He's probably right,* Phoenix thought.

"Well if they're all going to the square and we haven't moved in this long, that means that we're not going to move anymore. Come on. We're walking now," Phoenix said, killing the engine and slipping the keys in his pocket as he stepped out into the street filled with halted traffic. Harold grumbled as they all got out of the car about his poor hooves. The smell and smoke of car exhaust was thick in the air, making everyone except for Phoenix cough, since he didn't need to breathe in the first place. He led the group over to the sidewalk.

"It's this way, right?" he asked, glancing over his shoulder at Rumple.

"Yup," Rumple replied.

"What's Kile going to do at this ceremony?" Phoenix asked.

"We don't really know yet, but we'll get back to you whenever we do," Rumple said.

"Wait. We're just going to barge in there when we don't even know what's going to happen?" Phoenix asked, his eyebrows raised.

"You are correct, sir," Rumple said.

"You are all crazy," Phoenix observed.

"It's *them*. I just got involved because I don't want to live with my mom anymore," Harold said.

Phoenix snorted. *This goat is hilarious,* he thought.

"Okay, then," Phoenix muttered.

"What time is it, Phoenix?" She asked. He turned his head to look at her. She was actually quite beautiful, with a soft-featured face, silky curly brown hair, and bright blue eyes. He tried not to stare and forced himself to glance at his watch.

"11:47," he said.

"Crap, we've got thirteen minutes," Rumple said, then started walking faster, to the point where he might as well have been jogging.

"I know, I can do math," Harold said dryly. Rumple shot him a withering glare over his shoulder but didn't say anything, despite looking like he desperately wanted to. On the road, imaginary friends were beginning to get out of their cars, realizing what Phoenix had realized a few minutes ago.

"Perfect. A wave of people will go onto the sidewalks with us and we can blend in with them, then just get close enough to Joanne and Kafa to rescue them before we attempt to kill Kile," Alexai said, a pleased smile on his face.

"We're killing him?" Phoenix asked in surprise.

"We shall try, but if Joanne is too weak, we shan't kill him and we shall run instead," Edmund explained.

"Do you think they'll even be at the ceremony?" Phoenix asked.

"Well, he's a new threat, so it's very likely that he'll bring them as a show of his power to frighten everyone further," Alexai said.

"Oh," Phoenix said, images of what the ceremony might be racing around his head.

"Do you think he shall sacrifice one of them?" Edmund asked. Rumple paled considerably and looked sick beside Phoenix.

Alexai looked thoughtful, scratching the back of his head.

"It's definitely possi-"

"Probably not," Harold said hurriedly, surprising everyone that he was trying to keep Rumple from freaking out as he shot Alexai a warning look.

'Shut up,' Harold mouthed to Alexai. Alexai looked mildly annoyed that he couldn't speak his mind, but rolled his eyes and sighed quietly.

'Fine,' he mouthed back. Phoenix looked over at Rumple and could practically see the guilty thoughts that swirled around his head. He looked like he might vomit, so Phoenix placed a hand on Rumple's shoulder.

"Hey, it'll be fine. We'll get Joanne and Kafa back. Just you wait," he said.

Rumple nodded and gave him a weak, grateful smile. Just as Alexai said, people flowed into the sidewalk, and soon, She, Edmund, Harold, Alexai, Phoenix, and Rumple were just another few faces in a crowd of hundreds. Hopefully it would be enough, though Phoenix wasn't really sure if it would be or not.

They gushed towards the square in the very center of the City, near the Imaginists Palace. As Phoenix looked around at all of the faces, he noticed that every one of them looked scared. Scared of what was going to happen at the ceremony, and scared of Kile. Phoenix couldn't blame them, since he felt the same way. Kile had the Stone of Existence. He could do anything he wanted. And they could do nothing about it.

The tallest of all the skyscrapers in the center of the City were around a huge expanse of earth-toned cobblestones in the shape of a square. The skyscrapers towered so high that the square was usually shadowed by them, only completely lit up at noon, when the sun was directly above the square. There was a stage on one side that held plays every holiday. Chairs were set up whenever that happened, the area big enough to seat hundreds. Now it had to hold thousands. There was no doubt that Kile would use the stage. It was perfect, it was theatrical. Most of the square was already filled up, but thankfully, there was still room for Phoenix and the others. He noticed vampires sticking to the shadows of the skyscrapers, which were almost nonexistent due to where the sun was in the sky. Phoenix could feel the tension in the air, so thick it was intoxicating. People were worried, scared and tense, making a tense combination that was contagious to everyone else.

"Are you guys ready?" She asked. Everyone looked at one another and nodded, though nervousness twisted in Phoenix's stomach. There was a church, the biggest one in Imagine, about a mile away from the square. The church bell chimed in the distance, twelve times to dignify the time, each chime sounding like another nail in everyone's coffins. The quiet, nervous chatter died down by the time the bell finished chiming. Then there was silence and suspense. Everyone was looking around, ready for when Kile would make his appearance. Suddenly, his voice echoed around the square, though nobody could see where it was coming from.

"Citizens of Imagine! Welcome to the show! You are about to experience history. This will go down in books forever, and this day will always be remembered. So, enjoy yourselves. Relax. For I am your new leader. I am Kile," his voice rang out.

People began pointing at the tallest skyscraper in the City, which was directly opposite from the stage on the edge of the square. Phoenix turned and squinted up at the skyscraper, his eyes just making out a figure standing on the edge of the roof.

"I can't see anything," Rumple muttered.

"I can," Phoenix whispered.

"Frickin' vampire sight. What do you see?" Rumple whispered.

"Somebody's on the edge of the skyscraper roof," Phoenix answered.

"What?" Rumple asked, forgetting to be quiet.

"Shh!" Phoenix said, pressing a finger to Rumple's lips.

Kile began to speak again.

"Now, I will show you my power. I guarantee that, being the wielder of the Stone, I have an abundance of it and can destroy any of you at any moment. For example, watch this," he said, then stepped off the skyscraper. Imaginary friends shrieked as he pummeled towards the ground, never slowing. Phoenix almost looked away in fears of seeing a Kile-puddle on the pavement, but no such thing happened. Instead, at the last possible second right before he would've slammed into the pavement, he disappeared. The imaginary friends stopped screaming and instead looked at the space where he should have been in wonder.

"Nice little trick, isn't it?" Kile said from behind them. Imaginary friends, including Phoenix, whirled around in surprise, not expecting to hear his voice again. He now stood on the stage, grinning like a child on Christmas morning.

"How the kale!?" said one imaginary friend that sounded suspiciously like Harold's mother.

"Now, I will show you your first show of entertainment. Behold, Joanne Raider and Kafa Dux," Kile said, gesturing grandly to the stage behind them and stepping to the side. Phoenix heard Rumple suppress a gasp beside him, and Phoenix tried not to wince at the sight of the two of them. She put a hand against her mouth, which had been open in surprise and horror. Edmund's mouth opened slightly and his eyebrows raised. Harold couldn't see and flapped his wings a few times so he hovered in the air and was the same height as most everyone else. His eyes narrowed in anger. Kafa and Joanne were both a mess, to say the least. Kafa's eyes looked wild but ready, as if he was mentally preparing himself for whatever Kile was going to throw at them. His hair was a little wilder than usual, and that was really saying something. It almost looked as if he had been shocked and his hair had puffed out. There were dark circles underneath his eyes, as if he hadn't slept well. His eyeliner and eyeshadow were smudged to the point where they were almost gone. Otherwise, he looked fine. Joanne looked tired but determined in the way where if somebody struck her, she wouldn't cry. She had a red line across her face, like a healing cut. Parts of her blond hair stuck together with her dried blood, staining it. Her jacket was on, but the white shirt she wore underneath's back looked like it had been dropped in dark reddish-brown dye. With horror, Phoenix realized that it was blood. Her blood. They were both tied at opposite ends of a stake, facing away from each other, though they kept craning their necks to look at each other. They both looked ready for the end, but they also looked determined to not go out silently. The crowd was silent in shock. Kile walked over to them, Kafa glaring at him all the while.

"May I present Kafa Dux, former King of the Unavenged, who proved too weak to keep his position as their leader. And... now Joanne Raider, the stupid girl who tried to save everyone but failed miserably. You shouldn't have even tried, Joanne. You should have stayed at home and out of my way. And now, Joanne, you will die. But first, you will all watch the main feature of my little show. Behold, the East Border," he said, throwing his hand out and pointing to the East. Everyone turned to look in the direction of the East Border. Before Phoenix knew what was happening, Alexai paled.

"No. No," he muttered, looking terrified for the first time. All the other imaginary friends looked confused, including Phoenix.

"The East border is what protects us from Create and the characters inside of it. Because we all know that characters can kill one another and most certainly kill imaginary friends. It's almost like they're real to us. Funny, isn't it? You all have taken the East Border for granted. You've taken all the borders for granted. But no longer will you do such a thing. For today, the East border will fall! And so will the Imaginists! All of you will bow down to ME! I WILL RULE! If you want safety, you follow me. You bow to me. You obey and worship me. Understand?" he said, his voice raising to a crazed shout at times before falling back to its normal volume.

Then he took a deep breath and said, "Let the show begin!" and then threw his arms out wide, his eyes glowing a bright red as red tendrils of energy and power curled around his hands and rippled like water. Screams began to rise in the crowd. Phoenix tried to move but found that he couldn't. He was stuck. He could hear Rumple swearing beside him as he also tried to move.

Kile then threw his hands up to the sky and then brought them down slowly. A loud tearing, shattering noise filled the air, making Phoenix desperately wish that he could move his hands to cover his already-sensitive ears. It sounded like shattering glass, crunching metal, and tearing paper all at once, all of it unbearably loud. In the direction of the East border, the sky pulsed red, spilling the color out onto the once-blue sky until the entire sky was blood red. The sun was a weak yellowish sphere in the scarlet afternoon sky, the few clouds seeming to smoke and burn away into nothing.

*It looks like hell,* thought Phoenix. The screams of terror rose, mixed with gasps. Glancing over at the stage, Phoenix saw that Kafa was staring up at the sky open-mouthed as if he couldn't believe what he was seeing. Joanne was also looking up in shock. The air suddenly grew very, very frigid, unusual for the City's usual perfect temperature. Phoenix shivered, and time seemed to slow. It was almost like something from a horror movie. To Phoenix, it seemed like something from a movie. *None of this is happening. It can't be real. It just can't be,* Phoenix thought. Then there was a loud boom, and the sounds of tearing and shattering stopped abruptly. Everyone looked around slowly, waiting for something to happen. Kile finally lowered his hands, breathing hard. There was a sheen of sweat on his forehead, but his eyes were wild with excitement and something else. He threw his black hair out of his eyes and spoke again.

"Those of you who survive the rest of today and the night are worthy of serving me. The rest of you…" he laughed sharply and mirthlessly. "The rest of you, have a nice death!" he said, then walked off the stage and disappeared between two buildings, leaving everyone in the square. Suddenly Phoenix heard high, unnatural screeches in the distance.

"Do you hear that?" Alexai asked.

"Yes. What do you think it is?" Phoenix said.

"Nothing good," Alexai muttered, the terrified look crossing his face again.

"Wait, what are you guys hearing?" Rumple asked. The screeches were gradually getting louder. They sounded unhuman and strange, even tortured. They sent shivers up Phoenix's spine.

"Something's coming," Alexai muttered.

"But we can't move!" Rumple said.

"Well, we need to!" Alexai said. At that moment, Phoenix found that he could move again. Everyone could. Everyone was still for a moment, before chaos erupted. Imaginary friends ran every which way in search of safety, but it was no use. The screeches were getting louder, to the point where even Rumple and She could hear them. A man hit Phoenix's shoulder as he sprinted past them in the direction of the screeches.

"Wait! That's where the-" Phoenix started saying, but stopped in revulsion when the man ran straight into a moving, pulsing shadow that was at the edge of the square. The man's flesh sizzled up and he crumpled to the ground, his face now just a hole. Phoenix paled and his eyes widened in horror. He grabbed Rumple's arm and yanked him in the direction away from the East side of the square, where terrors were spilling in. There were pulsing shadows, things with no faces, grotesque monsters, flickering figures that were all white that were riddled with bullet holes, animals with glowing eyes and blood-stained teeth, clowns with no eyes, zombies with half of their faces missing, dagger-teethed hunched figures, and other unnamable terrors. It was like something from every horror film had come to life. It was like a doorway to nightmares had been opened, and everything was spilling out from within with nothing to stop it.

"GO! EVERYONE, MOVE IT!" Alexai shouted to the crowd, pointing like a traffic officer in the direction away from the things. People shoved, pushed, and ran through the square, pure fear on their faces.

"Come on!" Harold said, galloping in front of the group, leading them away. Edmund had a hold on She's hand and was yanking her while Alexai sprinted behind them and shot arrows at the monsters behind them. Phoenix was still gripping Rumple's hand, even when Rumple tried to stop.

"Wait!" Rumple shouted over the noise of imaginary friends' cries.

"What?" Phoenix shouted back.

"We have to save them!" he insisted, gesturing towards Joanne and Rumple on the stage.

Alexai looked at Rumple, sadness in his eyes.

"I'm terribly sorry, Rumple, there's just no time! We won't make it if we try!" he said, shaking his head sadly.

"And *they* won't make it if *we* don't try!" Rumple exclaimed.

Alexai sighed, something like pity on his face. And strangely, understanding.

"Rumple, we have to go!" he said, shooting another arrow.

"You go! I'm getting them!" Rumple said, determination in his eyes as he yanked his arm out of Phoenix's grasp and turned around, sprinting back through the river of people to the stage.

"WAIT! RUMPLE!" Phoenix called, but he was already gone.

Harold made a move to go after him, but Alexai held him back.

"We have to go. He's on his own now. Come on!" he said, before starting to run again. With slight hesitation, everyone followed. Phoenix glanced back at the space where he had seen Rumple one last time, but followed after Alexai and the others, feeling sick. Alexai was right. Rumple was on his own now. And now, he was Joanne and Kafa's only hope.

## Chapter Twenty-Two

Rumple shoved through the imaginary friends, trying desperately to get to the stage. The waves of monsters were getting closer. Soon they would get to the stage. Soon they would reach Joanne. Just thinking of his Creator and the trouble she was in gave him an extra surge of adrenaline. He broke through the edge of the mob and onto the steps leading up to the stage. He raced up them, somehow not tripping, as the monsters grew closer. He probably had around twenty seconds before they reached the stage, then another five until they reached Kafa and Joanne. Joanne's eyes widened.

"RUMPLE!" she yelled. Kafa's eyes widened in surprise as he struggled against the ropes. Rumple ran over to the stake and started trying to untie it.

"Don't worry, I'm going to get you guys out! We're going to get out! We're going to do fine!" Rumple said, talking more to himself then Joanne and Rumple as his shaking hands fumbled with the rough rope.

"It doesn't have a knot! You're going to have to cut it!" Joanne said.

"You've got to be kidding me!" Rumple exclaimed, springing away from the post and yanking out the pistol. He held it in his shaking hands, forcing them to stop so he wouldn't misfire.

"Wait, you're going to shoot a gun?" Joanne asked shrilly.

"Do you have a better idea?" Rumple demanded. Joanne squeezed her eyes shut as he took a deep breath and pulled the trigger. The first rope out of four fell to the ground. Rumple adjusted his aim and fired again, and again. He just had one more to go. Eleven seconds were left. He pulled the trigger again, but nothing happened. He was out of bullets. He swore and tried in vain one more time, but remained unsuccessful. He looked up at Joanne, his eyes meeting hers. She looked horrified as she realized what was going to happen. He wasn't going to be able to save her, and now it was too late for him to run. Rumple was going to die. And so were Kafa and Joanne.

"Joanne, I'm sorry. I'm so, so sorry," he said, shaking his head as tears threatened to spill out from his eyes. He was going to have to watch her die. And it was his fault that she was even here. His fault she had stayed. His fault that she was about to have her life cut short. She shook her head at him.

"Don't cry. It's okay. I'll be okay. We'll be fine. Alright?" she said, her voice breaking as tears ran down her face. Rumple nodded, his own tears escaping his eyes. Suddenly, like an angel sent from heaven, a small rocket zoomed around Rumple and hit the last rope, causing it to break and fall away. Joanne and Kafa were free. Rumple whirled around and saw Harold standing at the edge of the stage, one of the rocket things he had attached to himself smoking. Rumple started to smile, but at that moment the monsters descended upon them. Rumple saw a flash of teeth and glowing blue eyes before he squeezed his eyes shut and grabbed Joanne's hand, ready for the end. But the end didn't happen. Instead, Rumple felt nothing. He slowly opened his eyes to see that the monsters were now filtering around them in a circle, as if they were a rock in a stream. It is as if they couldn't or wouldn't get up onto the stage. Joanne stood beside him, clutching his hand, as she glared at the monsters, her eyes focused and concentrated. Kafa was staring at the scene around them in awe, as if he really couldn't believe what was happening. Rumple couldn't either, but he didn't show it.

"Rumple and Kafa, get on Harold and go," Joanne said through gritted teeth.

"I can't carry an adult and a kid successfully. It is too much weight," Harold said, shaking his head.

Joanne looked at Kafa and Rumple, clearly torn between them.

"I'll stay," Rumple said.

"Rumple, no!" Kafa protested, shaking his head. Rumple tightened his grip on Joanne's hand.

"She's my Creator. I'm not leaving her even if there was room on the goat. Go now, Kafa! Save yourself and others!" he shouted.

Kafa looked at him and let out a slow breath.

"Very well, Rumple, it's been great. Just in case we don't make it out of here, I want you to know that you and Joanne were great friends. Keep fighting, even if some of us aren't around to fight anymore," he said.

Rumple nodded.

"Same goes for you, Kafa," he said, giving him a salute. With a small smile, Kafa returned the salute before climbing onto Harold. They all looked at each other for what might have been the last time. What might have been goodbye forever.

"I'm really glad I met all of you. Even if I might die, I'm still happy that I was able to hang out with all of you for a little bit before this," Joanne said.

"Keep going, kid. You're gonna make it," Harold said, glancing back at Rumple and Joanne. Then, with one last look at them, he flapped his wings, and Kafa and Harold were gone. Rumple looked at Joanne, who still seemed very concentrated.

"I'm going to find Kile. And then I am going to kill him," Joanne said, her teeth gritted. Rumple nodded.

"I'll go with you. Because we're together until the end," he said, courage with an unknown source flaring up inside him.

"I know," Joanne said, then turned and still holding Rumple's hand, led him straight into the throng of monsters.

<p style="text-align:center">~~~</p>

"Come on! We have to hurry if we are to make it!" Alexai said, sprinting as fast as he could while shooting arrow after arrow at the surging tide of monsters behind them. No matter how fast the imaginary friends seemed to run, the monsters ran faster. They were slowly getting closer and closer to Alexai and the others.

*We're not going to make it,* Alexai thought with a sudden cold feeling in his stomach as one of the monsters tore into an imaginary girl five yards away from him. She was clutching Edmund's hand, who leaped and darted through the crowd with elf grace. Harold had flown off in hopes of rescuing Rumple, though Alexai thought it was too late. He had told Harold it would be suicide to go after them, but Harold had gone off anyway. Alexai had watched him go with respect but not much else.

Alexai wasn't one that usually let himself feel emotions. He tried to be stone cold and heartless since the death of his Creator nine years ago. John had been an amazing, yet emotional man. In the end, the death of John's wife had led him to sink into a state where he just had given up the will to live and just died simply because he no longer cared for himself. It had been hard, so hard that he had never wanted to feel emotions again. So, he hadn't. He knew he was heartless for it, at least a little. But what did he care? To love was to be weak in his mind.

Suddenly, Phoenix tripped and sprawled on the ground. Alexai kneeled down beside him while shouting at Edmund and She to keep going. He grabbed Phoenix's hand and yanked him up off the ground, Phoenix almost stumbling in the process. Alexai glanced behind them and saw that the monsters were only a matter of feet away. In that moment, Alexai made a decision. His last decision.

*For John,* he thought, remembering how brave his Creator had been until the very end.

"Tell them I'm sorry," he leaned in and whispered in Phoenix's ear. Then he put his hands on Phoenix's back and shoved hard, sending Phoenix away from the monsters. Then they were upon Alexai all at once, tearing and chomping and howling. They tore at his cloak, knocking the pieces aside like paper before digging into him, sinking their teeth into his body and biting and shaking it around. Alexai screamed in pain, his vision going blinding white with it, before they moved on to the crowd, dropping him to the ground. He hit the concrete, seeing stars as he laid on his side as the last of the monsters passed by him. He could see imaginary friends of all kinds all around him in similar states, bleeding out and dying. As they died, their bodies faded away into nothing, as if they had never existed. Alexai suddenly felt no pain even though he was aware of the blood running down his face from a gash in his forehead and the various other places where he had been severely injured.

Suddenly, he saw John in front of him, as clear as day, who was smiling at Alexai and extending his hand towards him.

"Come on, Alexai. Come on, take my hand. It's alright. We can go back to Burn Street and play again just like we did as kids. Wouldn't you like that, Alexai?"

John's voice was just as gentle as Alexai remembered. For the first time in nine years, Alexai felt a surge of happiness. It was His John. The happy John. The one that always helped those in need. The one that had always comforted people without a second thought. A smile crept across Alexai's face as he reached out and took John's hand. He was so happy in that moment, even as he saw his legs disappear, then his torso and his arms, as if he was being submerged in invisibility. He was fading. But he was with John, and that was all that mattered.

"Do you want to come with me, Alexai?" John asked. Alexai smiled wider.

"Always, John. Always," he said, then disappeared completely with John, no sign that he had ever been there at all. Just the ground, for Alexai was dead.

~~~

Kafa soared above the square on Harold's back as they scanned the crowd for their friends. Kafa suddenly spotted Alexai, but he was lying on the ground and bleeding.

"NO!" Kafa yelled. Harold twisted his head around to see what Kafa was looking at in horror. Harold swooped down as Kafa stared down at Alexai's broken form. Alexai had begun to fade. And fast. As they landed beside him, Alexai smiled. Kafa leaped off Harold and got down on his knees by Alexai just as Alexai smiled bigger and said,

"Always, John. Always." Then he disappeared, no trace left of him.

"ALEXAI!" Kafa shouted at the empty air, as if calling his name would make him come back. But alas, nothing happened, and Harold and Kafa were left to crowd around nothing in the thick afternoon air. Kafa suddenly felt a hoof on his shoulder. He looked up and saw Harold looking at him, sadness deep and dark in his goat eyes.

"We have to go. I'm sorry, Kafa. I'm so sorry," he said, his deep voice somber. Kafa felt some surprise to feel his eyes watering. He hadn't known Alexai for very long, but he had still cared about Alexai's safety as much as anybody else's. The fact that Alexai had died almost made it feel like it was Kafa's fault that he hadn't been there to protect him.

"It's not your fault. We have to keep going, no matter what happens," Kafa said, shaking his head as he stood up. Harold nodded, then saw something over Kafa's shoulder. Harold's eyes widened and before he could warn him, Kafa whirled around and drew out his sword, stabbing it deep into the stomach of a hooded figure. They made a quiet gurgling noise before toppling over, their hood falling back to reveal a hole where the face should have been. Kafa shuddered, taking a step back and making Harold yelp as his heel collided with Harold's hoof.

"That was kind of cool," Harold said after a beat of silence. Kafa threw his hair out of his face.

"Well, get ready to do it again, because we've got company," he said, tipping his head in the direction of a few monsters that were rushing towards them. Kafa heard Harold's rockets start hissing. They looked at one another, and nodding, they charged at the monsters, ready for anything.

~~~

Edmund yanked She along, his elf grace making him faster than her.

"Edmund! Slow down!" She exclaimed frustratedly as Edmund leaped over a downed flower cart.

"I am afraid that I cannot do that!" Edmund said with no trace of apology in his voice. Suddenly he heard She screech in terror in his ear. He glanced over his shoulder to see monsters ripping into Alexai behind them and a surprised looking Phoenix stumbling towards them. Edmund paled and almost fell down in shock. Alexai had been strong. Alexai had been brave and the leader of the Darkness. Alexai was invincible... or so Edmund thought.

*Why, cruel Imagine? Why must Alexai join my fallen brethren?* Edmund wondered.

"We must keep moving!" he said to She.

She reached behind her and grabbed Phoenix's hand. Edmund spotted a tall hotel ahead of them and ran for it, dragging them both behind him.

"EDMUND! WHAT THE HELL ARE YOU *DOING*?" She shrieked as he yanked her hand hard in the direction of the hotel.

"Inside of the hotel! Get inside of the hotel!" he shouted. They ran towards the hotel, bursting through the already-broken glass doors and into the lavishly decorated lobby. Nobody else was there. Edmund didn't know if that was good or bad at the time, though he figured he'd soon find out. She let go of his hand and rushed ahead of him to the elevators where she began pushing buttons desperately while Edmund ran for the stairs.

"What are you doing now!?" She asked, her eyes wild with fear and nervousness. Edmund grasped the handle of the door to the stairs and flung it open.

"It reads use stairs in case of emergency. This is an emergency, is it not?" Edmund explained, pointing to a sign by the stairs. She rolled her eyes.

"The elevators will be faster!" she said.

"Hate to break it to you guys, but I think the monsters found out that we went in here," Phoenix said. Edmund turned and glanced at him in slight surprise. With everything going on, he had almost forgotten that Phoenix was even there. Sure enough, some of the monsters were breaking away from the group and heading for the hotel.

"I no longer care if you chose the stairs or not, for I am taking them myself!" Edmund declared as he began to run up the stairs. Edmund heard She swear before following him, and Phoenix followed She. He took the stairs two at a time, never faltering due to his grace. He heard Phoenix slam the stairway door behind him before he and She also set up the stairs.

"What floor are we going to?" Phoenix asked, not even sounding winded because he didn't need to breathe.

"I don't know! Just keep going!" She said, sounding breathless. As they ran, possibilities raced through Edmund's mind. Possibilities of how they might get away from the monsters and possibilities of them surviving the day. Edmund hoped that they would survive, though he honestly wasn't sure that they would. Alexai had already died. There was no telling who would be next. Just the thought of dying sent shivers down Edmund's spine. It was something he thought he'd never have to do. After all, they were imaginary. They were supposed to exist forever. Supposed to. But now they weren't even sure of that. Suddenly, the stairs shook like they would in an earthquake, causing Edmund to fall over and slam against the railing. He heard She give a cry of surprise behind him.

"What was tha-?" Phoenix started saying when the staircase shook again and the sound of tearing, screeching metal filled the narrow space.

"THEY'RE HERE! RUN!" She shouted to Edmund and Phoenix. They had reached the fifth floor, though they now had no time to make it any farther up. She raced past Edmund, grabbing his hand and shoving the door to the fifth floor open with her shoulder. They burst into a hallway that had patterned carpet and small lamps on the walls with multiple doors lining the halls. She sprinted over to the doors and started jiggling the handles as if it would open them.

"It's a hotel, they're not going to have unlocked doors!" Phoenix said as he raced down the hallway ahead of them. She sighed in aggravation and followed him.

"Where might we be going?" Edmund asked, but She and Phoenix didn't answer him. Instead, they saw the hallway ended and both screamed out. Edmund heard the door burst open as the monsters started pouring into the hallway, their snarls and cries making Edmund pale.

"We're trapped!" Phoenix said, his already pale skin somehow paling even more.

"The window!" Edmund exclaimed, pointing to a window at the end of the hallway. She looked at Edmund like he was crazy.

"Are you-?"

"Mad? 'Tis terribly likely. Now come hither! Or else we shall not survive!" Edmund said as he started to run for the window. He squeezed his eyes shut as he hit it, the glass slicing into his skin. Then there was nothing touching him, and he was falling, falling, falling into the street below without anything to stop him.

~~~

Joanne could feel sweat forming on her brow as she and Rumple raced in the direction that Kile had disappeared. The alley between the two buildings led to another road, this one with few imaginary friends, all of them running from the monsters, who didn't touch Rumple and Joanne due to her keeping them at bay by imagining. The constant use of her imagination was beginning to tire her, but she wasn't about to tell Rumple about that.

"There!" Rumple said, pointing to the Imaginists Palace, where Kile could just be seen passing through the doors and shutting them behind him. The guards were nowhere in sight.

*They're probably dead,* Joanne thought darkly. She ran faster, leaving a huffing Rumple no choice but to match her pace.

"I see him!" Joanne said just as a monster leaped in front of them, pink maw open-wide and ready to consume them. Rumple swore and tripped as Joanne raised her hand and clenched it into a fist. The monster yelped, an invisible force lifting it off the ground, before it was thrown through the air like a toy to the side when Joanne jerked her fist to the right. Rumple looked up at her in amazement from the ground, his eyebrows raised.

"Holy crap, that was frickin'-"

"Cool? Right, sure. Come on, we really got to go!" Joanne said dismissively, yanking him off the ground with her imagination instead of her hand. She felt a little sick as the monster landed on the ground meters away, its bones crunching on impact. She couldn't help but remember when Kile had raised her up and then let her fall. *YOU ARE NOTHING!* Joanne shook her head, suddenly wishing she hadn't handled the monster so violently.

*I'm not like Kile, though. Right?* Joanne wondered. Imaginary friends were running to and fro, with monsters on their tails, some of them getting tackled. Joanne tried to ignore it and kept running. They made it to the doors and Rumple tried the handle. Joanne looked at him like he was an idiot.

"What? I had to try," he said, shrugging. Joanne rolled her eyes and shoved her hands forward, making them fly open. Joanne gestured for him to follow her as she set foot inside of the Imaginists Palace.

"Which way did he go?" Rumple asked. Joanne shut her eyes and sent out waves of energy.

*Find him, find him,* she thought. Suddenly she could sense his presence. She felt a tugging sensation up and to the right.

"He's this way!" she said, her eyes flying open as she started down the hallway.

"Wait, aren't you going to need a weapon?" Rumple asked.

"Hmm, you're right..." Joanne muttered. Her mind ran through the possibilities. She was good with a Nerf gun, but she had no idea how to shoot a real one. She had used a toy lightsaber before, and she was also good with that. She had shot a bow and arrow, but she had been quite terrible at that.

*A sword, then. But it's got to be a good one...,* Joanne thought. She stopped and closed her eyes, breathing deeply as she imagined it in detail. Suddenly it was in her hand. She opened her eyes and there it was. It was just as she had pictured it. The hilt was a black rock that looked slick and glinted in the light. The blade was a mixture of crystal and diamond, the color of it shades of blues and whites that sparkled and looked almost like a blade of water. The word IMAGINE was etched on the side of the blade that seemed to glow. Rumple whistled beside her.

"Holy crap, that is some sword," he said, his eyes wide. Joanne just grinned as she moved it through the air, causing Rumple to take a cautious step back.

"Woah, some of us are fragile. Please keep that to yourself," he said, holding his hands in front of him as he eyed the sword. Joanne laughed.

"You don't need to worry about that. Come on, he's this way," Joanne said, lowering the sword and continuing down the hallway, Rumple following as he took out his pistol, its silver paint glinting in the red light of the bloodred sky from the windows. The floor echoed with the sounds of their footsteps as the noise of chaos raged just outside the palace. Joanne stopped, the feeling above her.

"He's up there," she said, pointing up. They both looked up at the ceiling, but nothing was there except for a mural of the Forest.

"That means he's on a different floor. Did you see any stairs by any chance?" Rumple said, looking over at Joanne.

"Uh... there's some over there," she said, pointing to a staircase farther down the hallway.

"Nice," Rumple muttered as they started towards it. As they began to ascend the stairs, Joanne looked over at Rumple.

"Make sure you have your pistol ready. Kile is dangerous. Be careful or at least stay behind me," she said. Rumple waved his hand dismissively through the air.

"Don't worry, sis, I'll be fine," he said nonchalantly. Joanne nodded, not fully convinced.

"Okay," she muttered, half to herself,

"I think he's on the third floor. Be quiet and follow my lead," she said. Rumple gave a sarcastic salute but nodded after he did so. The staircase was made of a dark, polished wood and looked to be years old, yet it didn't creak or make any sound whatsoever as they stepped up it. They passed the exit to the second floor and continued up to the third. The tugging feeling was slowly getting stronger, making Joanne feel like a fish on a hook. They stepped off the stairs and onto the third floor. This floor was most definitely smaller, with a small, broken window on the far wall and a vault door on the other. The walls were painted a dark red and the floors were dark brown wood. There were a few splatters of darker red on the walls near the vault. Joanne shuddered as she realized it was blood. Old blood, but blood all the same. Joanne put a finger to her lips and motioned for Rumple to follow her as she began to slowly walk to the vault. The tugging was coming from the vault.

*He's in there,* she mouthed to Rumple.

*Okay,* he mouthed back. The noises of battle and screams could be heard from the broken window, the wind whistling through it at the same time and producing a bit of an ominous sound. When they reached the vault, Joanne stopped and put her hand on the handle. She jerked her head to the side and the metal crumpled like paper, making the vault door fall open an inch or two. Joanne slowly brought her hand to the side and the door swung all the way open, revealing a large space lit only by glowing and humming computer terminals. Rumple opened his mouth but then closed it when he remembered he was supposed to remain silent.

The terminals were arranged so they looked like a maze of some sort, the terminals too tall to see over. Joanne tilted her head to the right to signal Rumple to follow her as she turned left in the maze. She was beginning to feel dizzy from using her imagination, but she ignored it and kept going. They turned multiple times, to the left and then the right, then right again and then left, so many turns that Joanne couldn't keep up with them. Everything looked exactly the same, and Joanne knew that she surely would've gotten lost if she couldn't feel where Kile was. The tugging feeling got so strong Joanne felt as if she was about to fall over- and then it suddenly went away. Joanne held up a fist to Rumple, and thankfully, he understood and stopped walking. Suddenly, Kile's voice echoed throughout the vault.

"Hello, Joanne! So nice of you to come and see me here in this vault. It's kind of lonely without some company and- oh! Who's this? Ah yes, your *idiot* little brother. What's his name? It was something really stupid," he said, chuckling. Rumple's eyes narrowed into angry slits beside Joanne.

"What was it? Rump? Rumpy? Oh no, it was Rumple. How silly of me to forget. Sorry, my little memory slips sometimes. It comes with age, I'm afraid," he said, now sounding bored and not sorry at all. Then he continued.

"But that is inevitable. I assume you've come to try and defeat me." He laughed, though it came out sounding more of an evil, mirthless cackle.

"Kids are stupid. Always believing that everyone is special and everyone is a hero. Well, let me tell you this now. You will not be able to defeat me. Heroes *don't exist*. Heroes are points of view, as are villains, something you probably view me as now. I don't care, though. Really, opinions are stupid in the endgame. What matters is who has the power, hero or villain.

So, I will give you an option. Leave now and just go run away, let my plan run without any little bumps in the road. Or, you could stay and I could destroy you both. Remember that little whipping, Joanne? Remember when your face didn't have that ugly little to-be scar? I could do *so* much worse than that. And I don't mean physically. I mean mentally. Your mind was never that stable in the first place. I could tear your little mind apart. I could rip your emotions, your heart, out of you, leave you an unfeeling, numb little girl. And your brother... well, I think just killing him would be enough. So, what will it be, Joanne? Die with nothing, not even honor? Or fleeing like the wannabe heroes you are?" he said.

Joanne felt a flare of rage inside of her.

"I am not afraid of you, Kile! I am not a coward. I will face you and I will beat you!" Joanne declared, stepping out from behind the terminal she and Rumple were standing behind. And there was Kile. He was standing in front of a normal pedestal that must have served some purpose at some point in time, or else why would it be there? His pitch-black hair was visible by lines of color from the terminal light. His brown eyes seemed to be shot with red, as if the color of the Stone had leaked into his irises. He was wearing the same simple black clothes as earlier, Kafa's old black crown glinting menacingly on his head. The Stone was still on a chain around his neck, giving off red pulses of light that cast a red glow on Kile's neck and face. Even though he wasn't wearing anything elaborate, it was intimidating all the same. He smirked.

"Oh, really? You had an imaginary brother that only you could see and hear for eight years. That doesn't sound very mentally stable to me. Besides, I can defeat you. Easily. Last chance, Joanne. Three, two-"

"No! Don't hurt her! Joanne, we need to just go. We need to go while we still can!" Rumple interrupted, suddenly leaping out from behind the terminal. Kile's smirk grew into a twisted smile.

"Oh, somebody's being smart! Guess you're not that much of an idiot after all," he said before starting to examine his nails. Rumple glared at him and held up one finger before looking at Joanne with a look of pleading and dropping his hand.

"Joanne, please. I don't know if we're gonna be able to defeat this guy! We should go now, while we still can!" he said, grabbing Joanne's hand with his own.

"But we've gotten so far! He's right here! We can do it!" Joanne said, feeling a spark of surprise at Rumple's sudden change of mindset. Rumple had never been brave, but for him to change his mind last second was unlike him. He slumped a bit, as if he had been hoping that she would give up.

"Okay. Fine. Have it your way. But I'm not fighting with you," he said, suddenly straightening up. Joanne blinked in surprise as her eyebrows raised.

*Not fighting with me? What is he talking about? What does he mean?* Joanne wondered as cold dread pooled in her stomach. His eyes hardened.

"Maybe I'm not a total idiot. Maybe I know the right side to be on," he spat, his voice cold. Joanne's mouth fell open in shock as she flinched as if she had been hit.

*Rumple would never say that. What's wrong with him?* She thought desperately, confusion and fear racing through her.

"Rumple? What's wrong? Why are you acting so weird?" she asked, taking a step towards him.

"Nothing's wrong with him. He's fine, see? Just the same old brother you always had," Kile said soothingly.

"I'm not acting weird. I'm just growing up and noticing things, that's all. Like, how you never thought about how I felt when you kept me around for eight years and then suddenly told me I had to go. You never wondered if I was okay after I was discarded. You were just sad, you were just thinking about how *you* needed me, never about how *I* needed you. And now you want me to charge at an undefeatable enemy? Ha. Good luck with that, Joanne, because I'm not going to be standing by your side anymore. Nobody will," he said unfeelingly, shaking his head and giving her a venomous look. Joanne stumbled back as if she had been punched. Each word had felt like a knife to the heart, each one a razor-sharp dagger from the person she trusted the most. The blood had drained from her face and she was paper-white from shock. She felt hot tears began to gather in her eyes.

"Rumple, I'm so sorry. I never meant to-" she started saying, but suddenly Rumple's fist darted out and punched her in the stomach, making her choke on her words and double over, almost falling to the ground due to how unexpected the action had been.

"Rumple!" Joanne gasped, looking up at him. She almost recoiled in shock. Rumple's once blue green eyes were now tinged with red that looked like it was coming from his pupil. She looked over at Kile.

"What did you *do* to him?" she asked, a lump in her throat. Kile grinned at her.

"I didn't do anything to him. You did though, Joanne. You're only just now seeing it," he said innocently.

She shook her head in denial, not wanting to believe the words leaving his mouth.

"No. No, Rumple would never say that. I don't care what you say, this isn't Rumple. You did something to him," she said, her voice shaking as she spoke. His grin became evil.

"I told you that you should've run. You didn't take the chance. I told you that you couldn't win. Well, not when your dear brother is the one you're fighting," he said.

"No. No!" Joanne exclaimed, looking back at Rumple as if it would make what he said false. But there was no trace of the nerdy Rumple she once knew. No trace of the kind one. Just the cruel, red-eyed one. Rumple took out his pistol and aimed it at Joanne.

"Say goodnight, *sis*," he said, saying the last word like an insult. Joanne's eyes widened in fear. Just as he pulled the trigger, she threw up her hands, and there was a huge flash of blinding white light. Joanne felt herself fall to the floor, and then the light changed to something else. A memory.

> *It was a hot June day and Joanne was practically jumping with nervousness. Somehow, her mom had persuaded her to go on a scary ride, and now she was in line for it as she questioned her decisions.* Holy crap, what was I thinking? *Joanne wondered. But then it was time to get on. She wiped her damp hands on her shirt and climbed onto the spinning ride that had seats along the perimeter. The instructor told them basic things, like to sit down and hold on while the ride was in motion and not to get up, though Joanne only half paid attention as he talked. Then the safety barrier thunked onto everyone's backs, leaving them stuck in their chairs until the ride was over.*

Joanne looked around nervously. She could see her father and sister waving and smiling encouragingly from under the shade of the tree. Suddenly, the ride started, moving them back and forth, slowly at first, then faster and faster as it began to spin them around as it did so. Joanne's surroundings blurred past her eyes like a bad photograph, and she wanted to close them to badly, but found that she was too scared to. And suddenly, he was there, sitting in the once-empty seat beside her.

"Woah, calm down, man. This is just a ride. Heck, I'm here. You are fine. You will not die. We are good," Rumple said to Joanne, using a calm tone.

"Okay. Deep BreaaaAAAA!" Joanne's words turned into a scream of terror as they hurled the ride upwards while Joanne was spinning out, and for one split second, it felt as if the ride would fly off the rails. But they weren't, it was just the ride reaching as high as it could go, going as fast as it could spin.

"Hey, it's alright. We're not on this ride. We're... how about this. Instead of being on this ride, we are waltzing in the church bathroom. Remember that? Remember how every Sunday during church we'd go to the bathroom and waltz to keep you from getting too bored? Pretend we're doing that now. We're in the hold, and we're in the bathroom, and we are waltzing. And one, two, three. And one, two, three. One, two, three. One, two, three. One, two, three," he said soothingly, as if what he was saying was actually happening. Joanne breathed deeply as she pictured it in her head. So peaceful. So calm. Then the ride went all the way up again and Joanne almost screamed, but Rumple said,

"Hey, it's okay, I'm just spinning you. You hear that? I'm just spinning you." Then the ride went back down again, and he spoke again.

"Now we're just doing the steps again. And one, two, three. And one, two, three. One, two, three. One, two, three." Joanne breathed in deeply and imagined it again. And then the ride was over. Just like that.

"Hey look, it's done. See, that wasn't so bad, was it?" Rumple said, smiling over at her. Joanne nodded, a small smile on her face. Pretending to waltz with Rumple had made it not as bad as she had first thought, distracted her from how fast and frightening the ride was.

*"No, it wasn't that bad. Thanks to you. Thank you, Rumple," she said, looking over at Rumple with sisterly affection. He nodded.*

*"Anytime, Joanne. Anytime."*

The memory went away and so did the light. Even though the length of the memory was a few minutes, it had only been a matter of seconds. Kile looked at them, seeming confused.

*Did he even see the memory?* Joanne wondered. Rumple was on the ground a foot or two away, blinking and shaking his head. Joanne looked at his eyes and saw with a sinking heart that his eyes still had red in them.

"What are you doing? End her!" Kile ordered Rumple as he pointed at Joanne. Rumple got up and pointed the pistol at her again.

*No. I am not going to end this way. I have to get him to snap out of it,* Joanne thought. With one smooth motion, she moved her sword through the air until it was positioned protectively in front of her.

"Do it now!" Kile barked. Rumple's eyes hardened as he clicked the safety off the pistol.

"Rumple, look at me. Really look at me. This isn't you. This is Kile. He's controlling you somehow. You don't actually want to kill me. You don't actually want to shoot your sister," Joanne said, forcing her voice to sound calm and not jump with emotion despite how much it wanted to.

"No, this is me. You just don't know. You haven't been with me in three years. People change, Joanne. I did too," he said flatly, shaking his head.

"No, you haven't. You came back and you were the same boy you were. The same kind nerd that I loved so much," Joanne said, her voice breaking despite her trying to keep it from doing so. Rumple's eyes flickered for one second back to their blue green, but then they went right back to being tinged with red.

"That kid is gone. Forever. Goodbye, Joanne," he said, then pulled the trigger. Joanne focused and the bullet exploded midair on its way to her. He fired again and again, but each bullet had the same end.

Finally, Kile sighed and waved his hand through the air. A blood red sword suddenly appeared in Rumple's hand instead of a gun.

"Come on. Fight it out like soldiers," Kile said, waving his hand at them. They looked at each other for a second before Rumple charged at Joanne, sword raised high. He brought it down and Joanne blocked it, the sound of clanging metal reverberating throughout the vault.

"Wake up, Rumple! Wake up!" Joanne said as he swung again and she jumped away with grace she had only because of her imagination. He huffed and tried again.

*What would make him stop? What would make Rumple come back?* Joanne wondered as she blocked another blow.

"Come on, fight back, Joanne! Strike your brother down! Don't be weak! Don't let your memories get to you!" he exclaimed, gritting his teeth.

*Memories. That's it.* Joanne thought. She jumped away from Rumple, doing some sort of flip only a skilled gymnast would've been able to do.

"Rumple, look at me! Just look, please!" Joanne begged. Rumple looked at her, his red eyes meeting her blue ones.

"Remember when I was scared to go on that ride and you told me to pretend we were waltzing? Remember that, Rumple? Remember how you were the only reason I wasn't scared?" she said.

His eyes seemed to become unfocused as the red slowly began to disappear.

"What? No!" Kile said, clenching his fist, and suddenly the red-eyed Rumple was back, eyes full of hatred and loathing so strong Joanne almost flinched away. Joanne took a deep breath.

"Remember waltzing in church? Remember how we'd dance over the tile floor? One, two, three, one, two, three to the music the choir was making? Remember how their voices echoed and the drum made the perfect beat to follow?" she said. Rumple had started walking towards her but now he slowed, as if he was lost in his own memories.

"Remember how you'd always help me with math, because you were better at it than me? Remember how when I first started to learn to waltz, I was so bad at it and you were so much better? Remember how you made me better at it? How you were so patient? And one, and two, and three. That's what you used to tell me as we waltzed to the sound of the rain outside my window. And one, two, three,"

Joanne said gently, tears gathering in her eyes as she remembered herself the days where she and Rumple thought he'd stay forever and never leave her life.

"And one, two, three."

"And one, two, three."

"And one, two, three."

Rumple stopped and looked at her, his eyes blue green without any red in them.

"Joanne," he said, so quietly she almost didn't hear him.

"Joanne, run," he said softly, then twitched so violently it was if a rope had been yanked that he was on. Suddenly his eyes were all red as he leaped at her. Surprised, Joanne almost didn't raise her sword in time.

"And one, two, three. And one, two, three. And one, two, three!" Joanne repeated as they danced around the space, Rumple leaping and her dodging. Slowly, his attacks became less violent, less focused and angry. Then he stopped. There was sweat all over his face, soaking his Batman hoodie. His eyes were flickering rapidly from red to blue green, so fast that it made Joanne dizzy just to watch.

"I- I can't fight him. I'm s-sorry, Joanne. I can't let myself kill y-you. There's- there's not another way," he stuttered, squeezing his eyes shut as he fought for control over himself. Holding the sword in his hand, he turned it so the tip was against his stomach, pressing into the cloth of his hoodie.

"Goodbye, Joanne," he whispered, tears running down his face. The realization of what was about to happen hit Joanne at that moment.

"RUMPLE, NO!" she screamed, lunging for him, but he was already plunging it into himself. He gasped and looked down; all the red gone from his eyes as a darker red spread across his clothes. Then he looked at Joanne, his blue green eyes soft and sad. Then his knees buckled, and he fell to the ground, the sound of his body hitting the floor sounding far away to Joanne. She screamed, but she couldn't hear it. All she could see, all she could focus on, was her little brother on the ground, his breaths so weak that they were almost unnoticeable.

"Aww, such a sad ending for our little hero and her brother. Such a shame," Kile said with mock pity, shaking his head.

Joanne looked up at him, a white-hot rage filling her. She screamed, and suddenly there was an explosion, and Joanne could feel herself falling, falling, falling.

## Chapter Twenty-Three

*He was there. She knew he was. Somehow, even though she had never met him before, she just knew. She walked down the stairs nervously. She didn't meet new people very much, and she really wanted to be friends with him. She just hoped that he liked her. Her feet hit the wood floor and she crossed the room into the carpeted area with a TV and shelves with toys and movies on them. And there he was, standing there by himself, looking around. Then he saw her and gave her a shy smile. He was a little bit shorter than her, with a mop of messy brown hair and blue green eyes. He was wearing a long-sleeved brown shirt with a puffy red vest and black pants. A small yellow scarf was wrapped around his neck. She walked up to him, her white dress fluttering as she moved. She stopped in front of him.*

*"Hi. I'm Joanne. What's your name?" she said, rocking back and forth on her heels nervously.*

*"I'm Rumpelstiltskin. Do you live here?" he asked, looking around at the house they were in.*

*"Yeah, I live here with my family. Where's yours?" she said, looking around him as if she would see two parents hiding behind the boy.*

*"My parents are dead," he said flatly, as if he felt no emotions about the subject, even though most children would. Joanne blinked in surprise. She had never thought that his parents would be dead. Nobody she knew had ever died either, so she wasn't sure what to say.*

*"Oh. Who did you live with then?" she asked, curiosity on her face.*

*"I lived at an orphanage, but all the other kids were mean. So, I ran away," he said, shrugging.*

*"Oh, well, you can live with me now. If you want to. You can be my brother, because I've always wanted one and I don't have one," Joanne explained.*

*"Really?" he asked.*

*"Yeah. I don't think my mommy and daddy would care," she said, shrugging. A smile broke out over his face.*

*"Are you my sister now?" he asked.*

*"Yes. And now you're my brother," she said, smiling herself and nodding.*

*"You promise?" he asked.*

*"I promise. You'll be my brother forever. And I'll be your sister forever,"
she said.*

*"I like that idea," he said happily.*

*"I do, too. But I don't want to call you Rumpelstiltskin. It's too long.
Instead, I'll call you something else. What about Rumple?" she said.*

*"I like that name," he said, nodding. She smiled.*

*"Great! You wanna go play in my room? I share it with my sister but she's
not there right now. You can meet her later with my mommy and daddy.
Come on!" she said, taking his tiny hand in her own tiny hand and leading
him upstairs.*

Joanne's eyes snapped open, her breaths fast and hard. She looked around in
shock. The roof and most of the computer terminals were gone, only piles of ash
left where they once were. Scorch marks adorned the floors and walls. The
pedestal was still there, blackened by the explosion. Kile was gone. But Rumple
was not. He lay a foot or two away on the ground, his breaths so shallow his chest
was barely moving at all. The sword was gone, so nothing was stopping the blood
from leaving him. He was lying in a pool of his own blood, his hoodie no longer
gray. Joanne gasped and crawled over to him, leaning over him once she reached
him.

"Rumple. Rumple, can you hear me? Rumple?" she said desperately, tears welling
in her eyes. His eyes fluttered open.

"Joanne. Did we beat him? Is he dead?" he asked weakly, his eyes moving around
in search of Kile but not his head. Then he noticed the tears that had begun to fall
from her eyes.

"Oh, Joanne. It's okay, man. I'm- I'm fine. I'll be okay, and so will you," he said,
reaching up and wiping the tears from her face despite the fact that he winced
when he did so.

"No. No, no. Why did you do that? You are not going to die. I am going to make sure of it," she sobbed. He shook his head sadly.

"I didn't want to kill you, even if I wasn't in control. I wouldn't be able to live with myself. Besides, I think it is actually time for me to die, sis. There's nothing anybody can do. That sword was made by the Stone. It can kill imaginary friends- and it will kill me," he said, gasping in pain. Joanne shook her head determinedly.

"No, there's something I can do. I can heal you; I know I can," she said.

"Joanne, I don't think you know how bad it is," he said gently. Joanne looked down at his wound. It did look really bad.

"No, we can do it. Just keep breathing and keep your heart beating," Joanne said, taking one of his hands in hers.

"Easier said than done. Joanne, I really don't think-"

"It will happen. Now, come on. Keep breathing," she said, cutting him off. She put her other hand on his wounded stomach, causing him to inhale sharply, the sound whistling through his teeth.

"Keep breathing," Joanne repeated.

"Oh, I'm breathing! Just get it over with please!" Rumple said. Joanne closed her eyes and focused on the wound. She could feel it, feel where his flesh and organs were torn, feel where they were bleeding and where they needed to be knit back together. Taking a deep breath, she sent waves of power through Rumple. He swore.

"That feels so frickin' weird- OW! Watch it!" he said.

"Sorry," Joanne muttered as she began to knit his broken insides back together. His pulse quickened and he whimpered as he squeezed her hand hard. Soon, he had stopped bleeding and all that was left was a few more muscles, but his breathing was so weak it was barely there, and his pulse was just a weak beat. He swallowed and suddenly gasped.

"Joanne! Joanne, look at me. I'm not going to make it. I've-I've lost too much blood. No matter how much you heal me, I've lost too much and- and… my heart wants to give up. I can feel it. It's tired, Joanne. I'm tired. Let me fall asleep. Let me go," he said weakly, his voice already quiet voice quieting even more as he spoke.

She shook her head.

"No. We can make it. We can do it," she said.

He looked at her sadly, his blue green eyes sparking with sadness and affection.

"Oh, Joanne. You were the best sister I could have ever asked for. You made my life perfect, the best an imaginary friend's could ever be. I want to say thank you. Thank you for the life you gave me. Thank you for being you. Thank you for try- for trying to save me," he said, his voice breaking once or twice.

"Rumple, no. This isn't the end. It wasn't last time, and it's not this time," Joanne said, her voice pleading.

"Last time I was just going to Imagine, not dying. Trust me, I'm dying this time," he whispered, his voice soaked with sadness. He coughed, sending a little spray of blood out.

"Rumple-"

"Let me finish. I want you to keep trying to defeat Kile. I know you can. I'm sorry that I brought you into this, but there's no going back now. You can defeat him. You can save everyone. I know you have it in you. Just because I'm going to be dead doesn't mean that you should give up. Keep going. Keep going! I love you, Joanne. Remember that. I'll love you forever, even when I'm gone," he said, his voice so soft and gentle that Joanne almost couldn't hear him. Tears escaped from her eyes and landed on Rumple's hoodie.

"I love you, too, Rumple. I always have and I always will."

She could feel his pulse. It was so weak now, so slow. A slow waltz.

One, two, three.

One, two, three.

One, two, three.

He took a shaky breath and for the last time, the blue-green eyes met the icy blue ones. The eyes she knew so well. The eyes that he knew better than his own.

"Goodbye, Joanne."

"Goodbye, Rumple."

One, two... three.

One… two… three.

One……………….

# Chapter Twenty-Four

The blue-green eyes went glassy as the icy blue ones filled and spilled over with tears as she called out his name, over and over again, her voice hoarse from screaming and crying.

But he didn't respond.

His eyes didn't open.

His lips never moved.

His chest never rose.

His heartbeat never continued waltzing on.

Just silence and stillness.

# Chapter Twenty-Five

The explosion knocked Kafa and Harold off their feet and hooves.

"What was that?" Harold asked. Kafa shook his head.

"I don't know. It came from...." he trailed off as he saw the smoking Imaginists Palace. Or at least what was left of it. Out of the corner of his eye, he saw Edmund and She jump out a window of a hotel and land on the ground, Edmund rolling and then catching She. They looked back at the window, as if expecting something else to come out after them. Instead, a spray of vampire blood hit the window.

*Phoenix. That was Phoenix,* Kafa thought with horror.

"Is that Joanne?" Harold asked.

Kafa turned in confusion.

"Where do you-" he started saying, but broke off and paled when he saw Harold was looking at the Imaginists Palace. On the third floor was a room with the walls gone that was filled with burnt computer terminals. And around one of them, Kafa could see a very familiar head of hair and jacket.

*Wait, why is she in there? Why was she where the explosion was? Unless she made the explosion... but why? And what is she doing?* Kafa wondered, squinting at her. She seemed to be crawling over to something, but Kafa's view of whatever it was was blocked by a computer terminal.

"Yes, that's Joanne. But what is she doing?" Kafa said.

"I don't know. Hey, Kafa?" Harold said.

Kafa didn't even glance at Harold when he spoke to him.

"What?" he asked.

"Where did all the monsters go?" Harold asked. Kafa looked at him in surprise, then looked around. All of the imaginary friends were picking themselves off the ground and looking around. It seemed as if all the monsters had simply vanished out of thin air.

"Umm... you know what, that's a good question, Harold. I don't know," Kafa said slowly as he looked around again, confusion stopping his thoughts about Joanne.

"Kafa! Harold! Thank goodness you're alright!" She's voice called out to them. Kafa turned and saw that a tearful She and a shocked looking Edmund were sprinting towards them.

"She! Edmund! Are you alright?" Kafa asked as he jogged towards them, the sound of Harold's hoof steps letting him know that Harold was following him.

"We are fine, thank you. But Phoenix and Alexai… they didn't make it," Edmund said. Harold made a sad noise beside him while Kafa looked at Edmund in slight confusion as he felt a pang of sadness from Alexai's name.

"Who's Phoenix?" he asked.

"Somebody that wanted to help. We were both jumping out the window and-" She started saying, but broke out into wild sobs. Edmund pulled her into a hug as he patted her back. Kafa hung his head. Somebody had been trying to help them and they had died because of it, and he hadn't even known.

"Where's Joanne and Rumple?" Edmund asked as he continued to pat She's shaking back. Kafa scratched his head.

"They went after Kile, and then there was that big explosion, and I'm not really sure where they are-"

"Joanne's up in that room that the explosion came from. I don't know where Rumple is, but chances are he's with her," Harold said over Kafa.

Edmund nodded, looking over at the Imaginists Palace.

"We should go get them. Then we shall regroup and decide on what we must do next," Edmund said. Kafa nodded.

"Okay, let's go. I don't like them being up there by themselves. Makes me uneasy," Harold said, then started trotting towards the Imaginists Palace. With one last pat on the back, Edmund let go of She and followed him. She trailed after Edmund, and after one last look around, Kafa followed them, hoping that Joanne and Rumple were okay.

The streets were stained with blood, both monster blood and imaginary friend blood. Imaginary friends were slowly getting up and walking around fearfully, as if the monsters would suddenly spring upon them again. Some buildings were half-destroyed from monsters, and some near the Imaginists Palace were just piles of ash now from the explosion that may have been Joanne or something else. As they neared the Imaginists Palace, Kafa was able to see that most of it was just gone.

*Such a shame. It was such a beautiful place,* Kafa thought with disappointment that it had been destroyed, though he was mainly curious about what exactly had made the explosion. They stopped where the gates were. Most of the walls had been diminished, so to reach the remains of the stairs, all they had to do was walk through the ankle-deep heaps of ashes. They walked in silence, partially in fear of what they might find. Joanne and Rumple had gone to follow Kile. If they were here and an explosion had gone off, where was Kile? They climbed the stairs carefully, staying to the less scorched parts of it. They got off on the third floor and Kafa recognized the metal door that was still there.

*The vault. Where the Stone was kept. Oh no. Oh, no, no, no. What happened?* Kafa thought, his steps quickening and a cold ball of dread forming in his stomach.

"I see her!" Harold said, pointing with his hoof in between two computer terminals. Kafa stopped walking and stood behind Harold so he could see what Harold was pointing at. It was Joanne. She was huddled over… something. She was sobbing uncontrollably, clutching her stomach as if she was shattering from the inside and she was trying to keep herself from falling apart. Whatever it was, it seemed to be disappearing.

Kafa suddenly felt sick. There was only one thing that would be disappearing in Imagine that Joanne would be crying over that hard.

*Rumple,* Kafa thought, feeling like he needed to sit down. And then he was running, sprinting towards Joanne and what was left of Rumple without realizing he was even moving until he noticed that Joanne was growing closer. He stopped beside Joanne, making ashes cloud around them. Joanne didn't even seem to notice. And there, on the ground, was a very slowly fading away, dead Rumple.

Not laughing.

Not smiling.

Not breathing.

Not even blinking.

Just nothing.

Silence and stillness.

Kafa fell down to his knees, sending up clouds of ash. He could hear Edmund, She, and Harold walking up to them, slowly due to their horror and shock.

Rumple was gone.

Rumple, whom Kafa had known for three years. Rumple, who had been the first person Kafa had considered a friend since Kile. Rumple, who was immature but would make anyone laugh with his sassy attitude. Rumple, who put on a happy face even when he was hurting, a laugh when he felt like crying just to make others feel better. Rumple, who was brave and serious when he needed to be but was the perfect nerdy friend the rest of the time. And now, he was most definitely dead. *He was fifteen and now he's dead. He was just a kid. And now he's gone,* Kafa thought.

"Joanne? Joanne, are you okay?" Kafa asked softly, trying to brush away his own tears that were starting to run down his face. But Joanne didn't answer, lost in her own memories. Lost in another time.

*My brother is dead.*

*Rumple is dead.*

*He is dead and I am alive.*

*Why?*

Harold felt a sudden wave of sadness and shock when he saw the fading away boy. His mouth fell open as a goat-like sob escaped from it.

*He was just a kid. A bit of an idiot and kind of annoying, but he was a good kid. He was a good kid. And now he's a dead kid. Rumple didn't deserve to die. I know that much. Whoever did this to him is going to pay. I am going to make sure of it,* Harold thought, shaking his head as the fur around his eyes became wet and transparent.

Rumple's body became completely see-through, just barely visible.

And then he fully disappeared, a patch of ground where a boy once was.

Harold just stared at it and then looked at Joanne, who was staring blankly at the space where Rumple had been, tear tracks down her face but no new tears falling.

She looked … Empty. Broken. Lost. As if she would never feel emotion again. Maybe she wouldn't. Harold wasn't an expert on emotions. After all, he had hardly ever felt them. Harold never thought he would die, never thought that somebody he knew would die either. And yet, somebody did. Not himself, but probably the first person that Harold had ever begun to become friends with. It was Earth-shattering. First Alexai, then Phoenix, and then Rumple.

But they would have to keep moving, Kafa knew that much. They would have to find Kile and kill him, it was the only way to have any chance of success. No matter how much Kafa hated the idea of his former best friend dying, it was the only way that they could possibly prevail. The old Kile was gone. There was no longer any room for former emotions. But they would have to do it together. Just without the leader of the Darkness, the half-vampire, or the nerdy kid. Kafa felt a burning fire within him for revenge. After all, it was Kile's fault that Rumple was dead. That Alexai was dead. That Phoenix was dead. It was Kile's fault that hundreds of imaginary friends were dead, never to be seen again. And he would pay. Kafa would make sure of it.

At some point in time, Edmund got Kafa and Joanne off the ground. Edmund started walking away, down towards the road. Having no better options, they all followed, Joanne looking like a ghost. Kafa put his arm around Joanne, since she looked like she'd collapse to the ground again if she didn't have someone to hold her up. The roads were covered in wreckage and blood while ash rained down from buildings that had caught fire. The streets were deserted, all alive imaginary friends having fled. But they walked right through it, no longer caring about such things.

Where they were going, nobody knew. But nobody asked, either. They were going the way they were supposed to go.

They were going to defeat Kile.

The battle was over.

But the war had only just begun.

Acknowledgements

First, I'd like to thank my mom for editing this book. I know it wasn't easy since I'm not always grammatically correct and it wasn't very short, so the fact that she made it through the entire thing without murdering me is somewhat of a miracle. I'm lucky to have someone like her who's willing to sit and stare at my books for hours at a time to try and improve them. I'd also like to thank the rest of my family for their support.

Next, I'd like to thank two of my past teachers, Mrs. Isonhood and Mrs. Green, whose encouragement and excitement about my books inspires me to keep writing them, no matter how long it takes me to do so.

Then, I'd like to thank everyone who has encouraged me over the years, whether they be teachers, friends, family, or others. Your positivity has let me know that people really do care about my writing and has given me the perseverance to start and finish my books.

Now I'd like to thank R. S. R., who stuck with me and encouraged me for years far before anyone else did, telling me to keep dreaming, writing, and being weird until the end. They gave me inspiration for this book series, and were always there through thick and thin. For that, I'm thankful.

Last, I'd like to thank all of the readers of this book. I'm so glad you stayed with the main characters throughout their entire journey, and I do hope you enjoyed it as much as I enjoyed writing it! I'm so thankful for all of you. Without you, this book may as well have never existed in the first place.

Stay weird!

-Jolene

# About the Author

Jolene Reed is an eighth grader that likes to spend her time writing, reading, and acting. She loves hugs and nice hot cups of coffee and is so thankful for everyone in her life. In her opinion, she spends too much time staring at nothing as she tries to think of book ideas. She lives in North East Texas with her family and three dogs.

Made in the USA
Columbia, SC
21 September 2021